SCIENCE
SEX
SPIRITUALITY

SCIENCE SEX SPIRITUALITY

A MAN'S SEARING JOURNEY INTO THE SOUL OF GOD

YURESH SINHA

olive turtle

NIYOGI BOOKS

Published by
NIYOGI BOOKS
Block D, Building No. 77,
Okhla Industrial Area, Phase-I,
New Delhi-110 020, INDIA
Tel: 91-11-26816301, 26818960
Email: niyogibooks@gmail.com
Website: www.niyogibooksindia.com

Editor: K.E. Priyamvada
Design: Shraboni Roy

ISBN: 978-93-85285-79-0
Publication: 2017

This is a work of fiction. The names, characters and incidents portrayed in it are the work of the author's imagination. Any resemblance to actual persons, living or dead, events or places is purely coincidental.

Printed at: Niyogi Offset Pvt. Ltd., New Delhi, India

mayādhyakṣheṇa prakṛitiḥ sūyate sa-charācharam
hetunānena kaunteya jagad viparivartate

O Arjun under my aegis, Nature brings forth the whole creation,
consisting of both sentient and insentient beings;
it is due to this cause that the wheel of Samsara goes around.

—

Bhagavadgita, 9:10

CONTENTS

PROLOGUE

I sat at my desk and looked out at the view. Even after all these years, it was dramatic.

My reverie was interrupted by a knock on the door.

'Come in!' I barked out impatiently. Rupen should have known better than to knock. The standing instructions were that he could come in straightaway. If I didn't want to be disturbed, he would find the door remote-locked from my desk.

It wasn't him. It was my 9 am appointment, slightly early. A young man in a suit tip-toed in nervously.

I didn't blame him for being overawed. My office and its surroundings tended to have that effect on first-time visitors. The impact of the journey and the destination was striking. After all, would you expect to find a modern steel and glass-encased office jostling for space on a mountain ridge with a 22,000 feet high snow-covered Himalayan massif in the background?

The young man found me sitting, framed by the latest in curtain-glass windows, on a desk that had been taken from the mountains around—a square cut mono-bloc of rough-hewn granite. My office was large for its single occupant—me. It sprawled 50 feet by 25 feet, the space curving along the mountain slope out of which it had been carved.

This was my home and workplace. I lived in the Himalayas, tucked into the hollow of an alpine meadow at the base of the Swargarohini peaks.

Getting to me was a three-stage process. First a hop to Jolly Grant airport, then a bumpy eight-hour-long ride along the Yamuna river to Osla village and finally a bone-rattling climb of 4,000 plus feet along a jeep trail that wound its way through earthquake-tilted villages. The end result was a lung-wrenching view of the Himalayas from 10,000 feet above sea level.

I loved to call this home.

I had moved here many years ago, increasingly permanently, as my needs simplified and my attachments and duties to an urban life dwindled. Initially I would come and stay over the long weekends as local masons built this place, stone by stone, but as my ideas took off to become inventions and as the royalties from my inventions increased, I was able to spend far more time here than I would have ever thought possible.

The young man now poised at my office door was from a magazine that had expressed a desire to interview me. My secretary in Delhi had briefed me that the magazine was running a series titled 'High Achievers with Unusual Lives'. To me it seemed more of a section on mavericks and crackpots, since that always sells more copies. I didn't mind, though; as Anusuya says, sanity is highly overrated.

'Come on in,' I welcomed him.

'Sir, I am Ashish and I am from the *Business-Quarter* magazine,' he ventured, stammering a bit.

'I know who you are. It is rather difficult to wander in here by mistake!' I quipped to put him at ease as I rang the bell. Two short sharp blasts meant that Rupen would come in with tea and biscuits.

'Why don't you take a seat?' I pointed him to an old leather sofa that offered a panoramic view of the mountains from the corner window.

My Man Friday came in and we busied ourselves with pleasantries—small talk about the weather, the politics and the pollution of Delhi.

'So what can I do for you?' I finally asked him when we were comfortably seated, with steaming cups of tea in our hands.

'Sir, I wanted to interview you about your life and your remarkable inventions.'

'What of it? My inventions are all well known.' I paused, sipped my tea and continued, 'As far as I am concerned, it's been an ordinary life. I am a recluse by choice, a fact that should hardly be of any interest to the general public.' I waited to see his reaction, but he didn't offer any so I continued, 'I consider myself fortunate that I have been well rewarded for putting two and two together to make four. Why would your readers want to know more about me?'

That too didn't incite any significant response, so I provoked him further. 'In any case, talking about what I have done in the past bores me, apart from reminding me of my advancing years! I am flattered, of course, but I don't see why it's worth an interview.'

Finally, I got a rise out of the young man sitting across me. 'That's not true, sir!' Ashish protested, his earnestness transparently obvious. 'That's not how you are perceived. We look upon you as one of the most original thinkers we have, apart from being an unconventional man…' Ashish's voice trailed off as he looked down sheepishly.

'A crackpot, you mean?' I joked to put him at ease.

'No, sir!' Exclaimed Ashish, finally coming out of his deferential shell. 'The products and processes that you have invented cover such a wide spectrum that people get inspired by the sheer range. Our readers want to understand how, in this day of specialization and information overload, you can so easily cut through the fog of complexity and figure out the perfect solution—and that too across such a wide range of subjects.

'And this is what we want to pinpoint in this interview,' he continued. 'The magazine wants you to take us through the thought process behind your inventions. That's something we believe that our readers would be most interested in understanding.'

Hmm, I thought. The idea was certainly interesting. *How to think* was something that I had found sadly lacking in the general population. To me, the prevailing system of education with its focus on specialization seemed to bind rather than free the mind. At the beginning of my career, I recalled, I had been most surprised at the opposition I faced from the very people from whom I had expected support—the experts of the field in which I was working. Initially I had been naïve enough to think that when I explained my ideas to them, and how those ideas reduced the complications entailed in the earlier ways of doing things, the experts of that domain would be equally excited. Little did I know then that most people are petty-hearted, the experts being unable to stomach the fact that as an outsider, with very little technical knowledge of their field, I could better their products and processes. All I ended up doing was to arouse their insecurity and jealousy.

Not that I minded; I was a very rich man today simply because the so-called experts didn't think, as they say, *out of the box* or *through their hats*, and that left a very niche and very lucrative field of work open to people like me.

I smiled at Ashish. 'It may sound hard to believe but there is an essential and common thread to all that you think is diverse in my inventions. The difficult thing to grasp is that original thinking just cannot be compartmentalized. Catch one right thread and you can unravel the whole mess that is the world today.' The young man listened attentively as I mused, 'Anyone could do this if they set their mind to it. In fact, I am just an ordinary man with an average brain; the only difference is that I am in pursuit of an extraordinary goal…'

'That would be a nice caption for the article!' Ashish interrupted excitedly, 'Can I write that down?'

I repeated aloud, 'An ordinary man in search of an extraordinary goal. Yes, that sounds good.'

Ashish took out his recorder and asked, 'Would it be possible to record this conversation? Of course, I will send you the recording and print only what you approve.'

'Feel free,' I replied. 'I don't believe that knowledge should be proprietary in any case. We all learn from each other.'

Ashish began, 'Sir, I would like you to speak about three things. One—the significant moments of your life and when exactly did you start on the path of being an inventor? Two—what were the thought processes that created your inventions? And three—what do you consider as your greatest invention till date?'

I shot back, 'Which of them do you like the most?'

Replied Ashish, 'I don't know, sir. They are all intriguing and, believe me, all of us kick ourselves when we understand how they work! They are really simple once you think of the basic idea.' Ashish rattled off the names, 'The car heat-shield; the friction-condom; the airport-security system; the efficient water-heating system; the lean-energy building; the earthquake-proof building foundation design; the beating-heart bypass spigot; the non-invasive heart stent; the pollution filter/mask; the very short takeoff-aircraft concept; the Uber killer; the ultimate defender; the virtual tank armour; the extreme data compression software...they are all extraordinary in their achievement and simple in their conception, not to mention the wide reach of their impacts. Of course, though you have not revealed the design logic of many of these inventions, 'I won't be surprised that they would be simple in their conception as well.'

He paused and I could see that he was struggling to be eloquent. 'I can't really choose. Each of them has its own *wow* factor but, personally, what really intrigues me is the fact that they are all based on pre-existing concepts and technologies. That is what has all of us kicking ourselves!'

'Yes,' I agreed, 'that's what's unique—that most of them are based on the power of common sense and on well-established scientific facts, rather than on the latest path-breaking discoveries in science. As we go along with the interview, you will realize that this is no coincidence. This is in the very nature of how I think. I believe in working with whatever resources we have—materials and knowledge, rather than having to depend on advanced research breakthroughs, that haven't happened as yet.'

Ashish nodded. 'That's the appeal for all of us. And it is inspiring, the fact that we could, if we bended our minds just a little, do the same! Personally for me, what I find most interesting is the process by which you arrived at these products rather than the products themselves.' I quirked an eyebrow and he hastened to add, 'Not that the products aren't impressive in themselves, but to me it seems that your inventions are just a few fruits of a very prolific tree.'

This young man was perceptive, I thought appreciatively. He was pinpointing a fact that was generally not understood well. People knew me as an inventor of well-known products; little did they know that the products in the market were just a few amongst the many in my design book.

'Yes, you have hit the nail on its head,' I admitted cheerfully. 'Ideas flow by all the time and most are unpatentable. The system of patenting, in any case, is tilted heavily in favour of the corporations and, rather than encouraging home-grown inventors, it actually discourages most individuals from even trying to file a patent for their ideas. Now that I am well-off, I am putting down most of my ideas in a book form and letting them out in the public domain. The basic thread to all that I have done can be stated in one line: All these products were born out of a fundamental inefficiency I was able to spot that the experts in that field were unable—or unwilling—to see. I guess that will become clearer as we go along. So,' I enquired, 'how do you want to do this? Should I speak generally or will it be a question-answer session?'

'Sir, maybe you could start with your, uh, your own story—the start of your journey, so to speak,' he suggested diffidently.

'You could then take me through the salient points of your life. Depending on how it goes, I will fill in the gaps at the end with some questions.'

'Ok,' I agreed and took a moment to gather my thoughts; my mind flying back through the years, looking for the beginning of what had been an incredible journey. It had been a long road. I had traversed from the convictions of childhood to the uncertainties of youth, before reaching the clarities of today. From surety to delusion and back—I had come a full circle. 'Where did it all start?' I asked myself, and a sudden image of a lean, gangly adolescent standing in a dusty classroom came to me. I found myself smiling. Yes! That's where it had all started… leading me to where I was today…

To Ashish I said, 'It all began with my asking the most important question that anyone can ask: Why?…'

WHY

I was in the eighth standard when I first asked my physics teacher a question that has been with me ever since: 'Why does every action have an equal and opposite reaction?'

The question was innocent. The teacher was teaching us Newton's three laws of motion.

He looked at me and said, 'Boy, never ask *why*. All you can ask is *how*.'

'Why can't I ask *why*, sir?' I persisted, puzzled.

'I just said…don't ask *why*, that's why!' he snapped back.

Seeing my blank expression he relented. 'You don't ask *why* because no one knows why the laws of physics work. We can speculate only upon *how* they work but not *why* they work.'

That, I thought, was rather strange, since I always had a *why*, a reason for doing whatever I did. If I bunked school, there was a reason—usually to watch a film. If I took a detour on my cycle route, again there was a reason—usually so that I could cycle past my latest heartthrob's house. Even on the rare occasions when I behaved perfectly, there would be a compelling reason. Usually that happened only when I wanted something really badly! And I wasn't unique. This was how kids operated! The question then was, if this was so commonplace, why was this question invalid in my science class?

I let it pass that day. Maybe the teacher was having a bad day—or was it simply that he didn't know the answer? Yes, that must be it! He must be covering up his deficiencies by being officious. How typical of adults!

But I didn't give up long-term. I tried again next year with another teacher and again the year after that. The answer always remained the same. It was as if the teachers' association had briefed all the teachers that this should be their standard answer to the *why* question.

I have never liked being stymied and asking *why* had been the standard way I had operated till then. That a lot of adults got frustrated with this style of questioning was part of the charm. I also knew that some grownups (the ones related to me by blood) secretly admired me for my pesky qualities even though they were loath to admit it to my face.

I remember a conversation with my father that was typical of my style.

'Why does it rain?' I asked him one day.

'That's because clouds, which hold water in vapour form, can't hold it anymore and as a result they burst into raindrops that fall on the ground as rain,' my father replied.

'Why do they burst?' I instantly volleyed back.

'That's because when extra evaporation takes place due to the heat, the cloud is unable to hold it within. Therefore, as soon as the holding capacity of the clouds is exceeded, they burst.'

'Where does the extra heat come from?'

'It comes from the summer season, of course. That's why we have the monsoons immediately after.' he explained.

Pat came my next question. 'Why do we have seasons?'

'Well, that's because the earth revolves around the sun with its axis tilted at 22 degrees which results in the northern hemisphere facing the sun more for one part of the year and the southern hemisphere for the remaining part of the year. That causes the summer and winter seasons.'

As you can make out, my father was a reasonably well-read man, even though he had not been educated in the sciences. However, his patience and, more critically, his knowledge would start running thin when I persisted.

'Why is the earth's axis tilted at 22 degrees and why does the earth revolve around the sun?'

To that he replied, 'Ask your science teacher.' And that's when I knew that I had run to the end of that particular conversation.

My father, bless his soul, would usually not get off that easy since I would inevitably go off on a corollary, after what I thought was a suitable break to cool things down.

'What is evaporation?' I had asked after what I considered an appropriate cooling-off period. Five minutes was usually the maximum to which I could stretch myself.

'Evaporation is the process by which water, on getting hot, changes into water vapour,' he replied warily, since he didn't want another question chain starting. He was also conscious that he should not appear brusque or, worse, ill-informed.

I knew that I was beginning to skate on thin ice but the urge to find out was too strong.

'Why does water change into water vapour?'

With a resigned expression he parroted what we all have been taught. 'Because the molecules of water, on getting hot, gain extra energy, break down their molecular bonds and become gaseous at 100 degrees Celsius.'

With the temptation of imminent discovery flashing in my brain, I helplessly hooked on to this interesting new knowledge. 'Why do the molecules of water break down at 100 degrees and not at any other temperature?'

'That's easy!' The sweat droplets on my father's brow suggested that it was anything but. 'Different liquid molecular bonds break down at different temperatures because their molecular bonds have different strengths. For water, it just so happens that that point comes at 100 degrees Celsius. And *that* is because,'—in an attempt to preempt my next question—'that's the way the water molecule is structured.'

As to why the molecule is structured in a way that it breaks down at a particular point, his answer was, 'Ask your chemistry teacher.'

I know that my incessant questioning was appreciated even though it must have grated on his nerves sometimes. I knew this for a fact since I would often eavesdrop on him bragging with filial pride about my intellectual prowess to anyone who cared to listen. In my presence, however, it was a different story. He would prick my balloon usually by declaring, 'Even a fool can ask a question that a wise man cannot answer!'

I realized that most people (adults), including teachers, could handle a maximum of about six levels of *why's* before throwing up their hands in despair and admitting that they did not know—a fact that makes any child extremely happy.

As you can imagine, since the question *why* had been my standard weapon as far back as I could remember, its sudden ineffectiveness with my physics teacher was disconcerting to say the least. As I grew into adolescence, the *why* question remained unanswered from my teachers, so I turned the question inwards and continued my quest and as I reached the senior classes, I gradually realized that there was a genuine reason for the failure of the teachers to answer and it wasn't just the obstinacy of the teachers union at play. It seemed that science was built like an onion. You peeled away one layer and another layer appeared and just when you thought that you had reached the end, it all disappeared into nothingness and the basic *why* still remained.

It all boiled down to one central fact—how could an orderly place like the universe, where things happened so precisely—from the stellar to the subatomic scale—not have a reason, a *why* for existing? The lack of an answer left me feeling both disappointed and exhilarated. Was science, for all its claims, a puerile subject that could not explain in true depth anything at all or was it far deeper than what I, or for that matter anyone else, had been able to fathom?

Even as my initial stab into this fundamental question got no answers from my teachers, my quest continued. I explored the world of books and libraries, going through the immense work done by scientists. While my friends progressed in their reading habits from The Hardy Boys to Agatha Christie and on to Alistair McLean, James Hadley Chase, Nick Carter and beyond, I was reading Einstein, Newton and the rest of the quantum gang. I soon figured out that these scientists were kindred spirits, cheerfully acknowledging the fact that they did not know! Newton, in fact, modestly admitted that what he had discovered was just the equivalent of a pebble on a beach, even as the ocean of truth lay undiscovered before him. And that was the big difference between the ignorance of the scientists and that of the teachers! The teachers did not know that they did not know, while the scientists were well aware that they knew very little.

As I read further, I discovered that science was not the all-knowing, unequivocal subject that we as children have been taught to believe, but was essentially a stab in the dark, using certain conditional knowns to try and figure out the unknowns. From Galileo to Newton, to Einstein, to quantum mechanics and now down to String Theory, one could observe scientists frequently applying band-aids on already band-aided situations. The irony was that we, the general public, believed in the scientists far more than they believed in themselves!

This is how I spent most days and my vacations—reading the tomes of science and scientific biographies. Einstein in particular had a humorous style of writing that I really liked and I was struck by the fact that he would often mock his own theory of relativity.

For the readers let me summarize how the scientific process works. Typically, the job of scientists is to observe natural phenomena and then form a logical thought process that creates a theory that explains why that phenomena happens. The new theory ideally should do two things: one, better explain what was previously already explained by the existing theories and two, the postulates of the new theory should go one step further—they should also be able to predict certain phenomena that are as yet unexplained or even as yet unknown. And if the new theory did all this, the inventing scientist was considered a great man worthy of respect. But it must be said that all this is easier said than done and the guillotine of a failed future experiment always hangs over every theory, however respected and however successful it may have been in the past. It is salutary to remember that Aristotle's theory of the earth being the centre of the universe had been the accepted model for more than 2,000 years before being proved to be complete and utter rubbish!

I also learnt that the final frontier, the holy grail of physics, was the *Theory of Everything* that had been Einstein's greatest unfulfilled ambition. So obsessed was Einstein with it that even as he lay dying in hospital, he had scribbled equations on a bedside notepad. Einstein had fervently believed and had famously said, *'God does not play dice'*. He had never been able to accept that the contradictions between classical and quantum mechanics could be a fundamental design paradigm and had fervently believed that an as yet undiscovered underlying unity would explain this apparent duality. He had believed that there had to be a simple and elegant way to explain the common beginnings of all matter and all the known forces in the universe. He had pursued this stream of logic even in the face of subtle ridicule from his peers who did not say so openly, but had thought of him as a dinosaur in his twilight years.

I, in my adolescent certainty, instantly sided with Einstein. I believed he was the one who was right! And in the bravado that only extreme youth can bring, I also instantly decided that I would be the one to solve this last great mystery and be the one to formulate the theory of everything.

Thus I passed my school years, daydreaming about the cosmos and getting sucked deeper into the world of science. The answers that I got raised more questions than they answered and I didn't get any closer to solving the theory of everything. What did happen, however, was that I gained far more knowledge than my teachers were comfortable with. I used my power to the full extent, playing the joker in class and tripping up my teachers at every opportunity till I became notorious, someone to avoid, with my reputation preceding me. The teachers disliked and feared me, since my aim was to make them look like fools. It didn't help, obviously, that I ended up routinely topping the exams in all science subjects.

I entered college with the avowed aim of becoming a theoretical physicist.

St. Stephen's college in Delhi University, for all its exalted status, was a bit of a bore. I quickly discovered that the professors were going over syllabii that I had covered a long time ago. That being the case, I decided that there wasn't much point in attending too many classes for the next few months at least.

That was not the only reason for distancing myself from classes. I had discovered the hidden mysteries and equations of puppy love.

My love was just the wisp of an idea. I had spent but a week of enchanting togetherness with my love, whose hometown was Mumbai (then called Bombay). Her father and mine were college buddies and she had come to my home for a short visit and we had fallen for each other like a ton of bricks. But that was quickly followed by separation after the discovery of our proximity by our heartless parents. Banishment had followed as our parents scrambled to separate us as quickly as possible. The solution that my parents decided on was that I was to be exiled to my maternal grandparents' place where my access to the phone would be strictly limited. My grandparents didn't have a phone and calls, if any, had to be made through a payphone in the local post office.

Concepts of physics that had been my ideals suddenly started looking like boring lectures from graying uncles, while my love—a bejewelled angel wrapped in stardust and golden light—beckoned me sweetly in my fevered imagination.

As a result of this disillusionment with studies and the newfound introduction to the mysterious formulae of love, I spent a lot of my time in college bunking lectures, having coffee in the canteen and dispatching love letters through snail mail, since that was the only way to communicate in the era before the internet, mobile phones and Facebook. The only hope of any speed was the Quick Mail Service of the postal department. Yes, I am talking about an era that didn't even have Speed Post! Thus my English improved far more than my physics, and my college years would have been a complete washout if I had not discovered, in a corner of the St. Stephen's library, a book on philosophy. But I am running ahead of the story.

That day, I walked into class and could instantly figure out that there was trouble brewing. I hadn't attended this particular professor's classes in a long time. Most other professors didn't really care, but this one was especially nasty. A slim whiplash of a man, he loved taking students apart—especially those who slighted his beloved subject.

The professor peered at me over the top of his frameless spectacles. 'Good morning, Mr Kashyap.' His sarcasm was evident. '…Nice to have you with us today!'

I shuffled uneasily to my seat. I didn't want to provoke him. The fact was that I hardly knew anything about what he was teaching, having skipped a majority of his classes over the last three months. Mathematical Physics, M.P. for short, wasn't a subject that I cared for much, since it consisted mostly of mugging up a series of equations. For me, physics was a thing of beauty—the concepts were what mattered, not the equations! The professor, I am sure, didn't sympathize with this line of thinking.

I sat at the back thinking about Roli, wondering what she would be doing. Would she have received the letter that I wrote her two days ago? Would she even now be writing back?

'Mr Kashyap. Would you help us with the question on the board?'

My reverie thus abruptly interrupted, I looked at the board. I could see some indecipherable equations chalked out.

'I don't know this particular equation sir,' I said, hoping that he would let me off.

'That's okay, you aren't expected to know everything' he said generously. I looked up and so did the class. The old man seemed in an expansive mood. 'You aren't expected to know everything,' he restated. I relaxed and started to sit down. As I did, he swooped in for the kill, 'But...Mr Kashyap, do you know *anything* at all?'

I felt anger beginning to uncoil at the base of my spine, trickling up. I controlled myself. This was not the time to reply. He was right, after all, about my lack of attention—not to mention my lack of attendance.

He turned to the class. 'These people, getting admission into St. Stephen's, joining the physics course and wasting everyone's time! They know nothing, they are not interested in physics and they block a valuable seat from some deserving candidate.'

I looked at my shoes, hoping he would blow off some steam and get on with the lecture. He didn't. 'Let me repeat the question, Mr Kashyap. Do you know anything at all about physics?'

'I am sorry, sir. I am unprepared for your class, but I will study and catch up, sir,' I said, genuinely contrite.

'Do you think that you can catch up by putting in some extra studies, Mr Kashyap?'

'Yes sir. I can, sir.' How hard could it be, after all?

'That would be possible if you cared anything at all about physics,' he retorted. 'You can't catch up if you aren't interested—and that's assuming that you have a brain.' I could see he was waiting for me to say something, and when I didn't oblige, he continued, 'Why don't you take a transfer to the pass course?'

The whole class gave a collective shudder. That was the ultimate insult. The pass course was for the dregs of student society—mostly a rag-tag bunch of the academically challenged.

'I *am* interested in physics sir,' I stuttered, staggered at the enormity of the insult.

'Oh really? Is that so?' He turned to the board and started scribbling something on it while he spoke. 'In that case, can you solve this one?'

I peered at the board. What was written there was equally indecipherable. 'No, sir,' I had to admit. 'I don't know this one either.'

'That's what I said earlier, Mr Kashyap. You don't know anything and obviously you aren't interested in the subject. I suggest you stop wasting everyone's time and take a transfer to the pass course. I will personally sign the transfer papers.'

The boy next to me tittered nervously, looking at me with amused and fearful eyes. For all he knew, he could be next on the firing line. I said nothing, staring into space, remembering the time when I was five, standing in the path of an enraged bull that was charging towards me, watching it all as if it was happening in slow motion. Those ember-red, glaring eyes, the foaming mouth and the rancid smell of unnamed fury…I had survived that day because some passerby had plucked me out of the bull's path at the last minute. I still remember the excitement, the calmness, the feeling of time standing still and the thrill of standing my ground.

'Sir, not knowing is quite common in physics. That is how physics has been progressively invented.' My voice emerged from an unknown cavern inside me.

The entire class turned and looked at me, fear and awe in their faces. No one had gone toe-to-toe with this guy and survived. This guy was one of the contenders, even if distant, for the Nobel Prize, after all.

'What did you say?' The shock in the professor's voice was apparent.

Now was the time to keep quiet. Instead, I heard myself speak, 'I said that no one knows the basics beyond a point... sir. All scientists start from assumptions and spend their lives fighting the state of not knowing. As far as my interest in physics is concerned, let me assure you that I love physics. Newton, Einstein, Niels Bohr and others are my heroes, sir.'

The professor looked like he was having an apoplexy. It was a fearsome sight, yet no more than the bull, I reminded myself.

'How dare you compare your asinine lack of knowledge with the lifelong quest of these great men?' he roared. 'If you actually had even a bit of interest in physics you would know that we are on the verge of a momentous discovery—the last of the great mysteries is about to be solved. The Higgs boson! Once we do find it, and I am sure we will, the standard model will be complete and everything explainable. We will know the last little bits very soon.' He preened before the class. 'I myself am the head of the Indian chapter of the global team of the European Organization for Nuclear Research, CERN, as some of you may know.'

We all knew that, of course. It had been announced with great fanfare just a couple of months ago and he had been felicitated in the college auditorium. Dr Sood was a feather in St. Stephen's cap.

He turned away from me, his anger spent with this reiteration of his achievements. I was evidently not worth it, the mere lowly student that I was. 'Ok, turn to chapter six, page 85…'

'What about gravity, sir?' I asked softly but clearly. 'Can the standard model be said to be anywhere near completion with such an important part missing? Can you actually claim that the scientific quest is nearly over when something as important as gravity hasn't been explained as yet?'

The professor turned, not quite believing that I was challenging him like this. He had assumed that I would be glad that he had let me go. 'What about gravity, eh?' he snapped. 'Don't you know that Newton explained how to calculate it and Einstein explained its nature? The standard model does not need to account for gravity since it is not a force. It is a sag in the space-time fabric which bends the paths of travelling bodies. The extent of the sag is created by the relative masses of the celestial bodies.' The professor sneered. 'This is exactly what I said in the beginning. You don't know anything and I suggest that you stop wasting my time and sit down before I really lose my temper.'

'I will, sir, if you answer three questions,' I retorted firmly. The professor looked at me, stunned by my brazenness. I could feel the class staring at me. His silence spurred me on. 'First question: can you explain why the space-time fabric bends only downwards when the celestial bodies rest on it? Why not upwards, sideways or in any other direction? When a body encounters this dip in the space-time fabric, why does it follow the contour *downwards*? Doesn't that presuppose that there is an existing force pulling it downwards? In effect, isn't gravity being defined by using another, as yet unknown, force?'

The professor gaped at me like a gold fish. He looked ludicrous. It gave me the courage to go on.

'Second question,' I continued. 'Can you explain why the space-time fabric, assuming that it actually exists, is able to hold—offer resistance—to a heavy object like a star and yet we are unable to detect it even with the most sensitive of instruments?'

Still no response.

I ploughed on. 'And lastly sir, the entire mass of the universe is said to be far greater than the objects in it, in a ratio of 80:20, in fact. Therefore isn't it a bit presumptuous of you to say that the scientific quest is almost over when 80 per cent of the universe is unknown to us, as on date?'

It was as if time stood still and the world went silent. We could all have been frozen in the alleged space-time fabric except for the chirping of the birds outside. The class was staring at me, in their eyes a mixture of fear, horror, pity—and something approaching hero-worship on a couple of faces for the sheer daring of what I was doing. And there was a girl, a couple benches away, who was looking at me with something in her eyes that I couldn't quite place. The professor, too, was quite a sight. He was speechless, his mouth hanging open on a word he couldn't seem to utter.

I thought that the time to quit—or, rather, escape—was now, while I was still ahead. 'Sir, I will wait for your answers and will come to your class once you have them.'

On that immortal line—which, I am told, became the stuff of legend over the years—I picked up my bag and walked out with grace, dignity and, I admit, a bit of a swagger.

If I'd survived the bull, I would survive this as well.

That must have been a first in any college in the world—a student boycotting a class because he did not get an answer to a scientific question from an eminent professor!

I headed out onto the road towards Jai Singh's tea stall. The guy made great tea and I badly needed a cup at that very moment. Overboiled and heavily sweetened, just the way I liked it—*kaadhaa*, as it is colloquially called—with the best bun-samosas in town. I had struck up quite a friendship with Jai Singh over the last few months, since I usually took my evening tea with him before boarding the U-Special home.

He looked up. 'What's the matter? Not attending class today?' Jai Singh knew the timetables of Hindu and St. Stephen's College by heart. That directly affected his business, after all.

'I chucked the great Dr Sood out of the class today.' I quipped. It was true in a way.

'All you guys brag,' Jai Singh said placidly.

'No, Jai Singh, this is really what happened. I asked that son of a bitch a question that left him with his mouth hanging open in front of the whole class. He didn't chuck me out; I walked out when he couldn't answer my question!' Jai Singh quirked his eyebrows, disbelief written large on his face. 'If you don't believe me,' I offered, 'ask *any* of my classmates when they come out.'

'Just what did you ask that the great Professor Sood couldn't answer?' Jai Singh asked placatingly. He could make out that I was a bit hyper. Jai Singh had the well-deserved reputation of being a friendly and non-judgmental kind of guy—a repository of all the love affairs and one-sided attachments going around, apart from being an adviser and a discreet message passer! You could trust him to keep your secrets and that helped to make him a great confidante and adviser.

'It's nothing that you would understand, Jai Singh,' I told him condescendingly. 'It's a scientific question. The point is that these professors think that they know everything. They forget that there are many questions that haven't yet been answered by man.'

'Physics-visics I don't know, but I do know a man who can answer any question that you may have, and that too to your satisfaction,' Jai replied.

'Who is that?' I asked idly, my mind dwelling back on the scene in the class. The adrenaline was still pumping and I was actually physically aroused. That look that Saloni had given me was definitely not pity. My idle thoughts were interrupted by Jai Singh.

'I consider him my Guru,' he informed me. 'He is a doctor by profession but he cures all problems—mental, spiritual and emotional, apart from the physical. You can ask him anything.'

Humph, a doctor guru. What will they think of next?—I thought to myself wryly. Well, at least he'd be better than those charlatans who came begging for food in saffron clothes and had the reputation of being kid stealers. I had more pressing engagements on my mind, though. What I had done was crazy. On the face of it, it was enough to get me suspended at the very least, but on another level I had done something that would make me a hero to my fellow students. All I had to do was to figure out how to tread the tightrope of enjoying the acclaim and avoiding the pitfalls. St. Stephen's College, for all its reputation for academic excellence, frowned heavily upon impertinence to teachers—unlike other Delhi University colleges, where the teachers were treated in a far more cavalier manner. In that sense, St. Stephen's was more like a school than a free-spirited college. We were probably the only college in the world where the students had to attend morning assembly thrice a week!

I finished my tea and went to the park behind the college church and lay down on the grass. I had spent many quiet moments there over the last few months, wrapped up in Roli's letters, dreaming of her. Today, however, my thoughts were on what had happened in class and the questions that I had asked. I may have asked them in response to the insults that I had faced, but—tomfoolery apart—the questions had been genuine. The lack of answers and, more than that, the lack of curiosity regarding the lack of answers was intriguing and frustrating. I wished Einstein was still alive. I would have loved to bat the breeze with him.

Lost in my reverie, I felt a shadow fall over me as a breath of perfume enveloped me.

'Hi!' lilted Saloni. I looked up to find her standing over me. 'That was awesome! I didn't know that you were so intelligent!'

As I peered up at her, she tilted her head and unclasped the clip that held her hair in a prim ponytail. Waist-length hair cascaded down like waves. The angle was steep, as she was standing and I was flat on the ground. Her long slim legs looked even longer than they were in real life and the sun made a halo around her hair. Warning lights flashed as I peered up at her. '*When a woman opens her hair on seeing you, that means that she's got the hots for you and, if you play it right, she will open her legs as well!*' an older, wiser cousin—a man far more experienced than I could ever hope to be in these matters—had once advised me.

'What happened after I left?' I asked anxiously. The reaction to what I had done was finally setting in as the adrenaline-high disappeared. I was feeling a bit weak-kneed. For all my bravado, I really didn't want trouble. I could imagine the scenes playing out at home when my parents were informed. 'Dear Mr Kashyap, please meet the principal regarding the (mis) conduct of your son in college!' My mother was likely to have a fit, although my dad, I thought, would take it far more lightly.

'Nothing, actually,' said Saloni, interrupting my reverie. 'The old man didn't say a word, just quietly continued with the class. That's what impressed all of us—and me particularly,' she trilled.

'What?' I gave her a blank look.

'That you actually shut him up, silly!'

'Well, he asked for it! He is such a pompous guy. Anyway, I will be off now,' I said, getting up.

'What's the hurry?' Saloni pouted. 'The next class is a good two hours away.'

'I don't know if I want to attend that. It's been quite a nerve-wracking day for me.'

'That's true. Poor you! It must have been tough to stand up to that bully.' She waited for me to say something and when I didn't, she continued, 'What you did in class was unbelievable. How did you argue so well?'

'That's because I've been thinking and reading about these things for a long time. In fact I think about almost nothing else,' I admitted with a shrug.

'That's not true,' Saloni smiled at me, her eyes curious. 'I have seen you reading stuff that doesn't look like physics textbooks to me. More like letters from your girlfriend!'

'Well, I do read all kinds of stuff,' I said defensively. I hadn't known that my solitary activities were so well known. 'Anyway, I need to get going. Bye, see you.' No point in admitting to a pretty girl that you had a girlfriend, just in case. Better to have a bird in hand and be in a couple of bushes!

'Oh Saagar, I was meaning to ask you something.'

Saagar! So we were on a first-name basis now. Wow!

'Yes?'

'Can you help me with the Electro-Magnetism class tutorials? I can't seem to get the hang of the concepts.'

'What's so difficult about them?' I said impatiently. 'They are so simple.'

'That's exactly what I am saying! I just can't understand them and you find them so easy.'

'Just study harder and I am sure you will get it.' I tried to dismiss something that sounded like a bore—teaching a girl who was slow on the uptake.

'Won't you help me out?' she frowned. 'I thought we were classmates!' Really? I thought to myself. I couldn't recall her saying even a hello to me in the almost six months of togetherness in the same class.

'Or is it that you are scared of girls?' her tone teased me.

'Of course not!' I stuttered.

'Good, that's settled then. Now you are responsible for getting me through the Electro-Mag. paper. If I fail, I will blame you.' She fluttered her lashes and posed.

I looked at her. Outmanoeuvred by a silly girl! 'Ok,' I said lamely and walked off.

I took the U-special home. As I have mentioned, home was temporarily my maternal grandparents' place where I had been shunted off so that my budding romance with Roli in Mumbai could be nipped in the bud. Nani—my mother's mother—had been recruited to play the good cop to my parents' bad cop routine. I didn't mind the situation since I enjoyed Nani's company, not to mention her cooking. Also, it didn't seriously affect my communication with Roli since we usually wrote letters to each other. In any case the market did have a Subscriber Trunk Dialling booth for the very occasional phone calls, which I mostly couldn't afford. My temporary abode was in Anand Parbat—the last hillock of the once mighty Aravalli Mountains that stretched all the way from Gujarat, through Rajasthan and Haryana, before petering out at the north-western tip of Delhi.

A long weekend stretched ahead and I didn't have much to do except worry so I put down my bag and went for a walk. Anand Parbat, unlike today, was a beautiful, Summer-of-42 kind of place in those days. Eternally breezy, unlike the rest of muggy Delhi, it had meadows undulating down to Karol Bagh on the south-east side. Patel Nagar—a partition refugee haven—flanked it on the south side and the Jaipur railway track ringed it on its sheer north face. The best direction was the south-west where I would go for my walks. Threading through sheep-dotted meadows, the goat trail ended in a cluster of long-abandoned mica mines.

Countless days of my childhood years had been spent here exploring these hills with my many cousins—multiples of the four children my Nana-Nani had produced. We cousins would get together and get into the mica mines, collecting shards of golden mica, convinced we had discovered nuggets of gold. We would carry back these pieces proudly and deposit them with Nani for safekeeping. What we didn't know was that they had no value and Nani would quietly chuck them into the trash once we had forgotten about them!

The sun was setting and the shepherds were taking their sheep back home as I entered the house. I quietly went into my room and went to sleep since I didn't really want to talk to anyone. What I had done today was finally hitting me. My knees trembled and I felt completely alone. Not that this feeling was anything new. All my life I had felt a misfit, unable to groove with the concerns of others. I was like no one I knew, thought like no one I knew and there really was no one who liked me. Except Roli, of course, but she was in another city and I was here, parked with my grandparents so that I wouldn't be able to communicate with her. On top of that I had gone toe-to-toe with the strictest professor of St. Stephen's College. Life could definitely be better than what it was right now...

I dozed fitfully and thought of Roli and the time we had spent together—a short magical time of togetherness under our parents' noses. With those pleasant thoughts wafting through my head, I finally drifted off into an uneasy sleep.

I walked into St. Stephen's on Monday morning, bright and early. Thankfully I didn't have a M.P. lecture today. I still hadn't worked out how I would get back into that class since I was the one who had made that grand declaration and walked out. I must admit that my heart was thumping a bit as I walked past the bulletin board. Any student in trouble would typically be called by the principal and, always, the first step was to see your name on the noticeboard. I checked carefully. Mine wasn't up there—at least, not yet. To be doubly sure, I checked with the clerk inside.

'Hello, sir,' I said. All of us students were extra sweet to this guy since he was the advance warning system for any upcoming unpleasantness. He was a likeable kind of chap, so it wasn't any hardship to keep him buttered up.

'Hi Saagar, how's life? How is it going?'

'Fine, sir,' I replied. 'Just the usual, boring lectures and all…and how's work?' I asked, reminding him of his work, to jog his memory, in case he wanted to share something personal and confidential with me.

'All fine,' he replied. 'Things are going smoothly right now since the old man is away on tour. But I expect it will get busier when the college festival starts.'

'Okay, sir, see you around,' I said and began to walk away.

I was about to turn the corner when I heard his voice, 'Saagar, I forgot. Professor Sood wants to see you in his room at noon today. I was just going to put it up on the bulletin board.'

My heart hammering in my throat, I asked, 'What about?' trying to act casual.

'Don't know, he didn't say. Just that he wants to discuss something with you.'

'Okay,' I said, acting cool, even as my heart started a slow thump. I knew it. What I had done had to have some repercussions. There was no way I was going to get off scot-free. With a bravado that I wasn't feeling, I went for my Electro-Mag. class. The professor was a favourite of mine. He had a way of speaking that would clear the fog of electro-magnetic equations even before it formed. The fact that magnetism occurs perpendicular to the flow of electric current was known to all students; the formula said so. But that the perpendicular was in a three-dimensional plane was cleared in one second by a gentle wave of his hands. Twelve years of schooling had missed that little detail for me. I had been mugging it till I met this professor. This is what a good teacher can do, I would think to myself as I attended his class.

Saloni was already sitting there, notebook out, right in the first row. She glanced at me and gestured for me to join her. I ignored her and went to my favourite place—the middle row. The front was too claustrophobic and the back was out of bounds since I had slight myopia and was too vain to wear spectacles.

As I sat and waited for the professor to come, my mind slipped to the conversation I was going to have with Prof Sood. I thought and rehearsed how the conversation would go—what he would say and how I would defeat him with the force of my arguments…I dreamt on.

The class ended and I woke up from my reverie. Phew! It was 12. I couldn't avoid Dr Sood anymore. I walked slowly towards the professors' chambers—past the auditorium, the library and the patch of garden where I would often sit. I knocked and entered as he barked his permission.

The professor looked up. 'Come in, Saagar,' he said effusively. Strange, I thought, my senses on full alert. He actually sounds happy to see me! It was too good to be true, surely. In any case, the professor was known to be deceptive in his demeanor. Better be careful.

Heart hammering, I tiptoed in. This was the first time I had been in any professor's chamber. The room was not too big but managed to look spacious; the high-domed ceilings giving a feeling of space that did not exist in reality. And that was not the only illusion. The whole room looked decidedly tilted with Newton, Einstein and others staring down at me from their lofty framed perches that were off-centred and the skewed book-shelves adding to the effect by threatening to unload their top-heavy overflowing weights at any time. I craned my neck and looked curiously at the titles—Sri Aurobindo jostling for space with J. Krishnamurthy, along with the usual scientific journals. The room also had a lovely brick-lined arched window that looked down on a serene garden, one of the many that St. Stephen's is well known for.

Hold it! Wasn't that the very patch of grass where I usually lounged around, reading Roli's letters? The actual spot where I would frolic in the grass was directly in front of my eyes. And this must be the opaque window I would see from the other side…Holy crap! It was definitely not opaque from this side.

The realization sank in. I must have spent a lot of time here right under the professor's nose.

'Yes, Saagar, I have seen you there many times, especially when I am leaving to take your class, for which you would usually never turn up. And you were clearly not studying anything serious, as I recall!' He sounded rather amused and I flamed with embarrassment. This guy had directly observed my ungainly lovelorn antics on the grass. This was the very patch of grass that was responsible for the frequent grass stains on my slacks that my mother would crib about. No wonder the good professor was pissed! This was worse than I'd imagined. The episode in class wasn't just the professor being whimsically nasty. In short, I had deserved what I got that day.

All my fantasies about 'the boy stood on the burning deck…', confrontations and victories of David over Goliath disappeared like air escaping from a deflating tire. The time for discretion and apologies was now. Thank God there was no one around to witness my rout.

'I am sorry, sir; I was really rude to you,' I heard myself babbling. 'The fault is entirely mine. I didn't study your subject and yet I behaved so badly. I am extremely sorry, sir. Please forgive me, sir.'

The professor looked at me with a twinkle in his eyes as I stammered to a stop. It made him look almost likable. 'It's forgotten, my boy. I too was your age once upon a time.'

I did a double take. Be careful. I told myself. Something is definitely brewing. He could be fattening me up for the kill in his usually deceptive style.

The professor continued, 'Why I called you here was because I must answer your questions so that you may be able to come back to my class!' The old man was being sarcastic, I decided. He really wants to rub my nose in it.

'That was highly rude, sir,' I insisted earnestly. 'I must apologize once again.' The professor seemed impervious to my protestations, so I blabbered on, 'Of course I didn't mean that, sir, even though my questions were genuine…' I stammered on manfully. 'I would never have the temerity to actually expect such a thing from you, sir…'

'Oh that's fine, apologies accepted and all that,' the professor waved a dismissive hand; '…although if you know these scientists as well as you claim, you would also know that they were highly eccentric and extremely rude sometimes! Social niceties weren't their forte. So I say, just forget it. It's all part of the scientific spirit.' The old man seemed to be genuinely magnanimous. I wondered why as he continued, 'Yet your questions remain. I might ignore your rudeness but I can't ignore your questions, my boy.'

'Why not, sir? Can we not forget that I had ever asked them, sir? That won't be a problem from my end, sir,' I offered anxiously. Anything to escape the sword that hung over me!

'No, I can't, Saagar, and that's because, even while your rudeness might have been intentional, your questions are completely valid and, in fact, extremely astute, and therefore deserving of an answer,' the professor retorted. 'I myself and many others have been seeking answers to these questions for a long time. No one has found them yet, but together we can try to solve this great mystery.'

This was strange. The great Dr Sood—the head of the Indian chapter of the CERN project that was trying to find the God particle—was asking me for help? It just didn't add up.

I asked, 'Why me, sir? There are scientists all over the world looking into these things with multi-billion dollar particle accelerators. As far as I am concerned, it is true that I have studied and loved physics all my life (and it's not been a very long life either, I added silently to myself) but I have come up with only questions and no answers, as yet.'

'That's exactly why I am offering you this collaboration—because you independently asked the crucial questions.' Seeing my blank look, he explained, 'Saagar, the world of cutting-edge physics is very different from what you imagine it to be. The stereotypical image that you may have of scientists is not real. We no longer have eccentric and brilliant lone-rangers looking for answers in their makeshift labs or their sitting rooms—like Einstein, Faraday or Maxwell. What we have instead are large teams of people working together on multi-billion dollar projects.'

'That's what I said, sir…' I interrupted, but he interrupted me right back.

'Wait. Let me finish. The end result is that we are creating scientific bureaucracies whose basic interest is to show that they are doing something to justify the money that is granted to them. For these groups of people, real science is not the first thing on their minds. Most physicists treat Einstein as God and they never really question the basic premises that he made. They all try to understand the theory of relativity and construct experiments to validate it but they never question the basic tenets themselves or try to find a new way to explain things. Tell me,' he queried, 'if Einstein had treated Newton like an invincible God, could he have ever dared to develop the theory of relativity?'

I did a double take. He had a point, I decided. 'No, sir. Probably not, sir.'

'Yet that's what is happening today,' he shrugged. 'You are too young and inexperienced to know this but most academic institutes the world over are in the grip of professors who cannot be retired or fired and who have opinions set in stone. Most so-called cutting edge research in science today happens only with their express concurrence. Anyone who comes up unconventionally from outside the university system is simply ignored by these prima donnas. It's like an exclusive club membership. Very few original minds are able to get in today.'

I could make out that this was Dr Sood's pet peeve. He warmed up to the theme further. 'It's a fiefdom! Yes, that's what it is today with no one able to gatecrash the scientific party! Do you know the amount of money that the government puts into scientific research today?' I didn't answer the rhetorical question—he clearly didn't expect me to. 'Billlions upon billions! Do you know that there are scientific organizations today whose accounting departments employ more people than their research departments?'

'No sir, I didn't know that. That is indeed strange!' I replied and the professor continued his mini tirade. 'Yes Saagar. It is a shocking fact but how else can they consume all the money that the government throws at them?'

What the professor was saying started to make sense. It triggered a memory of what I had read in a magazine interview. The interview was with a doctor—a conscientious researcher—who had said that he would never go into cancer research since it involved too much money and too little science. And hadn't Einstein's own doctoral thesis been rejected by the University of Berne, after which he had no recourse but to work as a clerk—a patent examiner in the Swiss Patent office—and that too at level III, while he wrote his famous theory? What seemed like scientific folklore appeared to have its far seamier modern avatar.

'Yes, Saagar.' The professor could probably see the wheels clicking and grinding in my brain. 'If you don't have a post doctorate from Harvard or MIT, they won't even entertain your theory, which I am sure you are working on. Aren't you?' I nodded as he continued. 'Scientific journals don't have the time to read your papers, much less understand what you have written, so the only thing they look at are your qualifications and what your peers—the old boys' network—think of you. It all depends on where you have done your PhD from.'

I was nonplussed. This was the last thing I had expected to hear when I walked in. 'Sir,' I commented hesitantly and deferentially, '...all this sounds wrong, somehow, but I still can't understand what does this have to do with me.'

'Sit down, my boy. Let me explain. What I am saying is that the real scientific spirit is in real short supply these days. It is strained out by the education system till all that is left is scientific yes-men. And they are more mice than men!' Professor Sood laughed at his own joke as he continued, 'We throw the baby out with the bath water in these fancy colleges. In fact, college is better known for, as they say, dulling diamonds and polishing stones than the other way around! We need to go back to finding the original spirit and once again take a look at the fundamental issues facing science.' He paused to eye me and continued, 'That's where you come in. I am getting together some of the best scientific minds that I know at my house this weekend. The idea is to talk pure science while thinking totally out of the box and using nothing more than thought experiments and existing data banks, to try and make original headway in the field of physics.'

I gawked at the professor and he raised his eyebrows. 'You have heard of the theory of everything, I presume?' He knew he had struck a chord, the way my eyes lit up. Had I ever?

'Yes I have, sir!' I said, overcome with emotion. While my classmates from school had been dreaming of girls and cars, my fantasies usually revolved around finding the theory of everything, receiving the Nobel Prize and having beautiful women looking up to me with adoring eyes. The professor was offering me a shot at my dream. Yet, something was still off-centre here. 'Sir, but that means that you probably don't believe in the God particle that they are looking for,' I blurted out, words tripping over each other. 'Since it seems so much of an afterthought to somehow make the standard model work mathematically…' I trailed off. I didn't understand the standard model very well and nor did I like the whole approach to it. But that meant nothing. Far better minds than mine had worked on it, yet for me it somehow just didn't add up.

The professor gave me a keen look. 'Yes, Saagar, one has to live and earn money and fame in the real world also, but it is shrewd of you to understand that so quickly. But I want to make a real difference to science and not just be acknowledged by a bunch of illiterates; hence this is my pet project—my life's goal, in the real sense. As I said, I am the organizer of this group of people who meet once a month to talk about physics. And I would like to invite you to join this group. We meet at 4 pm every third Saturday of the month at my house. You know where my house is, don't you?' he boomed.

'Yes, sir,' I said, quite overcome. This is what I had been looking for all my life!

'Good! I will see you then, Saagar?'

'Yes, sir, I will be there, sir.'

The rest of the day passed in a happy daze. This was cool! This was surreal! After years of not finding my way, here I was knocking at the door of a club that consisted of like-minded people. What could be better? This was the best vindication possible of the years of lonely splendour that I had spent in musty libraries looking for things that made no sense to any of the people I knew. I sat in class the rest of the day, not hearing a word. After class I went to my favourite corner of the library and thought about all the things that I wanted to find out and hadn't known whom to ask. How does the universe really work? Maybe I was closer to finding out! And as evening fell, with that happy thought I went home to grandmother.

Naani was in the kitchen, cooking. She loved it there and that's where she was usually to be found. The kitchen wasn't like the modern kitchens of today. The cook sat on the floor that was kept spic and span and we all ate there, sitting on wooden slats. Shoes had to be kept out, of course. The food was served piping hot and the place was extremely cozy in the winters with the hot rotis coming off the gas-stove right in front of us.

'So, Saagar, what's happening with you?' Naani asked me cheerfully. 'You have been in your own world for the last few days.' She must have been told to pump me about what I was up to—basically, whether I was getting over my lady love or not. I was sure a report was being sent regularly to my parents, but I didn't blame her for her inquisitiveness. She was far too sweet for that, with not a single crooked bone in her body.

'Yes, Granny,' I told her, growling out the word as though I were a lion. I preferred to use the English version of Naani when I addressed her, 'Something strange and interesting has been happening in college.'

'What?' Naani's birdlike eyes sparkled with a childish curiosity that belied her age.

'Well, one of my professors, Dr Sood, has invited me to be part of a group of people who are going to find out about how the universe was created.' I told her the story as simply as I could.

'Bah. However hard they may try, science can never find that out!' Naani announced imperiously.

'And why is that, my dear granny?' I shot back, growling out the g's.

'Because what is made of the five elements can never discover what lies beyond the five elements,' she replied. I had heard this theme before. Her Guruji—Charan Singh Maharaj, of the Radha Soami sect, had spoken often on this subject. Some words had fallen into my ears as well, since I was her chaperone to the satsangs—spiritual talks—which she would regularly attend. Not that I had understood much as a child.

'Well, Naani, in that case, since we are all—including your guru—made of the five elements; we can never discover the fundamentals of creation anyway!' I quipped. We had been having this running argument for years now. It was the old debate between science and spirituality. After years of observation, I had concluded that gurus were lazy people who didn't want to go through the rigours of scientific validation. They would claim big things but I had yet to hear a guru give a formula which could be cross-checked to back his pet theory of creation. Empty talk was easy.

My bias was understandable. I had been brought up by a diehard Nehruvian father for whom industrial plants and universities were the real temples of modern India, rather than the ancient ones that dotted literally every banyan tree in the country. Not to blame my father entirely; I had taken to the atheist line of thinking like a duck to water, since that dovetailed with my interest in science.

I leaned back in my chair and thought back to those wonder years, when all of my life still lay ahead and Naani was still alive. God, I missed her so! Over the years as I changed my perspectives, I thought of her often. She most-of-all would have loved to see what I had become and what I had achieved. Yet that's what life is usually about. The people you love and whose approval you seek, or the ones who you obsessively want to prove wrong, are usually never around to see the results…

'I hope I am not digressing from the topic for your article, Ashish,' I asked the young man sitting across the table. 'I am not sure if all this is relevant.'

'It is!' Ashish blurted out. 'This is fascinating copy! Please do continue. We need our readers to understand the man behind the icon and this is compelling background stuff.'

'Ok. Don't say I didn't warn you!' I laughed and continued, 'As I was saying, back then, the Science versus Spirituality debate was a no-brainer for me. The glaring loopholes and the logical fallacies in the spiritual argument were obvious and I will recount a few of them here.'

I looked at Ashish, who was giving me his full attention. Reassured, I started. 'Firstly, in this world of spirituality and

God, we are all imperfect, living in an imperfect world, but we must be seen as striving towards perfection. The question is—why would a perfect God make this imperfect world in the first place? And if God is as kind, just, gentle and compassionate as most religions and gurus claimed, why would he create misery, injustice, anger, hatred and all the stuff that one could see around in abundance? Why would he create pain, disease, death? Why would he have children born handicapped and dying of cancer even before they have had a chance to live?'

I continued, 'Secondly, why did we need to be vegetarians to enter God's kingdom? If killing and eating another living thing was so wrong, then why was it the norm in the first place? Why was that inbuilt into the design of creation? The fact is that even the most die-hard vegetarian could not survive if he or she did not ingest something that had been alive shortly before being consumed! The point was that if God preferred us to be totally non violent and not take any life, He would have designed us to be able to digest things such as stones and earth. The vegetarian argument that plants, though alive, don't have enough consciousness and hence are spiritually acceptable as food, sounded more like a convenience to me than logically robust. Didn't the *Bhagavadgita* say that all living things had the same soul inside? So why were plants supposed to be lesser beings? The whole thing was bizarre!'

I continued, warming up to the theme further, 'Thirdly, I couldn't, back then, understand the concept of self-denial—of fasting and torturing oneself to find the path to God. To me, all our rituals seemed nothing but exercises in puerile superstition. For example, did it make sense for non-vegetarians to eat meat on all days of the week except Tuesdays and on the nine days of the Navaratras? And what was the link between poverty and spirituality? After all why would God make a virtue out of poverty when he himself had created all the riches of the world?'

I paused, took a breath and raised an eyebrow at Ashish. 'I could go on and on! In short, the ways of a capricious creator were beyond me and because of that I thought, back then, that religion wasn't worth pursuing, science was the thing for me. After all, everything should have a reason and logic. Our job was to find out how things worked in a scientific manner. End of story.'

'And yet, Ashish,' I continued, '...My pat and straightforward arguments would come up short against something that I couldn't quite place. There was something about Naani's demeanour that left a question mark. Not what she said or the logic of her statements (which I found silly) but how she behaved. The ignorant optimism that she generated and the glow of peace that I saw on her countenance were things that I couldn't see in the faces of those who were intellectually superior and more scientifically advanced than her. Scientific inquiry, doubt and reason, would lead me to the theory of everything one day, of that I was sure, and that was sure to make me happy, but that was still a long way off. Naani, on the other hand, was happy today—in the here and now and in the completely unreasonable belief that her guru loved her and that was apparently enough for her to lead a perfectly happy life.'

I continued as Ashish listened raptly. 'What would really get my goat was that her optimistic beliefs were never borne out by the harsh realities of her own life. She remained an incorrigible optimist, however hard life knocked her down. The fact was that Naani had had a really tough life. Difficulties had come in droves. A refugee from the Partition days, she and Naana—my maternal grandfather—had come to Delhi with nothing more than the clothes on their backs and two young children to look after. After 30 years, and the addition of two more kids to their brood, the weight of putting four children through college had literally bent her at the waist; she now walked with her upper body stooped at an impossible angle of 30 degrees. Yet, despite the physical frailty and her advancing years—she was 70 at that time—she kept a punishing schedule that would shame people half her age. The normal start to her day was at an unearthly 4:00 am and bedtime was rarely before 10:00 pm at night.

As I talked to Ashish, I slipped back in time and reverted to the tale I was recounting…

I remembered a conversation when I had been sitting in the kitchen on a cold wintery day, like it was today. 'Naani,' I said, as I stole a delicious slice of the potatoes she had just finished shallow-frying, 'how can you live like this year after year?'

She smiled, spooned some of the potatoes into a small bowl and handed it to me. 'Why, what's wrong with this?' she asked. 'This is my life.'

'But you work so hard and never take a break! How do you find the strength to do all this? Your ungrateful children never help you.' I added my two bits to the eternal battle that I had had with my mother all my life.

'You can't help your circumstances, dear child. All you can do is to do what you need to do under *your* circumstances.'

'But don't you get disheartened sometimes? Especially when people don't return the favours that you do for them?'

I persisted. I had constantly observed what she would unilaterally do for others, who scarcely bothered to even thank her in return—especially her ungrateful elder son, my elder mama-maternal uncle, who had moved away and literally abandoned her when he had found a lucrative job abroad!

'No, beta, that's their karma. I can only do what I believe is right,' she told me with deep conviction. 'In any case, Guruji lends me the strength whenever I need it.'

Invariably, no matter what we were talking about—including my amazing news that day—the conversation would veer back to her guru since she loved talking about him.

'That's just wishful thinking!' I protested.

'No, Saagar. He has been known to appear before different people in his glorious form across vast distances, when they needed his help. He has been there and will be there whenever I need him, even when he or I are not in this world anymore.'

I rolled my eyes. That sounded seriously optimistic to me, bordering on delusional, since I had never ever seen her communicating with him even through a postcard. I grilled her further about the mechanics of this communication. 'How do you let your Guruji know that you need his help?'

'I pray,' she said with utmost sincerity.

That took the cake! That reply infuriated me in a humorous sort of way. Typical spiritual self-fulfilling logic! 'And how long does it take for your wishes to reach him?'

'It's instantaneous,' Naani replied.

'Naani, don't you know that even light takes a fraction of a second to reach anywhere on the planet?' I asked her patiently, in slow motion, as if I was talking to an idiot child.

'Saagar, the speed of thought, unlike the speed of light, is instantaneous and my Guru helps me because I believe in him,' she returned equally patiently. 'The only condition is that I maintain the constancy of complete faith. And mind you, the results are dependent on my ultimate good and not some temporary relief that I may want.'

I shook my head in exasperation. 'Yes, Naani, and I believe the moon is made of cheese! I am allergic to cheese, otherwise I would have eaten a good portion of it by now.' I rolled my eyes again—something I'd end up doing often with her.

Usually I would leave it at that. The differences of opinion that I had with Naani were in any case more in the nature of a sparring game. One has to humour old people, right? Our way of thinking cannot be their way since they are looking at the end of their lives. They say that as one approaches death, one tries to find some way to defeat it—by extending this life into the next. Finding God and the promise of eternal life is the only way to do that. You can't deny an old person this mental solace!

As I thought these uncharitable thoughts about old people, I found Naani looking at me with a twinkle in her eyes. 'Don't worry, Saagar, I know that sooner or later you will stop flirting with science and go on the spiritual path. You are my spiritual heir in this family of non-believers.' For some reason she would always reiterate that.

'Humph. That's just not possible, Naani. I love my chicken curry far too much!' I retorted with a grin. Our bantering continued, as it usually did, as evening fell. Soon, it was time to sleep, since the day began very early in this household.

My classmates gave me curious glances as I walked into the M.P. class the next day. They looked at me, looked at the professor, tittered a bit and waited for the fireworks to start. Nothing happened and the class rolled on—a quiet affair with the professor writing down a series of equations. I dutifully noted them down. As class broke up, Saloni walked up to me, touched me on the shoulder and asked, 'How come you are here?'

Now was the time to brag a bit, so I said, 'I thought I'd let Dr Sood off the hook, let bygones be bygones, and come to class.' A couple of guys walked up as well. Guys who had never ever spoken to me till now—the breed called the front-benchers.

'So, Saagar, what's happening?' said someone as the group surrounded me. I was definitely the flavour of the day. Notoriety is not necessarily a bad thing, I was discovering.

'Nothing much, guys. It's all good.' It was obvious that they were all curious about what I was doing back in class and Dr Sood's nonchalant response to my presence. I said nothing and let them stew as I basked in the attention.

Pankaj the Brain walked up and came straight to the point, 'I saw your name on the noticeboard. The professor had asked to see you at 12:00 yesterday. What happened when you met him?' He didn't beat about the bush, my man Pankaj. Everyone standing around turned and looked at me, eyes bright with interest. Being on the noticeboard brought instant—well, notice! I sighed. The cat was out of the bag. Pankaj was sharp, with a P.C.M. (Physics-Chemistry-Maths, for the uninitiated) aggregate of 100 per cent. He had enjoyed an exalted status till then. Even the professors talked to him with deference. In our first unit tests he had created a major buzz in the college by answering all eight questions, as against the five we were supposed to answer. Next to the directive on the first page, 'Answer any five,' he'd written imperiously, 'Check any five!'

I wondered if he was jealous of all the attention I was getting. 'Well…the old man and I had a talk about the questions I had asked in class,' I revealed.

'He must have really taken your pants off!' Pankaj chortled, beady eyes glinting. He was very clear that I deserved it for my rudeness.

'Not really!' I shot back. 'He actually invited me to dinner.'

'What!' exclaimed Rajiv, another front bencher, 'How come?'

'That's because the questions I asked actually impressed the old man,' I explained, pretending to be modest. 'He told me that he has been pursuing the very same questions all his life and he appreciated me for thinking of those questions at this young age.'

There was an incredulous silence.

'What bull! What do you mean? That can't be true…' Pankaj blustered.

'Why not?' I interrupted.

He shot back, 'Your comments on gravity can't be right…' He stuttered, 'be…because science is precise about everything! Gravity is well documented and the paths of the planets and of satellites are precisely calculated. All the other formulae are crystal clear and science has explained almost everything. The nuclear bomb, satellites and the moon mission are proof that science is right—all the way from the large details to the micro picture. And look at the world—built by technologies which are all based on science! All this is evidence that scientists are right about their theories…' Pankaj tailed off, obviously disturbed. I didn't blame him. He couldn't stomach his formulae driven,

100 per cent C.B.S.E.[1] approved, scientific world disappearing into a chimera of uncertainties.

I couldn't resist a barb. 'Look, Pankaj, if you step out of our N.C.E.R.T.[2] text books and really look at the mysteries of the universe and of life, you will be forced to conclude that we don't know all that much.' I got an uncomprehending glare in return, and sighed. 'Pankaj, it will take a long time to explain what I am saying, and…'

'And Saagar is not free right now since he's helping me out with the Electro-Magnetic lectures!' Saloni butted in.

All the guys—and all the girls as well—turned around and looked at her and then at me. That too was a first. The best-looking girl in the first semester of St. Stephen's College was obviously making a very public statement; a statement of intent. This would be front-page news for the college gossip rag and hard to miss and hard to swallow for all the hopeful males around. I ignored her more out of shock than any attempt at being cool. Turning my back on her, I addressed Pankaj. 'Pankaj, I don't blame you for what you believe, but you haven't thought about things deeply enough. Learn to ask why and you will discover a black hole right under your feet.'

Everyone looked at Pankaj's feet.

'I would really like to understand what you are saying,' said Rajiv thoughtfully, 'What you said in class about gravity and the space-time continuum.'

'I will be happy to explain, but not today, Rajiv. Right now I have to go off to the library and make a list of discussion points for my meeting with the professor.'

---

[1] CB.S.E.: Central Board of Secondary Education

[2] N.C.E.R.T.: National Council Of Educational Research and Training

'I thought you said dinner!' Pankaj said accusingly, blinked and demanded, 'Hold on. Have you been invited to his Saturday meeting?' Pankaj trailed off as the import of what he was saying sank into the gathered crowd.

'As a matter of fact, I have,' I replied, and thought, so what's the big deal?

You could hear a pin drop—a rare feature when no teacher is around. As Saloni told me later, the silence lasted a few minutes after I had walked off. No student had ever been invited for this meeting—only professors and scientists. The who's who of the premier scientific establishments in India, in fact. This last fact I came to know only when I attended the meeting—and it was a good thing too. Had I known that in advance, I'd have been too petrified to attend.

The week passed peacefully after that. People kept their distance. It seemed that I had created an aura around myself, which people didn't know how to deal with. I too liked the solitude, wrapped up as I was in my thoughts about the theory of everything. I did, however, go over to Saloni's place to help her out with her studies.

Life moved on and, just a week later, my exile in Anand Parbat was over as abruptly as it had started and I was summarily recalled home, no reason given. Home was government quarters at Pragati Vihar on Lodhi Road. As I took the public bus home, I wondered at the sudden recall. Could it be because my parents thought that I had gotten over my infatuation with Mumbai? Not true, unfortunately. I was still persona non grata! The reason for the recall, as I discovered as I walked in through the main door, was that my cousin Vinod, from our ancestral village, had arrived and was sitting on the sofa grinning from ear to ear as he spotted me walking in.

Alas, I had not been forgiven or pardoned and it had been Vinod's insistence on seeing me at once that had forced my parents to end my exile at Naani's house. After exchanging basic pleasantries, Vinod got down to what he liked to discuss best—girls. I quickly told him about Saloni since I badly needed his advice on what to do. I also wanted to brag about getting a girl interested in me. I had to tell someone, for God's sake, and who better than this rustic connoisseur of women?

But before that I asked and he explained the reason for his visit. He had come not only because my father had arranged a job for him—a long-held promise to his sister, but also because the village was becoming increasingly unsafe for him. He had made far too many enemies, given the developing caste equations there. If you were the leader type you had to join the appropriate *sena*—local caste army—or else you would be killed by one local *sena* or the other.

Vinod was the proverbial son of the soil, born in the cowshed and brought up on the back of a tractor. A rough and active young man of average height, with broad shoulders tapering down to a slim waist, he had a style of walking that reminded you of Raj Kumar—the iconic Bollywood actor. He and I were very different. I was studious and impractical and he was cheerful about his lack of higher education. Yet he made up for it with a refreshing practicality and homely intelligence that made him good at negotiations and business. He was also a very good reader of character and invariably his opinions of the people he met were spot on, whether in the village or the city. The most important point was that, in spite of our differences, we got along famously. He probably admired my scholarly intelligence and I admired his practical skills and his consummate ease around women. We probably also got along because we didn't have to compete in anything. I guess I secretly wanted to be a bit like him and he probably wanted to be a bit like me. He was also a very energetic kind of guy and he would just get up and do whatever he decided to do. He had forced my homecoming simply by cheerfully refusing to read the subtle undertones in the explanations my parents offered and insisting that I meet him immediately.

I had met Vinod for the first time when we had all gone to the village five years ago. It was my first trip to our ancestral village and it had been all new, exciting and a trifle strange. Vinod had taken me under his wing immediately and had given me a guided tour of the fields which he insisted belonged to me and not to my village bumpkin of an uncle. He had also advised me to stake my claim on my lands as my scheming uncle had no desire to split the property with my dad. My uncle believed that the lands belonged to him since my dad had left decades ago to live in Delhi in pursuit of higher education and finally a career in the Indian Civil Services and had never shown any interest in farming them. Vinod's opinion was that my dad may well be a Class I officer in the Indian Railways, but was far too much of a sentimental fool to deal with his wily younger brother whose sole ambition was to somehow usurp our portion of the land.

Our village lay in the heart of Sherghati near the ancient town of Gaya on what used to be known as the Grand Trunk Road and was now called Sher Shah Suri Marg. As I think of my village now, fond memories of ancient mountains in the background and mango trees around our house come to me. I remember the river that winds its way close to our thatched mud house and that's where I had heard the oft-repeated stories of my dad almost drowning as he was learning to swim.

The scene was idyllic and I have pleasant memories of the serene riverfront. I vividly recall the view of cranes standing on one leg, waiting patiently to catch fish, as the tall grass gently swayed in the breeze. Back then, the left bank of the river also housed a village school and that's where my Chaachi—paternal aunt—taught. As was the norm in most village schools in Bihar back then, there was only one classroom and only one teacher for the entire school, which held classes from the nursery to the fifth standard. To handle the workload, the older students were drafted to teach the younger ones. And when Chaachi went on leave, as she did when we visited, the entire school had to shut down. As they say, it happens only in India…

I remember walking through the narrow bylanes of the village that smelled of freshly plastered mud—not an unpleasant smell—and I would often find the village women looking at me and giggling. I assumed that Dinkar's (my father's) family was a novelty to be gawked at and I learnt to ignore the giggles. The women were very different from the city ones but really beautiful and graceful all the same, with their clunky silver jewellery and swaying waist bands that really showed off their walking abilities. Although decorously dressed from head to toe, they unclothed themselves figuratively with the way they looked at us with frank eyes and flirty smiles—when the village men weren't around, that is. They would look at us—Vinod and me—give us sidelong glances and talk amongst ourselves in Magadhi, a language that I did not understand. What they would say was obviously funny and frequently Vinod would reply to them in the same lingo with a laugh. When I cross-examined him, his usual reply was that I was too young to hear such things. When I insisted, he told me that some of the girls wanted to marry me and that he'd told them to wait for a couple of years till I was of age. It was obvious even to my tender ears that Vinod wasn't telling me the entire truth, but I let it slide since I found the whole experience slightly unnerving. Vinod would often proceed to give me a personal piece of information about some woman we had crossed on the streets—personal bordering on the intimate. What he usually said sounded so unbelievable that I would tell him that he was talking through his hat. That challenge led me to the incident where I lost my virginity, but that's again running ahead of the story.

The next time I met Vinod was when we returned to the village a couple of years later. Papa's dear friend had just lost his son-in-law. A Rajput by caste, the young man had been gunned down by the Naxalites. That was the first brush I had with the quagmire that is the caste politics of Bihar. Now of course the situation is much worse and there is no way that I can even think of ever returning to the village, so ridden is the area with Naxalites and their opponents, but in those days things were far more innocent; the first rounds of vengeance were just starting back then.

Papa was busy with his friend's family and I spent the next few days with Vinod since my chaacha—paternal uncle—was also not around. Vinod was made my keeper and given strict instructions about keeping me out of harm's way. I wasn't to be taken anywhere outside the village, especially to Murli Parbat (Flute Mountain) which was infested with Naxalites. This was sad, since that particular hillock had been our favourite haunt the last time I had been to the village. Not only that, I was supposed to ask for permission to even go to the local market. The result was that we were restricted to the village and its fields. It was quite boring and Vinod and I would spend the day fishing in the river and taking a dip when the sun got too hot. At night Vinod would disappear and I would be left alone at home, along with my aunt and my other cousins—a gaggle of giggly kids. After a couple of nights of boredom I told Vinod that I would come to his house and stay with Bua—my father's sister—and him.

'But I am not staying at home,' Vinod told me.

'Where, then?' I asked him.

'I go off to the machan, you know, the watchtower to guard the crops at night.'

'Okay, so I'll come with you,' I announced. The idea sounded exciting since the men on the watchtowers carried guns to guard against wild animals. Leopards had been known to enter the village and elephants regularly raided the fields to get into the sugarcane patches.

Vinod looked at me thoughtfully for a moment and said, 'You are a bit too young. Although…' he paused and then continued, 'although it would actually be safer on the watchtower with all those armed men around, but…' he trailed off.

'But what?' I said impatiently. I couldn't understand what Vinod was up to. Why was he acting so mysterious?

'You can come but…if you come you will see things that you might not want to see or hear, a tender-eared city kid that you are, still tied to his mother's sari.' There was a taunt and a challenge in Vinod's voice.

Challenges had always provoked me since the days of the bull. 'I am not a kid, Vinod. I am 15 years old now. I won't take offence and I won't tell anyone. What happens there anyway?' My voice started angry, went through petulant and ended up pleading.

'Well, what do men do when they have to stay awake at night and have nothing else to do?' he asked me challengingly.

'What?'

'Drink, gamble, talk shit and screw women.' Vinod said with a smug smile.

'What!' I could understand the drinking and gambling but where did the women come from at that time of the night?

'Are they whores?' I demanded, trying to sound like a man of the world.

'Humph, I've never needed to screw a whore as yet, although the other men in the watchtowers frequently call them from the bazaar in the market.' Vinod snorted. 'Have you seen that large house that stands by itself at the corner of the market towards the river?'

'Yes,' I said.

'Well, that's a whorehouse and that's where the whores come from.'

I digested this piece of information. 'So if you don't screw whores and yet you don't want me to come, then who do you, uh…?' I tapered off, the Hindi word for sex being a bit too direct for me to use with ease.

Vinod looked at me with a smile 'That's why I was warning you. You are too innocent for such wiles. Stay home with your

Chaachi and the kids or go over to my place and stay with your Bua.'

'Look, Vinod, I think you are trying to simply fob me off. I insist that I will come.' I could feel an excitement growing within me.

'Suit yourself,' Vinod said laconically. 'Just remember that I warned you and also that since it is too dangerous to wander around at that time of night, you will have to stay on the watchtower, whatever happens. If you want to chicken out and run home in the middle of the night, you just can't. Remember also that the watchtower is just 10 feet by 10 feet and there is no place to hide. And I will not be escorting a crybaby back home at that time of night. Our houses will be barricaded anyway. If you can promise me this, then I will think about it.'

I digested all this information. Suddenly the whole thing started sounding far scarier than I could handle. 'I don't have to do anything, I hope?' There was a tremble in my voice. I suddenly lost heart. My experience of the carnal type was zero. All I had done was spy upon some relatives when I was 12. What I had seen was strange and exciting and consisted of glimpses of naked skin and lots of to-and-fro movements and noises that sounded as if the woman was in some kind of pain. I couldn't really make out what was happening, but it all looked forbidden and exciting. Since then I had managed to acquire some knowledge about the birds and the bees by picking the lock on my father's briefcase and browsing through the graphic pictures and stories that I found in the books and magazines inside - obviously stuff that he had retained from his university days in London. I knew for sure what was involved between a man and a woman, but there is a scary difference between theory and practice.

Vinod looked at me perceptively. He could make out that I was scared. 'No you don't have to do anything, unless you want to, of course. Remember, it's all supposed to be fun and it's definitely not like doing your homework,' he chortled.

'Good,' I gulped. 'That's settled then.'

'If you decide to come, reach my house after dinner, but before 8 pm and carry some bedding, some mosquito repellent, something to eat, and a torch and drinking water, of course.'

I ran home and told my Chaachi that I would be off to the watchtower with Vinod for the night. She grumbled a bit, but I insisted that I was going and that Vinod had said that it was safe. 'Watch out for that Vinod. He is too smart for his own good. What will your mother say if you get spoiled in his company?' she demanded, clearly unhappy.

'Chaachi, as it is, I spend my entire day with Vinod, and that is time enough for him to spoil me if he wanted to! I am going and that's final.' I had discovered that village women listened to and obeyed men far more than city women did and if you said what you wanted strongly enough, they deferred to you even if you were 15 and the woman 45!

With a thumping heart I headed off to Bua's house and found Vinod standing at the door, his ancient 12-bore double loader slung on his shoulder. 'We will swing by the village shop before we head off to the watchtower. I have to pick up something,' he told me. As we turned the last corner of the village, Vinod stopped and lit up a cigarette. It was a bit odd as I had never seen him smoke before. Obviously he wasn't an expert as he started coughing after the first couple of puffs. He soon ground it out and we headed towards our fields. Surprisingly, he didn't pick up anything from any shop. We arrived at the watchtower, clambered up and surveyed our surroundings. I had been to the watchtower before during the day. It was a just a kilometer from the house but it seemed much further at night. It commanded a clear view, especially on a moonlit night like this one. We could see a couple of other machans or watchtowers in the distance. Vinod flashed his torchlight and explained the distress code to me—three long flashes interspersed with three short ones. He then flashed the 'Hello' code and our neighbour promptly replied with flashes of his own, after which Vinod and he had a hollered conversation. They exchanged some pleasantries and then we settled comfortably onto the watchtower.

As I sat and looked around, I could view the silvery expanse of the fields surrounding us—a beautiful sight. In the stillness, I could see silver strands of wheat stretching far into the distance—rather like a panoramic shot in a David Lean film. Vinod took out a bottle of country liquor and started swigging it. He didn't even offer it to me!

My excitement wore off as the minutes stretched on. It had been a long day and my physical exertions had tired me out. I dozed off, lulled into a dreamless sleep by the monotonous soothing sounds of crickets. Suddenly I woke up, startled by a noise. As I groggily sat up, I could hear Vinod talking, whispering in fact. He seemed to be just under the machan. As I was wondering who it could be, the ladder started to creak. I put my eye onto a crack in the floor but all I could make out was that he was helping someone up the steep ladder… I peered out into the darkness. Hold it! Wasn't it the girl we had passed that day on my last visit, the one with whom Vinod had exchanged some joke that I hadn't been able to understand? My heart started thumping. Vinod hadn't been joking about getting girls over to the machan. I pretended to sleep while he helped the girl up to the watchtower. She looked different somehow. It wasn't the dress since that was the same. Oh, okay—her chunni was missing and she had some kind of bright lipstick on, which made her look rather like an over-painted doll. She had grown up a bit since the last time I had seen her two years ago—from a slip of a girl to one with a voluptuous figure and a slender waist, whose curves were glinting in the silvery moonlight.

She didn't notice me since I was lying in a corner and the lantern was throwing long shadows in my direction. Before she could really look around, Vinod had grabbed her and was kissing her hard. She struggled a bit and then sagged against him. Vinod swung her around with her feet flying off the ground so that she had her back towards me. She giggled and clutched him while he put his finger to his lips and winked at me. Then he went to work on her. Rather, it would be fairer to say that they went to work on each other.

I watched fascinated as the girl responded eagerly to what Vinod was doing. He unhooked her blouse and she helped him take it off. I could see that he was roughly squeezing her nipples and rather than crying out in pain she was egging him on. They both seemed to be in a tearing hurry and Vinod soon had her stepping out of her skirts. There she was—my first live naked woman, standing with her figure displayed to my staring eyes! Vinod's hands were everywhere, kneading her buttocks, squeezing her breasts and stroking her on the nape of her neck. She seemed to really like that. Vinod was constantly kissing her and she responded by gently thrusting her hips against him. Vinod then pushed her down on her knees and she willingly complied. Before I realized what was happening, she was doing something that I had only heard about, though it was obvious that they had done it before. Vinod, being the devil that he is, kept telling her to take it in deeper. 'Suck it harder, you bitch—*saali kutiyaa*!' I was stunned by the language he was using and the way she responded to that so eagerly. He then looked at me, smiled and said to her (probably for my benefit) *'Badaa mazaa aa rahaa hai*—I am really enjoying this. You really know how to suck cock. Your husband-to-be is one lucky man!'

At that she took her mouth off him and said, 'I am not going to do all this with him. He will think I am a slut.' She coyly arched her back and seemed to chide him while gently fisting him. 'And I do this for you because I love you.' Her voice softened. 'I will do anything for you.' That seemed to be the cue that Vinod had been waiting for. He pulled her up, put his arms around her hips and effortlessly lifted her high in the air. She knew what to do. She wrapped her legs around his waist and with one swift thrust he entered her. She sighed and started rocking in his arms.

Vinod looked at me and crooked his finger, silently mouthing an invitation.

The blood was roaring in my ears. The sight before me was amazing. The gently swaying enticing hips, the silver waist-chain tinkling and glinting in the moonlight, the naked skin glimmering and soft feminine sighs of pleasure renting the air. As if in a dream, I found myself moving forward into the short distance between us. Vinod saw me coming and quickly moved his mouth to cover hers and started kissing her deeply. And then I was with them…

The girl gave a short muffled scream and started struggling as she felt me embracing her from behind. Vinod let go of her lips and said, 'Don't be scared. He is the boy you wanted to marry two years ago. See how much I care for you. I keep track of all your demands!' Vinod's eyes twinkled at me as he started thrusting into her harder. The girl twisted around wild-eyed to confirm my identity for herself. She found me staring at her as if in a trance, sighed, gave up and relaxed against me. I stood there not knowing what to do. 'Squeeze her breasts, Saagar baba! She really likes that,' advised Vinod and so I did. They felt soft, like candy floss, feeling far less substantial to my touch than they were to look at.

I could feel the girl beginning to really relax and enjoy what we were doing. She started moaning and rubbing her neck against my face. 'Have you ever kissed a girl?' Vinod huffed and puffed at me.

'No, *bhaiya* (brother),' I replied, continuing to squeeze her nipples methodically since she really seemed to like that.

'Kiss her, then,' Vinod commanded.

'How, *bhaiya*? Her face is towards you!' I clumsily tried to kiss her on her cheek.

'Kusum, teach Saagar baba how to kiss,' Vinod told her, and just like that she turned her face towards me and kissed me. As she did, Vinod started really thrusting into her and her mouth turned more and more insistent on mine.

It was all over rather soon. She slid down his legs and they leaned against each other. I stood awkwardly behind them feeling like the odd man out. I was now extremely aroused. As she slipped further down his legs to curl up on the floor, Vinod brusquely told me. 'Now take your turn with her.'

'But I don't know what to do!' I whispered, the excitement choking my voice.

'She will help you.' Vinod was brusque for some reason. 'I am going down for a smoke.'

'What if she gets pregnant?' I stammered. I knew everything about how a girl gets pregnant since we'd had our biology class on the human reproductive system just a few weeks ago.

'Don't think so much and don't worry,' he suggested. 'She is getting married in a week's time anyway. Hurry up. She has to go home soon.'

Vinod left and I turned back to look at her lying on the floor of the machan. Kusum gave me a smile and spread her legs. I got between her thighs, pulled my pants down, freeing my erect cock, thrust forward clumsily—and didn't get anywhere. I tried again, with no better results. 'Wait!' Kusum murmured, and I felt her fingers on me, holding me and placing me where I could feel myself enclosed. 'Now push it in,' she told me huskily. I shoved forward eagerly and found myself entering a tight moist tunnel. She gasped and so did I. It was just too exciting and I came. As I began to roll off her sheepishly, she stopped me, keeping me inside. 'Stay,' she said. 'Don't worry, it happens like this the first time,' and wrapped her legs around me. I was instantly hard again. This time it was much better. I pushed in hard. She seemed to like that. I looked at her face. Her eyes were closed and her mouth slack with desire. Every time I stopped, she'd push forward and make those mewling sounds that really excited me. Just as I finished thrusting into her and ejaculating, Vinod came back.

'Jaldi khatam karo, bahut der ho gayi hai,' he said in a hard voice. *'Kusum, tujhe mushkil ho jaayegi!'*[3]—And just like that,

[3]*Jaldi khatam karo, bahut der ho gayi hai. Kusum, tujhe mushkil ho jaayegi!*: Finish fast, it's late. Kusum, you will get into trouble!

the girl put on her clothes and left—my first fuck, disappearing into the night mist!

The rest of the night was uneventful. I was quiet and so was Vinod, who continued to drink steadily. I dozed off soon after and the next thing I remember is Vinod shaking me awake. It was morning.

I saw Kusum again the next day. She was the same coy giggly girl that I had seen the first time. Last night didn't seem to have changed her even a little bit. The following week we attended her wedding. She was dressed up like a traditional bride—an epitome of shyness and virginity, her head and face covered so that all you could see were her henna-decorated palms and feet. It was hard to convince myself, as I watched her in this new avatar, that she was the same girl whose mouth had been wrapped around Vinod's cock just a week ago.

The contrast really troubled me. This girl sitting under her wedding *mandap* was making a lifetime commitment to the man she was marrying, but that commitment itself was based on lies and pretence. Mind you, I was not being a hypocrite, or at least trying not to be one, moralizing about what she should or shouldn't have done with us. It was just that I found it difficult to stomach the utter dishonesty that lay at the base of what should be an honest relationship.

I said as much to Vinod, who looked at me with amazement. 'Are you crazy?' he demanded. 'Do you know what will happen if she is honest, confessing all to her husband about her experiences? He is not going to appreciate her honesty; instead he will pack her off the very next day. She would be lynched for being a slut. What a thought, Saagar baba!' Vinod shook his head, apparently stumped by my naivety. 'And I thought we village people were conservative psychos!'

I was also at a loss for an answer. What I was suggesting was impractical in the real world—even I realized that, and yet… 'What then is real, *bhaiya*? The girl we see right now getting married or the girl who was with us that night? They seem the complete opposite of each other.'

Vinod looked at me. 'Saagar baba, both are real. Just because she slept with us, does it make her bad? The fact that she hides it simply makes her a normal person, not a slut.' I let that sink in, holding my opinion. Vinod could make out that I wasn't convinced. 'Haven't you hidden inconvenient facts from your parents?'

'Yes I have, but…'

'Saagar, you must remember that women in society—especially in the villages—have no say and are completely dependent on the men,' Vinod explained seriously. 'We don't have divorces and remarriages. Women have to adjust to anything and everything that the men folk do—fair or unfair. Don't you think that they resent that somewhere?'

'Yes I suppose so…' I mumbled.

'What do you do when you dislike someone and can't do anything about it openly? Won't you cheat to take revenge, or do something underhand?'

I pondered over what Vinod was saying. He was right, as usual, yet what I had experienced was the beginning of an eternal conflict within.

Vinod continued, 'The trouble is that these women have no outlet for their sexual desires with their husbands since, if they show their real sexual selves, they would be branded as characterless. Thus they have two sides to them; one for their husbands and society and one for the lucky guy who gets to see them alone and in close-up. For him, they will do anything, and I mean anything at all!' Vinod said with reminiscences in his voice. 'Do you know why marriages are shunned between boys and girls of the same village?' I didn't say anything, waiting for him to continue. 'The official reason is that we are considered brothers and sisters as we share the same gotra or clan, but the real reasons are that the men in the village have no faith in the women they have grown up with, having observed them over the years and having slept with many of them on the sly. After all, we all live in the same small spaces and some amount of attraction and interaction is inevitable. Spying on naked women having a bath in the river is part of our folklore but what's to prevent it from going much further? Believe me, it does go much further!' he smirked. 'And who do we do it with? Our very own so-called aunts and sisters! What do you say in English? Age no bar, caste no bar, sex *bar bar*[4]. Ha-ha-ha!'

I didn't laugh.

He continued on a more serious note, 'We grow up lusting incestuously and when we marry we want a stranger so that we can start with a clean slate. Don't we know that the slate would probably not be clean? Of course we do, but at least my local buddies would not have slept with my wife.'

'But, *bhaiya*, isn't that a very unsatisfying way to live?' I queried, 'To marry someone who is too afraid to show her love or affection or attraction to you? And having to find it with someone you can't marry, and to forever suspect your wife of

[4] *bar bar*: again and again

cheating and lying to you or at least being unnatural with you…' I trailed off. These adult complications were just beginning to strike me. After a moment I continued, 'I thought marriage is meant to be for real love, togetherness, friendship and honesty. This seems to be outright duplicity. Can you ever be happy with this two-faced existence all your life?'

Vinod looked thoughtful. 'You are right, little brother. I agree that marriage should be the way you have described it, but in real life it doesn't happen. Shall I tell you something? I grew up with this girl, Kusum, and I love her.' I was shocked. He shrugged and continued, 'But I knew all along that I cannot marry her. Sure we could have run away but that usually never works out. I was ready to do even that and had proposed it to her, but she was the one who refused. She is ready to sleep with me, even have my child as a keepsake and pass it off as her husband's but she is unwilling to marry me. I called her that night and let you use her so that I could get over her.'

'*Bhaiya*…' I didn't quite know what to say. It hadn't been the casual fuck that I had assumed it was for Vinod.

'It's okay, Saagar baba, you don't have to feel bad about it,' Vinod said heavily. I had never seen him this serious. He continued talking as if to himself, 'This was the only way to get her out of my system. Besides,'—a quick smile—'we had to do something about making you a man.' Vinod's mood switches were like that—instantaneous. 'So tell me, brother, did you like what you did?'

I felt embarrassed, but what the hell. 'Yes I did,' I grinned, 'And, *bhaiya*…thanks for everything!' I was suddenly overcome with affection for this cousin of mine.

That was three years ago. Today we were together again with Vinod prodding me on about Saloni—not that I needed much prodding to confess whatever little had happened.

'Well, I go to her house and help her with the class lectures. And, Vinod, before you say anything, let me tell you that the door to the room is always open and her mother is prowling next door,' I said, my words piling on top of each other, since I knew Vinod would pounce on me the moment I stopped speaking. Even my inexperienced radar was telling me that there were possibilities with Saloni. I needed to get Vinod to advise me, but without looking too amateurish about it.

Vinod spoke placatingly, keeping my adolescent ego in mind, 'Ok, ok, it's your business, baba.' After a pause he asked an innocuous question 'Tell me, what does she usually wear when you go to see her?'

'At home it is pretty casual,' I revealed, 'usually a t-shirt, not a skimpy one, and before you ask, the skirts are long.'

'Hmm…any makeup?'

'At home?' I hedged.

'Yes, that's what we are discussing right now, aren't we?' Vinod replied sarcastically.

'Well she seems to put on a bit of lipstick,' I offered, '… maybe it is just lip gloss…and kajal around her eyes, definitely.'

'Hmmm…' Vinod went into a long silence. I waited. 'I want you to do something for me Saagar baba, just to test things out,' said Vinod finally, a devilish glint in his eyes.

'What?' I asked, my heart beginning a slow thump. This is why I had told him all this - for some experienced advice on how to proceed. I didn't want to blunder around in Saloni's house, with her parents around, and make a fool of myself or worse.

'You said that you sit next to her, didn't you?'

'Yes,' I confirmed.

'Next time you…' Vinod paused.

'Yes?' I prompted eagerly.

'Drop your pencil and…' Vinod paused dramatically before continuing, as I waited eagerly. '…Bend down and…put your hand on her ankle or calf, wherever you can touch her naked skin, and then…' again a dramatic pause, '…run your hand all the way up to right between her legs.'

'What!' I jumped up from the chair on which I was sitting.

'You heard me.' Vinod said evenly.

'What on earth are you…?' I began but was interrupted.

'You must take care of just one thing,' he continued, quite unfazed. 'You must do it firmly and quickly and make sure you touch her *you know what* and get your fingers in, if possible; if not, cup her mound at the very least.'

I gaped at Vinod. What was he saying; what was I hearing?

'Are you trying to get me killed?' I demanded. 'And what do I do when and if I am able to reach the umm…target?'

'Well, that depends on what she does,' said Vinod with a straight face. 'If she screams, tell her that there was a cockroach getting up her skirts and that will probably make her scream again. If she doesn't scream then look into her eyes and finger her nicely and pretend that nothing is happening. Be careful about one thing, though.' Here comes the rider, I thought.

'Don't be gentle with her. And make sure she knows that it's no accident. Don't let her confuse it with a romantic gesture.' A pause. 'Unless you like her romantically, of course.'

'No, I don't.' I mumbled.

'Then make sure that she believes that you will not stop, whatever she may do.'

This was interesting. This was completely contrary to what I would have done. I would probably have stopped the moment Saloni protested—that is, if I ever carried out all the preceding actions. 'Why do you say that?' I asked.

'That's because girls like being overwhelmed physically so that later they can tell themselves that it wasn't their fault—helps with their guilt! And if she does take offence, the best line to trot out is that you were overwhelmed with her charms and couldn't help what you did. Flattery always softens them.'

I pondered over this earthy wisdom. In a strange way it made sense.

Vinod could probably see the wheels grinding in my head, 'Yes, my city dwelling, smart brother. Most nice, clean, educated, good-looking boys—like you, dear cousin—don't get anywhere simply because they stop when they are told to stop, while ordinary looking guys like me get to home base with almost every woman we like! Be a man, baba. There is only one way to find out…'

I looked at my watch. It was midday. I could tell that by the way the sun glinted off the Swargarohini peaks. 'Let's take a break, shall we?' I told Ashish who had been listening with rapt attention.

'Okay, sir.' He sat back reluctantly. It was obvious that he was completely entranced by my story.

I didn't blame him. It did sound like a compelling story even in the telling of it. I called Rupen in with lunch and we tucked in.

Lunch was basic but delicious—soup made of local flour and rough-cut mountain vegetables, home-baked bread along with freshly made spicy chutney and of course piles of fresh salad with black mountain salt for that zippy flavour.

'We didn't know that you had studied science,' Ashish talked even as we ate. 'The general impression is that you are this unbelievable dude who has invented all these things in a fit of artistic inspiration. Your blurb describes you as a maverick inventor whose education is…let me see,' Ashish referred to some papers he had in front of him, 'A Bachelors in Economics and a Masters in Project Finance from King's College, London.'

I chuckled. 'My usual bio—the one that circulates on the internet and Wikipedia—misses out on my first year at St. Stephen's and the fact that I was a starry-eyed nerd dreaming of being a scientist all my life—two significant facts that would otherwise have demystified my success.'

'I see what you mean.' Ashish nodded. 'The story around you is far more dramatic because this one fact is not known. The story of a maverick, who appears out of nowhere and beats the experts at their own game, and that too without the benefit of a formal education in that subject is a far more romantic idea. Puts you in the category of people like Steve Jobs, doesn't it?'

I said nothing, although there definitely were similarities.

Ashish continued, 'Sir, for people with your background, your education would not be in the straight-jacketed Science, Commerce or Arts stream. You would probably be getting ideas from any subject you may be studying.'

'Yes,' I agreed. That's how it indeed was. To Ashish I said, 'That's right. For instance, Steve Jobs talks about the learning experience of a calligraphy course in designing his computer products. The way I would put it is that when one studies any subject in its true spirit, then that subject loses its compartmentalization and becomes a useful building block in the understanding of life itself.

'To set the record straight, since you will be publishing all this, it is not all that strange that I ended up inventing all this stuff. The fact is that I have been engaged in the study of scientific subjects all my life, even though I formally studied science for only six months at St. Stephen's.'

Interjected Ashish, 'So the timeline, as I understand it, indicates that you made the switch soon after your meeting with the professor?'

'Yes,' I responded.

'That is indeed strange!' exclaimed Ashish and, on seeing my bemused expression, added hastily, 'And interesting. I would have thought that a meeting like that, with India's top scientists, would have inspired you further towards a career in science!'

'I considered his question—a fair one—and thought about how to reply, since it started a chain of thoughts and memories that took me down an uncomfortable road. There were things in the past that I was still affected by.

'Yes, Ashish,' I began my reply, '...but as I have learnt the hard way, life dictates terms and one really does not have any control over what happens to you.'

Ashish gave me a quizzical look. 'I would have thought that you, of all people would not be a fatalist, since you have achieved so much in life because of your own efforts?' he ended with a question.

'What I say isn't fatalism, and your question does require a serious answer, but I won't go into it now, since that will derail the chain of the story. But I will take it up later since it is an important question. All I will say now is that people struggle against things that they can't change and are passive in circumstances where they could have done something to change their lives. Most of us simply don't know how to tell the difference. Learning when to make efforts to change and when to let go is an important milestone in one's journey through life.'

I took a pause to marshal my thoughts. 'Ashish, look at my life through this prism.' Ashish looked back blankly so I explained, 'My lifelong aim, till that point, had been to discover the theory of everything and I had focused my entire effort in that direction. But what happened was that life knocked me into a completely different loop. My path shifted dramatically and yet my desire finally bore fruit, but in a way that I could never ever have imagined. The result was that I did end up figuring out the theory of everything but from a completely different angle.'

'What are you saying, sir?' Ashish stammered, looking startled. 'That you formulated the theory of everything? The one that scientists are trying to solve?'

'Yes,' I said simply.

Ashish shook his head slowly, eyes wide. 'I don't understand. Why haven't you presented it to the world, then? Or is it that you formulated it only recently?'

I replied, 'No, it was done many moons ago! It was the very first thing that I formulated—before all my other inventions, in fact.'

'But I don't understand, sir. Such a feat, and you didn't even mention it to anyone…' Ashish trailed off.

'That's because the theory that I have discovered is really the theory of creation and not just the unified laws of physics.

Its scope is vast—far larger than what the scientists envisage, far beyond the purview of those subjects that are collectively called the Sciences,' I said, selecting my words carefully. 'It seems rather puerile to present it for the approval of what is basically a well-meaning but very limited jury.'

'Can we talk about it, sir?' Ashish asked tentatively. 'Or is it a secret? And is that why you haven't put it in the public domain?'

'Oh, it is not a secret! I haven't disclosed it because of two reasons. One—it is of no extra help in developing any new technologies, at least not as yet, although I am working on it, so to disclose it would be needlessly tom-tomming my name. That leads to the second reason, which is that the person who helped me formulate it will never take credit for it and if he doesn't then I won't either. I am not qualified to own a copyright over something like this and till such time as it is of some use to the world, I see no benefit in putting it in the public domain. I may talk about this theory later but to give you a hint—as I mentioned earlier, what I had found unacceptable about gurus was that they would talk about the origins of creation but they would talk only qualitatively. Scientists, on the other hand, would refuse to talk about any concept of a Creator. They do talk about creation, of course—something that they can hope to quantify, formulate or trap with their scientific equipment. Are you getting the drift of what I am saying?'

'Yes, sir,' replied Ashish.

The problem is that scientists typically start from the Big Bang since it was only after that that Space and Time—the measurable stuff—happened. The Creator lies beyond that, although he permeates the built universe as well—which is God made flesh, as the Bible puts it. Gurus talk about the beyond—the realm of which no proof can be found in the physical sense. Gurus find it unimportant to explain the construction of the universe but it does leave them open to the charge of intellectual laziness.'

I continued further, 'So I resolved to bridge this gap, aiming to start from where the gurus and the religious scriptures started but not stopping where they stopped. That way I would avoid the divides and contradictions of modern-day physics and arrive at a genuine theory of everything.' Ashish looked blank so I explained, 'As you may be aware, as of today, physics is divided into exclusive and contradictory branches and multiple objects and forces paradigms. Classical physics, Relativity, Quantum mechanics, particle physics—all these are disparate and contradictory aspects of a science that logically should come from a single source. Scientists believe that physical matter and the laws of nature are separate entities, while. I, have found that the laws of physics don't create the universe. They are simply symptoms of the act of creation.'

Ashish was looking thoroughly confused, so I paused, trying to make what I was saying simpler for him to understand. 'For example, can you explain why our bodies show a temperature of about 98.4 degree Fahrenheit under normal health? Who can say why or even explain why it isn't 100 degrees or any other arbitrary number?'

Ashish didn't answer and I continued, 'This is akin to asking why light travels at 300,000 km per second, right?'

Ashish had this beatific expression, as if he was meditating! I raised an eyebrow at him since Ashish was looking at me as if I was some kind of a strange being descended to this earth, or as though he had died and gone to heaven! I stopped. This was sidetracking the main conversation and I wasn't sure whether Ashish understood any of it.

Ashish waited for me to say something more and, when I didn't, enquired tentatively, 'Can we talk about this now, sir? Unless, of course, you don't want to talk about the theory of everything through the means of my interview...'

'It's not that I don't want to talk about it, Ashish.' I paused and thought my way through the welter of emotions that were swirling through me as the past, present and future all came together. In the long silence that followed, I thought about how to explain my reluctance. The fact was that the theory of everything had been preceded by events that had shaken my safe little world—a world where fathers were pillars of strength and where mothers were unconditionally loving. A world where honesty, loyalty and being there for each other were supposed to be the default expectations from life. An idyllic world where, if one was a good person, one would be protected from misfortune—a world of inviolable truths where the definition of right and wrong was set in stone. A bit like kindergarten!

Earlier, I had been a typical young man who had known what he wanted to do and how it was to be done. Happiness was supposed to be an inescapable by-product of following these principles and guidelines. Yet I had been twisted around and dumped by life, even though I had followed the straight and narrow path. I had lost—not by being a rebel, but by following the righteous path, as defined by the accepted moral code.

Yet in all that losing I had actually gained!

I said nothing of all this to Ashish and instead joked with him, 'Complicated, huh? Ok, let me try to explain my reservations. Let me explain why I am a bit reluctant to discuss the theory of everything here with you. It is not because it is some state secret but because, before I discovered the theory of everything, I had to go through a really turbulent time and the memories are a bit painful. Before I finally found my way to the theory of everything, I was destined to first face real loss. I had to lose all that really mattered to me at that time, and face betrayal by what had mattered very little in the end. And yet ultimately I had gained from it all.'

I took a deep breath and tried to calm myself. I hadn't thought about these things for a long time and had forgotten the power they still had over my equanimity. And yet, even as I thought about past memories and old times, I also remembered all that my guru had said to me over the years and I began to feel better. Loss is not a problem; that is bound to come at its own sweet pace, but how to live with loss is a problem, since the mind craves for what it has chosen as a yardstick for happiness.

I took a decision and turned back to Ashish, who had been waiting patiently. 'Let me go back to this fine tale that I was telling you,' I offered, 'and maybe in the telling of it you will get to hear the theory of everything.'

'Yes sir.' Ashish looked relieved. 'Let's do that.' He settled back onto the leather couch.

I continued, 'As I was saying, the period that followed changed my life completely. Seduced me; misled me and betrayed me,' I said slowly. 'Sometimes, what feels like progress is actually a regression and what you think of as regression is actually what leads you on to your wish fulfillment. Before I became an inventor I had to experience both these truths.'

CHASING FALSE GODS

'Hello, you must be Saagar.' The short woman who had opened the door smiled at me. Pleasantly plump with a beaming countenance, she made me feel instantly welcome.

'Yes ma'am, I was invited for this meeting by Professor Sood,' I replied, a trifle diffidently.

'Yes, yes, I know who you are and why you were invited. The professor just can't stop talking about you and what happened in class!' She placed a hand on my elbow and guided me through a narrow passage that opened into a large sitting area. *That is strange*, I thought to myself as I walked in. The episode in class could hardly be described as flattering for the professor and yet he seemed to be telling people about it as if it had been a victory for him!

Mrs Sood leaned towards me, birdlike eyes twinkling, and whispered conspiratorially, 'I hope you won't feel too out of place with all these fuddy-duddies. Most of them think that they are charmers but to the less brainy plebeians like us, they are nothing but crashing bores! They might have huge reputations as scientists, and that intimidates most people, but strictly between you and me,' she winked, 'they are mostly a bunch of garrulous old men who can't even balance their cheque books properly. So don't be too overawed by their bragging!'

I followed her into a room which was overpopulated with quaint odds and ends. Paintings, carpets masquerading as wall-hangings, table-top sculptures that were obviously works in progress, mismatched pieces of furniture—most of which had seen better days—and bookshelves competed for the limited space and yet the eclectic mix seemed to work. It was a bit like the interiors of a Chor Bizarre restaurant, where everything was mismatched and yet added to the atmosphere. The room had a charm that was hard to pinpoint. The main sofa tilted comfortably to one side, draped with an old fraying cover that had seen better days. The centre-table was piled with magazines with a half-drunk cup of tea acting as a paper weight!

What, however, added depth and a dramatic effect to the rather long and narrow room was a set of large and graceful French windows that ran along the entire length of the outer wall. These windows opened into an expansive garden that was ringed by alcoved stone walls. These walls were back-lit with subtle hidden lighting, a fact I discovered as the evening progressed. Since the walls blocked any further view, the effect created was that of a serene private space. There was a waterfall gurgling in the back and a birdhouse nestled in one of the corners, but what grabbed the eye was a striking sculpture in the centre of the garden—unlike anything I had ever seen before. Made of black unshorn stone, it was neither modern-abstract, nor classical-traditional; it depicted a kneeling man with his hands seemingly lifted in prayer. The body was a study in appeal and the hands reached up, as if for salvation.

'What do you make of it, eh?' The professor joined us. The words were aimed at me and the barbs at his wife, even as he looked at her with a twinkle in his eyes.

I thought for a bit and chose my words carefully since I didn't want to take sides in what was obviously a triangular conversation. 'Sir, this looks like a man praying.'

'Yes, a mendicant Asha had photographed praying on the ghats in Banaras. I had told her to choose a less scrawny subject. It spoils the reputation of our country with all the foreign scientists who come here. They end up thinking that we are all malnourished!'

I looked at Mrs Sood who rolled her eyes while the Prof. deliberately provoked her further. 'I keep telling Asha to make something more traditional for such a central spot in our garden,' he announced, 'such as Krishna playing his flute, or better still, the Natraj. The Natraj would be good since it is rather well known in the western world. You may know that it is placed at the entrance to the headquarters of CERN. People, even scientists, relate to that. Who, I ask you, would want to have a statue of some unknown person—and a beggar, at that, in their house!'

Out of the corner of my eye, I could see Mrs Sood turning purple, so I thought I should interject and divert the upcoming storm, by asking a question.

'But, sir,' I began diffidently, 'the statue doesn't seem to be that of a beggar, at least not in the typical sense. If he is begging, it is definitely not for food or money…' I felt my way through the words that seemed inadequate for what I wanted to say. 'In a way, he seems to be supplicating the higher powers for…umm, deliverance, maybe?'

'Go on!' Mrs Sood encouraged me, sounding very pleased for some reason.

I paused, searching for the right words. 'The man seems to be in some kind of pain but the pain doesn't seem physical…or even mental.' What I wanted to say suddenly came to me. 'The pain seems to be within his being…' I felt through my words, 'I don't have much experience with art, though, and could be completely wrong about what I am saying…' I trailed off.

Mrs Sood beamed at me and turned to her husband. 'See! This young man with little or no experience of art can still see something evocative in my sculpture, while you scientists, who claim to be visionaries, don't understand even basic human emotions.' She placed her fists on her waist imperiously as she spoke and Prof. Sood stepped back and smiled at her. It was obvious that he loved provoking her. 'If you can't sense what lies right in front of your eyes, how can you claim to fathom the mysteries of the universe?' Her eyes flashed like a dancer's emoting through an *abhinaya*. 'I tell you, Saagar, the more I stay around these scientific types, the more I believe that there has to be a God up there somewhere!'

I took another look at the sculpture. There definitely was something evocative about it—the way the half-figure seemed to reach up, as if to strive higher. There was a movement, a longing, a wish, and it had all been created by carving what was essentially just a lump of rough black stone.

'Ma'am, how do you go about creating a sculpture?' I felt compelled to ask. 'I mean, where do you get the ideas from and what are the rules that you follow?' My question was natural. All my life this was the approach I had followed—the scientific method of problem solving. You followed induction and deduction and built structures that led from the known to the unknown. It was like climbing a ladder; each rung helped in climbing higher to the next rung for a better view. Simple! Follow these principles and you were alright. But I could see that this particular sculpture didn't fit that mould and definitely hadn't been created this way.

'That's an interesting question,' Mrs Sood replied. 'Art is creation; something which, even when put together from known materials, creates something new—if it is worthy of being called Art, that is. Based in the familiar, it must still be original.' She paused before adding, 'It must make the viewer pause for a moment and think. Bend their mind, so to speak.'

'But Ma'am, isn't there some standard way? Isn't the artist lost without some blueprint or directions, some rules or formulae?' I enquired inquisitively. 'I am not suggesting spoon-feeding, but should there not be some methodologies of making a work of art?'

'What formulae do you mean? What are you referring to, young man?' Mrs Sood asked.

'Symmetry? Balance? Composition?' I ventured. I had heard these words and had been explained their meanings in our art class in school.

Mrs Sood smiled and I couldn't quite understand why. 'Do you really think,' she queried, 'that once you follow these principles, you would have created a worthy piece of art? Mind you, I am not saying that these principles are wrong in themselves.'

'Yes, I believe I could make a good painting if I followed these guidelines.' I waited for the riposte since I knew that this was a trick question.

Mrs Sood shook her head, 'These qualities are useful only after the concept is crystallized. If the basic concept is not clear and if these principles are your starting point, then you will only end up duplicating things that you have already seen. Like a series of Mughal gardens, which essentially all look the same!' she laughed. 'The truth is that symmetry and balance are only tools and they tend to create their own limitations. They can never be the only or even the main yardsticks.'

I listened attentively, and that seemed to please her. 'Therefore,' she concluded, 'these rules of design are double-edged weapons. They help, no doubt, in achieving art but they can at best be a tool, not the main guiding principles.'

That's the opposite of the scientific approach, I thought to myself, and enquired, 'But then how does an artist decide what to do, what shape to give, or even decide on something as basic as what colour to choose?'

'The artist decides by sense and feeling—intuition, let's say,' she explained. 'He or she starts with an idea or an inspiration and pursues it through intuition and open-minded exploration. As you can guess, these are all qualities that are missing in all these gentlemen over there!'—pointing to the room that was now full of people, all of whom seemed to be well over 60.

I pondered over what she was saying. This was truly intriguing. She was talking about no specific formulae at all. How was that possible? I found her looking at me perceptively. She could probably figure that I didn't have much of a clue about what she was saying.

'Integrity!' she finally spoke, and paused dramatically before continuing, 'That's where it all flows from. I look for integrity in my work. Integrity to the concept that the artist wants to develop, in case you were wondering what integrity I am talking about! From that flow all secondary qualities such as the ones you've mentioned.'

'What do you mean by integrity?' I asked, getting into my childhood Q&A&Q mode. Integrity did mean something to me even if it wasn't quantifiable, and even though it couldn't be trapped in a scientific formula that one could master, I couldn't dismiss it out of hand.

'What it means is that since a piece of art flows from an idea, a feeling or a wish that the artist may have, he should construct the design in such a manner that the central idea is conveyed lucidly and without having to be explained through words. The artist may take any material or a combination of materials that he may like. Paints and colours, if the artist is a painter; fabrics, stone, glass etc., if the artist is a sculptor; a musical instrument or the artist's own voice, if he is a musician; or the artist's own body, if he is a dancer or an actor. Today artists tend to cross the traditional barriers of materials and this is called *Mixed Media*. She paused before continuing, 'As I said, the true test is that the idea that the artist expresses is communicated to the viewer without having to be explained through words and that the idea inspires the viewer.'

The penny dropped. 'And I did that when I spoke about what the statue conveyed to me without being prompted?'

'Yes!' Mrs Sood smiled at me approvingly. 'That's the ultimate compliment to the artist.'

'That's a very different approach to the way we are taught in our science classes, where it all comes down to right versus wrong,' I ventured.

'Yes,' she nodded, 'but you have to realize that there is more to life than just being right or wrong.'

I looked back at the statue to confirm what Mrs Sood had been saying. The statute definitely spoke to me—that was a fact that I couldn't deny. It didn't speak just to me but to others as well, and the idea it conveyed seemed consistent. The message it conveyed could not be characterized as right or wrong. There was some principle that had been followed to create this art—*Integrity*, Mrs Sood called it—but this principle was not quantifiable in the scientific sense.

Hmm, I thought to myself. There was something of value here that could not be contained within the prism of scientific thinking. Could there be a world out there, I wondered, that had nothing to do with the certainties of science? And still be of value? Interesting!

'How do you learn all this?' I asked her. 'Or are artists born with this knowledge?'

'I wouldn't put it that way,' she responded thoughtfully, 'but usually you must have some talent, or at least an interest. If you have that, you can hone those skills through a design school, but it is not strictly necessary to have a formal education. Many of the artistic greats had no formal education in their subjects. Vincent Van Gogh, for example, took up painting after failing at various other things.'

'Ma'am, I have always looked at everything through the prism of science and I find this fascinating. I must ask you a question which may help me understand this better,' I said.

'Go ahead, then!' she smiled.

'Art and Science seem very different and that leads to the question—what's the relationship between Art and Science?'

'That's simple enough to answer,' she stated. 'It is like the relationship between a master and a servant.'

'In other words, it is like the relationship between my wife and me—she being the master, of course, in case you were wondering.' Prof. Sood butted in and laughed uproariously at his own joke. 'A fact that any married man will testify to!'

'Very funny!' Mrs Sood gave him a cutting look and proceeded to ignore him. 'Every act of creation starts with an idea. That creation could be anything—a painting, a statue, a book, a building, software—or even the universe itself. For me, God is an artist who must have first imagined the universe in his mind and then proceeded to create the tools that he used to physically make the world. The study of those tools and logic are called Science,' she concluded imperiously 'In short, Science is just a tool.'

'Yes, master; absolutely, master!' Professor Sood was in high spirits. '...A tool that is studied by fools! Sorry to interrupt your lecture, master, but can I take this young man and introduce him around, since we are about to start the evening's discussions?' He bowed low to his wife, who gave him a long-suffering look.

'Oh, for heaven's sake!' she muttered in exasperation. 'Take him, then. I'll see to the snacks.' Mrs Sood stomped off as the professor placed an arm around my shoulder and herded me into the drawing room, which was now a packed mix of people and clinking glasses.

I was introduced to everyone we met as the student who had asked uncomfortable and original questions in class. We meandered through the crowd, with Prof. Sood having something to say to everyone. Finally we ended in front of a nattily dressed gentleman in a deep navy blue waistcoat—a Nehru jacket, as it was called. That's when the professor was called away and I was left standing awkwardly with my new acquaintance, whose name I hadn't quite caught during the hasty introduction. The gentleman had an interesting face that seemed vaguely familiar, framed by flowing salt-and-pepper locks that placed his age above 50, and yet he seemed to exude a childlike innocence and curiosity. As I stood quietly by his side with my soft-drink glass in my hand, he chatted me up. 'So, young man, what do you intend to take up as your career?'

'Sir, I want to be a theoretical physicist,' I confessed shyly, and he laughed.

'That's obvious, seeing the company you are in!' he responded. 'The only question is—why?'

'Sir, I'd like to find out the answers to the deepest mysteries of the universe.' I made my answer poetic—Mrs Sood's effect, no doubt!

'But why did you choose theoretical physics?' The man wanted to know. 'I hope that you know that physics is no longer the preserve of the idle intelligentsia. The romantic idea that brainy people sitting in their drawing rooms are formulating universes in their heads, like Einstein, isn't true anymore—not by a long shot! Countries that spend billions of dollars experimenting with particle accelerators are the ones who now hold all the aces. Maybe you intend to join one of those corporations for a handsome salary?' He peered at me from under bushy eyebrows, throwing out a challenge.

'No way, sir!' I snorted.

'An idealist! Hmm…And why not?' He gave me a quizzical look, so I thought I should explain.

'According to me, that's a silly way. It is futile and doomed to failure!'

The gentleman looked intrigued. 'Oh, really? Pray tell me—why do you say that?'

I hastily backtracked. 'Of course what I am saying is just my opinion—and I'm merely a first-year student,' I said quickly.

My interlocutor waved his hands dismissively. 'Age doesn't matter! What matters is how much you have thought about what you are saying and whether you have thought things through. Remember, most chess champions win their titles in their early twenties. That's when the brain is at its quickest.'

I took a moment to gather my thoughts and spoke. 'Maybe what I have just said is far too emphatic, but I feel that there is an inherent limitation to this kind of approach, sir.' I hesitated, since what I had to say sounded very presumptuous.

'Go on, go on! What kind of approach do you mean?' my new friend prodded. 'And do stop calling me *sir*, will you?'

I thought for a minute. 'Ok, sir, and…I feel that there is a basic flaw in this Star Wars approach.'

'Star Wars approach! That's a good one!' the old man chuckled. 'Maybe I can use this expression in one of my speeches, if you would allow me. I will, of course, acknowledge you as the source of this pithy quote. But do go on with what you were saying.'

I continued, rather charmed by this quaint gentleman and his encouragement, 'Scientists today are trying to make progress by smashing subatomic particles into smaller bits, right? Isn't that what they essentially do in those particle accelerators?'

'Yes, more or less,' he acknowledged.

'The idea being that if they can smash these particles hard enough, they would obtain pieces that may be the fundamental building blocks of matter,' I continued, and he nodded. 'But what they seem to be discovering instead, is that the particles they obtain on smashing subatomic particles are very different animals. There are literally hundreds of them and that's not the only problem. The total of the parts—the sub-subatomic particles, I mean—don't add up to the whole—the subatomic particles—in any way. Don't even come close, in fact.'

'And how have you come to that conclusion, may I ask?' my companion enquired. 'I presume that you haven't studied the results in any detail since they are a closely and jealously guarded secret as of now.'

'You are right, sir,' I admitted. 'I haven't studied the results in any great depth but my conclusion is based simply on an obvious and well-known fact.'

'Uh-huh, I'm listening,' he nodded, looking intrigued. 'Particularly since you are, let me point out, dismissing billions of dollars' worth of effort and research by the best scientific brains as useless!'

I blushed but went on bravely, 'I am basing my conjecture on the fact that sub-subatomic particles are exceedingly fleeting, while the subatomic particles are extremely long lasting—almost eternal, so to say,' I paused. Whoever this gentleman was, it was certain that he was a top scientist and I'd better formulate my thoughts and words carefully. 'What do you get when you break a piece of wood into two?'

'Two pieces of wood, I presume?' the gentleman grinned.

'Yes,' I nodded. 'Now let's take a proton.'

'Yes, do let's!' he agreed in all good humour.

'What do you get when you smash a proton?' I soldiered on, answering my own question. 'Not two solid part-protons but pieces that are extremely fleeting. Quarks, I believe they are called.'

'Yes, that's true.' My companion looked thoughtful for a change.

'So we have a situation where an extremely stable entity called the proton literally disappears when it is broken into its sub-atomic components. Isn't that right, sir?' I asked.

'Yes I would agree with your statement,' the man nodded, flatteringly focused on what I was saying. 'The quarks that emerge when we break down the proton have a very—ah, ephemeral life.'

I continued, 'What would you say if a length of wood disappeared when you broke it into two pieces?'

'Magic?' smiled the gentleman.

'Now you are pulling my leg, sir,' I protested, and the man laughed, but very kindly. I drew a deep breath before stepping off into the unknown. 'Therefore, my conclusion is that the particles that help create the atom—the proton, the electron and the neutron—come from some other reality, a reality that is non-material and one about which we have no clue as yet.'

'Hmm,' hummed the gentleman, his tone and demeanour open and encouraging.

'And it is a reality which cannot be discovered by the machines that we have invented,' I added. 'After all, how can any machine, however sophisticated, ever detect what is essentially one step *beneath* the physical world?'

'How so, young man?'

I paraphrased my grandmother, although I didn't say that to the gentleman. 'What lies beneath the material world cannot be seen by an instrument made by the material world!'

'Well…' remarked my new friend.

'Ok, let me give you an example to explain what I am saying,' I offered, and he nodded expectantly. 'Professor Higgs of the

Higgs-Boson fame says—and my source is simply a popular newspaper—that mass originates from an invisible field that fills up all space,' I proceeded cautiously. 'He says that even when the universe was empty this field still existed. Particles acquire mass due to contact with this field. What I understand is that these particles emerge from somewhere, get entangled with this mass field in various degrees and therefore acquire different quanta of mass.'

'Quite so,' acknowledged my interlocutor. 'In fact, Professor Higgs explained this through a metaphor. He describes it as three types of objects going through heavy snow and experiencing three different types of drag. The first object goes through like a bird and is scarcely affected by the drag; the second object is like a man on skis who feels the drag but only to a limited extent, and the third object is like a man trudging through the snow with heavy boots on. The third object has to really struggle to wade through the snow.'

'Absolutely, sir!' I agreed enthusiastically. 'In the world of Higgs, the man with the heavy boots will have the heaviest drag and therefore the maximum mass, while the bird will scarcely feel the drag and will have the minimum mass. The degree of drag defines the extent of the mass. Light photons are like the bird while protons are like the man with the heavy shoes.'

'The allegory sounds reasonable enough, doesn't it?' he quirked a bushy eyebrow at me.

'It does, sir, superficially, but the fact is that it is all based on assumptions of which there is no material evidence,' I batted back quickly. 'Firstly, there's supposed to be an invisible field that no one has ever seen. Secondly, there's the mechanism of the drag—the variable attraction that different particles feel for this so-called field—which is equally unknown. And no one is answering one basic question about this field—how is it so different from a field that was discredited just a hundred years ago due to lack of evidence?'

'And that field would be?' probed my companion.

'Ether!' I reminded him eagerly. 'You'd recall that it was discredited by the Mickelson Morley experiment, sir. Before that, everyone was convinced that ether had to be there—how else could light travel through empty space? Yet it was proved that there was no such thing. It was a big shock to everyone when it couldn't be found at all! Yet what scientists are saying today about this gravitation field sounds suspiciously like ether by another name—a fancy explanation for something that has no proof! Don't you agree, sir?'

'Hmm!' was the gentleman's noncommittal response. He seemed lost in deep thought.

'Therefore,' I continued, 'My conclusion is this: how can these kinds of non-provable assumptions ever lead to the theory of everything? Isn't it obvious that we are starting from an intermediate point rather than the beginning? And how is it different from any of the suppositions that our forefathers made and at which we laugh today—such as angels with wings pushing the earth through space?'

The gentleman seemed to be lost in deep contemplation. I shut up, suddenly conscious of having said more than enough already. My interlocutor suddenly looked across the room and called out, 'Hey, Sood! This young man here has an excellent head on his shoulders; I must say you weren't wrong!' Professor Sood gave me a thumbs-up sign and a grin, and the gentleman turned back to me. 'Let me get this straight. Are you essentially saying that the origin of the universe can never be detected?'

'It can be,' I clarified, 'but not in this manner, sir. I mean, not through these machines alone.'

'In that case why do you want to be a physicist at all—err, Saagar, isn't it?'

'Yes sir, it is and my aim is to formulate the theory of everything,' I offered somewhat diffidently, 'and logic tells me that I must study all that has been discovered already. There is no sense in re-inventing the wheel, is there?'

'But what if this theory has no wheels?'

'I'm sorry, what do you mean?' I asked, slightly nonplussed.

'What's there not to understand?' My interlocutor's eyes were bird-bright. 'There might not be any wheels to re-invent. By travelling on the same beaten path you will endlessly roll down the same channels—or wheels, as you said, on a path that has been trodden by thousands of scientists before you, only to arrive at the very same dead-ends. My point is that all your diligent study could simply be a waste of time.'

'I…I suppose so,' I stammered. That hadn't struck me before and it was a disconcerting thought.

'I am not trying to discourage you, my friend, but we do need to think out of the box,' he elaborated. 'This is the dilemma that I face, as do all these scientists here today. Whichever way we look at it, we come to the same logical conclusion—as you have—that we are not starting at the base of it all and, because of that, we can never create a theory of everything. Not by using the present approach, at any rate. The fact is that we haven't dug deep enough. That is why we fail. All we do is pay lip service to the idea of starting afresh and spend large sums of money on what you so aptly call the Star Wars approach!'

He had a faraway look in his eyes as he continued, 'The question is, as Einstein mused—*if I were God, how would*

I design the universe? Would I create a universe as complicated as the one being propounded today by our theorists, one where hundreds of sub-atomic particles are blinking in and out existence? Would I build a universe based on random chance?' He cocked an eyebrow at me and asked, 'What do you say, eh?'

'Completely agree, sir, but I have a practical question.'

'Shoot.'

'If physics is not the starting point, where *does* one start, then?'

'Hmm…Fair question,' he agreed. 'Let me give you a clue. Start from philosophy, since philosophy and metaphysics are two subjects that approach this in a logical manner. The trouble is that metaphysics and philosophy deal with these questions qualitatively but ignore quantities and formulae. On the other hand scientists insist that they will only believe what they can see. The eternal questions about the beginning can be found in any good book on philosophy. Let me recommend two to you. One is *The Tao of Physics*, which tries to establish a link between ancient religion and modern science. The other is a conversation between Jiddu Krishnamurthy and David Bohm—one a spiritual master and the other a renowned scientist. This book is about the nature of intelligence and whether artificial intelligence can ever surpass human intelligence.'

'I saw several books on Krishnamurthy in Professor Sood's office,' I ventured.

'I am not surprised! Most scientists read Jiddu because he is one philosopher who talks philosophy using scientific rigour in his arguments,' the gentleman inclined his head. 'Unfortunately, he doesn't give any answers! That aside, he does teach how to use the intellect to ask the right questions.'

We were interrupted as Dr Sood clanked his glass with a spoon and called for attention. 'Ladies and gentlemen, if you've all had enough to drink, let us begin the evening's proceedings. And don't worry; the bar will be open throughout!' Laughter rippled through the room. 'I will be the M.C. for the evening since none of you volunteered for this onerous task. So please make yourself comfortable and do laugh at my silly jokes! I hope we will all have a wonderful evening discussing subjects that fascinate us.'

Someone yelled, 'I don't know about the others, but, I come here more for Mrs Sood's delicious *pakora*s than for the boring science that is repeated here month after month!'

A chorus of hear-hears followed.

Dr Sood held up his hands to call the meeting to order and said in a mock whisper, 'Don't say that to our sponsor who happens to be our local confectioners! He has high hopes from us! And that is why he gives these highly discounted rates!' Again a roar of laughter went through the room. When it died down, Dr Sood continued, 'Who am I to question your motives for being here? Even an apple falling from a tree can be of use to a scientist, so why should I question the creative potential of my wife's *pakora*s? I do hope, however, that our ears will remain open even if our mouths are full—and that's the way it should be when someone else is speaking! So the purpose of the evening will be well served in any case!' There was again a chuckle all around, and he took a modest bow. 'I now invite Dr K to kick off the evening and summarize where we are with regards to our knowledge on the law of gravitation. Please welcome him with a big round of applause.'

At that, the gentleman who had been talking so amiably to me took my leave and started to move towards the head of the room. *Holy s**t!* I thought dazedly. *I had been chatting with India's missile man!*

Dr K could make out my shock and turned and gave me a wink. 'When you do read those books and if there are things that you want to discuss, give me a call. Sood will give you my phone number.' With that, he walked leisurely to the head of the room, calling out as he went, 'Friends, a very good evening to all of you!' A chorus of good evenings answered him. Dr K reached the head of the room, where a temporary platform had been set up with a podium on it. Dr K let a technician help set up his collar mike, even as he spoke to the various people milling around. Once the mike was fixed, he turned to face the audience and started.

'Good evening, friends. I am here today to summarize where we are with regards to our understanding of gravity and the unknowns thereof. Why the honour of talking about gravity has been bestowed on me is no mystery.' The audience tittered and he smiled back. 'As all of you know, I am the one in India who is responsible for sending our rockets and missiles into space. That duty includes making sure that the ones that are supposed to come back—the missiles, I mean—don't land in the wrong spot, while the ones that aren't supposed to come back—the satellites—don't surprise us by returning! It's all a bit like throwing stones accurately to bring down mangoes, something I used to do rather well as a child, so they appointed me to do it officially! As you all know, the Agni series is the result.' Again the audience roared, stomped their feet and whistled.

Dr K paused and let the audience express their enthusiasm before holding up his hands to ask for silence. 'To do that job well,' he continued, 'one needs to understand gravitation extremely well. Therefore it could be assumed that I am pretty familiar with the laws of gravitation, more than many of you absent-minded professors would be with your grandchildren's academic progress, in fact.' People laughed, and he went on, 'What would surprise you, though, is the fact that, even though I know the law intimately, I don't really know much about its real nature—what gravity is and how it works across time and space.'

Someone from the audience called out, 'We do know that gravity is a bitch!'

Dr K instantly riposted, 'Yes, it is! And hence the need to know it intimately…'

The audience leaned forward attentively; it was obvious that Dr K was getting into the meat of his subject. My ears perked up. Gravitation was an ancient law and a ubiquitous one. Even an eighth standard student knew about it. Yet it was the start of a scientific discussion of this calibre. I heard him say, 'We know, of course, how to calculate the force of gravitation and I will not go into the history of the law here since I expect most of us to have known it before forgetting it.' Chuckles again erupted. 'Let me state the problem again. We know how to calculate the force of gravitation but we have no clue about the *nature* of Gravity.' His voice dropped to a conspiratorial whisper, 'Don't tell anyone outside this room, but the fact is that we have no idea about something that has been described as the greatest generalization achieved by the human mind. I didn't say that, the great Feynman did.'

'Anyway, there are three, or rather four major unknowns about the law of gravitation. Firstly—just what is gravitation? We have absolutely no clue about its nature.' Dr K gave a dramatic pause, 'Secondly—why is gravity only attractive in nature unlike the other forces which have both positive and negative components? Why is there no anti-gravity—outside Hollywood, that is?'

Dr K gave us a few seconds to digest what he was saying before continuing. 'Thirdly, a fact that is a common mystery in all forces that we know of—how do these forces travel across time and space? We all know the concept of the field—including the gravitational field—but that is no explanation at all, really, since space is supposed to be completely without form—empty, as laymen would call it. Fourthly—and this one is quite confounding—how do these objects calculate the magnitude of the forces that are generated across the vast distances over which they operate? In effect, how do they actually communicate their attraction for each other across vast distances? Do they play Chinese whispers? Lastly—oh, I forgot to include this one in my initial headcount. Why does gravity not work at the atomic scale? There is, as you all know, no quantum theory of gravity that fits in with present day quantum mechanics.

'There are other tantalizing indications that common factors operate across the entire spectrum of all the laws that we know. For example, we are aware that gravitational attraction is inversely proportional to the square of the distance, which means that every time you move two objects closer by a distance of one unit, the force of gravitational attraction increases between them by not one unit as expected but by two units—inversely to the square of the distance. That same effect can be seen in the forces of electro-magnetism as well. We all know that the force of gravitation is miniscule as compared to the electromagnetic force and yet they both obey this basic relationship. That hints at the fact that the square-of-the-distance relationship is a basic building block of the way most forces interact in the universe. If we have to find the theory of everything, we need to be able to pinpoint the inherent reason why this is so. Any ideas on that, gentlemen?'

I glanced around at the others, who appeared to be glued to every word Dr K was saying. Fascinating stuff, I thought, and looked back at the speaker.

What ensued was a lively debate about paths of least resistance and action-at-a-distance versus local actions. Most of it flew over my head. But the gist was gratifying. Something as common as the law of gravitation was a virtual mystery. And I had not been wrong when I had posed those questions to Prof. Sood in class. I had earned this invitation.

That evening I came back home with electrons, protons and photons whizzing around in my head and the rest of the week passed in a blur. I constantly thought of that meeting and not just the bits on science. The lecture on the known and unknown scientific facts of the day had been fascinating, but talking to Mrs Sood had also been an eye-opener, and the conversation with India's missile man had frankly been a shocker. If I couldn't find the theory of everything through studying physics, just how was I supposed do so? Besides, what was the use of studying science when the top scientists were still expressing their frustrations after decades of study?

With my mind seduced by the unfolding vistas of new knowledge, I headed for the library the first thing on Monday morning. I had never been to the philosophy section and I located it just behind the carrel where I used to study my physics lessons. The Krishnamurthy book sprang out at me almost immediately but *The Tao of Physics* wasn't available. I placed a request for it with the librarian and started reading the K book at once.

This book was unlike any of the books that I had read so far and yet I could make out that the rigours in the arguments used were all based on science. But there were many words in it that simply did not fit the scientific terminologies we were familiar with. 'Consciousness', was one such word that I frequently encountered. The book explained that all living things were conscious but consciousness could not be observed scientifically. Neither could thoughts! Nor intelligence! So could we say that thoughts did not exist because they couldn't be observed? As I read the book, I realized that there were many things that we knew existed, but which had no basis in science. Could we simply dismiss them? The obvious answer was no. And this led to a larger question. Could we dismiss all that we could not comprehend with our senses as non-existing? Mind you, our senses (the technological ones) were getting better every day so we could see today what we had not been able to see yesterday. The only conclusion could be that it would be foolish, to dismiss what we couldn't perceive today as simply not being there just because we couldn't see it. *Consciousness, soul; desire; hope; beliefs*—all these were words that could not be denied but they had no place in the dictionary of science. That immediately led to one conclusion, which no scientist could argue against—that science tried to explain the material universe but, in the totality of existence, the material universe seemed just one part of the whole…

In short, science wasn't the complete boss that I had thought it was…

The next few days were quiet ones. These glimpses into a brand-new world engaged me completely and I was a silent ghost flitting in and out of college. To get a grip on this new subject, I even tried to attend classes in the philosophy department. The students turned to look and so did the teacher, but no one objected to my sitting there. I gave up when I realized that I would have to do more than attend a few lectures, as it would require systematic study to reach even a passing familiarity with these subjects.

CHANGING COURSE

A few days later, I walked into my house to find Mr Mehta or Uncle Mehta, as I called him, chatting with my father in the drawing room. Like all good Indian kids of my generation, I'd been taught to address all my parents' friends and acquaintances as uncle and aunty. Uncle Mehta and Papa were old buddies and batchmates in the Indian Railways, but their career profiles had diverged significantly over the years. While my father had continued to serve the iron monsters of the world's second-largest railway network, Mr Mehta had taken voluntary retirement after serving for 20 years, not to gracefully ride into the sunset early, as you might think, but to become a builder—one of the new dynamic ones who were beginning to challenge the hegemony of the holy trinity of DLF, Ansal and Unitech, the leaders at that time. Mr Mehta was known as the bright spark of his batch—a rare man who had given up the cushy comfort of the air-conditioned office of a Class-I government officer in the days when air-conditioning was a real luxury. He had opted instead to step out into the heat and dust of India's fledgling private sector.

I had once asked him about where he had found the courage to take such a bold step. I was curious as to why he had not been scared to leave the safety and prestige of a top-level government job. Uncle Mehta had laughed in reply and avoided answering, but I persisted.

No, he did not regret leaving. What he did indeed regret, he said, was that he had not left sooner, since if he had, he would have had more time and would have become a much bigger builder than he had till then. I hadn't been fully convinced by his answer and when I prodded him further, he confessed to some worry when he resigned, but he had had a couple of things going for him. Firstly, his grandfather had been the Nawaab of Khatauli—a small princely state in Uttar Pradesh, and his family still owned a lot of land there. That meant that day-to-day living expenses had never been a cause of concern and since he had worked for the mandatory 20 years required to get a pension, he always had a monthly paycheck to fall back on, not to mention the travel and medical perks that all railway officers enjoyed till the end of their lives. For him, that was enough of a backup if his gamble failed and so he had taken a chance and plunged into the deep end.

'Come, come, Saagar,' my father called to me as I crossed the lobby on the way to my room, 'Uncle Mehta wants to talk to you.'

'Oh what about? Wait, I will be right back!' I said over my shoulder, as I walked to my room. I dumped my bag on the bed, splashed some water on my face, towelled it dry and went back to the drawing room.

'Hello, Uncle!' I greeted the visitor on returning to the sitting room.

'Good to see you, son,' Mr Mehta nodded amicably.

'So, how was college?' Dad enquired.

'Fine,' I was noncommittal. There was no particular reason for my reticence, but far too much had been happening on various fronts for me to formulate a coherent reply.

Uncle Mehta and I had always got along like a house on fire. I would visit his construction sites whenever I got the chance and he would happily show me around. I had always found the whole business of construction fascinating. Something about seeing a building emerge from its two-dimensional blueprints into a three-dimensional reality really enthralled me. What I also liked was the sheer practicality of the construction process. And when I would visit any of Uncle Mehta's sites, I would pepper him or his supervisors with questions. I soon figured that everything that was done on site was done for a reason and done in the most cost-effective way possible. There was no space for bullshit. For some reason that really appealed to me. These random memories of mine were interrupted as my dad spoke, 'Uncle Mehta has an offer for you.' My ears perked up. 'He wants to borrow you for a couple of years.'

'Borrow me?' I gawked, not understanding what that meant.

'Well,' Papa elaborated, 'he has recently started this big outstation project in Pune and he wants your help in constructing it.' He turned to Mr Mehta and invited, 'Here, Mahendar, why don't you explain it to Saagar yourself?'

'It is rather simple, son,' our guest took over smoothly. 'As your father mentioned, I have just been awarded a project in Pune. What's different about this project from the ones that I have done till now is the sheer size and scale. I have no hesitation in saying that this project is not only my largest by far but also the riskiest. The bottom line is that if things don't go well, it could bring down my company. If all goes well, though, I will break into the big league. There's no question that this is a game changer for me and my company.'

I listened attentively, wondering where I fitted into this whole scheme.

'To handle this project properly,' he continued, 'I am putting together a team of people both here in Delhi as well as on the site. I would like you to be part of the team based in Pune, to act as my eyes and ears there.'

'But…' I was stunned by the statement and couldn't, for a moment, figure out how to respond. '…but what about my studies?' I finally blurted out. 'I am only halfway through my first year of college! Besides, I have no experience in the construction line and—and aren't I too young, not to mention completely inexperienced, for all this?' I looked appealingly at Papa, surprised that he hadn't already said no to something that sounded so outlandish.

'Well,' my father began, 'we always wanted you to be an engineer and if you…'

Uncle Mehta cut him off and said bluntly, 'I am offering to sponsor your education abroad in any course and any university of your choice once you finish the project, Saagar. I will also, as I have already told your father, pay you a handsome stipend apart from all your living expenses in Pune in case you agree to do this.'

Wow! I thought to myself. *This is something! So what's the catch?*

'The sky would be the limit for you, Saagar! Besides, it's only for a couple of years,' my father spoke placating. He, of course, knew of my lifelong ambition of wanting to be a scientist. He also knew that I considered even engineering—let alone the job of a site supervisor—a step down from the pursuit of the pure sciences. So why did he think I'd even consider an offer such as this?

Silence hung heavy in the room for a long moment before Papa spoke again. 'Why I think we should consider this seriously,' he volunteered, 'is because this way, you'll be able to join a course of your choosing, in a university that you like anywhere in the world, once you've seen this project through. Think about it.' I still didn't respond, so he tried again. 'Look, I know you have your heart set on becoming a theoretical physicist, but you know that our financial situation is not great. We could never imagine sending you to study in the US or UK. If you do this, you could ultimately end up studying at one of the best colleges in the world. Harvard, MIT, Oxford—you name it. It can't get any better than that. The only drawback would be the two-year gap in your education.'

'Well, Dinkar, three-and-a-half years would be a more realistic estimate,' Mehta uncle intervened. 'The project deadline may be two years, as I told you, but the project is likely to go through a couple of extensions. However, I don't see it stretching beyond three to three-and-a-half years at the most.'

'Three years,' I repeated slowly. 'And, uh, when would I be expected to start—if I accept, that is?' My brain was in overdrive. A week ago, I would have rejected this offer outright since I was already where I wanted to be—in India's premier college, pursuing a degree in the pure sciences, but after the meeting at Professor Sood's house I had begun to see other interesting possibilities. My first cursory look at the books on philosophy that Dr K had recommended had proved fascinating. Those books seemed to lay down the conceptual map for the structure of the universe and it seemed a little surprising to me that scientists had not yet used these channels to create pathways towards the theory of everything. To me the linkages seemed fairly straightforward. It appeared to my brash eyes that physics and metaphysics needed to combine their diverse strengths and the one to do it—me—would need to approach it through a combination of diverse subjects. St. Stephens (like any other college in Delhi University), for all its reputation for academic excellence, did not permit cross-subject study. In any good international university, I could do so with ease. Another fact that could not be ignored was that Pune was just 3-4 hours from Bombay. Bombay was where Roli lived. A stipend, all expenses met. Wow! I could buy that Yamaha 350 cc that I had always desired. This definitely had possibilities.

Uncle Mehta interrupted my reverie. 'In one month,' he said.

'Huh?'

'I said that you will have to move in a month's time.'

I reached my decision but didn't blurt it out. It was time to get the maximum juice out of this! I put on a serious face. 'That would mean, Uncle, that in essence I would be giving up three years of my life to this project.'

'True, but don't forget that you'll then be enrolled in a college of your choosing,' he pointed out. 'In the meanwhile, you would also be earning good money!'

Uncle Mehta was a tough cookie, I knew, and a great negotiator, but what these guys hadn't yet realized was that they were preaching to the converted. I was already sold on the idea—a win-win situation for me all around. Still, there was no harm in making them feel a bit guilty—or letting them think that I was doing them a favour. So I argued, 'But, Uncle, quitting St Stephens is unheard of. People kill to get in there. And doesn't it leave my future very—err, uncertain? My classmates would be studying while I'm working, and I would be studying when they would be off getting jobs!'

'You should look upon that as a plus rather than a minus,' our smart guest interjected. 'You would be entering college with a wealth of practical experience for which many of your classmates would give an arm and a leg! Besides, age doesn't truly matter when it comes to academic pursuits does it?'

I pretended to give this some serious consideration. 'Before I decide,' I finally said, 'I want to ask you a question, Uncle.'

'Shoot,' he invited me.

'I'm not sure why you want me to join you,' I said. 'I have neither the experience nor the qualifications.'

'Ah! That's an easy one!' he smiled. 'I need someone reliable in Pune since this is an outstation project. I can trust no one completely, paid employees being paid employees. As I have said, this project is critical for me and I have very little margin for errors. It's far larger than anything I have ever done and I need a coordinator I can trust. As you know,' his eyes softened as he looked at me, 'I have always regarded you as the son I never had. If I can't trust you, who can I trust?'

The truth of that one statement touched me somewhere deep inside, and I suddenly didn't want to play games any more. I took a deep breath and asked doubtfully, 'I will do it, but—will I be able to handle it, Uncle?'

He sat up, looking relieved and pleased. 'Oh yes, believe me,' he insisted. 'A large part of construction is common sense and timely management; it's experiential rather than having to mug complicated formulae or theories. In any case there already are technical people—architects and engineers—on the job. All I need now is someone to keep an eye on the whole thing from our end and to keep the deliverables on track. For me having someone sincere and honest as a fulcrum is the most important thing; that's why I want you there, Saagar. These architects and engineers are nutcases with fragile egos. Every esoteric point on the building code can be the potential scene for a no-holds-barred battle. It is so incredibly petty sometimes that it is hard for me to even explain it. You will experience it yourself, I am sure!' said Mr Mehta with a laugh, 'To achieve the deadlines we need to be well ahead in terms of our requests for drawings, design decisions, work orders—and personal egos. To keep to the schedule and to keep the pressure on the clients we need to stick to the P.E.R.T. charts. Only then will we be able to ensure timely achievements of targets and therefore get our payments out. Cash flow is critical since the amount I can overdraw from the banks is a pittance as compared to what I need to execute this project. My only hope is to keep billing the client on time and receiving the payments on time as well. So I need a bright mind which, more importantly, is of a person whose integrity I can trust.'

He reached out to pat my shoulder, and concluded, 'Trust me, it is not as complicated as you think and you will pick it up very quickly.'

&

I leaned back in my chair. The Swargarohini twin peaks were glittering in the twilight and the table in front of us was littered with empty cups of tea and plates of half-eaten snacks.

'Wow!' said Ashish as he rested his shoulders against the sofa-back and stretched. 'What a story. This will make a great read when printed! And this is certainly not turning out to be the straight and narrow scholar's story I had assumed it would be when I boarded my flight to Dehradun! This could easily be a movie script.'

I laughed, 'Come on, Ashish, it's really not as dramatic as that!'

Ashish countered, his passion evident, 'I don't agree, Sir. It really is dramatic, just like a Bollywood film! The hero a sincere single-minded nerd—pardon the expression,' Ashish grinned, '...with the sole objective of discovering the theory of everything, goes on to have a major fracas with his teacher, gets invited to dinner instead of being chastised, where he meets the Missile Man himself who, instead of encouraging him onto the straightforward career path in physics, gives him completely contrarian advice. Just when you think that the story couldn't turn out any stranger, the biggest whammy hits with the protagonist getting this offer to become a project manager—and that too with no relevant education or experience! If that's not dramatic enough, I'd like to know what is! Were I the reader or the movie-goer, I would be on the edge of my seat wondering what'll happen next!'

Ashish paused and said, 'So what does happen next, sir?'

'Well,' I shrugged, 'There were many outside forces in play, taking me in a direction that I hadn't foreseen. I was simply swept along.'

'I assume you took up Mr Mehta's offer?' Ashish queried, and I nodded.

'You bet I did!' I corroborated. 'It was just too seductive. Talking to Dr K had broken the linearity of my thought process just enough for this new idea to seep through and take root. I had always assumed that I would be heading for a post-doctorate in physics down the line but this comfortable sequence suddenly had broadened into a maze of possibilities…I was at a loss with no real sense of direction and this career move seemed as good as any. Better, in fact, since I could get the best education possible without having to burden my father financially.

'So there I was, just a month later—packing my bags and heading off to try my fortune in Pune.'

'Poor Saloni!' Ashish chuckled. 'She must have been quite heartbroken!'

'Yes,' I smiled reminiscently, 'but she does come back into the story for a brief interlude a while later.'

MAYA

I walked into the nightclub. The Rhythms Cafe on Senapati Bapat Road was our current favourite. The chrome floor was pulsating to the heavy beat; the night was young; the dance-floor sparsely populated and happy hours were on. My friends were already there. Two couples—Sumit and Radhika, and Vikrant and Suvernika—waved to me from the balcony above, laughing hysterically. From the crazy angle that the girls were being held at, I could make out that they had already had a few drinks.

These were my latest sets of best friends after a year and a half in Pune. Delhi seemed a distant dream and my life was bright and exciting like the laser lights that revolved on the dance floor. This was *it* for me. This was how life should be. Every moment, whether at work or afterwards in the evening, had that hard excitement that only youth can sustain.

Uncle Mehta was more than pleased with my performance. I had taken to the work like a duck to water. I had quickly realized that if I got to the bottom of things before I was required to, there was ample time to stay ahead of trouble since the lead times available to us were usually weeks, if not months. This wasn't touch and go, or like launching the space shuttle at all! The work was certainly hydra-headed but everything happened in super-slow motion. The architects needed time to come up with their designs and then needed more time to revise them repeatedly till they were finalized. Even after the so-called sign-offs there were many back-and-forth's and umpteen revisions on site to boot. Mind you, all this after the contracts had been signed and sealed! We, the contractors, had to simply wait it out, with our subcontractors ready to roll, and pretend that great damage was being caused to us because of the delays, for which the clients and architects, of course, were responsible. Since our teams did not need much time—usually only days to mobilize—it was no skin off our nose, but we never let that on to the clients. Guilty clients and defensive architects release payments quicker! I quickly learnt the good builder trick of sending off letters just as soon as some commitment/deadline of the client or the architects slipped. These so called gentle reminders had implicit threats built into their flowery language since the letters had legal implications that led to panic at the clients' end. Any delays from the clients/architects' side could be compelling grounds for us to demand suitable financial compensation for time slippages. And those compensations, in the days of the money-order economy that India then was, were huge—usually 18 per cent per annum on the outstanding amounts!

The P.E.R.T. charts became objects of deep study for me and I became an avid student of the mechanics of work. I had always had a thirst for new knowledge and I turned my learning skills towards the practical art of getting a building designed and constructed. I quickly realized that building construction was like an octopus with the various tentacles requiring various lead times to complete. Many targets depended on other targets being achieved, and those in turn depended on still other targets. That sounds complicated but the process could be streamlined and speeded up tremendously—not by working faster in selected areas but by ensuring that various things pulled together better as a team. I learnt literally hundreds of deadlines and what they entailed. Even a small thing like a pavement had to be first designed and then re-designed a million times till the clients were satisfied. It had then to be run through the mechanical engineer's, the structural engineer's, the landscape consultant's and the plumbing engineer's office before it could be finally issued to us after many back and forth's. All this while, we could act as the injured party who were suffering great losses because of these delays.

I quickly realized that most of these guys never talked to each other and as a result there were mistakes galore. Their king-sized egos were the problem, as Uncle Mehta had pointed out. Architects pretended that their disorganization was the result of artistic virtue but the truth was that they were simply run off their feet with last-minute changes and had no proper systems in place to create mistake-free drawings. The clients, to take care of this massive coordination exercise, had appointed a reputed project management company to keep things running smoothly, but all that the company could really manage to do was to make sure that the paperwork was processed in time. They simply had no way to check the quality of the paperwork. Very often we would point out mistakes and anomalies in the design and construction drawings to which they could only respond by sending our observations back to the clients and architects. This again resulted in delays and protracted correspondence.

It's not that we nitpicked unnecessarily; we, too, had an interest in moving things along. Sometimes, though, the mistakes were really substantial, couldn't be handled on site and had to be underlined.

I will mention one substantial mistake that I spotted, that garnered kudos for me, delayed the project by a couple of months and led to a lot of red faces. This was a drawing that gave the details of a pyramidal steel column. There was nothing wrong with the drawing except for the fact that the column so indicated in that drawing was designed to hold up to a 5 mts x 5 mts span roof, the drawing even carrying a warning note—'Not to be used for more than a 5 x 5 metre span'. This specific column detail had been pulled into another drawing where the column-spacing was shown as 7 mts x 7 mts! The mistake was basic, more in the nature of a typographical error, since the wrong detailed drawing had been called in, but one that—if I hadn't spotted it—could have led to catastrophic structural failure. That one caused quite a flap, with the Chief Architect being summoned from Bombay and a great deal of acrimony between the clients, the project management team and the architects, while we watched with serious faces and glee in our hearts! C.Y.A.—Cover Your Ass—was the norm and it was funny to see grown people scurrying around like errant school kids, trying to hide their mistakes. We almost felt sorry for them but, well, business is business!

We—or rather I was the guy everyone came to plead with. Architects would plead with me to let them change their incorrect drawings on the sly—and believe me; some of these mistakes were staggering. The clients would come and pump me for information about the real speed of the work, since their marketing and sales depended on it. My own contractors would plead for payments. The suppliers would plead for their money as well, although we made sure that they pleaded the least. I had learnt from Uncle Mehta that the way to builder paradise was through two basic rules—keep the pressure on the architects and clients for drawings and specs, and keep your material suppliers happy. Happy material suppliers gave a long line of credit without interest and that was vital for our financial well-being.

It was staggering to see how much of an impact interest payments made to the health of the balance sheets and the profit-and-loss statements of a company. Companies that had no loans were far better off than the ones that had, even if both companies had similar profits. Sure, being cash-rich was the ideal solution but that was usually never possible and with little cash in hand, sticking to the two golden rules mentioned earlier was crucial. If one could do this—implement those two rules—the contractor would not need to invest any of his own money; he could simply pass off part of the money received from the clients to the material suppliers and subcontractors, and pocket the rest. I was rather proud to report that I ran the entire project in exactly that way!

'So you were enjoying being practical, huh?' Ashish interrupted the narration to ask.

This was Day 2 of our rolling conversation. The sun was out; we were having our tea on the open terrace and admiring the view. From here, one could see down the edge of the cliff to the bottom of the river. I had a clear view of the corkscrew road with a toy-sized jeep winding its way up its hairpin bends.

That would be the transport that would be carrying some of our provisions and the newspaper as well.

'Yes,' I nodded. 'I had always had a chip on my shoulder about being regarded as a dreamy-eyed, impractical nerd, with my nose stuck in books. And I found myself taking great pride in doing stuff literally with my bare hands. Believe me, there is something greatly satisfying about watching a mere sketch on paper emerging in concrete and stone. By the way, Ashish, there was another entity in that long and distinguished list of pleaders who I forgot to mention—someone you would never ever guess.'

'Who?' enquired Ashish with a sparkle in his eyes.

'The local Architecture College!'

'What? How?' Ashish quirked disbelieving eyebrows.

'Simple. We had six places for architectural apprentices, and architecture colleges from across India vied for those positions for their students. This local College of Architecture was relatively new and desperate to establish its credentials. It was important for it to place its students well for their on-the-job training, and it pleaded with us without shame. For them to be able to place some of their students' right in Pune itself and on such a flagship project was very important. We didn't mind; after all, for a mere pittance, we ended up with bright-eyed, sincere young people who knew something, if not a whole lot, about design and construction.'

I took a pause before continuing, remembering those frantic, exciting days. 'The systems of construction that were employed on this project were so different from the traditional methods that we had to re-train our experienced employees in any case. That meant that existing knowledge had to be literally unlearnt - something that the old geezers of Uncle Mehta's company had a real problem with.'

I laughed at the memories. 'I too, was a perfect example of the same logic, having started from a slate that couldn't be any cleaner! You can imagine me, Ashish—a 20-year-old boy, being kowtowed to by much older professors and the dean of a college!' Ashish laughed at that imagery and I continued, 'I replaced all my frontline paid supervisors with these students who were paid peanuts for the same job!'

I sat back, remembering those heady days.

There I was, pretty much on top of the world. I had my own apartment, my own Yamaha 350 cc and no responsibilities. I worked hard and partied even harder as my bank balance zoomed. What more could a youngster ask for?

So why was my heart so sad and the parties I threw so brittle? Why would the glittering lifestyle not make me happy? It was certainly true that the work was extremely hard and the hours long, but I enjoyed it and the high profile that went with it, but what I valued more was the relief it provided by making me forget, for a few blessed hours, the big hole in my life—Roli. One of the reasons I had come to Pune was to be with her but, even as the geographical distance between us diminished, I found that the emotional distance had widened. In simple words, she had moved on. I had written to Roli as soon as I reached Pune and told her that I was finally footloose and fancy free and would be able to take care of all her complaints of not being able to spend any time together. Instead of effusion and enthusiasm I received a bright, cheery and impersonal response which basically said, *good to know that you are finally getting free of your parent's shackles.*

I wrote back to say that I had been expecting a more personal letter, that I was finally available and that I was really looking forward to seeing her and being with her again. She replied with what was essentially a *Dear John* letter, saying that she liked me and wished me all the pretty young things in the world, but she herself had moved on and found someone else. She had simply been unable to handle the conflicts that our relationship had generated. Couching it in diplomatic words, she told me that I had some growing up to do; I was stepping into adulthood and it wasn't good for me to settle down with the first girl that I fell for. I would soon find a beautiful girl more appropriate for me, she said, who would appreciate me for who I was.

I tried calling her, but it was always her mother who picked up the phone and I would hastily hang up! Once, though, it was her brother Saurabh who answered and, even though I said nothing, he somehow guessed it was me and proceeded to give me some unilateral advice. He told me to forget Roli, period! He also had some very unflattering things to say about her, the gist being that, for his sister, relationships were like tubes of toothpaste; once the paste was gone, she simply discarded the empty tube—which was what I'd now become, evidently. I'd listened quietly, hanging up when he had finished. What Saurabh said had the ring of truth. I could make out that it wasn't just his attempt to fob me off. The writing on the wall was clear; she had dumped me.

The realization that I had lost her hit me like a stab in my heart but I couldn't generate any anger. All I could feel was this deep and dark despair that seemed to have no bottom—

devastation so total that I find it hard to think about it even now. And all I could feel for her was love even when all she expressed was disinterest. I wondered what to do. Should I go and confront her? I would read and re-read her letters a million times. I read them when I was sober; I read them when I was drunk. I even read them holding the paper upside down! Did her words offer some chance? Was there something that I could do to make it all ok? But no, the words were plain as Jane and more than what they said, it was the tone of her last letter that completely deflated me. It was bright and impersonal and indicated a real moving on.

What do you do when someone you truly care for expresses such indifference? Do you remind them of the eternal promises that had been made and were now being squashed underfoot without a thought?

I decided to let it go. Can you ever revive a love that has died? All that the reminders of the promises made would achieve, would be to embarrass her. As the famous couplet says,

Unhoney maangaa bhi to kyaa maangaa,judaii maangi
Aur ek hum they, jinhey inkaar bhi naa karnaa aayaa.

(When I asked my lover what I could do to please her,
she asked for separation,
And I loved her too much to deny her even that.)

I gave up on Roli that day but I couldn't stop the endless flow of feelings. She may have moved on, but I simply couldn't. Whenever I was with another girl, all I could do was compare her to Roli and the girl in question, however charming, always came off second best.

So here I was, onto my third set of architecture students, having a blast and yet not able to really connect with anyone.

This last group was particularly brash. Rich kids from builder families, they knew they had established businesses at home to go back to; life was a series of parties and fun. And they were not wrong. The saying goes that you cannot be a good architect unless you experience the spaces you have to design. After all can you design a Japanese restaurant without having had Sushi? Can you design a bar without knowing the subtleties of handling beer, whisky and other intoxicants? After all if you don't know that you can't serve white wine with ice and therefore it needs to be chilled beforehand and that whisky bottles don't need to be refrigerated because the beverage could be served on the rocks, then how can you design the right services for a bar? How can you figure out all these things unless you have had some experience with drinking? Similarly, could you do justice to a wellness project unless you have spent a few hours of your life getting pampered in a spa or a healing facility?

This is what makes architectural learning very different from any other subject. It is experiential and books are the last place where you can learn it. A guy or girl who doesn't smoke, drink, have an active social life and is a vegetarian will typically not make a good architect. The bottom line is that you need to be a hedonist, always looking for an experience. The usual terrifying admonishment that parents scold their children with—'Study or you will be a failure in life!'—is completely the wrong way to go about being a good architect.

My latest group of friends was good at that—experiencing, that is—and they did it in style. I found myself yo-yoing between the guilt of living it up and saying 'why the hell not!'

&

'You know, Ashish,' I said to my interlocutor in an aside, 'I have this maverick reputation now for creative thinking, but in those days I used to be really hidebound. Quite the proper little conformist with concepts of right and wrong stitched firmly into my psyche. Interacting with these groups of architecture students helped me to open up my closed little mind. Mind you, I am not suggesting that promiscuity, alcohol and drugs are the way towards originality, but that's a subject we will talk about later since even the opposite is not true.'

I continued my story.

&

I made the perfect friend for them. A guy their age, yet with his own means and his own pad while they had to make do with their allowances which, though admittedly large, couldn't compete with my handsome salary. What more could a student ask for? Only the fact that I was project head and technically their boss kept the girls halfway decent with me—but only halfway.

It was one such early morning when we had all stumbled into my apartment after a session at the night club. I was sitting quietly in my chair with the deep strains of *The Scorpions* flowing seductively around me. The party was on the wane and most people had left. My friends were amongst the few still remaining and I could see them in the far corners of the room, necking. I continued drinking steadily as the night deepened and my living room emptied out, with even my hard-core drinking friends finally staggering to their feet and heading off to their hostels. As the night deepened and the sounds of the city quietened, I closed my eyes, leaned back and let the music wash over me. I had grown to love the Scorpions and liked them far more than the usual popular choices of our generation—*Pink Floyd, Deep Purple* and *JethroTull*. I found their guitaring clean, the dependence on techno music less and the lyrics far more understandable. They sang their songs straight and true and the words of this particular song sliced straight into my gut.

Time, it needs time
To win back your love again…
Love, only love
Can bring back your love someday…

I admit I was fairly maudlin by then, well into my fifth large rum and coke when the track changed to the latest hit song from Michael Learns to Rock, again a favourite of mine for its lyrics and its plaintive tone. The first time I had heard *Complicated Heart*, Roli had been in my arms and hearing it always brought back heartache. Tears sprang into my eyes and a lump formed in my throat as the song reached my favourite lines:

…You tell me you are leaving, but I just have to say
Before you throw it all away,
Even if you want to go alone
I will be waiting when you're coming home…

Unquestionably, I was drunk, close to blubbering like a boy when I felt two slim arms slip around my waist from the back. I was enveloped in that familiar heady musk of Roli's perfume. Chanel No. 5 it was, as I recalled from our time together. Roli placed her soft cheek against mine and snuggled up to me. 'Hi, baby,' she whispered softly, throatily, her breath tickling my ear, and I was overcome with emotion. I knew Roli had to come back.

My love for her was too strong and too true for her to resist for long. Nothing in the world could match up to it. Our separation was finally over. I had been right to believe all these months that we would ultimately be together. 'I love you,' she was murmuring, 'I have missed you and I have thought about you all these months. And I just can't forget all the times we have spent together… and I just had to come and be with you again…'

Tears slid down my face as I heard that. I looked on straight ahead to stop her from seeing them. 'Come make love to me,' she whispered and took my hand to pull me up. I tried to get up but couldn't. I was simply too drunk. I staggered and nearly pulled her off her feet. 'Never mind,' she giggled and settled onto my lap.

I could feel her weight settling on me, comforting and warm, the heat radiating off her body in waves. Those beautiful legs that I had touched only fleetingly before were on my thighs with her bare anklet-clad feet tinkling as they dangled in the air. I buried my nose in her body, wrapped my arms around her and just breathed her in. 'So beautiful...I will never let you go...' my words were an incoherent whisper muffled against her breasts.

She hugged me back, her breath ragged, and proceeded to kiss me all over. 'Nor will I, sweetheart.' And she started really kissing me. Deep kisses that showed how much she loved me. I knew that this time I would not disappoint her. I kissed her back hard till she squealed, her lips and teeth mashed up against mine, but I didn't stop. She would have to pay for leaving me like that. At that moment I didn't care for niceties—just my need for her and the urge to make her mine and claim her body.

And that's how it was. We made love right there. With her sitting on my lap, with only the starlight outside the window to show me glimpses of her beautiful curvaceous body that fitted into mine so well, with her face hidden in the shadows of the night. Our love-making was all that I had thought it would be. Soft and gentle, wild and physical, nurturing and feral. We made love to each other as if there was no tomorrow. Afterwards I fell into a deep dreamless sleep, satiated and content. This was it for me. The girl I wanted to be with all my life was finally back with me…

The phone jangled into my ear and I was startled awake. The events of last night flooded into my mind and I felt the goodness of life wash over me. Last night seemed like a dream and I looked at Roli's sleeping form for reassurance. There she was, curled up on the carpet on the floor beneath the duvet I had tucked around her. I looked at my watch. It was eight in the morning—early by construction industry standards. Who would be calling at this time?

I crawled to the phone on my hands and knees on the thick pile carpet and took it off its cradle. 'Hello,' I said groggily.

'Hello, Saagar, how are you?' It was my dad, from Delhi, sounding bright and cheery.

'Yes, Papa, hi! Good morning! I am great!' I replied. The world was a sunny place for me today.

Dad batted the breeze with nothing much to say, except to repeat the news that all was well and that Uncle Mehta was very happy with me. For some reason he sounded more cheery than usual, rather excitable in fact. And he kept talking about inane things. I didn't mind. I could see Roli's tousled head emerging from the duvet on the drawing room carpet as I doodled on her bare shoulder. She stirred and started to turn towards me, beginning to wake up. Suddenly I needed to be with her again.

'Papa, I have to go now.'

'J-Just one second, son.' For some reason, Papa stuttered a bit as he spoke. 'Just wanted to tell you that—er, that Roli got married last week.'

I dropped the receiver onto the carpeted floor. It made no sound. I turned to look at the girl lying on the carpet as she turned towards me. It was Saloni, not Roli, turning, stretching and purring. There were superficial similarities to the shape of the head and the body structure and last night, I had been too drunk to know the difference…

Saloni spoke, 'Boy, you really were something, but you know it is bad manners to call out another woman's name. Who is this Roli, by the way?'

I was stricken, unable to say a word and I guess it showed in my face. Saloni came close and softly hugged me. 'Its my fault. I shouldn't have surprised you like this, but I have been thinking about our time together in Delhi and when dad said that he had some work in Pune, I just had to come and see you…'

I still didn't say anything so she chattered on, 'She must be quite a woman, this Roli, to fire you up like that. Now I know why you wouldn't look at any other girl in St Stephens—apart from talking to them, I mean.'

I slid down against the bare wall to the floor and looked at my ruined life. I had lost Roli. Finally and irrevocably. That was the long and short of it. 'You know,' Saloni said perceptively, 'love cannot survive unilaterally. Let it go. You can't endlessly hold a candle for someone who doesn't love you back. And it certainly is not the end of the world.'

'For me it is.' The words somehow emerged from my choked throat, the voice of a stranger.

'Ok, promise me just one thing, then,' said Saloni gently.

'What?' I said dully. How did it matter? My life was over, in any case.

'That you won't go into a blue funk, will carry on as usual and live your life normally.'

'Huh?' was all I could manage. Did she think that I would commit suicide the moment she stepped out of the door?

'Use this sorrow, this angst and this sense of betrayal to achieve something in life, rather than let it eat you up like acid.'

'Why?' I shrugged, my head pounding. 'What will that achieve? How will that help?'

'Well, you know what they say—it's better to be rich and unhappy than poor and unhappy!' Her smile was bittersweet.

Well...I thought to myself, that makes sense. To her I said, 'Thanks for everything, Saloni, but I need to be alone.'

'That sounds like a goodbye and I will not allow that!' she pouted. 'And have you forgotten that I am your guest, even if uninvited, and you have to show me the sights of Pune?'

'I know,' I mumbled. 'Of course I will...'

'So get up, then, sleepy-head, and let's get going!'

She was right. I picked myself up off the floor, picked up the broken pieces of my life and started over.

I took her around, showed her the sights and acted normal. We went for a long drive to Khadakwasla and to the fort where the National Defence Academy cadets were sent for their 42 km runs. As the day wore on, I cheered up. If everyone else in the world was having a party, why should I be the only one to suffer from Obsessive Compulsive Disorder? I tried hard to be cheerful and being around Saloni helped. When I was lugubrious, Saloni more than made up for it with the sheer excitement that only a tourist can have. She kept saying that this was her first trip away from parental supervision, and since this would be probably her last, she wanted to make the most of it. After the umpteenth time she had said that, I finally asked her why this would be her last such trip, she told me that her parents were looking for a husband for her…

'You wouldn't be interested in applying, by any chance, would you?' she asked with a coy, half-serious smile. When I didn't say anything, she nodded as if to confirm a fact that she already knew and insisted that she wanted to just live without a thought for the next couple of days, and who better to do it with than the one person her parents admired the most—me!

The next two days were a whirlwind of parties and outings interspersed with drinking binges and she kept talking about me to anyone who would listen. It became embarrassing after a point. She would tell everyone who'd listen how intelligent I was, how I had stood up to Professor Sood in class, how that had led to that famous invitation to the professor's house, even how much her parents liked me and how everyone was amazed at this crazy career move that I had made! As she got progressively drunker, she even told everyone, at the top of her voice, about how I had put my hand up her skirt while tutoring her! Everyone had a good laugh at that, with Suvernika winking at me and giving me a thumbs-up more than once! We drank and danced as if there was no tomorrow. I joined in the brittle excitement of the moment and later each night I re-discovered that I did share a great chemistry with her. Drunk and filled with desire, we literally pounded into each other, trying to rid ourselves of our respective ghosts. I learnt how to pleasure a woman, if not with my heart then with my body. As they say, sex is like pizza—

when it's good, it's really great, and when it is bad, it's still pretty good! I also discovered that, at least for me, the body and the mind were two different entities that lived together in the same person. I found that I could love someone and still have great sex with someone else…

But no question, I had changed. I just couldn't be romantic anymore. That moment when I had discovered that it wasn't Roli beside me—that had broken me into a thousand pieces. Those pieces had come back together but the image through the glass was fundamentally altered.

My life carried on. The minutes from that fateful day slowly became hours and then slid gently into weeks and months. Alcohol became a constant companion—dependable and unquestioning in its reliable company. The parties carried on and I would end up on most occasions with a splitting head and a strange girl on my pillow in the morning. The more I tried to fuck Roli out of my life the more I ached for her. The more intimate I became with a woman physically, the more I was reminded of the alabaster perfection of Roli's body. Everything that I did, instead of making me forget, further reminded me of the love that I had lost. *The more I indulged myself physically, the further I drifted away from my pristine self.* I blamed myself for not being man enough, interesting enough or capable enough to hold Roli's attention and heart. I drove myself more and more into my work and into these shallow relationships so that I could convince myself that I was good enough.

The remaining one-and-a-half years of the project went by in a blur. The project turned out to be a blazing success with all our parameters met. It became a first-of-its-kind project in India where an Indian builder gave a product that met international standards in its planning and execution. A grateful Uncle Mehta, true to his promise, sent me off to study—all expenses paid as per our agreement, with a Mitsubishi Spyder convertible as a thank you gift waiting for me in London. But my objectives had changed forever. I was no longer the callow boy who had wanted to find out the deepest secrets of the universe. You need a certain innocence to want to do something like that. Instead, my objective now was to be truly successful and financially wealthy. I reasoned to myself that if all relationships were based on half-truths, if not on downright lies, with people only interested in using each other for self-appointed reasons, then I should be the one who held all the aces. If everyone was a seeker of self-interest, success was only a matter of figuring out each person's weak spot and purchasing them.

This cynical belief of mine was reinforced under Uncle Mehta's tutelage. While in Pune, I had closely examined how his company worked and as a corollary, how all companies worked. I had learnt that the employees of the company could make or break it. And I understood why he had wanted me so desperately. Integrity is the key. And as I looked at our payroll, one man had stuck out like a sore thumb. He was our accountant, a soft-spoken man who would never look you in the eye and who handled oodles of cash. That had been the initial red flag that had made me look closer at him. That man dealt with all our cash and we seemed to have no checks or balances over him. We, like any typical contractor, generated a lot of cash. Since there is a big price difference between buying things with bills and without bills, we ended up saving a lot of money by dealing in cash. When translated into purchases of tens of crores, tens of lakhs could be saved. The rub was that this meant that a lot of cash was always lying around and had to be counted and secured from theft—and kept carefully unaccounted for! That's where the accountant came in. He was the sole person in charge of the cash and there was no one to keep an eye on his dealings. I questioned Uncle Mehta about what to me appeared as a straight and imminent danger to our finances.

'Oh, he's fine—don't worry about him!' the usually conservative Mr Mehta told me emphatically.

I was intrigued. The faith that he manifested in the accountant's honesty was a faith that I'd rarely seen him exhibit towards anyone else.

'And why is that, Uncle?' I asked.

'That's because I own him,' he said seriously, and I frowned. Modern day slavery, huh?

'Own him? What do you mean?' I asked, intrigued.

'Son, a few years ago, when Ved Prakash was a just a couple of years old in my company, he suffered a devastating personal tragedy. His wife was badly burnt in an accidental fire. He came to me with a request for money for her treatment. Even he did not believe that I would give it to him since the amount was huge, his salary was low, his job not permanent and unemployed accountants a dime a dozen. He asked me only because he was clutching at straws.'

'So what did you do, Uncle?'

'Gave him the money, of course!' he shrugged. 'On a salary of 10,000 rupees a month, I loaned him 6 lakhs of rupees!'

'What?' I knew my eyes were round with incredulity. 'But—why, Uncle? He surely would have had everyone's sympathies but I am sure that no one expected you to do that. And did you ask for collateral?'

'He had none to give. Anyway, I didn't do that, by the way, to earn the halo of a saint or a philanthropist, although that was the inevitable byproduct of my act. You see…' He paused and sipped on his glass of gin-and-tonic, 'with that one act of calculated kindness, I bought his eternal gratitude, in the shape of his undying loyalty. I bought my own peace of mind, knowing that my accountant would be completely honest with me forever after. Can you put a price to peace of mind?'

'I guess not!' I had to admit. Typical Uncle Mehta!

He continued, 'That's what I have learnt. Everything can be bought or sold. Everything and just about everyone—no exceptions. When you figure out what a person really wants, you can purchase him. Mind you, it's not a transaction in the exploitative sense. What I do is that I stick to what I have promised and the other person usually does what his conscience dictates. And you will be surprised that it's not always money that people want.'

He'd done the same with me, I thought to myself wryly. He had plugged together my interest in higher education with my father's middle-class financial stature and his own need for an honest project manager to recruit me to create a successful project. A win-win situation for all concerned. Could I call him calculating? Yes! A great judge of human nature? Yes! Someone who used people? Again the answer would have to be yes, but not in the purely selfish, exploitative sense. My respect for my dad's friend and my mentor grew but my faith in the unconditional things of life such as love, loyalty and friendship, receded into the pages of fairy tales. The bottom-line was that, since people always wanted something from you, why not put a price to what you could do for them?

I became a machine of a man—aloof, exclusive, unapproachable and eerily competent at what I did. I started coming across as far above the reach of ordinary mortals. I guess it started to show in my face and people stopped asking me my age or commenting that I was the youngest project manager they had ever seen.

There were, of course, moments when I regretted what I had lost. When I looked at the photos of my younger, far more innocent self, clear lucid eyes bright with hope stared back at me, searching for some reflection of themselves in me, but the eyes that looked at those photos had forever altered—hooded and probing for the first sign of weakness or desire in others.

I reached London for the fall semester. My break from the pure sciences was complete. What I now chose to pursue was not a Bachelors in Physics but a Bachelors in Economics with a specialization in Project Finance.

Uncle Mehta had been right as usual. After the work experience I'd had, I knew exactly what I wanted to study—unlike those who first stumbled on a subject almost by accident and then hoped to get a job as per their qualifications. I had also realized that technical competence could be easily hired but there was a paucity of originality. A Eureka moment, an original idea—as Mrs Sood had said all those eons ago—these were definitely in short supply. Most people simply didn't have the balls to stretch out into something new, preferring to be told what to do with the safety of a salary cheque at the end of the month. Surprisingly, even if they looked confident, most intelligent people were timid, and didn't want to step out of their narrow field of expertise. It was always a mystery to me why otherwise intelligent people with high IQs could never conceive of working across platforms to produce original products that the masses would like—while I found myself effortless at that. And over the next few years, I learnt the economics behind innovation.

'The theory of everything seems to have been the last thing on your mind at this stage of your life,' observed Ashish, as Rupen laid out the dinner on a table on the verandah. The sun had set and it was a quiet evening bejewelled with stars that hung so low that they seemed like apples hanging on the trees in the orchards below. The moon was a slice of watermelon throwing its pale red light on the Swargarohini that lived up to their name: the golden Heavenly Peaks.

'Absolutely,' I admitted softly.

'But then how did you become an inventor?' Ashish asked, dipping enthusiastically into his plate. 'What you have told me indicates that you were set on a brilliant, though straightforward, career as a corporate honcho.'

'Yes, just when I thought that I was set on a path to all the brilliance and success life could offer, my life changed again.' I yawned and stretched. 'But that's a tale for tomorrow.'

RE-BIRTH

'Saagar, where are you? Can you come home right now?' There was panic in my mother's voice on the phone.

'What happened?' I asked, her tone triggering an instant alarm in my mind.

Her reply confirmed my worst fears.

'Your father is having severe chest pains.'

I heard those words like a clang in my heart. In my fearful nightmares over the last several years, ever since he had been diagnosed with cardiac disease, I had imagined hearing these very words.

As luck would have it, I was in India that week, attending a conference on city planning. The seminar had been a free-wheeling discussion on the nature of fast-growing Indian cities and what ought to be the paradigms for sustainable city planning.

Ten years had passed since I had left India for London and I had never returned except as a visitor. I was now a senior cog in the wheel of the world's largest real-estate developer, based out of London. My area of operations was South-East Asia and my company had sent me to explore the burgeoning Indian real-estate market. This is how I found myself back in Delhi when mummy's call came.

I thought quickly. 'Can you call a taxi and take him to a hospital? It will take me some time to reach home.' Hyatt Intercontinental was at least an hour's drive from my parents' home in Janakpuri.

I knew the answer to that would be a 'No' even as I asked the question. Bull-headed in the extreme and hating all things medical, my father would probably simply refuse to go.

'He is refusing to go,' mummy replied, her voice desperate, seconding my thoughts. 'You know how he is.'

'Ok, I am leaving from here right now, but it will still take me an hour to reach home. Try to convince him to go in any case.' I said and quickly hung up as I dashed for the lobby.

As I was driven home, I tried to send him Pranic energy. I had done a course on that a few months ago. The teacher had explained that the energy would flow automatically from the healer to the patient once the bond was established. In the workshop, all I had felt was a minor tingling in my fingertips as we practised on each other and I had dismissed that as a figment of my imagination. Now I could feel a river of sensation flowing out of my hands. Endless. Unstoppable. As familiar landmarks whizzed by, my mind and heart went through a turmoil of thoughts and emotions—a quagmire of unexpressed angers, suppressed affections, unshared love and unadulterated fear. There had been many unresolved issues with my father over the years—sticking points and long-held hurts. So many things that I had wanted to say and had never been able to say. Right now none of them seemed important. I prayed throughout that unending drive. I prayed that it would be a false alarm, but the river of energy flowing out of my hands continued unabated. I wondered what that meant.

As I sat numbly on the passenger seat of the hired sedan, I mulled over all the things that would need to be done if it was serious. Ambulances, doctors, hospitals, money—all that could be handled, but there was a complication that even I couldn't deal with. My dad himself.

My mother and I had long known that the day Papa needed to be taken to a doctor would be a day of big trouble. My dad had always been dead set against doctors and the couple of times I had to take him to one had been major trials of wills. He would simply refuse to go on the rare occasions when he was unwell. Luckily for us it had worked so far, since he had been as strong as an ox all his life.

At one level I could understand his reluctance since he was a self-made man with oodles of will power and no situation where he hadn't been in control of his own life! He was also a man who believed that he could heal himself through yoga, long walks and, if that didn't work, sheer will power! For him, going to the hospital, on the rare occasions he had to go, was always an admission of defeat. The last time he had been seriously unwell, almost a decade back, he had refused all treatment. He had healed himself, as he proudly claimed, from a bout of typhoid, without any allopathic medication. In the last five years, since being diagnosed with 95 per cent blockage in all of his cardiac arteries, he had visited a doctor only twice. And on top of that he had trekked to Gaumukh to show all of us that he could still do it!

We finally headed to hospital after I reached home. I could see that he was in terrible pain and was sweating bullets.

They say that the pain of a heart attack is unbearable and it did turn out to be a heart attack, not some gastric disturbance as I had hoped. Yet there he was, still larger than life and joking with the E.C.G. technician. The attending doctor told me later that the brave ones are the ones who usually die since they ignore their pain; the cowards go to hospital in the first instance and live to tell the tale.

And die my father did that day, just a short while later. We had left it too late and his heart was literally not in it. True to his wish of never getting into the grip of doctors, his last visit to the hospital was short—just 50 minutes from entry to exit. The cause of death? Complete cardiac blockage! The doctors said that they had rarely seen anything like it, where every part of the heart stops functioning due to blockages all over! I was with him, watching as he fought his losing battle, his body convulsing as if electricity was running through it. Strangely, he seemed to be smiling through it—as if he was seeing some glorious vision as he left his body. Towards the end, he somehow propped himself up on the stretcher, looked up towards me as if he couldn't see too well and then fell back as we ran desperately through the hospital corridors towards the cardiac care unit.

It is strange and unreal to watch someone die. To see the light in the eyes dim and disappear, till what is left resembles a wax model of the same person as in Madame Tussauds. The room looked as if a battle had been fought there. There were medical equipment, rubber gloves, wires and pipes strewn all over the place and in the middle lay my father looking as handsome as ever, open eyes staring up into eternity, while the nursing staff went about quietly removing the equipment that had failed to save him.

Duty takes over when someone you love dies. You find solace in ritual and in doing things. Things that are designed to make you forget the large fact that your loved one has gone and will never come back...

The first of many tasks was to buy a white sheet, from a shop outside the hospital gates, to cover his body before, we could take him home and then make arrangements for the cremation.

As I lit the funeral pyre the next day, I saw my father's body melt in the flames and disappear from the face of the earth. Two days later, I went to Haridwar to immerse the ashes.

There is something bleak and desolate in emptying the urn into the black swirling waters. Even the fire of the crematorium does not destroy the illusion of life as does this simple act. As I let the ashes flow through my fingers, it occurred to me that I was wiping a human being out of life into eternity, as if he had never existed—that his presence or disappearance from the face of the earth made no difference to anything or anyone. Was our life of no significance and were we just a recycling process for nature? I wondered to myself.

Yet the world around me looked exactly the same. My world had come crashing down, but the world wasn't crashing down. It seemed painfully obvious to me that what was important to me was meaningless in the larger scheme of things. I wondered at my own stupidity and lack of understanding of this fact earlier. That moment as I stood in the river, I lost faith in the way I thought. In what I believed to be true and in my own infallibility. All the unshakeable pillars of my life that I had created so meticulously seemed to be sinking into quicksand.

The question that stared me in the face was this—wasn't my life till today, successful by most standards, built completely on the wrong premises? What could I, a small pitiful person, do against the vastness of the cycle of creation itself? Whether I became a corporate king or formulated the theory of everything, could I prevent what was happening now?

My dad was gone. For eternity. Eternity is such a small crisp word but is so infinite in its reach. I had never appreciated that in my creative writing class.

Standing in the Ganga up to my thighs, with the hot sun on my back, the cold air blowing into my face and the hired pandit muttering ancient mantras, I felt like sinking and disappearing into the softly swirling water along with my father's ashes—a pitifully small amount of wet grey dust, all that was left of what had once been a living, breathing human being. Where would this dust scatter? What would happen to my fathers' ashes? I staggered in the water, struck by the enormity of what I was letting go. I was scattering my father across the vastness of the universe itself.

Till then, death had been a concept, something to gawk at, on the obituary pages of *The Times of India*. I had always had a ghoulish attraction for those eulogies. I would look at the photos and wonder what the person had been like in real life. They must have been loved by their families for them to publish those expensive 'in memoriams'. All those people in those photos must have left behind unfulfilled ambitions, heartaches and memories. Yet, none had been spared by death.

Now my dad was one of those eulogies; reduced to a cutting in a newspaper. Was his life, great by average standards, worth only that much? Yellowing frayed newsprint fading over time to be recycled into paper envelopes? Like falling leaves in autumn… And if all greatness and/or mediocrity ended like this, what was the worth of that greatness? What was the value of the familiar pillars of my universe that I had been constantly chasing and had been so intent on preserving? In the face of the inevitability of death, was I not stupid to believe in my own special place or the permanence of my personal universe? What was the worth of my hopes, ambitions, beliefs and attachments? Were they worth anything at all? Why would nature in its vastness even look at my specific concerns? And what was the point of pursuing all my petty ambitions when the final outcome of all ambition, all relationships and all hope was this—being emptied into the river, burnt to cinders?

Was all of life in its multiple hues just a blind march towards death? I looked around the river, pole-axed by my own thoughts. The Ganga was flowing serenely by, as it had done for thousands of years. There were birds calling in the distance and the reeds on the far bank swayed in the soothing breeze. Buses were crossing the bridge above, heading into the Rajaji National Park with their loads of people. It all appeared normal. As I looked at the scene before me, I suddenly realized that this wasn't real—that every single thing that I saw was actually going to turn to dust. Every leaf, every blade of grass, every man, woman and child, every animal and even every rock in the universe would end its existence sooner or later.

I marvelled at this thought. Why hadn't this struck me before? Death was indeed the ultimate leveller, the great equalizer and neutralizer. As I looked around I could see it everywhere, all of a sudden. I saw it lying in wait in the decaying walls of the ancient architecture of the ghats; in the mould that grew in damp places under the great banyan tree in the distance; in the vine that crept up the tree even as it strangled it slowly; in the rust hidden under the shoddy paint of the Public Works Department guesthouse gate that I could see hanging on its hinges. All of us were just helpless lambs being readied for slaughter.

I turned and stepped out of the river. I needed to get away, anywhere, somewhere, as long it was away from the known, the familiar and the ephemeral.

I needed to find out what was truly eternal, or if anything at all.

'God, help me…' The Lord's name was wrung out of my heart for the very first time and flung echoing into the universe. I had no clue as to where I could find the answers to these questions. In this maze of unknowing, what basic certainty could I start from? Where was the firm ground where I could plant my feet? Was this what motivated people to look for answers in religion and go to gurus? To seek the eternal, the absolute and the unshakeable, as opposed to the shifting vagaries of life? To seek that something that could be depended on to not betray, to not end and to not leave, as my father suddenly had, without even a goodbye.

I suddenly realized that looking for answers to these questions wasn't the airy-fairy escapism that I had always derided. It was a living, practical, urgent concern.

I looked around. The curve of the hills that cradled the Ganga as it emerged into the great plains of India yawned back at me. A strong breeze blew in from the funnel that my dad and I had traversed many a time. Badrinath, Kedarnath and Gangotri lay beyond—eternal evocative names that truth seekers had been going to, as far back as history and legend recorded. The river; the breeze; the swaying reeds on the bank and the calling birds were just a mirage. A limited shifting scene that cloaked the eternal truth lying beneath. How could I find that truth? I didn't know where to start but the memories of my childhood trips with my father beckoned me. Maybe I could find it in the lap of the Himalayan peaks? After all, why would seekers head there for centuries if they found no answers there?

My feet charted a course to the Haridwar bus stand. I called home and informed my mother that I needed a few days to myself. I caught the first bus that left for Gangotri the next day at an unearthly 4:00 am.

The buses that leave for Gangotri—one of the four Himalayan pilgrimage destinations—are full of pilgrims who have an expectant air and who chant God's name as the bus travels. And the recitations become even more fervent when the bus takes a sudden and perilous turn or jerk! As we left the plains a group of devotees began chanting Sanskrit hymns. They sounded melodious but I couldn't understand a word. I asked my fellow traveler who had the markings of a pandit, 'What sloka is this?'

'That's the famous Gayatri mantra!' he exclaimed, his voice betraying his surprise that I didn't know something so ubiquitous.

'Sounds nice.' I hedged, embarrassed, 'Er, what does it mean?' It had been a long time since I hadn't known something that seemed common knowledge.

'It is a prayer to almighty God, which asks him to give us the necessary wisdom to find the right purpose and direction of our limited life.'

'Wait!' I exclaimed 'Can I write the full meaning down?'

I was shaken. This was exactly what I had been praying for in my heart! What I had thought of as my unique, personal pain seemed to be a well-travelled gripe—the most common and ancient prayer of India. Obviously I wasn't the first one to go through something like this.

The pandit looked at me, 'Have you lost your father?'

I nodded. His guess was hardly rocket science, since my tonsured head was a dead giveaway. The pandit looked sympathetic. That spurred me to go on. To share some of what I was feeling.

I marshalled my feelings and started, 'I don't know what to think or do. My father who was alive and well only four days ago, is not there anymore and I regret so many things…'

'That happens,' said the priest sympathetically and lapsed into silence.

'Tell me, panditji,' I persisted. 'Where does the soul go after death?'

'I don't know personally, son, but our scriptures say that the soul is first purged of its sins and then, depending on its karmas, goes to an appropriate world where it resides till it is time to come back to earth to live out its balance karmas.' The pandit continued after a pause, 'The *Garuda Purana*—the Hindu book of the dead—and similar books of other religions say that the soul lingers around its body and its family due to grief and attachment. This is especially true if the death is sudden, violent and in any way not anticipated by the soul. In that situation, the soul is disoriented on losing its body. It can still feel the body and is troubled by all bodily needs such as hunger, thirst, pain, heat, cold, etc., except that these needs are greatly magnified and cannot be fulfilled since the body does not exist anymore. Since the deluded soul has no way of satisfying these cravings, which are said to be seven times stronger than normal, it is always in danger of taking a quick rebirth into any species just so that it can escape the hardship.' The pandit continued reflectively, 'Even a pious soul can get lost in the cycle of birth and death due to pain, disorientation and fear and the wrong choices of those terror-filled moments can derail a soul's journey.'

I digested all this. 'Is there anything I can do to help my father's soul?'

The pandit replied, 'Yes, son, our rituals are meant to offer relief and solace to the soul so that it may become calm, that it may detach itself from its existence in its previous birth and move on naturally. Performing the thirteenth-day ceremony and the yearly remembrance are all meant to offer this relief to the departed soul. One year in our life is equal to one day in the life of the departed soul, which is usually awaiting rebirth. As his son,' he concluded, 'you can directly help your father by chanting the Gayatri mantra 108 times every day. That's one of the best things that you can do since the mantra offers wisdom to the soul to find its true path.'

'What!' I sat up straight in my seat, 'You want *me* to recite the Gayatri mantra? I can't do this mumbo-jumbo! And I am sure it would take far too long! Besides, I used to fail my Sanskrit exams!' This was my public school upbringing speaking, and I felt ashamed the instant the words left my mouth.

'Not so,' said the priest, not put off at all by my rude words towards what would after all be his staple. 'You'll find 108 recitations will take less than 10 minutes. Also, do you still think this is mumbo-jumbo after understanding the meaning?'

He was right. Once I understood what it meant, I could not dismiss this as superstition. The Gayatri mantra was simply a prayer for guidance. So what if it was addressed to an entity that might not even exist, and if it did, may or may not respond? If you ignored these two basic questions, it all made perfect sense! Anyway, what else could you do in such a situation?

Another penny dropped in my atheist head, 'So that's why people resort to prayer!' I exclaimed aloud. This wasn't superstition—just a normal response in the face of complete helplessness.

We both fell silent as the bus hit the mountain-ghat section and started its long climb towards the source of the Ganga. I watched the river becoming a silvery thread as it receded far below as we wound our way higher through dense forests. The road twisted and turned and climbed, dipped and descended and we welcomed the stops to stretch our legs and sip the piping hot, heavily sweetened tea that was served at the wayside dhabas. Pine soon gave way to deodar and the wind turned cold. The open bus windows were quickly shuttered and we put on our jackets and sweaters as the long day slowly untwined itself into evening.

We crossed big rivers, turbulent rivulets, even a dam, and tunnelled our way through half-cut mountains. It was turning out to be a long journey—12 hours or so—but its monotony was frequently broken by dramatic changes in view. We went through narrow valleys, brimming with water-filled stepped fields lined with impossibly green lines of lush paddy, and onwards through gorges that seemed too narrow for anyone to pass through. From Rishikesh to Chamba we climbed, before descending towards the sinking town of Old Tehri and then winding our way along the Tehri Lake, onwards to the pilgrimage town of Uttarkashi. Uttarkashi is where the nature of the journey changes and the middle Himalayas start giving way to the really high peaks, the further climb simply stunning in its beauty and grandeur.

I had made friends with the bus driver at one of the tea breaks and he advised me to clamber onto the roof of the bus to get a better view. I did and sat there entranced, along with a bunch of raucous trekkers, and looked with awe at the scenery that extended in all three dimensions. We crossed the quaint and scenic towns of Harsil and Lanka. The river Bhagirathi followed us all the way up, sometimes stretching its girth placidly across the valley and sometimes showing its angry and turbulent nature as the gorges deepened and narrowed.

It was towards 4 o'clock in the evening when we finally reached our roadhead—the town of Gangotri. The town itself lay nestled in a forest of dense trees with no particular view. The only thing of note was the river roaring by and there was a single mountain trail heading off northwards that said 'Gaumukh 20 kilometers'. At the beginning of the trail were the small compact ghats on the banks of the young Bhagirathi that flanked an ancient Bhagirath temple whose age was said to be unknown. Legend has it that King Bhagirath had sat and prayed at this very spot for Ganga to descend to earth. This is where the glacier had apparently ended many eons ago. Since that day, the glacier had been steadily receding and had retreated 22 kilometers to its present spot, named Gaumukh, which translates to 'a cow's maw'. That's where the river emerges today from its icy womb.

I was mentally, emotionally and physically spent, so I checked into the first hotel I could find and went off to sleep as soon as my head touched the pillow. Early next morning, I started my walk to Gaumukh.

Everything about this walk is special. The view and the air that flows through the valley, the glaciers that feed the river one has to cross, the unfolding vistas of the Bhagirathi peaks on one side and the killer mountain Shivling—which extracts a toll from almost every mountaineering expedition—on the other side, the ancient trees whose bark peels off to make the parchment that our scriptures were originally written on, and last but not the least, the picturesque sadhus themselves who made for an exotic sight, dressed in nothing but loincloths and ashes. Everything about this trail indicates that it is an ancient walk, trodden for centuries by pilgrims, seekers and tourists.

My father and I had walked this path five years ago. That last trip together had been the one when we had finally begun to become friends, leaving behind the acrimony and heartburn of my growing-up years. This is where we had debated science and philosophy and argued whether a belief in the scientific way should preclude a belief in religion or if science and religion could coexist. My father had been a diehard atheist, the way only a self-made man can be. As a result, I had been brought up deriding religion. Yet my forays into the fundamentals of science all pointed to one fact—that there seemed to be a Creator and that most scientists, be they Einstein or Neil Bohr, strongly believed in the concept of a Creator. 'Something made something out of nothing, seemed easier to believe than nothing made something out of nothing' as the famous saying goes!

I had spent a lot of time on that trip putting together a rational argument to prove the existence of something beyond science or at least that all things physical seemed to emerge from a non-physical base. My father had a lot of difficulty with that. He had retorted that protons, electrons, neutrons and other compositions of matter were all proven by science, while the existence of God had never been proven. I quoted Osho and he was stunned into silence, whether by the force of the argument or by the revelation that his young son was reading Osho! Osho's argument went like this: Nobody has seen electrons, protons and neutrons, yet scientists say they are there simply because even if we can't see them, we can see their effects. The mystics say the same thing—that we cannot see God but we can see his effects! And so on and so forth we had chatted. We had talked and walked through the bracing air as it blew off the ancient ice of the Gangotri glacier. I could feel the same breeze today as well, but this time I was completely alone with nothing except my memories. *Memories are strange things; they give no indications at the time they are being formed, yet when one remembers them later, they add so many hues and feelings to an ordinary existence.*

Dusk was falling as I reached the Garhwal Mandal Vikas Nigam guesthouse at the base of the glacier. I checked in, turned in early and slept. I was physically and emotionally exhausted, yet something woke me up early the next morning. I looked at the radium dial of my watch; it was only 2:30 am. Unable to go back to sleep, I went to the window and peeked out. An amazing sight awaited me. A hitherto unknown peak—Om Parbat, as I learnt the name later—was glowing blue, standing right above my window. I saw a flag fluttering high above, on a ridge below the icy base of the peak.

'Who stays there?' I asked the waiter later in the morning as he served me a delicious breakfast of paranthas and white butter, with some pickled chillies as accompaniment.

'Oh, that is Science Baba, sir,' the waiter informed me cheerfully, in his sing-song hill dialect.

Science Baba! What a name—I thought to myself, and asked aloud, 'Why would he be called that?'

The waiter replied, 'I don't know, sir, but he has always been called that.'

'Since when has he lived here?' I wanted to know.

'I have no idea, sir,' the man scratched his head cheerfully. 'Since well before I joined duty at this lodge—let me see,' I could see the wheels grinding in his head, '...definitely, more than five years ago. And by then,' he added, 'he had been coming here for several years already.'

'How far would that place be?' I asked, my curiosity piqued.

'Not very far, just 5 km or so, but you'll need to cross a treacherous glacier and climb straight up. It is a nice walk.' The man paused and said, 'Sir, do you want to go there?' As I pondered the offer, he continued, 'If you do want to go, then you could accompany Vimal who is going up shortly to deliver the baba's supplies.'

The idea was tempting me, but Gaumukh was first priority. I shook my head. 'Not possible today, since I am planning to go up to the glacier, but I could go tomorrow if Vimal could take me again.'

'No problem, sir,' the man said placidly. 'Vimal can postpone the trip till tomorrow if you are certain that you want to go.'

'Yes, count me in. What else is up there?' I asked.

'The best view that you can imagine. The vast panorama of the Bhagirathi peaks and many unnamed ones stretch into the distance right up to China,' he told me. 'There is nothing else there—no villages, no tourists and not even sheep, since it is a rocky barren ridge. Most people are content to go towards Gaumukh, with the adventurous ones heading further to Tapovan and Nandanvan. This place, where Science Baba stays, is the base camp for the Om Parbat climb and it is to one side so no one goes there, unless there is a mountaineering expedition. There is no one up there but Science Baba. I guess that's why he likes it there.'

I finished my breakfast and then walked up to the maw of the glacier and immersed the last of my father's ashes. And with that, the last mortal remains of my father were assimilated with the elements of the earth.

Next morning, I trailed Vimal as we headed off to visit Science Baba. I discovered that the path wasn't really treacherous, just difficult to find. It was a maze through creaking, shifting ice and unless one knew which crevasse to get into, one couldn't reach the point on the river bank where it could be safely crossed. Once across the river, it was a hard, bracing climb of approximately three hours with breaks. Vimal soon outpaced me, even though he was carrying quite a load, but I didn't mind as I could see him clearly in the distance.

It was noon when I finally reached the ridge and the flag that I had seen from my hotel room window. Ramesh—the caretaker—had been right. The view was phenomenal. It looked down at the same panorama as from the hotel, but from a much higher elevation. We were a good 17,000 feet above sea-level, having climbed 4,000 feet straight up in a short 5 km. Across the rocky alpine meadow, I could see a small hut assembled from splintered rock. Outside the hut, on an elevated rock, was sitting a sadhu—Science Baba, I guessed.

I went up to him. His eyes were open, gazing into the distance and I touched his feet. A first for me, since I had never touched anyone's feet before. But with him it seemed the natural thing to do. In any case, how else do you say hello to a sadhu? 'Good morning' or even 'Namaskar' doesn't sound appropriate somehow! I straightened clumsily, my back a bit stiff from the rigorous climb, but couldn't say a word. I was suddenly overcome, my throat choked and my eyes full of unshed tears with the memory of my loss.

'You have done your duty towards your father, eh?' said the sadhu, my shaved head again providing the requisite explanation. He spoke in English, surprising me.

'*Aap angrezi*...? You speak English?' I exclaimed.

'Why not? Is there any law that states that sadhus can't speak English?' he retorted. It was strange but a relief somehow, reducing the enormous gap in our sensibilities. I stood there, not sure what to do or say next.

The sadhu looked at me perceptively and said in a matter-of-fact voice, 'This is the play of *Kaal*. The cycle goes on. The son cremates the father...' I half turned away, hiding the tears that I had temporarily forgotten in the last two arduous days. Who could understand my pain? Who cared? Specially a sadhu who had given up on a normal life anyway?

'Don't feel sorry for yourself.' His voice rang out strong in the clear air, reading my thoughts—not that it was very difficult to do so!

'How can I not?' I retorted. 'I have lost my father and along with that my sense of the familiar is gone. I do not know what is real and what isn't. What is worth pursuing and what is not. Life has lost its meaning. What is the point of living, planning and achieving anything, since the end is always like this? I don't expect you to understand or sympathize, of course,' I muttered half to myself.

The sadhu laughed, 'And you have understood this fact today? When you have lost your particular loved one? Where were you when others died and others suffered? Having fun,

I suppose? When you did not feel any pain for the suffering of others, why do you feel it now?'

'Because this time the pain is mine,' I retorted, stung to the quick by the sharpness of his words and the utter lack of sympathy in his tone.

'How utterly self-centered! How utterly childish! *Pain is flowing through creation like lava, but as long as it doesn't impinge on him personally, it's of no consequence to him. He has no sympathy for others but expects it for himself.*' I looked up at the sadhu in anger and amazement. What a rude, unfeeling man!

He appeared unfazed by my obvious anger. 'Don't you know that thousands of embodied beings—men, women, children and other living creatures—are disappearing back into the soup of creation even as we speak?' he asked rhetorically. 'Even the mighty Himalayas are fading away. And you grieve for just your particular loss!'

Stung to the quick, I retorted, 'Easy for you to say, Baba! Sadhus like you escape from life and then say that they are detached! You stay aloof and mock others who grieve over their lost relationships. You shirk your responsibilities in an effort to run away from pain even before it happens. You are cowards but you pretend that you are noble. You may escape from life this way but even you cannot escape from death by hiding here.'

The sadhu looked at me and smiled a gentle smile. 'Well spoken, boy! You seem to have some sense in your hot head!'

I gaped at his strange unpredictable reactions, mildly offended that he had addressed me as 'boy'. I thought I had long outgrown that epithet.

'You are right,' he conceded. '*Sanyaas*—renunciation—is usually an escape from life in most cases and an excuse to smoke pot! Real *sanyaas* is a state of mind. It can be practiced from anywhere, including your own home. As far as I am concerned, I come here when the living conditions in my hometown are difficult, typically the summer months. The rest of the time I live in Mumbai where I used to teach physics at Kalina University till I retired.'

A professor from Kalina University! That's why they called him Science Baba!

'The real intent of *sanyaas*,' he continued, 'is seclusion from sensory overload so that you may contemplate the real nature of the world and God, without getting unduly disturbed by the business of living.'

That's an interesting way to put it, I thought to myself.

'Boy, do you know how to figure out when you are really ready for sanyaas?'

'How?' I was intrigued in spite of the harsh words that we had exchanged earlier.

'When neither happiness nor sorrow affect you. That's when *sanyaas* or seclusion makes sense and not before. If you renounce the world simply to escape the toughness of life, then it doesn't work and all that happens is that the attractions and repulsions go to the mental plane. You may be sitting in your Himalayan cave but you would still be dwelling on the world back home! The *Gita* describes such a person as a hypocrite.'

There was a brief pause and I pondered over what the baba was saying.

He continued, 'You are right in the sense that most people you see wandering around are simply escapists and not true ascetics.' Again there was a gap before he spoke, 'yet a thousand pretenders don't take away from the real need for sanyaas that resides pristine in every soul.' He shrugged, 'Of course, that need may be active or may remain forever dormant. And as to your next probable question—why do renunciates abandon home and hearth, and why can all this not be done at home, the answer is simple. When you want to contemplate, reflect or go inwards, the sounds of an ordinary life—the noise outside, the whirring fan, the air-conditioner, neighbours gossiping and vehicles honking on the road—anything and everything has the power to disturb you, especially when you are new to the path. Even advanced yogis have to spend some amount of energy dealing with the world around. Meditation and contemplation need mental, emotional and physical stillness and the more trying the circumstances the more energy and time you waste. It's rather difficult to sit quietly when you are swatting flies, sweating in the heat and sniffing what the neighbours are cooking for dinner!'

'But isn't it equally difficult to live here at these inhospitable heights, all alone? Isn't it too cold here?' I asked curiously.

'Yes it is cold,' he admitted, 'but it is relatively easy to get immune to cold. A thick blanket inside a snug Himalayan cave does the trick quite effectively till you master the heat-creating *Pranayams*. After that you can walk around naked! You need less food and less water too. Heat, on the other hand, causes stress even in a yogi's body which has to do extra work to cool itself down. Precious Pranic energy is wasted in doing that.'

I pondered over what I was hearing.

'Let me ask you a counter question,' he broke into my thoughts. 'Why do you think yogis have this predilection for the Himalayas? Why have they been coming here, or going to the Vindhyachal Mountains in droves for centuries?'

'Umm—for seclusion?' I ventured.

'Seclusion could be found even in the forests of the plains,' the yogi pointed out.

I knew I was missing a trick here but I couldn't quite catch it. I hazarded another guess. 'Is it because these mountains are holy? This is said to be God's own country and there must be a reason why people say that. Maybe the Himalayas are imbued with the actual presence of God? If so, maybe it is easier to find God in these divinely charged surroundings...'

The sadhu smiled. 'Sorry to disabuse you of these fancy notions; it is nothing as exotic as that. The real reason is this: where else in India can you find perfect air-conditioning, clean non-polluted water and no disturbances, and that too without having to pay a penny! In the city that's available only in 5-star hotels! That way yogis have a lot in common with people who love a luxurious life!' Science Baba laughed uproariously at his own joke.

This time I wasn't offended by his lack of caring about my grieving state. There was definitely an intriguing edge to whatever the man had said. He seemed to be offering a no-nonsense practical explanation for what yogis and renunciates did—things that the rest of us found exotic and strange.

The basic conclusion seemed to be that to find God, one needed to be still and inward-focused. Therefore, by default, one needed peace, quiet and a comfortable living environment. The lack of clothes was also explained as the result of the heat that was generated by meditation. And voila—*sanyaas* was neatly explained!

Was this the real basis for the twisted rituals that monks and monasteries practiced?

'Yes, that's what it is, a practical exercise!' the sadhu exclaimed. It seemed he could read my mind as well.

'What is a practical exercise?' I asked, not too sure what he meant.

'Why, finding the meaning of life of course! What other purpose could there be to live?'

'Oh, really!' I could think of a few others, but on second thought, could I really? In the face of inescapable death?

'All things being natural,' Science Baba declared, 'contemplation and the search for the ultimate truth is hard-wired into the soul of every human. Remove the rubbish, the dead-weight and the ballast of karmas and the soul naturally rises higher like a hydrogen-filled balloon. *Even an idiot figures out sooner or later, as Gautama Buddha did, that all life is transitory, with happiness and sorrow scrolling by*. Of course the real idiocy is ignoring this fact once this awareness comes into one's mind.'

'What should I do now, Baba, now that my father is dead?' I asked, feeling suddenly humble.

'Exactly what you were doing before this happened, but this time with awareness!' the sadhu volleyed back.

'But that seems so meaningless now, in the face of death. Isn't life just a game of chance with all of us destined to lose?'

'Is that what you think it is?' he asked me quietly.

'Seems so to me at least. What was the result of my father's long life, after all?' I queried rhetorically.

'Ho! This boy is calling God's creation chance!' Science Baba sounded jovial. 'Don't you think you are too young to have such fixed opinions?'

'Am I?' I wondered. 'The world that I see around me seems meaningless at this point of time…or, come to think of it, at any point.' I paused, marshalling my thoughts. 'Does the world make any sense at all? Does it have any ultimate purpose? Or…' I answered my own question with another question, '…is it just a random reversal of random chaos?'

The sadhu said nothing so I continued, 'It seems to me that any resemblance to a meaningful well-ordered system is just a coincidence. After all if you give an infinite number of monkeys an infinite number of typewriters, one of them is bound to write a play of Shakespeare, as per the law of probability.'

The sadhu again said nothing but seemed to be giving me his full attention so I continued, 'And if all of life is just random chance, what is the point of doing anything at all?'

'Your example of monkeys with typewriters is rather puerile,' my interlocutor announced, just as I had begun to think that I had silenced him with my wise words. 'Have you thought of who gave those monkeys typewriters? Who made those typewriters and who invented the English language in which the Shakespearean play is written? Come to think of it, who made the monkeys in the first place? And that still leaves the question of who created Shakespeare!' Again the baba laughed, his belly shaking, and this time I laughed with him.

Shaking an admonitory head at me, after we had stopped laughing, Science Baba continued, 'All the things that you just listed out—the monkeys, the typewriters, the English language and the Shakespearean play—they all allude to the basic fact that all this,'—he gestured with his hands at everything around us—'is purposeful and has been created.'

I sat there totally intrigued. Here was not just a saadhu, I reminded myself, but a professor of physics well versed in logic. He was arguing with me rationally without getting God or the need for blind faith into the argument. With his strange combination of qualifications, I couldn't dismiss what he was saying.

Science Baba continued, 'You know what is the most compelling and straightforward proof of a divine purpose behind this vast creation?'

'No, what?' I asked.

'That any system descends into chaos when left to its own devices over a period of time.'

'You mean the Law of Entropy!' I exclaimed.

'Yes,' he replied. 'If systems naturally descend into chaos, then what and who reverses that inevitable trend? What prevents inevitable decay? Whether you see a star or a cell of your own body, you see this tussle playing out every day. Stars are dying and so are the cells of our bodies, yet stars and living things are being born as well. Death and decay can be somewhat explained by entropy but can creation ever be explained as a consequence of entropy? The question that we never ask is that if unravelling is the order of unattended nature, then how does creation ever take place without something—or someone—doing it? Have you ever thought about that? And if you consider what I have just said, would you still think that it is all just a matter of chance?'

There was a point to what this guy was saying. Science was full of realities whose origins simply could not be explained. Take the birth of stars, for instance. Science had established that stars were born in nurseries which held vast amounts of stellar dust composed of hydrogen gas, and science postulated that this stellar dust somehow came together to start those immense fires that powered the nuclear chain reactions. Yet science could not explain why those dispersed clouds of dust came together in the first place. Gravity wouldn't be powerful enough since it would be too weak until the dust particles had already compacted to a significant degree and none of the other known forces could explain this coming together either. So how did the dust come together to form those heavily condensed stars? Science couldn't say! And this wasn't just the only unexplainable in science. Come to think of it, the famous experiment that we were all taught as kids where scientists had created amino acids in the lab was actually a failed experiment since those amino acids never amounted to anything. The expected next step towards the formation of living organisms never ever took place in the laboratory. The ladder from inorganic lifeless chemicals—hydrogen, carbon and oxygen—to even the simplest amoebas could not be explained or recreated in the lab. And to top this, it had been statistically proven that even 5 billion years were just not enough to evolve a lowly amoeba into the complex species that have roamed the earth for hundreds of millions of years till now. The inevitable conclusion could only be that someone or something was kick-starting the process of evolution along high speed paths!

'Hmm...' was all I said. The point the baba was making was not disputed by known scientific facts. Rather, scientifically accepted facts seemed to be making his case stronger. Yet my aim was not to argue with him about the theory of evolution and the law of probability. I needed more urgent advice—how to carry on in the face of inevitable death.

'Baba,' I asked, 'Er...my point is that whatever I may achieve—and I have achieved a great deal so far—isn't it all pointless, since death will wipe my achievements clean sooner or later anyway?'

'What you are expressing may sound like detachment but it is nothing more than a grief-stricken reaction to your personal loss,' the heartless sadhu responded. 'Once the edge goes off your grief, your detachment will also disappear and you will be back to your self-indulgent ways, chasing your personal dreams. What you are suffering from at this moment is called *"Cremation ground renunciation"*. Its effects last a few days,' the man chortled, 'depending on how much you actually loved your father.'

'How can you say that, sir?' I protested, angry at his flippancy, yet shaken by the grain of truth in what he was saying. But what he was pointing to sounded so cynical somehow that I just couldn't take his statement lying down.

'Look,' he sighed, 'I don't have time to argue with you so I will say it one last time. Till such time as you don't know the real meaning or purpose of life and act accordingly, whatever you do, whatever you achieve, it is all futile. With that frame of mind, the suffering that you undergo will never come to an end.'

'Meaning?' I asked nonplussed and he took me literally. 'Exactly! There is a meaning to all that happens, the good and the bad, and till such time as you know the Why of it, you can never know peace.'

'I didn't understand, sir.'

'Till such time as you understand the real meaning and purpose of why you were born, your own death or your father's death or your dog's death or the death of anyone else you love will continue to be meaningless. Until you understand the purpose of creation itself and how it functions and what your role in it is, you cannot find peace. No one can. Without the *why*, it is all meaningless,' he concluded.

Who was this guy who was throwing the *why* question—my old friend—back at me? Beating me with my own shoe? I fell to my knees in the soft grass. 'Can you help me, sir? I am lost and confused. Nothing makes sense anymore.'

'Nothing will, till you find the right purpose to live,' he nodded, his eyes kind. 'Your father's death, though tragic, has opened a brief window for you. In this moment you are questioning your life and you are open to this fundamental question. Life is but shadows and dust, but most of us are immune to this fact till someone we truly care for passes away.'

The Sadhu continued, 'Don't let living an ordinary existence pull you back into that stupor, that comfortable numbness again. If you awaken, then your father's death would have achieved a worthwhile purpose. If not,' he shrugged his shoulders, '...well, people die every day.'

'So what *is* the purpose of life, Baba? How can I find it?'

'The purpose of life is to find the purpose of life! And to answer your second question—seek within. Examine the examiner. Try to find out who you are, without any judgments, fears, excuses or expectations. Because what you see outside is tainted by your inner beliefs. And remember, the answers you get are limited only by the questions you ask. Ask the right question and you will get all your questions answered!'

I listened intently as he continued, 'Your life is a laboratory. What you face are tests and lessons that the Creator sends to you so that you can understand, realize and enlighten yourself.'

'I don't want enlightenment—*moksha* or whatever you call it.' I protested. 'I think it is just escapism—running away from life!'

'That's what I was talking about,' he answered calmly. 'Pre-conceived notions must be done away with. In any case, enlightenment is not an escape, my friend. It simply means to lighten the loads that you are carrying. You still have to live your life even after you are enlightened. Enlightenment simply enables you to walk around with no unnecessary emotional or mental loads. To me it seems that you could do with that kind of enlightenment!' he quipped humorously.

He had a point, I conceded. 'Are there any guidelines that I should follow?' I asked tentatively.

'You mean rules, morals, codes of conduct such as not lying, not cheating, not committing adultery with your neighbour's wife, or things like waking up at 4:00 am and all that?' he chuckled.

'Uh—yes, sir.' The sadhu was embarrassingly direct.

'The only rule that you need to know is that there are no rules to follow…'

'But that doesn't make any sense!' I interrupted. 'I could simply go berserk that way. Besides, if rules weren't important, why do all religions start with a set of rules?'

'Let me finish!' he barked. 'Don't follow the rules that are not real to you. Better to have one rule that you believe from your heart rather than a hundred that you don't understand.' My face must have told him that I didn't understand, because he elaborated further. 'If I tell you not to lie, for example, but you still want to, then even if you don't lie, it will create a conflict that will disturb your equanimity and you will be unable to go inwards. Better, hence, to lie and face the karmic consequences of living in untruth so that you learn your lesson well. The idea is that the urge to lie finally becomes a stranger to you rather than you not lying because you want to be a good boy and because Gandhiji said so. That, of course, may take a few moments or a few lifetimes!' Science Baba chortled again. 'Blind rules—or belief systems, as I prefer to call them, are an impediment to the truth seeker and the hand-maiden of the hypocrite and the extremist, who pretend to be men of God. Don't let a rule stop you from acting one way or another. What is worthy of being your guide is only unadulterated, fearless consciousness. Your job is to find that level of consciousness within yourself. Believe me, it exists…'

I listened quietly as he went on. 'By the way, there is only one rule. Know that and you will know everything else that is worth knowing in the universe.'

'And what is that?' I asked eagerly.

'I can't tell you that! You must find it for yourself—that's the trouble.' My crestfallen face softened his voice. 'If I tell you, it will lose its effect—rather like a self-destruct button! The only hint I can give you is that God hides in plain sight.'

'What books should I read, Baba?' I asked, trying to puzzle my way through what he was telling me, 'and how do I proceed?'

'First step—stop pretending to yourself at least, if not to others. *The most destructive lies are the ones we tell ourselves*,' he replied. 'Guidance will come to all who seek it sincerely as and when they need it. As far as books are concerned—huh, quite useless, the lot of them. All they do is fill your head with airy-fairy concepts that actually hinder real progress and are mostly the opinions of mere mortals masquerading as God's word. And of course they are a good source of stories you can tell to impress others!'

'But, sir, I have heard of the Vedas, Upanishads and Puranas, not to mention the *Bible*, the *Quran* and the *Guru Granth Sahib*.' I reeled off the names I knew, 'They are all supposed to be Holy Scriptures that contain all there is to know…and everyone uses them as guides. Won't they be useful for me?'

Science Baba looked thoughtful and said after a pause, 'There is a difference between information and knowledge. All knowledge that is theoretical—mere information, shall we say—causes spiritual indigestion.

Yavaanarth udpaane sarvatah sampalutodakey
Taavaansarveshu vedeshu brahadasyaa vijaanatah

On seeing my mystified expression he translated, 'A person who has obtained enlightenment has as much use for the Vedas, as a person who stands in front of the ocean has for a pond of water!'

His eyes twinkled, 'That, by the way, is a sloka from the *Bhagavadgita*. There, I have told you about the uselessness of bookish knowledge—and that too with a quote from the most succinct and pithy of books! If you still insist on reading something, then your reading list can contain just one book for the moment. The *Bhagavadgita*. I refer it to you since you are a Hindu. This small book contains everything that you need to know and do—that is, if you are able to understand it. And being a slim book, it fits into your pocket conveniently, I tell you!' Science Baba chuckled again before continuing. This guy seems totally happy, I said to myself as the baba continued, 'In case you were wondering, had you been a Muslim, I would have asked you to read the Quran and if you had been a Christian it would have been the Bible that I would have referred you to. Not for any other reason than that there is no point in starting from scratch. We might as well use any residual racial memory that you may have, to give yourself a head-start. Just remember that a spiritual book is merely someone else's realization written down. They are useful for getting tips and information about the spiritual journey but until that knowledge is real to you, it is not worth much. It only adds another load to your already loaded being.'

I bowed to this man I had met just three hours ago! When I looked at Science Baba again, his eyes were closed once more and he seemed to have slipped back into meditation.

The sun was on its downward spiral. It was time to head back. At the risk of disturbing him, I spoke again. 'I will take your leave now, sir, it is getting late. Can I hope to see you again tomorrow?'

He opened his eyes and said, 'No, since I am heading off across the passes to Kedarnath tomorrow morning. You can meet me in Mumbai, though, or call me next month when I am back there.'

'How do I contact you, sir?' I asked hesitantly.

'Here, take my card.' I looked at him with amazement. A nearly naked ash-smeared ascetic was offering me his visiting card testifying that he was a professor with a post-doctorate from Harvard University. Yogis and sadhus aren't supposed to carry visiting cards! I wondered how many other post-doctorates were going around in disguise. Obviously I needed to revisit some of my firmly held opinions such as that sadhus were illiterate, ignorant escapists. Science Baba looked at me and smiled. 'Never judge a book by its cover! And the worth of education is only when you make it real for yourself.' Smiling at this parting shot, I touched his feet, this time without any embarrassment, and took his leave.

I headed down. As I looked back from the last turn in the trail, I could see Science Baba sitting there still as a stone—a position he had held as long as I had been with him! I walked back with a modicum of peace in my heart. I knew that something had happened here that was significant. I had been shown a path and a purpose. It was up to me to take it.

The journey back to the plains was a quiet one. As I descended, leaving my father's mortal remains in the lap of the Himalayas, to be reused as nature saw fit, I also left behind a certain way of life and a certain way of thinking. I had lost my father but at the same time I had been given a sense of purpose. The world wasn't just a cosmic chance. It seemed that it had a nature and a purpose. If only I could discover what this purpose was, I could align myself with it.

Having your father around gives you a sense of immortality and his passing puts you next in line—right in the jump seat! It gives you a sense of urgency about the whole business called life. You also find yourself wondering about the what-ifs. What if you were the one who had died? Would your life count for anything? Would you feel that you had ever truly lived? Would you go with a sense of satisfaction or would your last thoughts only be regrets about the things that you had done or not done? All these were uncomfortable thoughts. Had I done something, anything that I could be genuinely be proud of? In the rush to be a success in the usual terms, had I neglected my real interests and bypassed the road to real glory as I attempted to stay within a safe shell?

Papa's death and its suddenness constantly hammered one reality into my consciousness: That I was mortal and the uncomfortable conclusion from that truth could only be that if my time was limited and its duration unknown, then should I not focus on those things that were really important to me? I wondered how much of my life was of my own choosing and how much was constructed by the frenetic world that I had created? Was there meaning and intensity to what I did or was

I merely trying to prove myself to an uncaring universe? Was I working out of love or from a sense of inadequacy?

As I dwelled on these questions, I realized that a lot of my life was effectively a second-hand existence—an emotional house of cards that would tumble down during any moment of turmoil.

And that begat the next question. Did I want to live like this? A scared human being who did things simply because they were supposed to be done? As I examined my life in these terms, I realized that I wanted to change, to really live with every moment filled with meaning and intensity. I resolved that there would no longer be a gap between my inner and outer self…

It was with that resolve that I came back home. Life returned to a semblance of normality after that as I awaited, with great anticipation, the passing of a month before Science Baba would, as he had mentioned, be available once again in Mumbai and on the phone.

Time crawled by, but it passed.

And then I called him.

HOW

'Hello, this is Saagar.' I introduced myself as soon as I heard the call answered. There was a disturbance in the line but the *hello* was definitely Science Baba's. I would have recognized the booming tone anywhere, but he, on the other hand, didn't seem to recall me. There was only static from the other end, after his initial booming hello.

I tried to jog his memory. 'We met in Gaumukh a month ago. Remember?'

The silence prolonged itself so I reminded him again. 'I had gone to Gangotri to immerse my father's ashes and I met you at your cave at Om Parbat. We—umm, discussed a few things. You may recall that you had given me your visiting card and asked me to call you in a month's time...' I found myself stuttering. I had gone through a series of anxieties and doubts about whether he would remember me at all. Now my fear of being forgotten seemed to be coming true.

'Yes, of course—Saagar, right? Of course, I remember!' Suddenly the line improved and the voice came through clear and strong.

'Yes, sir! If you remember, I had wanted further guidance and—and you had asked me to call you when you returned to Mumbai…' I repeated lamely, my voice limp with relief.

'What do you want to know?'

That foxed me. What did I want to know? There were so many things skittering through my mind that I couldn't find a thing to say.

'Sir, I thought you could teach me meditation.' That sounded like a good starting point. If you can't find anything to say to a sadhu, ask him about meditation. That's a sure-shot safe topic and a great conversation starter!

'Hmm…' The voice fell silent for a moment but came back stronger.

'The aim of meditation is to make all of life a meditation—but it is rather difficult to explain all this on the phone. Where do you live?'

'I live in Gurgaon.'

'Goregaon or Gurgaon?'

'Gurgaon, Haryana, sir!'

'That's near Delhi, isn't it?'

'Yes, sir,' I replied.

'Good, in that case you can go and meet my guru who stays in Delhi.'

'Your guru?' I mentally gawked. Science Baba didn't seem like he needed a guru.

'Yes sir! Even a guru needs a guru! That's how the chain of command works,' said Science Baba, mind-reading as usual and laughing his trademark uproarious laugh. 'Never forget that every saint was a sinner in his past and every sinner is a potential saint in the future.'

'Alright sir,' I said meekly. It felt good to be recognized by Science Baba. But why was I so pleased with what was ultimately just a normal conversation with an unknown man?

Science Baba interrupted my thoughts. 'Take down his phone number then,' he commanded, and proceeded to dictate it to me along with the address, which seemed to be located somewhere in the north-western part of Delhi. Science Baba continued, 'You can give him a call and take it from there. I must warn you though, that he is difficult to meet. He tends to avoid new people but if and when you get past that initial resistance, he is the friendliest of men. So insist on an appointment even if he sounds less than enthusiastic. Give him my reference. That should, hopefully, help.'

I thanked Science Baba profusely, invited him to my home whenever he happened to be passing by Delhi next, and said my goodbyes.

I looked at the details I'd scribbled down. Dr Avinash Kumar. Was this person a medical doctor? And why did that sound familiar?

I jogged my memory. Ah yes! A half-remembered conversation from long ago came back to me. Jai Singh's tea-stall outside St. Stephen's college—that was where I had heard of a Doctor Guru. Could it be the same person? After all, two Doctor Gurus in the same city would be quite a coincidence.

With a thudding heart I called the number that Science Baba had just given me.

'Hello,' a soft voice answered.

'Is that Dr Avinash Kumar speaking?'

'Yes it is,' the voice on the phone replied.

'Sir, your name has been given to me by Science… excuse me, by Professor Menon from Bombay and I was hoping to learn meditation and understand the *Bhagavadgita* from you, sir…' I found myself speaking rapidly—something I used to do in college when I was nervous and hadn't done in a long time. My words were getting all jumbled up and I didn't know what to say first…

The fact was that I was simply too full of too many things, over too many lifetimes, to be coherent in the way I usually was in my corporate world. Even as my words skittered out, tumbling over themselves, I wondered at my own behaviour.Why was I so anxious and so hopeful? What was I expecting would happen?

Dr Kumar cut me short. 'I hold a Satsang—a talk—every Sunday at 10 am. You are most welcome to attend. You may find that many of your queries get answered in the talk itself. And if you like what you hear, we can go further into things like meditation.'

'That would be great, sir. I will be there this Sunday.' Again, I simply couldn't control my enthusiasm.

'Would you like to write down the address?' Dr Kumar enquired kindly.

'Science Baba, I mean Professor Menon has already given me the address,' I rushed to explain, 'but let me confirm it.' I read out the address I'd been given.

'That's correct,' Dr Kumar confirmed. 'Now let me give you the directions as well. Take the Ring Road from Dhaula Kuan towards Naraina and onwards to…'

The rest of the week passed quickly. My mind was a skittish horse, shying and neighing at every thought and expectation of the upcoming meeting. This was strange, I thought to myself

… high profile meetings and presentations to important people were common in my line of work and I was known as a cool cucumber when it came to high-pressure situations. Yet here I was, all wound up about a simple religious discourse, where all I was supposed to do was listen.

At least one thing seemed clear in all this turmoil—that deep down, this was really important to me. But I had no idea why. Nothing at work, however big, had ever fired me up like this. This was like the excitement I had felt when I'd attended that meeting at Professor Sood's house. It was as if I was going to be given the key that would unlock heaven's door! I can't describe the sheer euphoria of that moment—a moment when the blind alleys of my hopes seemed to be opening out into a highway that may actually lead somewhere. I couldn't wait for the week to pass.

I realized that however much we may pride ourselves on the achievements of our mind, what makes us feel alive comes only from the matters of the heart.

Sunday came and I was up at the crack of dawn, driving down an unfamiliar road. Dhaula Kuan, Raja Garden, Pitampura, Rohini and distant Rithala soon receded in my rear view mirror and I found myself driving on an unknown highway. The city gave way to lush open fields that seemed to have been carpet-bombed with sunflowers. I followed the black ribbon of the road till I reached the village of Barwala—my destination—without too much trouble. The village lay bang on one of the major highways that headed north-west through the urban sprawl of outer Delhi. This area had not yet been swallowed up by Delhi's explosive development, but the signs of imminent takeover were visible. The land on both sides of the road was still verdant green, but many of the portions of land had been fenced off with crudely made low-level brick boundary walls that heralded future construction. Large signboards of property dealers lined the roads.

I parked by the side of the main road under a shady neem tree. A couple of buffaloes were tied nearby, placidly chewing the cud. There was a park right next to the road, which carried the bust of a long-forgotten hero of the Indian army. *Havaldar Naik Singh laid down his life fighting the Chinese in Nathu-la* said the plaque. *And he also helped Saagar in finding his Guru, Amen!* I said silently to myself, since this was the point Guruji (I seemed to have already given him that denomination) had mentioned as the landmark that I was supposed to reach. I called the phone number I had been given and was soon trailing a smiling man dressed in white, through a labyrinth of strictly pedestrian streets—and there I was.

There was nothing special about the house as I came upon it. It looked like any other in the village, except that there was an orange and green flag fluttering in the breeze on top of it. I was directed to the first floor by a volunteer. The house seemed to be under renovation, with scaffolding spanning the front. The entire first floor was bare, with the rough concrete of the floor slab visible. There was no plaster on the walls and a fan whirred slowly from a hook in the roof. This was unprepossessing! Where had I landed up?

I took off my shoes, added them to the pile of footwear that already lay on the first floor landing, tip-toed into the room where the talk was to take place and looked around for my bearings.

The room was crowded and I could see an interesting mix of people. A group of men chatting at the back; a cluster of sari-clad women sitting on the floor; small children running around, a couple of men dressed in white who looked rather well-off. Their wealth was obvious since one of the men with gel-slicked hair had a heavy gold chain wrapped around his neck, while the other man had the fingers of both his hands covered with rings. One of the rings was the largest solitaire I had ever seen! There were a couple of saffron-clad sadhus sitting quietly in the corner and there was a very good-looking man with flowing hair and the most magnetic eyes that I had ever looked at. The women on the floor were singing a bhajan—a devotional song—together. And there was an expectant feel to the air.

Here I must admit that my first thought was to turn around and go back. The bhajan-kirtan crowd had always been an object of derision for me. I had always found it hard to simply let go and sing and dance my angst away. It didn't help that I could do neither very well, that is sing or dance, and I had always found it difficult to take things simply on faith. How could singing songs lead to God-realization or spiritual upliftment? Could the master of the universe be enticed so easily—especially by the tuneless Bollywood rip-offs that were usually sung at such gatherings?

I hesitated near the door, debating whether I should just slink off quietly, when a tall, sparely built man walked in. There was nothing special about him except for what he was carrying tucked under both arms. It was a thick load of books. Books! And in this surrounding? That seemed incongruous. I tilted my head and looked at the titles as the man walked past. *Srimad*

Bhagavatam (Bhagavata Purana), Skand Purana, Bhagavadgita, Garga Samhita, Mandukya Upanishad, the *Bible*, the *Quran* and the *Guru Granth Sahib*—these titles floated past my eyes. Some were familiar names, but the rest I had never heard of. That stopped me and I dropped the idea of retreating—at least for the moment. Books were something that I could relate to. Familiar and comfortable with them, I had always delved into them for answers. Instead of 'If you don't know, just ask', what had worked for me was 'if you don't know, just read the right book.' Lately, of course, this has morphed to 'If you don't know, just Google!'.

The books that the gentleman was carrying in must have been brought here for a purpose. I slipped further into the room, and sat down in a vacant chair, deciding to stay and, at least, give the good doctor a fair hearing!

When he walked in, along with a couple of men, we all stood up. Of average height and build, he was dark, like a storm cloud about to rain, and was dressed, of all things, in a western suit—a button-down snowy white shirt worn over navy blue pants. He even wore a tie, like a corporate CEO. This was unusual, quite a contrast to the flowing-robes that gurus inevitably sported on devotional TV channels! Well, I told myself, if his disciple Science Baba, a professor by trade, could sit in a loincloth and ashes high up in a Himalayan cave, why couldn't the Guru dress up like a corporate honcho? As Science Baba had admonished, a book should never be judged by its cover—nor, I thought to myself with a small mental chuckle, a guru by his attire!

He reached the head of the room, turned around and gently asked us to sit down. As we settled in, there was a sudden commotion at the back. A man came, pushing his way forward through the crowd and fell at Guruji's feet. The ushers, who had been taken by surprise, quickly leapt forward to pull the man up but Guruji stopped them with a gesture.

To the man who continued to crouch at his feet, Guruji said, reproach evident in his voice, 'Rameshji, where have you been these past six months? You promised me—mind you, I didn't ask you to, but you insisted—that you would be here once a week to help with the construction work?'

The man at Guruji's feet looked embarrassed. He mumbled something about being busy with some urgent commitments at home. Clearly Guruji didn't like his answer. He took a step back and said with a regal air, his voice taking on a booming tone, 'Do you remember that you had to crawl up these very stairs using both your hands and feet, the last time you were here? Do I have to remind you of your desperation as you yourself told me that all doctors had given up on you? Do you remember that you were ready to do anything to regain your health?' The man looked contritely at the floor as Guruji continued, 'I healed you on the promise that henceforth your first priority would be God's work. And here you are, surfacing after six long months!'

There was a pause; the man looked ready to sink into the ground. 'I am sorry, Guruji. I am free to work now,' he mumbled.

I looked at the tableau before me with curiosity. It seemed that some kind of miracle had occurred here six months ago.

Guruji's voice gentled in response to the mumbling man, 'Get up! Get up! The past doesn't matter; it is never too late to start over. And that's enough drama. Please take your seats, everyone.' Guruji stepped back and the man moved away, slinking off quietly to a corner of the room.

It was an Alice-in-Wonderland situation. The rag-tag audience; the dilapidated room with the fan whirling above in slow motion; the guru dressed up in formal corporate attire; the women singing tuneless devotional songs; the chair in front, piled with the scriptures of all the major religions of the world and the evidence of a genuine miracle.

Nothing matched with what I had expected so far. That is, till Guruji opened his mouth to speak.

'Why have we gathered here today?' he enquired, his voice easy.

There was an expectant silence in the audience.

He repeated. 'Why have all of you come here today, from near and far, leaving your work and your commitments? Not to mention your Sunday sleep!'

He paused again before continuing as if to give emphasis to every syllable. 'Is it because you are unwell and need treatment?' He paused again and looked around. 'Is it because you can't bear some personal grief or that you have suffered some loss that you can't handle?'

I listened, careful not to miss any word or gesture. He spoke every sentence forcefully, in a slow cadence and with gaps after each phrase, as if he wanted the words to sink in.

'Or is it because you have some kind of problem that you expect me to solve through a miracle, as I did for Ramesh here?' He pointed to the man who had just fallen at his feet.

'Could it be that you have no confidence in yourself and have come here to find a way to beg God for the things that you can't do for yourself?

'Or,' he looked around at everyone present, '...could there be an outside chance that you love God and want to know more about him without any other ulterior motive?'

He took another pause as if trying to sense something from the audience.

'...And are there any amongst you who want to know the purpose of your life and your place in this universe?'

I mentally raised my hand to that. Not that the rest weren't my goals. I could relate to all of them except the loving God bit. I was a bit ambivalent about loving an unproven concept. Besides, what exactly was love anyway? A quagmire of hormones acting up?

Guruji paused and looked around before continuing. 'Today I am not going to talk about God or even about what the scriptures say. I am not going to talk about religion or the moral codes of conduct that are supposed to lead us towards enlightenment.'

There was a rustle amidst the crowd gathered in the overflowing room, as if he had surprised everyone.

'Instead I am going to talk about the pursuit of happiness.' Guruji paused and looked around. 'The fact is that God is unknown to most of us. He is just a concept, a photo on a calendar. And most of us don't have any way of knowing if He really exists…But happiness is something that is real, something tangible. And it is something that we all want. Today let us discuss why it is so difficult to be happy and what we can do to achieve real happiness. And in finding that answer maybe we will find our other queries answered as well.'

He continued as we, the audience, listened with rapt attention. 'Let us start by finding out the state of happiness in this room! How many of you are happy? Raise your hands.'

Not a single hand went up.

'Hmmm…' said Guruji, with a sigh, 'I thought so! It seems I have chosen the right subject and I hope that my talk today will be of help to this sorrowful audience!'

He began, 'Do you find that, even though you try your best, even though you are sincere and hardworking, happiness and success elude you? Do you find that just the act of living itself causes cycles of difficulties that you just can't escape from? That, even as you build your safety nets and your fixed deposits with guaranteed 8 per cent interest, circumstances blow them away with the smallest of puffs? Does it seem to you that you are helpless puppets on the strings of an uncaring fate?'

Guruji paused for effect. 'Is that how you feel?' he demanded from the audience.

'Yes!' The audience, including me, chorused back.

'Why is there such a large gap between what we expect and what we get from life? Why is it that you constantly strive for happiness and permanence, and yet happiness is fleeting?'

Another pause.

'Do you all feel this dilemma? This gap between expectations and results?'

'Yes!' we roared back enthusiastically as one. It seemed that, whether rich or poor, the desire to be happy cut through all class barriers.

Someone from the audience piped up, 'Guruji, my dilemma is different. In the blink of an eye, I have reached old age. In my heart I feel as young as ever, as if I haven't lived at all, but my body and my wife tell me that I am an old and useless man!'

Laughter rippled through the room and I turned back to look. The man who had said that was sitting on the floor, his back ramrod straight and his arms wrapped around his knees. At first glance he did indeed look old with a mop of curly white hair as proof, but his skin was youthful with nary a wrinkle. His upright back belied his age, and his eyes were impish like a child's.

A woman sat next to him, dressed in the traditional manner with her head covered with the end of her sari. She looked both embarrassed and angry at the same time. Mulish would be the best way to describe her expression! That must be his long-suffering wife! I turned my attention back to Guruji.

Guruji was saying, 'That's not a different dilemma, Jagmohan! It is just a corollary of the point I am making. We live our life chasing desire after desire. As Ghalib said, *"Thousands of desires, each more entrancing than the one before."* And in that endless chase, before we know it, our life is drawing to a close and we still feel unsatisfied and unhappy. Isn't that the general rule?'

'Yes!' we chorused back again.

'To be happy is both easy and difficult. Things that give happiness and things that give sadness are enmeshed together like wheat grains in chaff. It is a matter of developing the right perspective.'

The jocular man interjected, 'I don't know about that, Guruji, but what I do know is that I would be happy if all the good things of my life remained and all the bad things disappeared!'

The audience laughed its agreement but Guruji took the question seriously. 'What are the bad things in your lives? Can you people name a few?' he asked us.

'I have to work hard for a living,' someone called out, 'and yet I can never meet my expenses…the more I earn, the more I pay out. The result is that I am always in debt.'

'I am not able to land a job even though I am well qualified and have given dozens of interviews. I get rejected for the strangest of reasons. In my last attempt, I finally got the appointment letter but this time it was the company that closed down!' said someone else, in a cheerful voice that belied his situation and we all chuckled in sympathy.

'I lost my only son when he drowned in Haridwar and I just can't find it in me to live anymore,' The quiet voice of a woman came from the back and the audience went silent. She continued, '…I have even prayed for death but even that does not come to relieve me of my suffering. Why would God do this to me?'

The audience went silent and it was after sometime that the next person spoke. 'My wife has cancer. I have run through my entire savings and I have no more money for further treatment,' said a man (who in a later meeting went on to report that his wife had been cured).

'I lost my father suddenly and I wonder what the purpose of my life is, when death is a certainty?' I asked myself silently.

Guruji held up his hands. 'I was right in thinking that this audience needs to be advised on how to seek happiness before it is ready to seek God! You may say that you desire God, but that is usually a lie. After all, can an unhappy man think of enlightenment?'

Guruji continued, 'Many people think that happiness is a spiritual goal but that's not true. Happiness is not a goal, it is a pre-requisite! If you are not happy or if you are full of fear then how can you take the right decisions? And that's the case with peace, or even health. Happiness, fearlessness and good health—these three things are the prerequisites for starting the spiritual journey. They can never be the end goals of a spiritual journey. To seek God if you are unhappy, troubled or unhealthy is only escapism. You can never find God that way…'

He continued, 'It seems to me that all of you are so weighed down by your troubles that you imagine that an escape from your sorrows should be your real goal. Not true! So today, let's talk about how to reach the starting point of the spiritual journey before we can talk about how to reach the end of it.'

A murmur of approval went through the audience and Guruji said, half to himself, 'I thought so! Why can't we find happiness is the question? Can anyone answer that?'

There was a bit of mumbling but no one volunteered an answer. Guruji continued, 'The trouble is not in seeking happiness but in seeking happiness in things that are by their very nature impermanent.'

The room turned silent.

'The mother mourns her lost son and the son mourns his father. Some here fear the lack of work and some feel the pressure of work! How can all this ever be resolved?' Guruji looked around. Again no one said anything.

'The fact that we must accept is that the world is constantly renewing itself. Change is permanent. How can we ever find happiness if we set store by something that is bound to change?'

'We change. Our friends and families change. Our children grow up and our parents grow old. Our financial situation grows better or worse. Sometimes times are good and sometimes things are not to our liking. We can't control any of that. Linking our mental and emotional state to the shifting sands of time, opens us to fear and sorrow.'

'But then how can we ever be happy?' asked the man with the magnetic eyes. 'I can't help but be attached to my family. They are my roots—my basis of happiness, my reason for living.

If I didn't have my family, my child and my society around me, how could I ever be happy? I have come here to you to seek advice because I constantly fear that something will happen to the perfect little world that I have worked so hard to create.'

'You have got it all wrong, brother,' said Guruji gently, 'I am not asking you to abandon your family or your life. All I am asking you to do is to accept the fact that change is constant and happiness needs to be found in every moment of that change. If you look only at the past moments to judge your level of happiness, then every new day will be a day of terror since you will fear losing what you had yesterday.'

Guruji turned to the rest of us. 'Another thing about happiness is that it can never be planned, organized or held on to. Moments of happiness are always unexpected. Look back at all the happy moments of your life. Were they not completely new and unexpected and isn't that why they delighted us?'

That's true, I thought to myself. Memories flashed through my head, of the times I had been really happy. Roli walking in through the door of my house all those years ago and the week that I spent with her. The shock of Professor Sood's invitation instead of the suspension I had been expecting. Saloni opening her hair as she stood over me with the sun making a halo around her head. That star-lit evening on the machan with Vinod and Kusum and the bracing walk to Gaumukh with my father…

Guruji was saying, 'The essential quality about happiness is that it is fresh. It takes you completely by surprise. That's why it is called happiness. Happiness just happens. It's happenstance!'

'My son makes me happy every day. And he is no surprise,' argued a man sitting at the back.

'How old is he?' asked Guruji.

'Just turning four. He was born after a lot of prayer and I find him delightful,' said the man.

'I am sure,' said Guruji gently. 'Every moment that you spend with him must fill you with joy.'

'Yes,' said the man simply, his eyes softening with the love he obviously felt for his son.

'His birth, his first steps, his first words? Which do you prefer? And how do you choose which memory to freeze as the yardstick of your happiness?'

'That's true. It's all good,' said the man, suddenly losing his aggression.

'And even though you love your son deeply, he makes you happy as you say, but have you never been happy before your son was born?'

The man became quiet.

Guruji looked around like a master surveying his craft. 'I repeat. I am not asking anyone here not to love their families or to abandon life. Sanyaas—renunciation—is a flawed concept. It may sound good to troubled souls, but does not work in real life. We can be happy only when we think of our life as a blessing that is meant to be lived and not to be avoided…But we can do that only when we don't form expectations based on past experiences. When we demand certain specific results based on our memories or belief systems, we only open ourselves to fear and unhappiness.'

'But then how can we ever be in control of our life? For me personally it is a terrifying thought—that I have no control over what may happen to me or my family at any time. And what should we do when something bad happens? And how can I not be angry with fate and God for taking my son away?' said the woman who had lost her son in Haridwar. As she finished, she burst into tears.

Guruji looked at her calmly till she quieted down.

'That gets us back to where we started from. Why is there such a large gap between what we expect from life and what we end up getting from it? Why is it that we constantly strive for happiness and permanence, and yet nothing in life is permanently happy?'

'Are you saying that it is wrong for us to expect to be happy?' asked someone.

'Not at all,' said Guruji unperturbed, 'Our intention of finding happiness is hard-wired into our soul. It's our expectation of what our life should be, that prevents happiness, creates fear and causes conflict.'

'But we need to rest our sense of well-being on something and if we can't trust the quicksand that is life, then what do we rest our sense of well-being on?' asked one of the mendicants in the room.

'You raise a valid point,' replied Guruji. 'Happiness needs a point of rest and succour. We instinctively associate certain qualities with happiness. What are these? Anyone?' asked Guruji.

'Happiness must be unexpected and delightful, as you said!' I ventured

'And good times that last forever?' said someone else.

'Yes,' said Guruji. 'Happiness is these things and yet it is something more. It overwhelms, it delights, it inspires and it makes us grateful for what we experience. Isn't that so? And happiness happens when we are in the domain of something larger than ourselves; when we know that we are in the presence of something that nourishes and protects us without us asking it to do so. Something that makes us feel special and showers us with love, like the way our parents coddled us when we were babies. Happiness is the way an infant feels in the lap of his mother or as he is being bounced in the air by his father.'

'And to answer your question,' Guruji pointed to the sadhu, 'yes, happiness does need a point of focus. That is the goal of any spiritual search—to find that point of rest. So, friends, this is the journey I want to take you on. I want to help you close the gap between what you expect and what you get. I want all of you to experience what it is to be truly happy! Who wants to take this journey?'

Every hand shot up in the air!

'Do you desire to know the secret to happiness in this sea of unhappiness?' Guruji's voice boomeranged across the walls, echoing in places in my heart that I didn't know existed.

'Yes!' Even the walls of the room seemed to be shouting back.

His voice grew softer, yet each word impacted the audience who listened with rapt attention. 'It is only when you desire to know what is real, as opposed to escaping from tough circumstances, that the search for happiness can begin. Most of the time we are just overwhelmed by life. We are not seeking happiness. We are only trying to avoid pain. We are either running towards or are running away from some object of desire or fear. And while we are in that state, no happiness is possible. It is only when we desire to know the ultimate reality without motive—God, divine consciousness, the perfect state of being ...it's been called by many names—can we start to walk on the real path to happiness.'

'So, how do we start, Guruji?' someone queried.

'The first step? Check your motives,' he replied. 'What do you really want? And do you really want it or are you just reacting to your circumstances? Before you look for God or even a better life, you must know why you are looking.'

I knew instinctively that I was listening to something critically important. It was the missing link in my struggle for peace. Guruji's words rang in my ears. 'If you truly know why you do something, it leads to achievement without conflict. And when you achieve what you had aimed for, you attain peace.'

Guruji sipped some water before continuing. 'Therefore, you must know the *Why* of whatever you do. Knowing the *Why* creates the sharp edge to the chisel as you hammer away at understanding your life. The *Why* creates the focus on your blind desire for a better life.'

As I pondered over what I was hearing, Guruji continued, 'When you go home today, I want all of you to observe the motives of whatever you do. Every time you do anything, or think anything, even the smallest, most ordinary of things, ask yourself—why did I just do or think what I did?'

There was something I had to ask at this point, 'Guruji...' I interrupted tentatively and he looked at me. 'Uh, everyone in the world is pursuing their desires, and even if, as you say, most people don't know their real intentions, they are still deeply attached to their personal universes. They spend their entire lives chasing their dreams, but—isn't it all ephemeral? Relationships, money and success—none of these seem capable, ultimately, of giving lasting happiness or even a sense of deep satisfaction. In any case, all the pillars of a good life—even our bodies—are fated to end. So even if I do understand my real intentions—which could be houses, cars, family-progress, money and social position—could I ever be ultimately happy in these pursuits? And if not, then how do I ever find peace and happiness?'

Guruji looked very pleased for some reason and replied, 'Permanent peace can be found only when one naturally aligns oneself to the Truth—to the eternal and the absolute and the real. Till that blessed day comes into the life of a seeker, all we can do is seek; find; get disappointed; seek again, and yet again. You will notice that we give a lot of emphasis to our actions but this is a good point to tell you that the acts per se are not very important. What is important is the *intention* behind your action. When your actions are aligned with your intention, that action is called *sacred action*. It is sacred because it takes you through the shortest path to your nearest higher self.'

Guruji again took a pause before continuing, 'When we pursue what we deeply desire to its satisfaction, whatever be that goal, it also takes us towards the ultimate goal. I would say that it is better to fully achieve your heartfelt worldly goals rather than end up with bits and pieces of unfinished agendas floating around you even as you claim to seek God. Once you complete a task, you can move on cleanly and you don't waste your time looking back over your shoulder...

'*The secret is that the route to self-realization lies through a series of genuine satisfactions. You may travel far but if there is no satisfaction on the way, you have scarcely travelled at all.*'

Guruji looked around at the assembly before continuing. 'As I have just said, any action is fine as long as we understand the intent that hides behind the action. Only this clears the fog of confusion. When you realize what your intentions are, even if they are worldly, sooner or later you will ask the fundamental question—what is the intention *behind* the intention? You will ask—what am I here for? You will ask—even if I do get what I desire, fame, money, worldly pleasures, will it make me everlastingly happy? You will wonder in your heart—can rising to the heights of personal glory in this temporary, ephemeral world ever be enough? When you ask this question genuinely from your heart, without being brainwashed or tutored or influenced, nothing is ever quite the same again. This question—*Who am I?*—is the start of the real journey.

'But let's not jump the gun. Let's take the first step first. Is what I have said so far clear to everyone?'

There was a bit of mumbling. Many in the audience looked uncertain and Guruji could make that out. 'Ok. Let's take a practical example to clear up this point. Let us take an action that most of us do on a daily basis. An activity that is of prime importance to most of us—earning our livelihood. Let's examine our motives about why we do the work that we do?'

The room waited and Guruji continued, 'The obvious answer is that we work to earn money; so that we can take care of our responsibilities and live a prosperous life. Some of us also work for social prestige. Most of us do the work that we think will give us money and prestige, but has anyone asked themselves—Do I love the work that I do?'

'Why is that important?' asked Jagmohan. 'If I earn a lot of money, that is sure to make me happy. So if I do a job that I don't like, but it earns me a lot of money, then what is wrong with that?'

'Because happiness is experiential!' Guruji instantly shot back. 'This is where everyone goes wrong. Money in the bank does give a sense of security but when you work without liking your work, you have condemned almost your entire life to living in unhappiness.'

Guruji continued on a softer note, 'Happiness is straightforward. It happens in the Now. If you take the approach Jagmohan just talked about, then you are getting into a straightforward contradiction. You are trying to be happy by doing things that make you unhappy!'

'But if I earn a lot of money, then I can better look after the people I love and that makes me happy,' said a man sitting next to me.

'True. Happiness is always related to abundance but I am not talking about working for free in any profession that you love. I am talking about making a choice between two professions based on whether you like the work or not, rather than making the salary the deciding factor. And let me remind you that in the long run the expected pay materialized only to those who do their work well.'

Guruji looked around the room and asked us. 'So we are back to the original question. How many of the people here love their work? Please raise your hands.'

Not a single hand went up. We all avoided his eyes, embarrassed. Even I couldn't in all honesty say that I did my work out of love. Sure, there were aspects of it that engaged me—but love? No, not quite.

I looked around the room at the hanging heads. '*Lives of quiet desperation*'—Thoreau's famous words came into my head. And was I any different from all the others in this crowd? I searched for an escape route. There must be degrees to this love that Guruji expected us to have. Yes, that must be it. After all I was good at my work, no doubt about it, and had enjoyed considerable success at it. But to Guruji, I said nothing...

Guruji continued, 'Since money is very important to all you here, let me ask the same question from the point of view of earning money. Listen carefully to what I say and speak up if you disagree: To get a lot of money and get promotions, etc., you have to be very good at your work, don't you?'

No one answered as Guruji looked around the room, 'Yes, isn't that so?' he asked again.

'Yes!' we chorused back.

'So my question is: How can you become really good at your work so that you may earn a lot of money and respect?' Again he looked around the room, 'Anyone?'

Again, nobody answered, so he went on, 'The answer is simple. Being good at anything comes from spending a considerable amount of time doing that activity. When you spend every waking moment immersed in thoughts of that work and you even dream of it when you sleep—it's only then that you become an expert at it. There is no other way. Isn't that so?'

We listened quietly, 'Now examine your motivations for doing whatever you do individually. You will find that your motives for working are usually negative. The usual refrain is—what will happen if I don't do this or how will I survive if I don't do that? Isn't that so?'

The hanging heads looking at the floor were the answer.

He continued, 'The fear of loss, the fear of being second best, the fear of being poor and that of being unable to take care of your loved ones, and of course the fear of social ridicule—these are some of the typical reasons we use to goad ourselves to do our work. In essence you do something not because you like doing it but because you don't know what else to do. Your work is like eating bitter gourd. You eat it because you know it is good for you, even though you hate the taste.'

'Now if the fear is strong, you may work hard and become very good at that activity and you may enjoy a great degree of success at it. But that activity will always cause you stress. Mediocrity is the constant companion of a person who lives like this since he hates and resents what he is doing. And the reality is that when we do what we don't like, and in which we have no interest and have no talent for, we become avoiders. We do the least amount of effort—just enough to get away with. Such a person becomes a shirker without even realizing it, so he can never excel in what he does or derive any pleasure from it. Nor can he derive much money from it, even if that was the original aim,' Guruji looked pointedly at Jagmohan, who grinned back unabashedly.

'But there is another way, another motive, which also leads to unhappiness even though superficially it sounds better. This time the goad is a positive one. That is when we desire something and then use our God-given talents and training to achieve it. That's a positive reason and the results are usually better than the negative goads. The stress generated is also less in this case. The positive goads are usually worldly—social prestige, wealth, admiration of peers and a luxurious life. The person with a positive goad is the one who has a strong ego and usually a talent that makes them naturally better than others in the field of their choosing. Such a person becomes some kind of expert in their field. He or she enjoys the perks of being someone who others look up to. Yet when something happens that shakes their perennial world-view—usually some tragedy—that person starts questioning their one-sided emphasis on their goal.'

I kept quiet. This was getting way too close to home. This was how I had been happily trundling along till my father died.

'There is another way and that is the way of real achievement,' Guruji went on. 'Those who are the outstanding leaders and pathfinders in the fields of their choosing follow this way. The greatest singers, performers, painters, scientists and such like. People whose achievements are far above the reach of ordinary mortals. Kalidasa, Beethoven, Mozart, Pablo Picasso, Ustad Vilayat Khan, Albert Einstein—these are a few examples of people who take such an approach.'

'And what way is that, Guruji?' I asked, completely hooked. My aim had always been the pursuit of excellence and Guruji was saying something I had never heard before. How to excel had been the subject of so many of the corporate seminars I had attended but no one had raised these points. At least not in my hearing.

'That's the way of love for what you do,' Guruji responded. 'You don't think about anything but the activity that you love. You forget hunger, sleep, even how much money you will earn out of it. Doing that activity is a reward in itself. Time itself disappears when you are engaged in that activity.

'*When you are in that frame of mind you are a subcontractor of God, part-creating the universe along with him.* Your results, by default, will be way above the reach of ordinary mortals.'

Guruji paused to take a sip of water. 'To summarize—the first is the way of fear and laziness. *Tamas*, as we call it. The second is the way of desire. *Rajas*, as we call it. And the third is the way of love and harmony. We call it *Sattva*. These are the three modes of action.

'In the first two ways—*tamas* and *rajas*, the activity is a means to an end while in the *sattvic* way; the activity is an end in itself—its own reward. By the way, there is a fourth way as well but we will talk about it some other time.'

Guruji looked around the room as if to emphasize this point. 'Now you know why you must figure out your motives. *Are you doing something out of fear, desire or love?* This motivation applies to all aspects of your life, not just work. Even if the act remains the same, the motivation—*the Why*—creates completely different impacts on your life. What are those impacts? If you do things out of fear, then its acid will corrode you. If desire is the motive, then its indulgence will deplete you and if you do things out of love then your life will have a balance that constantly keeps you charged and ever fresh. Money will pour in abundance. *Remember, the wages of a loving act can only be abundance...*'

Guruji looked around. 'Are you unhappy with your life? Now I am telling you why that is so! You are not doing what is in your heart. You are living in fear. You operate negatively and under duress. Can you ever be happy that way? Get out of living this way today itself. You can't change your despair with life by working harder at something that you basically dislike. People try harder and harder and in the end they have nothing left to give. So this is my diagnosis and if you believe me, then you already know the cure. Remember, trying harder at a wrong solution will not make it right. Going harder in the wrong direction will not make you reach your desired destination! If your compass itself is wrong, then by travelling faster you only go further away from the goal of fulfillment. And can happiness ever emerge from the womb of this contradiction?'

'But, Guruji,' Jagmohan again interrupted, 'I have done the work I do all my life and there is nothing else that I know. In my childhood, I was very good at the pure sciences and wanted to be a lecturer in my local college. I was a first-class first from my college but my father forced me to join the I.T.I. for a machine operator's course and he opened this factory for me. He spent lacs of rupees on the land and the machinery…He had to sell half his village land! And that was 30 years ago. I can't rewind all that!' Jagmohan cheerfully continued, his light tone not quite concealing the sadness that lay beneath his words as we all listened. We were all like him in one way or the other.

He continued, 'Sure I hate my work, I freely admit that! But what else can I do now? I can't become a teacher at this age! I am 60. That's when most people retire.'

'Sure,' said Guruji, 'but does anything prevent you from once again delving into the subjects that you loved? For an hour a day? So what if you earn nothing out of it. That one hour will be well spent. At least you will be happy and you will stop harassing your wife for that one hour! And if you do that, you may find that your natural talent will make you better than the average science teacher. The average teacher may have been forced to accept a teacher's job when he may have actually wanted to be a machine operator and ultimately run his own factory!'

We laughed at how Guruji turned the tables on Jagmohan, and he laughed with the rest as Guruji continued, 'And if you take tuitions, you may earn some money as well. Believe me, when you look at that money, there will be satisfaction in your heart and a sense of pride in yourself. Or you could join an organization that teaches street kids. The point is that the time you spend doing this will be a time when you are happy.'

He looked around at us. 'I may be a Guru who everyone looks to for guidance,' he said, 'all the way to *Moksha*! But I don't look at the future. I look only at the next 24 hours of my life. Out of those 24 hours, I sleep, eat and do other regular stuff for about 12 hours. That leaves 12 hours in my hands. Can I spend at least a bit of those 12 hours doing something that makes me happy?' Guruji paused and looked around before continuing, 'That, friends, is the only way to be happy! *And happiness has a peculiar quality. When you indulge in happiness, it tends to expand and bring prosperity in its wake.*'

'Come, let us sit quietly and reflect on what we have just heard.' Guruji lapsed into silence and the hall slipped into meditation…

I looked around the hall, at those faces that seemed so peaceful right now. Would I, could I ever reach that state where all was right with the world for me?

I, who had attended so many talks, seminars and workshops, had never heard anything like this. This was unique—an honest look at the base motives of how we lived.

Guruji woke from his reverie. 'Let me add one last point to what I have said, before we end,' he said as everyone else stirred.

I listened intently. I knew from deep within my heart that what I had heard was critical to the path to salvation. In this ramshackle little room with a rickety fan, in the middle of the anonymity of the urban jungle, I was being given the secret in black and white.

Guru continued, 'For God to free you from worldly troubles is child's play. For him to cure you of disease, to give you wealth and fame and other such things is also no big deal. For the person who created all this, can solving your petty problems be difficult? Yet even if God saves your life or heals you today, can even He prevent the ultimate decay of your body? If not, then why should He save your life today? Let me ask this audience here—if avoiding death today cannot save you from dying someday, then why do you ask to be saved today?'

He tilted his head and looked speculatively at us. 'Why grieve over something unpleasant happening in your life? Why grieve over losing your loved ones when you will lose them someday in any case? That *someday* has arrived today for someone, that's all.' Guruji looked squarely at me as he said that—almost as if he was speaking personally to me. 'Let me repeat. The world is transitory. It is the nature of this world; what comes must go, and one who is born must also die. In all this coming and going only the soul remains pristine, untouched by birth, death or the living experience. It is the only thing that is permanent in this transient world.'

Helplessly, my eyes locked with his as he continued softly, 'You have cremated your father today and he may have cremated you in some other life.' Tears sprang unbidden to my eyes and I found myself weeping silently. 'I say this to all of you: pain and fear are alien to the soul and yet all of us experience pain and fear. Why? Why are we in the grip of something that is alien to our true nature? Can anyone give me an answer?'

'Guruji, if we could answer that question, why would we come to you?' someone jocularly remarked. Everyone laughed, including Guruji, but then his face took on a grave aspect. 'I am not here,' he told us after the laughter had died down, 'to answer your silly and selfish questions about your petty concerns. I am here only to show you a higher way to live, to help you in that quest. But I can only do so much. I can only take a horse to the water; I cannot make it drink. If you show the intent, I can show you the way.'

'Let me tell you,' he smiled, 'where my train is going. I am here for one purpose and one purpose only. To lead you to *Moksha*, *Nirvana*, enlightenment, whatever you may call it. Please don't come to me for *naukri* (jobs), *chhokhri* (girls or brides), money or other worldly aims and ambitions. I'm not that kind of guru. If you want to see your highest self face-to-face, come to me. I will hold you by the hand and take you there. Are you ready for that?'

I was hooked. As the lecture ended, a crowd of people gathered around Guruji and I quietly slipped out of the room. My mind was in a whirl. As I put on my shoes outside the door, I pondered over what I had just heard. It was remarkable in its intention and scope. I had expected to hear stories from the scriptures—a blend of the *Ramayana* and the *Mahabharata*, and tales of the poster boys of Hinduism, with some quotes from the Vedas and the Upanishads thrown in for good measure. But what I had just heard was something else. The search for God, enlightenment, meaning and happiness in life were being defined and discussed as an intensely personal quest to which everyone was entitled and which was the only goal worth pursuing.

And that was when I experienced what was to be my first miracle…

'What?' asked Ashish eagerly.

I yawned and stretched. I was tired. Not surprising since I had been speaking for a good three hours. 'Let's take a walk,' I said to Ashish and we stepped out into the bracing air. I was suddenly restless. I was missing Anusuya and maybe a walk would distract me. The weather was wonderful at this time of year. There was a brisk breeze blowing, funnelling in from the gorge below and the sky was a brilliant blue.

'I hope you have brought some sun cream,' I said to Ashish. 'Otherwise you will get burnt in a jiffy.'

'I am pretty dark in any case,' laughed Ashish.

'I noticed, but didn't mention it as, firstly it doesn't matter, and secondly I didn't want to offend you.'

'The wages of years spent in hot and humid Mumbai as a crime beat reporter,' Ashish chuckled.

My curiosity piqued, I enquired, 'From reporting crime to interviewing people for a business magazine—how did that happen? Or is it one and the same thing?' I laughed at my own joke.

'No, sir,' Ashish grinned back. 'The crime beat has a high burnout rate. How long can you cover the baser human impulses and not get sickened by seeing what humans can do to each other on a daily basis? I shifted because I thought it was time to explore the highest motivations of the human mind rather than the lowest.'

'And do you like the move?'

'Yes sir, I do. It is very interesting to talk to people who step out of the usual mediocrities that smother us and do something original in life. I had been looking forward to meeting you, for this very reason, ever since I was assigned your interview.'

We lapsed into companionable silence as the trail steepened. We were soon at our destination, which was the village market where I bought a few things I needed. Then we headed back.

Ashish picked up the conversation where we had left off as we walked back. 'Sir, you left the story at a very interesting point…'

'At what point?' I pretended to have forgotten, amused by his enthusiasm.

'The miracle? Remember?' I gave him a blank look, enjoying his attempts to jog my memory. 'You were talking about experiencing your first miracle as you walked down after the satsang…'

'Yes, yes,' I said and resumed the tale. 'Do you remember that the talk was held in a room on the first floor?'

'Yes, I do,' said Ashish.

'Well, when the satsang concluded, I was the first to leave the room. The drive back home was a long one and it was getting late.' I paused and recalled the scene in my mind. It had happened decades ago, yet the feelings generated in that moment were still fresh and the scene crystal clear.

'The stairs were right next to the room and I scooted down after putting on my shoes,' I explained.

'And?' asked Ashish.

'Imagine my surprise when, on reaching the ground floor and turning left towards the exit, I saw Guruji standing far to the right!'

I paused before continuing, visualizing the scene, 'You must understand this carefully, Ashish. Guruji was standing on the right end of the building, on the ground floor, a good distance away, while I had left him just a minute ago, one floor above on the left side.'

'Really? That sounds strange!' exclaimed Ashish.

'Yes, you can imagine my surprise. To reach where I saw him, his path would have had to cross mine in a scissor fashion.

The only way he could have reached where he was, would be if he'd taken another staircase. But it was funny, because I hadn't seen any other staircase when I had been on the first floor.'

'Umm, did you look for the other set of stairs the next time you went?' Ashish demanded as we wound our way down the twisting path. We were crossing an orchard and the scent of apples in the air was intoxicating.

'Yes, I looked,' I assured him. 'It was the very first thing I did when I went there again...'

'And?' demanded Ashish.

'And…' I paused, enjoying the suspense I was creating, '…there was no other staircase in the entire building!' I shook my head at Ashish, reliving those incredible moments. 'You can imagine the intensity of that moment for me. Nothing out of the ordinary, that I could even remotely call a miracle, had ever occurred to me before that day and here I was witness to something that had no logical explanation. I thought and mulled over it for days but I couldn't figure out how what I had witnessed could have happened. I was forced to conclude, ultimately, that Guruji couldn't possibly have used normal means to surprise me that afternoon.'

&

My mind flew back in time and I was standing with Guruji once again, at the foot of the stairs and gaping at him as he called out genially, 'So how did you like the satsang, Saagarji?'

'It was really very good,' I replied, a trifle shyly. To break the ice, I made a conversational overture. 'Guruji, I was referred to you by Science Baba—Professor Menon…' References were very important in the world that I had come from. 'And I wanted to ask you a couple of things, if I may.'

'Please do,' Guruji said encouragingly.

'If knowledge has to be made real and books are not of much use, as you mentioned in your talk, why, then, do we consider the scriptures holy and why did you refer to all those books in your talk?'

'Books have their use,' he acknowledged easily, 'but in today's modern world, they are overemphasized. In our work, a book is essentially a guide map, simply a means to reach a specific destination. Follow the instructions of the correct book and you will reach your destination safely. That's all there is to a book. Would you worship your guide map or would you rather open it to read and follow it?' I smiled, enjoying the analogy. 'Keeping a book in a prayer room and treating it as some sort of holy relic is silly. A waste of time. Can the Bhagavadgita give you moksha? Yes, if you read it, understand it and make its precepts your own. Not if you simply keep it in a bound cover, dust it and bow to it every day.'

Again that made sense, I said to myself. Guruji continued, 'Knowledge has its uses no doubt, especially in the practical field. Doctors, architects and lawyers need to have technical knowledge about their work and books are essential for that, but for the purpose of realization all acquired knowledge has to be made real. Over-reading and under-implementing can only give you spiritual indigestion.'

'Yes,' I agreed. 'That's what Science Baba also told me.'

'That's why,' Guruji clarified further, '*Gyaan*-yoga—the knowledge-seeker's path to realization—is a difficult one.

A *Gyaan*-yogi thinks that he has reached somewhere because he knows so many things and because he can put together a metaphysical argument well. This is akin to knowing *ten ways to bake a cake*, but if you have never even lit a stove before, all that knowledge cannot feed you when the cook is on leave and you are hungry.'

Once again I marvelled at the practical way he explained a common confusion. I knew people who spent their entire life researching books and arguing what was the best way forward, but they never actually did anything practical with their knowledge.

'As to your question about why do I keep referring to the scriptures, the answer is simple. It is only to make you believe that what I say is true. If I say something without referencing it, your doubting nature will create barriers in your acceptance of it. However, if I tell you that the *Bhagavadgita* says the same thing, your inherent belief in that book will help you accept and digest what I am saying. This is like sugar-coating something to make it more palatable or tagging something unknown to something that is familiar. That's all there is to it. I do it to create belief, which is essential because it is only when you believe something that you start doing something about it. *When you believe something truly, your mind wraps itself around it and brings it to reality.*'

I found myself hanging on every word he uttered, fascinated by this utterly novel explanation of familiar things. 'Every truly holy book,' Guruji explained further, 'comes from the same source and what each of these books say is also the same, except that every such book is couched in the idiom, the social customs and the language of the time when the book was written. You may spend your entire life, as academicians tend to do, comparing and arguing about various texts and various philosophies but you will not reach anywhere on the spiritual journey. On the other hand, if you are a simpleton who has read no books—or maybe just one book, but are able to make that basic knowledge real to yourself, then you will progress.

He continued, anticipating my question. 'And before you ask, making the knowledge real means digesting and implementing it in the laboratory of your life.'

Why was Guruji constantly harping on the perils of knowledge?—I wondered. Was it a gentle hint at my rather academic approach to life? 'Guruji,' I said deferentially, bringing the conversation back on my track, 'I wanted to learn meditation.'

'I will teach you next time you come. What I teach has the potential to give instant results. If you do it properly then you will see the results right there and then!' With those encouraging words, I touched his feet and took his leave.

Guruji's satsang stayed with me. He seemed to promise a practical way forward; scientific in that sense. I wondered if it could be that easy. I felt charged up and better than I had felt in a long time. I was also greatly intrigued by the experience I'd had, of seeing him in two different places within the span of a couple of minutes. So the next time I visited Guruji's home, I asked one of the older disciples in an oblique manner about Guruji's whereabouts after that last talk—whether he had left immediately afterwards or had stayed back to handle more questions.

Sheeshpal, the tall spare man I had seen walking in with the books under his arm, replied, 'He stayed back, as he usually does, to hold his Sunday clinic. Why do you ask?'

I hesitated, feeling a bit foolish. 'Because,' I finally admitted, 'I saw him downstairs just a couple of minutes after the talk had finished. I was wondering how he came down so quickly…'

'But he didn't!' interrupted Sheeshpal.

'But he did!' I shot right back. 'We even had a conversation standing in the entrance lobby on the ground floor.' I let that sink in before I continued, 'How…how is that possible?' I faltered., 'Are you sure he didn't come down straightaway?'

'Sheeshpal looked at me perceptively. 'No he didn't. I was with him all the while.' I quirked my eyebrows as he continued, 'But don't be too surprised. These things are common around Guruji. You aren't the first to have seen something like this, you know.'

'Something like what?' I asked.

'Two people seeing him at two different places at the same time!'

The topic of Guruji's talk that second day was apt, almost as though he knew what was on my mind: What are miracles?

The answer, as I understood back then, was that miracles were the result of scientific methods and truths that are as yet undiscovered by man. For example, a light bulb or conversation on a mobile phone would be a miracle for someone from the 15th century who has never heard of electricity or seen a mobile phone. The difference between normal scientific phenomena and a bona-fide miracle is that while the scientific phenomenon can be reproduced by anyone in command of his five senses, a miracle can only be performed by a person in an elevated state of consciousness—someone, to put it differently, endowed with a sixth sense; someone who can alter the default settings of the laws of karma. Since that elevated state of consciousness is foreign to most of humanity, the manifestation is considered a miracle. Just as colour cannot be explained to someone born blind, miracles cannot be explained using the existing body of scientific knowledge.

The second important thing about miracles is that they should be performed only by someone who has a mandate to do so. And who gives that mandate? God himself, in case you were wondering! And miracles are never to be performed lightly or for the purpose of showing off but only when there is a specific need or wish of the Guru in order to achieve a certain task. Such a task is typically one that furthers God's cause. Why there are so many do's and don'ts for miracles is because miracles by their very nature violate the law of cause-and-effect and since this law is the basis of creation itself, it is not trifled with even by God himself. Gurus performed miracles usually to help their sincere devotees in difficult circumstances, so that their spiritual journey may not be derailed. At the same time, miracles are a medicine that should be used sparingly since a miracle cannot change ultimate realities. Everyone who had overused the laws of miracles had had to pay dearly for doing so...

INNER JOURNEY

As promised, Guruji started us off on meditation after the Satsang.

All of us sat expectantly on the carpeted floor facing him, as he settled in front of us on a low settee. We waited as a helper drew the drapes and switched on the air-conditioner . On seeing my quizzical expression, Guruji answered my unspoken question. 'We must be comfortable, otherwise our attention will never leave the mind-body complex.'

Why did Gautama Buddha torture himself in the forests of Bodh Gaya, in that case? The thought flitted through my head as Guruji started to speak, 'Why do we meditate?'

'Is it because we can find God through it, sir?' I ventured.

Guruji smiled. 'What is God but a belief that we have no experience of? How can we focus our attention on something that we have no acquaintance with?'

We waited as Guruji settled in. He folded his legs and sat, in what I learnt later was called the *Siddhasana* (Accomplished Pose). 'Let us start with first understanding what meditation is. Why do we meditate in the first place? If the purpose is to relax and de-stress, why not see a movie instead or watch a comedy show? Or why not take a nap after a sumptuous meal?' Guruji chortled and we laughed with him. 'Remember what I said about *why* it is important to know why we do something?'

'Yes, Sir,' I replied as if I was reciting a lesson. 'That's because if we know what our goal truly is and what meditation can do to help us achieve that goal, then our effort will be successful.'

'Well, that's more or less partially incorrect!' said Guruji humorously, 'A lot of confusion has developed around the word meditation. Meditation has become a fashion. That and having a Guru, of course! The media is full of advertisements glamorizing yoga and meditation. Slim girls in leotards, striking a graceful Padmasana, with the snow-clad Himalayas in the background, are the standard advertisement for premium spas. This multi-billion dollar business is driving a frenzy that takes us away from the core objective of meditation, which can be described as a process of achieving inner stillness.'

I interjected, 'It has reached a stage where western yoga teachers are even patenting yogic techniques that they claim to have invented, Guruji!'

'Oh really? I didn't know that it had gone that far!' Guruji exclaimed. 'That only reinforces the point I am making. Modern life and its stresses are creating a great demand for meditation and its de-stressing effect. From bad health to broken relationships, meditation has become a cure-all. Mind you, I am not pulling down anyone's right to make a living but the role of meditation goes far beyond just good health and mental peace. If done properly, meditation grants good health by default. That's just a small side-effect of meditation but unscrupulous teachers make that the main benefit. And that's because meditation for de-stressing is relatively easy to achieve. Mental peace is just the first step in real meditation. The irony is that what is given free by the real masters is made the final destination and a money spinner by the pretenders. The Indian tradition is to give free coriander and green chillies when you buy vegetables. Today, however, clever traders are selling the green chillies and not talking about the vegetables at all!'

We all laughed at the imagery as Guruji continued, 'If we are serious about learning meditation, we must go beyond the fancy names and look for the real stuff. Only then can we reach the highest levels. And I do hope the people who are sitting here are serious about learning real meditation and are not here for some glamourous version that has a film star promoting it.'

Guruji leaned back and continued, 'So today let's start from a clean slate. Let us unlearn what we may have read or heard about meditation. Let us forget the rituals, the mumbo-jumbo, the secret symbols, the different chants of the various schools and all the rest of the complicated rules that we may have been taught to remember. Let's simply explore what meditation should be in its essential avatar.'

He began. 'Meditation translates to the word *Dhyan* in Hindi. And if I convert it back to English, it simply means *Attention*. So meditation can be described as a process of giving attention to, or focusing attention on, our inner self.'

Guruji continued after a pause to let that sink in. 'The question that then arises is: How to focus inwards? Practitioners use a wide variety of focus-objects. Some people meditate on their breath, some try to reach the state of thoughtlessness, some meditate on a carefully cultivated inner vision, some chant mantras and some meditate on a candle flame. Many people meditate on their chakras—*pranic* energy whorls. Since there are so many varieties and schools of meditation, it becomes very confusing to the average seeker. The question that looms in his or her mind is: Where do I start and what process do I follow?'

Guruji paused and I tried to absorb what he was saying. 'My submission to all of you here today is that before we find a suitable method, or a focus object, we must fix our meditation goal. That means we must decide individually, for ourselves, what we desire to achieve through our meditation. That is the essential first step.

'And remember, your goal must be something that is close to *your* heart. The reason for failure in meditation is usually this: people choose politically correct goals rather than heartfelt goals. For us, it has become more important to look good in the eyes of others and even in such a private thing as meditation, we look to others for setting up a goal that is considered holy.'

'Let us get rid of this bad habit today. Let us get out of the passive-follower mode and set a goal that *we* believe in and are ready to work towards.'

'But Guruji, my goal, if I am permitted to choose just anything, may not be spiritual at all!' objected Sheeshpalji. 'Am I allowed to meditate on a worldly goal?'

'This is exactly the wrong habit I was pointing to just now. You are trying only to be a good boy when you choose a so-called spiritual goal. This attitude indicates that you are obsessed by worldly approval and that is far from being inwards! And what exactly is spiritual? Can someone tell me?'

When no one answered, Guruji sighed, 'Since all of you want to be spoon-fed, let me lay it out in black and white. Being spiritual is to be open-hearted. It is to be fearless. It is a state where you know instantly what is right and what is wrong from your perspective. A state where you are completely honest and there is no gap between your inner and outer self. A state in which thought flows instantly out as action. These are just a few of the symptoms of a spiritually enlightened person.'

'And if you are the above, your goal will leap out at you and grab you by the neck.' Guruji said indulgently. 'In any case even if you are not spiritual as per my definition, even then only what is real and heartfelt to *you* will occupy your mind as you try to meditate.'

'Isn't meditation the same as concentration?' asked someone. Good question, I thought to myself.

'No,' said Guruji. 'We must be aware of the difference between concentration and meditation. Both are very different things although they may appear superficially similar. And they lead to very different results. Concentration is about focussing on one object to the exclusion of everything else. A student studying for a specific subject for an impending exam is basically practicing the art of concentration. He ignores everything except the subject matter at hand. On the other hand meditation is about being totally aware. You still have an object of focus but you are aware of everything else in a way that could impact your focus.'

'What do you mean, Guruji?' I interrupted.

'Hmmm…' said Guruji, 'Let me explain with an example.'

'In the *Mahabharata*, when Arjuna was asked to shoot at the eye of the bird by his Guru Dronacharya, he only saw its eye. The question is—was that concentration or meditation?'

We all listened expectantly. Most of us had grown up on a steady diet of bedtime stories from the *Mahabharata*. This particular story was well known but Guruji was asking a question that I had never considered earlier.

Guruji continued as I leaned forward in my chair. 'Arjuna, as he focused on the eye of the bird, had also, at the same time, to be aware of all the things that could affect or spoil his aim. The angle of the light, the breeze blowing, the rustle of the leaves, etc, would have to be factored in. Only focusing on the eye while ignoring everything around the bird would be a recipe for a miss. This focused awareness is the essence of meditation and not to be confused with concentration.'

I listened, fascinated, as Guruji continued, '*Further, the aim of meditation is to make all of life a meditation. Meditation takes you higher and broadens your perspective while concentration takes you into the innards and narrows your focus.* Both are useful in the search for a higher life. We must remember always that there is no distinction between life and spirituality. You *think* that spirituality is different from life, and so you want to create a spiritual goal! You are filthy in your life and you want to be pristine in your spiritual goals! I ask you: Can a filthy person ever be clean at the same time?'

Guruji chuckled as he continued, 'This, my friends, is the hypocrisy you practice. You invent a noble goal but unfortunately that noble goal is not something that really interests you, like all those New Year resolutions people keep making and promptly breaking! So forget these fake distinctions and these hypocrisies. Go for something, *anything*, that you really want—from life or from yourself. Is that clear to everyone?'

Somewhat, I thought to myself, really impressed with what I had just heard. Everyone else either nodded or maintained a pensive silence.

'Let us move on, then,' said Guruji briskly. 'Let's take some examples of goals that people may have. Does anyone here want to share his meditation goal?'

As usual, Jagmohan was the first one to chime in, 'Guruji, all I know is that my mind is constantly active. I am told I think too much but what am I supposed to do? It's not that I *choose* to worry. It's the way my life is! All this worrying has led to so much stress that my blood pressure is high. My wife calls me mental and the doctor has told me to meditate to help bring it down. My meditation goal is to worry less.'

'Hmm,' said Guruji. 'Anyone else?'

'Umm, after my father's death,' I offered hesitantly, not sure I wanted to share something so personal with so many people I barely knew, 'I find my life meaningless. I have always been very goal oriented but the—the certainty of death tells me that all our efforts are ultimately futile. So what is the purpose of my life? I hope that meditation will help me find the answer.'

A young voice called out from the back of the room 'I have heard that yogis meditate to get higher powers. I too want to develop my psychic powers, Guruji!' And everyone laughed.

'Not only you, kid!' some wit wisecracked, provoking chuckles from the audience.

'Since I lost my son, I have lost my peace. Why was my son taken away? Maybe meditation will help me find peace…' said the woman who had so moved us the last time

'I am in the last stage of cancer and before I go, I want to atone for my sins and attach myself to God. I am told that meditation can establish the connection,' a woman said and we all sobered up. *Death was something that stalked us all*, but most of us chose to conveniently forget that.

'I want to increase my power of concentration and use it in my business. I want to be wealthy,' said the man with the golden rope around his neck.

'I want to see God face-to-face…' said a man I had not noticed before.

'Quite a wide and varied list, I can see,' quipped Guruji. 'You people have a lot of expectations, but don't worry. Meditation, when done properly, helps with all these things. Okay, let me now define what the process of meditation really is.'

I sat up and leaned forward. This was why I had come here.

Guruji started, 'Practically, meditation is a process of going inwards so that we may find a hidden doorway within our head. A doorway that exists in all of us, whether sinner or saint, and leads through a series of inner worlds, or a series of unravellings, back to our final resting place—the point of origin, where it all started. This is the place where we have come from and this is the place where we are essentially our true self. The word *Enlightenment* is nothing but re-discovering that essential self. The process of going into the inner world is called meditation and the state of enlightenment, when we finally reach our goal, is also called Meditation—the same word but with a capital M.'

Guruji continued again after taking a break, 'Let's first talk about meditation as a process. Simply put, meditation is a process that is designed to direct our attention inwards. Our attention is the most potent tool that we have, although we have no idea it is so, since it is sapped by the quicksand of multiple desires. For most of us, this attention has been flowing outwards our entire life through our senses. Meditation is an attempt to make a U-turn and redirect the flow of attention back to our core. That's it! That's all that needs to be done—at least in principle.'

'Now, before we go any further, I want all of you to try and meditate. Try out the nature of the beast! I want all of you to close your eyes, focus between your eyebrows and try to switch your attention from the outside world to the world that is inside. That's all you are supposed to do in this session. Let us give it ten minutes. And don't have any expectations. Just observe what you see, hear or feel. And before you start, please switch off your mobile phones, all of you. I don't want to hear even the vibration of your phones.'

There was some rustling and beeping as we all went about complying with his directions. I sat back in my spot, folded my knees and did as I had been told. As I closed my eyes and focused on the point between my eyebrows, I felt a swirling blackness engulf me. Sensations started crawling over my skin, over my hands and feet, my back and shoulders but there was nothing divine about them. They were, to tell the truth, rather unpleasant. There was the same nervous anxiety that I remembered from my exam days. My stomach tightened and butterflies winged their way through the canyons of my innards! There were no divine lights, no celestial music, and I definitely did not feel more peaceful. I clenched my teeth and tried harder. I peered with more focus into the opaque blackness but it was like clutching at water. What was I doing wrong? Why was I failing at this simple exercise even though I wanted so desperately to succeed? What would I do with myself if I could never learn the technique? Go back to the same life that I had been living? All kinds of unpleasant thoughts started to cross my mind.

'Time up!' announced Guruji, and I opened my eyes, far more disturbed than I had been before. I had been looking forward to meditation as a way to improve my life, but it seemed to be far harder that I had presumed.

'How was the experience? Would someone want to share what they felt?' Guruji enquired.

'All I felt were thoughts and fears rushing through my head,' I confessed, 'and—and there were unpleasant sensations rushing through my body. I actually felt dizzy!' There was no point being diplomatic. I had driven all this way to learn meditation and I was dammed if I would lie to myself that it had worked when it hadn't.

'Me too!' corroborated Jagmohan. 'I felt dizzy too.'

'I was beginning to feel very peaceful just before you ended it, Guruji,' said the woman who had cancer.

'Could any of you focus your attention inside?' asked Guruji.

There were sidelong glances among the audience, a general shaking of heads and a generalized negative murmur. Only the woman with the cancer raised her hand.

'Good!' said Guruji cheerfully. 'This is what I wanted you to experience—that what sounds like a simple task is actually not that simple.'

My ears perked up. It seemed that my failure was not a failure after all.

'Now the question is, why did you find it so difficult to focus your attention inwards?'

We all looked at Guruji for the answer.

'The answer,' Guruji informed us, 'is straightforward. Inside us, there is only darkness and no specific point to focus our attention on. The outside world, by contrast, is sharp, clear and vibrant—in Technicolor! Our attention naturally runs to the outside. Even a newborn baby can do it. All you have to do is to open your eyes and lo and behold—exciting things are happening right in front of you. This is why the average earth-bound soul finds it so difficult to turn its attention inwards. We try hard to meditate only because we are told of its benefits but we find that it's not easy to do in practice! If life is a school, then meditation is a mathematics class. If you were a kid with a choice which would you prefer? The math class or the playground?'

The audience tittered.

Guruji paused and sipped some water before continuing, 'Let's look at the mechanism of meditation in more detail.'

I leaned forward as Guruji spoke, 'The individual soul—a splinter of the divine soul—rushes into this world, greedy for experience. *Kaal*, the keeper of the universe, has designed creation in such a way that all the souls who come in are entranced with what they find here. The soul that is born into this world enters this playground by grabbing an appropriate body and mind. The soul, being fused intimately with the body and mind, believes itself to be this body and this mind rather than recognizing itself as the spirit of God.'

Guruji spread his hands expansively and shrugged his shoulders as he continued, 'Look at the irony. The soul is a vast and powerful entity but because of its union with the puny body and the untrained mind, it believes itself to be this limited self. This farce couldn't have continued for long but you see, *Kaal* keeps the charade going by sedating the soul into forgetting its true nature. Like Hanuman the Monkey God, the soul forgets what it truly is. This deluded soul, called the *Jeevatma* in our scriptures, or the Ego in western literature, is greedy for experience. Identifying with this body and this mind, it peers into the world through the narrow sensory aperture and clutches at whatever it can perceive with the senses.

'One's own family, job, parents, children, money, status, nation, religion and, of course, I, Me, Myself is the usual limit.'

'This is why,' Guruji chuckled, 'Jagmohan here is attached to his business and couldn't care less about yours! And this is why you, Sureshji, are attached to your business and couldn't care less about his, even though both of you claim to be best friends! This is why someone is sad when his or her father passes away, but is hardly concerned when it's someone else's turn to lose a parent or a sibling or a spouse.

'Because our interface with the world is narrow and our capacity to experience through the body is limited,' he went on, 'we relate only to what we think is ours. Therefore even though we are being constantly bombarded by all kinds of sensory inputs, we blank out most of them—except the ones we think will affect our own small little world. And it all boils down to the sensations we can feel. Pleasant is good; unpleasant is bad.

'And before you start blaming Mr *Kaal* for designing the pleasure/pain response mechanism like this, think why it is so. You will discover that this system is so because it is designed to help us survive for as long as possible in this dangerous world. The instinct to run away from a tiger is one example of the usefulness of this design. Snatching our hand away from a burning stove is another example—it saves us from injury. The trouble starts when this response starts triggering even when there is no physical danger. Running away at full speed when you come face-to-face with a tiger is a good thing, but getting your heart rate, blood pressure and breathing rate up just at the thought of a tiger—or losing your job—is neurosis, right?'

'Yes!' we chorused.

'So our being—the *Jeevatma*, as the seers call it—desires sensation and fears annihilation, and the body and mind, being faithful servants, do their best to provide these indulgences to the *Jeevatma*. This is the first obstacle you experience when you try to meditate. You are literally trying to change the course of a river! As you meditate, the body will show itself up through aches and pains that you never noticed before. The mind will also try to recreate sensations that you are addicted to and that are now missing since your eyes are closed. The mind will play re-runs of those experiences that affected you deeply in some way.'

Guruji again paused and looked around before continuing, 'So friends, this is the human condition. This is how we spend our life. Time after time, life after life—chasing pleasure, avoiding pain and fearing the loss of what we have. And when you start meditating, all this comes pouring out into your being. You are attempting to reverse a million years of greedy living. That's the nature of the beast that you are trying to tame.'

I listened quietly. No wonder I had felt dizzy! The room too was silent. No one spoke, because I think all of us understood the essential truth behind the statement. As Guruji had said so aptly, we were all coming face to face with the nature of the beast—our very own greedy self!

'So how do we get out of this whirlpool?' Guruji enquired softly, sweeping his gaze around the room. 'How do we stop being greedily reactive? Can anyone tell me?'

A respectful silence greeted his words and he continued, 'The only way to do it is by being in the eye of the storm—where it is all still. Meditation is not about controlling the whirlwind that comes in through our senses; it is about being one with our inner core that is always still. If life is a merry-go-around, it is to be in the centre of the wheel and not on any of the rides. To reach this point of being centred is the aim of meditation. As I said earlier, once we become centred, meditation as a process is over and true Meditation—the one with a capital 'M'—begins.'

'So let us try it again and this time when you meditate, don't try to control anything. Just throw out the question—Who am I?—and wait for the answer to come. And don't worry if the answer doesn't come immediately or even in this session. Let your mind and body run free. Don't try to nudge them along righteous paths. Come, let us start.'

I closed my eyes; my legs folded on the soft carpet, and turned my attention once again to the point between my eyebrows. The same blackness started swirling, but this time I wasn't disturbed by it. This was supposed to be normal. My aim this time was not to try and locate something within the darkness. I was only supposed to throw out a question and then wait for the answer. *Who am I?* I asked in all sincerity to the blackness and waited for the answer to come. This time there was no anxiety and as I waited, I started becoming aware of various things: the soft whirr of the air-conditioning, the sounds of life from the street outside, the chilled draft of air that bathed my skin...This carpet is rather comfortable, I thought to myself and I settled more deeply into it. I became aware of a crick in my ankle and I could feel the twinge of pain. My attention went down to my legs and at once I felt several sensations. There were many pain points and, as I chased them, the discomfort seemed to shift from point to point. As I watched them, they seemed to recede and I soon got bored of it.

Then I heard a sonorous sound in the distance—like a slow, rolling, thunder. Was it going to rain? Was the monsoon finally hitting Delhi? Or was it an aircraft landing at the distant Indira Gandhi Airport? I wondered as I meditated. Rain would be good since the land was parched and it needed the healing touch of the monsoon. The barren brown land would turn green and life would sprout almost overnight. The seeds that the farmers had sown would flourish and the economy would improve. The stock market would go up and so would my stock portfolio, since the farmers would have money to spend! Hindustan Lever should be a good buy. I thought to myself and with that happy thought, my body relaxed and I slipped into what can only be described as a light sleep. The only difference was that I seemed to be aware that I was sleeping! Instead of thoughts, like the first time, this time images and short dreams came to me. Of people from long ago, and of things that I had once wanted to do…The moment one short episode ended, another would start. It was all rather relaxing and pleasant.

'AUM…!' I soon heard Guruji's sonorous voice and I came out of my trance, dream, sleep—whatever you may want to call it. I felt completely refreshed and wide awake.

The rest were stirring as well and this time the atmosphere was different.

'So how was it this time?' asked Guruji.

I pondered over what to say. I definitely hadn't got the answer to who I was but…I looked around the room and checked the clock on the wall. Wow! I had been in that dream-like state for more than an hour! Had I been meditating or sleeping? It couldn't be sleep! My neck would have tilted to the side and I would surely have snapped awake…

'Very different this time,' I ventured tentatively, feeling through my thoughts, 'Instead of thoughts, I saw…dreams and images and I seemed to have relaxed enough to have fallen asleep.'

Guruji smiled and offered, 'When we meditate, we are attempting to regain the control from our senses and turn the gaze inwards. The inner world is the natural state and the outer world is the one that is unreal, although it appears the opposite to the inverted souls that you have all become. Although exciting, the outer world is the one that is unnatural and it costs energy to be in. That's why we get tired at the end of the day. And when the body gets depleted, it wants to sleep to recover. Sleep is a type of default meditation. And when we go into conscious meditation, the same relaxation hits us and if the body has been under stress, the first benefit of meditation is the rest and the repair of the body. You will tend to fall asleep when you attempt to meditate till your body has found its equilibrium. Once you regain your health, you will find that you remain awake even as you relax deeply. And that is when you will consciously climb the ladder of meditation!'

'But why the short dreams? And even though the thoughts seemed to be far fewer, they still came.' I countered.

'*Dreams are desires and thoughts are fears.* That's how to accurately place them,' explained Guruji, in response.

Guruji turned to the group and said, 'So friends, this is how you start to meditate. Resolve to know yourself and then dive into it without preconceived notions. It is an amazing journey and I want all of you to do it regularly since you need practice to succeed. Call me and share your experiences.'

I raised my hand. 'Guruji, I have understood the basic aim of meditation and I seem to have even glimpsed how I am supposed to proceed but the answer to the question—Who am I? Where does *that* come from?'

'That is something that you will discover as you find success in meditation. What I *can* tell you now is that when you get the answer to who you really are, the Soul that has rested, enmeshed heavily in the prison of the body and the mind, easily finds its freedom and rises up and away. John Magee's poem, made famous by his tragic death, says it perfectly, *"Oh I've slipped the surly bonds of earth and danced the skies on laughter-silvered wings."*'

Guruji paused and looked around the room, 'It is difficult to explain this state to those who haven't experienced it. You look down on your own body and you finally understand that you are not this body or even this mind that chatters to you all day long.

'What we have tried today is just the starting point. Once you know how to start your engines and take off, you will then need a guide map to the inner journey. You may think that this world is vast but let me assure you that the inner worlds are far larger. And it is easy to get lost or seduced by the things that you encounter in those progressively more and more subtle inner worlds. The journey back to enlightenment is essentially the reverse process of how our universe was created. If you know how the universe was systematically created from the subtle to the gross levels, all you have to do is to walk the path back to the source. Since that is the place you came from—your origin, that's where you will get the answer to the question of who you really are.'

My ears perked up. What did meditation have to do with how the universe was created? I leaned forward with rapt attention. Guruji could make out that I wanted to know more: 'Ok,' he said, 'I will give you a glimpse of the path that starts from the top of your head and takes you up to the source…'

INNER JOURNEY CONTINUED

The talks continued after a short loo break.

'The One, who is the source of all things, creates and continues to create the many by differentiating itself,' Guruji told us. 'Remember, he is neither male nor female in the beginning. All souls are essentially derived from that One Soul. Meditation with a capital "M" is simply being in that state of oneness with that over-Soul. If you understand how the differentiation was created in the first place, then you can reverse the process and climb back up the ladder that you came down from as you meditate.'

'Guruji, how did God create this universe?' I couldn't resist asking. This question had been with me my entire life, after all.

Guruji explained, 'What I am going to talk about is special knowledge. We call it *Tattva Gyaan* in Sanskrit and it roughly translates into: *That knowledge which is fundamental*. Since it is fundamental in nature, it is also a knowledge that liberates. This knowledge is critical for making spiritual progress since it is only by understanding and believing in this knowledge that we can head back to our spiritual homes. Believe me, it is simple. Ultimately the whole edifice of creation has one, just one basic root—something on which the whole superstructure rests. Grasp that one thread and the whole thing starts to make sense.'

I listened attentively.

'What is that root?' He asked us rhetorically as he looked around at the audience, 'It is the gaining of the answer to the three essential and eternal questions. One—*Who am I, the real I?* This is something that we have been speaking about today. This is also called self-realization. Two—*Who is the Creator and how did he create this universe?* This is also called God-realization. And three—*What is our relationship with him and how can we become one with him?* Ignorance of these basic questions is what keeps us stuck where we are. This same ignorance, permeating through every pore of the universe, is also what keeps creation going. Find the answer to these three questions and you can escape this *Maya-jaal*, this web of creation…'

'But enough said for today. I don't want to fry your brains! So we will take up more of this next week…'

I left Guruji's house in a complete daze. What I had heard, what I had glimpsed and the significance of what was promised, completely seduced and enchanted me. I couldn't wait for the week to pass and the next Sunday to come.

The entire week, I was a lost soul, and attempting to meditate the way Guruji had explained. I can't say that I made much headway, but I definitely experienced something. And I realized that what I had always thought of as a silent space—my insides—were actually full of sounds and sensations. And it wasn't just imaginary stuff but things that I could physically hear and feel.

The week passed and we were again all eagerly gathered at Guruji's feet. This time the crowd was much larger as word had been sent out that all those who wanted to attend the *Amar Katha*—the key to liberation—could attend.

'How can ignorance keep creation going, Guruji?' I asked as soon as the session started.

Guruji looked around approvingly at the large crowd. 'To answer your question,' he said, 'we must hear the story of creation. This is the story that Lord Shiva is said to have told his wife Parvati in the secret depths of a Himalayan cave. It is said that two pigeons heard the story and as a consequence became immortal. Lord Shiva called the story the *Amar Katha*, which roughly translates to *the knowledge that provides the key to eternal life*. This story is not some fable about the pantheon of gods and goddesses that our scriptures are full of, but is the blueprint of creation and, consequently, that of liberation as well.'

The crowd shifted and leaned forward as Guruji began the narration. 'Before creation took place in our particular universe,' he told us, 'there was nothing. All that existed was a limitless and omnipotent sea of undifferentiated nothingness. Time and space did not exist…'

'At one particular moment, a ripple emerged. We can call it the T=0 moment; time started ticking at that point, since something measurable had happened and because something had been created. Since what is born, modifies with time and is ultimately destroyed, therefore time becomes relevant as a tool of measurement only when anything is created. For God, time is simply a way of keeping score but let me not digress into the concept of time, which is a vast subject in itself. Let us instead stay with this ripple that was created at T=0. This ripple was nothing but a desire within that limitless, omnipotent nothingness—some call this nothingness the Creator—to create an object so as to experience it. Just as the simple act of throwing a pebble into a lake creates ever-widening ripples that reflect and merge and create complex patterns, this unstoppable desire of the Creator created ripples in this endless ocean of potent nothingness. Many debaters ask about the motive of the Creator in doing this. No one knows that, and for our purpose, it is sufficient to presume that the Creator did it out of the desire to experience itself. This original desire becomes the seed for all subsequent creation—from the stars that shine, to the earth we live on, down to the garbage that one sees piled on the road! This ripple-desire-vibration is the basis of creation; it creates everything before it like the bow of a mighty ship that cleaves the vast ocean as it slices through it. This is, Word made flesh, as the Bible describes it.'

'This vibration is called by various names. Hindus call it "*AUM*" and it is called "*LOGOS*" by the Christians. This sound continually reverberates through every pore of the universe and through all spectrums and frequencies. The word AUM is only a symbolic representation of this primordial sound which can be best described as the hum of the divine motor. Looked at another way, AUM represents the sound of the cleaving of the undifferentiated omnipotent reality into separate and distinct portions. The first part of AUM represents the material universe. The second part represents consciousnesses, which are the modes of action, and the balance part of AUM represents the Over-soul—the Creator himself coming down to live in and experience his own creation by pervading its every pore. This is like a child's electric toy complete, with battery and wiring, but which can only start working when someone flips the switch. That switching on happens when the Lord of the universe permeates every pore of the universe and makes the universe come alive.

'And there is an important thing to note here,' continued Guruji. 'This process goes on even as we speak. Creation isn't that one single act that birthed the universe, 14 billion years ago, with everything functioning on auto-pilot after that. It is an ongoing process as of this moment.'

I chewed on that interesting bit of information. If this was true then it turned the scientific understanding of how the universe was created on its head. Science assumes that all matter and all the forces that ran the universe were created in one flash at the time of the Big Bang and that everything was on auto-pilot after that as per the laws of physics. Guruji was implying the opposite. That the laws of physics were not the *creators* of the universe but simply the symptoms of an underlying reality. In effect, $E=mc^2$ was being constantly recalibrated every moment and so were all the other laws that we so took for granted. I decided that I would think about the ramifications on science later…

Guruji continued, 'Now what can we conclude from this basic knowledge that has a practical use/impact on our life?'

There was only an expectant silence.

'There are many ramifications of understanding this,' said Guruji. 'Firstly, since we—the one who asks, *Who am I*—are the ones experiencing our own limited creations, we are in a sense God's co-creators. We are He Himself, albeit in a deluded form. Aren't we?'

A pause. 'And if that is true then just knowing that provides us with a sense of relief, doesn't it?'

'Relief?' I enquired, puzzled. 'Why?'

'If we are an indivisible part of the Creator's soul, could we ever come to any harm?'

'No…I suppose not,' I said hesitantly, trying to figure out where he was going with this logic.

'And shouldn't knowing that give us a sense of relief? Think about it.' And Guruji fell into one of his long silences.

I sat quietly and thought about what Guruji had just said. If we, as he said, were a soul splinter of God, and if we had taken a body and a mind to take birth into this physical world, the worst that could happen was that we would lose the body and mind at the time of death. We—who were the soul and not the body—would always exist, in one form or the other; with this body or any other. We could never be destroyed…

Suddenly it clicked. What Guruji had just said started to make sense. If what Guruji was saying was true—if I was truly a co-creator of God, I would be part of something that had no beginning or end. I had nothing to fear.

'The second thing of note,' Guruji pointed out, '…is that, since I am part of God Himself, then something powerful would have to be done to seduce me into giving up my godly nature to come and take up ownership of this puny body and unruly mind. Isn't that so?'

True. It would be like a person volunteering to live a lifetime in a straightjacket, I said to myself as Guruji continued, 'Therefore, in order for creation to take place, the inseparable soul of God has to be separated into its soul droplets and then continually be kept separated by employing some devious technique. Only through deception will the soul give up its inheritance and chose a much worse state to be in than it was earlier. Isn't that logical?'

We listened quietly.

'And friends, that technique of maintaining the deception is called Ignorance, Darkness, Maya, Satan, Sin—whatever you may like to call it. If you look at it logically, ignorance of the truth is a necessary condition for creating a universe and to cleave the one into the many. We have a situation where one soul in one body is unaware that the other soul in the other body is the same as itself. This is like a bottle of water floating in a lake. The water in the bottle is the same as the water in the lake but they are separated by the cork of ignorance. And how does the keeper of this Creation—the creator of this deception technique, whom the Hindu scriptures call *Kaal*—prevent the individual soul from pulling out this cork of illusion?'

No-one answered, so Guruji continued, 'By continually distracting the individual soul from realizing the fallacy of its separation. Just as a mother distracts the cranky child by shaking a rattle, wily *Kaal* keeps the soul's attention engrossed, through various inducements and attachments. Mr *Kaal*, as I like to call him, does it with a simple trick. He has six armies at his command. Lust, Anger, Greed, Attachment, Fear and Ego—the sense of the petty I. He uses these entities to keep the *Jeevatma* engrossed lifetime after lifetime in petty pursuits. Our deluded soul is essentially running after not the Creator but his creation.'

Guruji continued after a pause, 'But however slick the whole operation; it is ultimately a Ponzi scheme. And sooner or later we, the individual souls, figure out that this is a trick being played on us.'

'What would we do when we realize that we are being taken for a ride?' Guruji turned to me. 'Saagarji, what would you do if you realized that you are being shortchanged? That you are being made a fool of?'

'I—er, I wouldn't like it one bit,' I stammered, surprised by his sudden attention, 'and I won't accept it!'

'Precisely!' Guruji chuckled. 'If only you knew, you would do something about it. The average soul that resides in the universe usually isn't that lucky, unfortunately. One soul believes itself to be a proton—and so it is. Another believes that it is superior to a mere proton and believes that it is the king of metals—the noble gold! Another soul believes that the highest achievement is to be a shady tree and, after lifetimes of struggle, it manages to become the giant redwood. Another soul believes that he is the king of the jungle and he roars like a lion. And of course we humans believe we are the crowning species—special because we are made in the image of God. What dolts we are! We aren't made in the image of God; we are God Himself!'

'So, friends and fellow souls, this is the story all around. The soul has forgotten its true nature, its true lineage and heritage and it remains forgotten because of the machinations and inducements that are offered by *Kaal*. These inducements, you can even call them bribes, may appear very exciting to the young soul fragment as it rushes in, greedy for experience, but ultimately all this is just a fraud that is perpetrated to make a king believe that he is a beggar.

'Just knowing and believing what I am just telling you is enough to start the process of escaping from this fraud.'

'Yes Guruji,' the crowd chorused.

I asked, 'So is that what meditation is? A tool that can reacquaint us with our true self?'

'Yes. And how does it do that?' asked Guruji rhetorically. 'As we have just practiced, we reverse the outward flow of our desire and attention, we stop getting seduced and short-changed by the six armies of *Kaal*, because we realize that these are fakes, designed to mislead us, and we turn our attention inwards, towards the eternal, omnipotent source that is our true nature.'

'Wow!' I said to myself. That was a succinct explanation. It wasn't that I had been ignorant of meditation before. I had dabbled in Buddhist meditation techniques, both Mindfulness and Vipassana, and Transcendental meditation (TM for short), as part of my corporate training. I had even done a weeklong camp of Raja Yoga meditation to subdue a truant episode of high blood pressure, which the doctor had said—shaking his head—that I was too young to have. All the techniques had appeared exotic to me—hard to understand and harder to practice.

Guruji had brought the talk around beautifully in a circle.

'Let me recap what we have learnt today,' he announced. 'The first objective of meditation is extremely simple. It is to go inwards—away from the created, towards the Creator, since only the Creator is the eternal, constant truth that we seek. The outer world, always being in flux, can never give us peace.

'Why will going inwards work? The reason is that the Creator, who resides in every pore of the universe, also resides in the physical container that we call our body. Why go looking for God in temples and pilgrimages when we can find Him in the comfort of our own self? Switch your air-conditioner on! Make the body comfortable and focus the mind inwards—and there you are!'

We all laughed at the imagery. 'The lazy man's guide to God,' I remarked and Guruji laughed his agreement. 'Saagarji, this is why saints call this body our temple where the Lord lives.

So, what is the first step? Since we have to achieve complete stillness—physical, mental as well as emotional—any route or technique by which we can achieve this state is the best method of meditation for us. The usual method is to sit still with the eyes closed—eyes being the major source of sensory experience—but there are other methods as well. Some people meditate well to music, some meditate as they cook and some meditate as they walk or drive a vehicle. Anything that gets us inwards is helpful and can serve the purpose of meditation.'

Jagmohan, the eternal comic in the group, remarked, 'Guruji, I have even seen people who take opium sit in what looks like blissful meditation!'

Everyone laughed but Guruji took it seriously. 'You are right!' he exclaimed. 'This state can be induced by drugs or alcohol as well!'

'Really?' the audience gasped.

'Yes! Why do you think it is so difficult to give up any addiction? Not because there is some great chemical dependence, as doctors say, but because these chemicals create a state of being that has the very same stillness and inwardness that successful meditation gives. You feel at your best when under the influence. The question that arises is—if that is the simplest way, bottled, labelled and available at a fixed price at the local liquor shop, why do the scriptures of all religions frown upon intoxicants?'

No one could think of a reply and as usual, Guruji answered his own question. 'Since our aim is freedom, crutches of any kind defeat the whole purpose. In the case of the addict, the state of Ananda is so deeply satisfying to his soul that once he has tasted that state through, shall we say, illegal means, he wants to keep intoxicating himself. Unfortunately for him, that state of satisfaction lasts as long as the effect lasts and he ends up damaging both his body and his wallet. This is why addictions are so difficult to get rid of, since giving up the intoxicant also means giving up that blissful state. So if you really wish to meditate truly, you can only ever use your own self—your body, heart and mind.'

With that, Guruji fell silent. I sat there with awe in my heart. What a short, succinct and practical delineation of an activity that religions made into rituals and teachers of Yoga made into hard-to-understand principles that earned them billions of dollars! A million questions were buzzing through my head. If this was so simple then why were there so many rules and admonishments that any aspirant had to follow? Why did all the religions of the world lay down so many regulations? I refrained from voicing these queries right away. All in good time, I thought.

'Are there any questions? Anyone?' asked Guruji indulgently, looking around the room.

'Sir, aren't we supposed to learn all the Asanas and Pranayams first?' someone from the audience asked.

'Hatha Yoga is good,' agreed Guruji, 'but it is meant to get us to the point where we can sit comfortably for a good length of time without the body troubling us. This is only preparatory to the practice of meditation and not a goal in itself.'

'But then, why is so much emphasis given to Yogic Asanas?' Another voice demanded. 'Why does Baba Anantdev spend so much time teaching Asanas rather than meditation? And he is followed by millions of people across the world.'

'Hmm, Well, let me give you an example,' Guruji responded. 'Suppose I have to go to India Gate and you, Jagmohan, have a car. Can I ask you for a lift?'

'Of course!' he replied cheekily giving a sidelong glance to his wife, 'If my wife permits!'

'What if your wife permits but your car is out of order?' Guruji volleyed back.

'Then I would request you for a bit of time so that I can get my car repaired, I suppose,' said Jagmohan. He was the one who usually drove Guruji around.

'Yes,' Guruji nodded. 'That's what you would do—go to the mechanic, get your car repaired and then pick me up. But is going to the mechanic the same as going to India Gate?'

'No!' we responded.

'Precisely! If going to India Gate is our purpose, and going to the mechanic is necessary to repair the vehicle so that we may be able to go to India Gate, then by the same logic, all exercises, diet and yoga are only facilitators to the main purpose, which is to achieve the goal of a realized life. Why I am belabouring this point is because it is easy to confuse Yogic Asanas and Pranayama—the facilitators—with the main practice, which is meditation. You could spend your entire life performing Pranayama and Hatha Yoga in the fond belief that you are a spiritual adept, while all you are doing is a sophisticated form of exercise!'

I listened quietly and sheepishly. I had been guilty of the same belief till just a moment ago!

Guruji continued, 'So do whatever it takes to keep the body healthy. Exercise, gym, yoga, diet, Pranayama and medication—all have their strong points. The only reason to choose one over the other would be because it fits your particular body type. Yoga is good since it is, pound for pound, the most effective way of staying healthy. But don't be squeamish about going to a doctor if you need to. Take the medication or get the operation done if required. A combination of cardio-vascular exercise, strength training and yoga is best for someone who is in basic good health. And of course diet is critical.

'Now let me speak a bit about diet, as people obsess over it. Diet is important in two ways. Firstly what you eat affects your physical body, but there is a karmic component to what you eat as well. Great spiritual progress is not possible if unnecessary harm, pain and fear is caused to the life you are taking to feed yourself, since that violence and pain accrue to you. While it is true that our first duty is to keep ourselves alive, we should try to do that by maintaining as light a karmic footprint as possible.'

'This was the time to ask a question that had always troubled me. I interjected, 'What if there is nothing available to eat, except meat? What if I live in Alaska, for instance?'

'Eat what is available.'

'That means you don't insist on us being vegetarian…' I concluded aloud.

'I don't,' shrugged Guruji. 'The fact no one can deny is that the entirety of creation feeds on itself. The law of karma says that what goes around comes around. When we kill, we are evicting a soul from its body abruptly and we become responsible for interrupting its natural life-cycle. Why do it unless it is essential?'

'But, Guruji, plants have life too!' I objected. 'The nature of the soul in any life-form is the same, so what is the difference between taking the life of a plant or that of an animal?'

'There is a difference,' Guruji reiterated calmly. 'Notice that when we eat a plant, we usually don't destroy the plant. We take its fruit. What is the fruit? It is an inducement or let me say, a transaction, that the plant offers us so that we may serve its purpose of pro-creation. We eat the fruit so that we may live, and we in turn offer the plant an eternal life by spreading its seed. Transaction completed. Quid pro quo! Observe that the same is not true when we kill an animal to feed ourselves. But as I said, this point should not be overemphasized. The truth is that there is not even a moment in our life when we do not kill. God knows how many insects we tread underfoot as we walk, and how many bacteria we ingest while eating or even just breathing. So it is foolish to feel pride in being vegetarian.'

'Ultimately, everything is a rearrangement of atoms and molecules and we kill and are killed constantly. It is only when we start to disassociate ourselves from our body, and start treating it as a place where we live rather than thinking of it as us, that the karma of killing starts to disappear.'

Gautama Buddha died of food poisoning while eating pork. The memory of reading that strange fact flashed through my brain. I had always wondered why a man who was considered the epitome of gentleness and peace wasn't a vegetarian. His rule was simple. He would accept whatever was offered to him as *Bhiksha*. Now Guruji had explained *why*.'

Guruji continued, 'All this indicates that meditation is a simple process, but the preparation has to be perfect. It is like having the right amount of salt in the meal. Less or more, both are unpalatable…'

Guruji went silent and closed his eyes. All of us also went quiet. I closed my eyes and thought about what I had heard. I wondered whether I could retain it all…

Guruji's voice woke me out of my trance. 'One last key point. Meditation is not just about being able to sit still with your eyes closed for a certain period of time with your attention between your eyebrows. As all of you would have experienced, when you do that typically two things happen. The mind takes over and the body starts going into repair mode. All kinds of thoughts, feelings and sensations start racing through your mind and it may seem to you that all is lost. The fault is not in your technique of meditation but in our urge to experience the world. The mind, being the efficient slave, wraps itself around the being's real desires and tries to create the conditions that enable that particular desire to materialize. When we sit in meditation and close our eyes, what we are essentially doing is to shut down the senses without shutting down the desire to indulge in the world. This is like shutting off the output of a water tank but not the input water-supply. Since the supply of water keeps coming in, the water tank will soon overflow and flood the entire house!'

'The real problem is not the senses but the attachment of the soul to the external world. That's what generates all this traffic. It is only when the desire to experience the outer world starts to quieten naturally, that the tap to the water tank supply is shut off, and the spirit or soul can come into play and lead one onto the path of realization.'

'Most of the spiritual literature, etc., that we read,' Guruji continued further, 'is aimed at taming the mind and quietening it by giving knowledge of the true nature of reality. *Yamas*, *Niyamas*, the Ten Commandments, and the Shariat—most codes of conducts in religious books—are written to gradually pacify the mind and give it less food for thought. Unfortunately people think that by following these rules blindly—paying lip service to these rules—they will progress towards salvation. The trouble with all this is that the word *taming* is in itself wrong. What happens when life turns this carefully cultivated existence topsy-turvy? What happens, for example, when you have carefully avoided women all you life and are proud of your unbroken celibacy, and suddenly, an *apsara*, a divine damsel, comes to seduce you? Wouldn't you end up behaving like a love-lorn idiot as the sage Vishvamitra did?'

The crowd laughed. Everyone knew the story of the famous sage who had been seduced by an *apsara* after spending years in *tapasya* (hard penance) and as a consequence, lost his powers.

'The essence of the being is the pursuit of desire. As I said, that's how the universe was created in the first place. We pursue our deeply held beliefs and desires until either they get sated, or we realize their futility. The objects desired vary from person to person. It could be material, temporal or even spiritual—or simply to escape the difficulties of life. Most people desire to meditate to either escape from their troubles or to release stress generated by their self-created situations, and some meditate to get supernatural powers through the awakening of the Siddhis so that they may get the objects they desire. Whatever may be the driving cause, it should be understood that when meditation is done with a motive, however noble, it fails to achieve its highest potential, which is the realization of the self. If enlightenment is the aim, then even the highest form of desire will prevent that from happening. Forcing yourself to have no desires, as many renunciates try, are all doomed to failure. The desire to have no desire is also, after all, a desire.'

'There seems to be a very thin line between spirituality and escapism!' I thought wryly.

'Success comes when the desires of a being naturally comes to rest on their own account,' I heard Guruji say. 'When the being reaches a point of equilibrium, when it neither gets attracted nor repelled, and nor is it fearful, then meditation happens spontaneously…'

And with that Guruji fell silent…

My mind reeled with all that I heard. My heart thrilled to these potent words that contained seeds within them for my future life.

That evening I sat at my bedside on a jute cushion and truly meditated for the first time in my life.

WHO AM I?

It was a Saturday and here I was, sitting in Guruji's drawing room with my list of questions.

Every time I had listened to Guruji in the last few weeks, I had come away with a feeling that this man knew what he was talking about. With his words resonating in my heart, shaking things up, I could literally feel the layers of hurts, defeats and unspoken hopelessness creaking and cracking in my bones. Like a dry waterway coming into flood, the feeling was emotional and overwhelming. What Guruji spoke of appealed not just to my emotional self, but to my rational mind as well. It explained both the logic and the practical aspects of the spiritual journey. For someone like me who was steeped in books, it was a refreshing way of looking at things.

My instincts told me that he could be the guide I was looking for, but I wanted to be sure. Choosing a guru is a major commitment. That's one thing that I had learnt from the books that I had read. As I advise others now, if you can get only one thing right in life, get this right. Find the right guru! If you get that right, you get everything right. Everything—and I mean everything, whether temporal or spiritual—all flows from that one fateful decision.

It is also no coincidence that all the major spiritual texts give an unparalleled position to the guru. But the difficulty lies not only in understanding this fact but also in handing yourself over so unilaterally to another person. The ego rebels, self-preservation mechanisms kick in and this unquestioning obedience flies in the face of the norms of the self-centred masculinity that society promotes. Since everyone aspires to be independent and supposedly without any need of a helping hand, showing vulnerability is considered a weakness. To break this mould is not easy and can happen only if you literally believe that the guru is a superman—a physical, mental and emotional giant. In effect, God himself on earth, sent just for you. Since people tend to misunderstand this sense of surrender as a passive giving up, they resist letting go. Because of this resistance, the guru has to wrestle the recalcitrant devotee into surrender and that usually involves some healthy debate and some miraculous tidings. With the ego's defeat and surrender at the hands of the guru comes the satisfaction of knowing that one is in capable hands. Only then can you trust someone enough, to let go of your petty defensive self. This is as difficult as signing away all one's properties, squandering one's bank balance and resigning from one's job on the verbal assurance of someone who says that everything will be alright but doesn't explain how!

So here I was, sitting in Guruji's drawing room, for the first round of jousting.

As I waited, I wondered—could Guruji really give me answers to the many questions running through my head?

Could he remove that vague sense of unease that life was passing me by and that I was stuck in the wrong place? Could he give me a sense of meaning and purpose?

I literally trembled as I sat there. Wanting to run away and postpone it to another day and at the same time, wanting to get it over with. It was a classic flight-or-fight response!

'Yes Saagarji, what can I do for you?' Guruji finally looked up from what he was doing.

'Thank you, Guruji, for seeing me. I will n-not take too much of your time,' I stuttered, my carefully prepared opening remarks forgotten. This was the first time I was sitting with him one-to-one and this time there was no anonymity of the crowd to disappear into.

Guruji looked at me calmly. He probably sensed my nervousness, 'Take all the time you want. It is very important to get your questions answered to your satisfaction.'

'Why?' That popped out before I could stop myself.

'Only when you get satisfactory answers to what you think are the important questions of your life, will you believe that you have come to the right place. And only then will you stop craning your neck for the next guru down the road.' Guruji chuckled and I laughed sheepishly as well.

'Why is that important?' I asked as our laughter subsided.

Guruji smiled his response, 'Only when you believe that you are in competent hands will you relax and surrender to the higher authority of the guru. The work to be done on the spiritual aspirant is so intense and so personal that it requires faith on part of the devotee. And before you ask, surrendering is nothing strange. Don't we believe in the teacher's infallibility before we let him teach us anything? This is like going to a surgeon for an operation. Only when you are convinced of the efficacy of the treatment and the competence of the doctor will you go under the knife. Not otherwise.'

'That makes sense,' I said to myself even as I wondered about how I could check out the competence of a guru...'

Again Guruji seemed to have anticipated my question. 'Going to a truly enlightened master is critical because only that special person—one who has actually been there and done that, shall we say—can take you there. The difficulty is, how can an ignorant devotee check the competence of a guru? A chicken-and-egg situation, yes? But there is a solution. Instead of your mind, trust your heart. The quality of your seeking attracts the kind of guru your seeking demands. There is tremendous power in your seeking. When you genuinely seek and pray for guidance, the Creator actually listens. *He takes your feelings seriously but not your words literally*! However inadequate your words may be, God understands what you are really trying to say and *that* is what is fulfilled.

'The Gita says it well and I am paraphrasing it here: those who seek the gods go to the gods; those who seek their forefathers reach their forefathers; those who seek the spirits, reach the spirits and those who seek Me reach my supreme abode.

'The sincerity of your seeking, whatever may be the object you seek, is the first necessity. And this is a good time to tell you that *the journey to enlightenment is a series of evolving beliefs and satisfactions that create continuing impetus for the individual to strike forth on his journey*. Remember, the only thing that is real to the individual is his desire to be happy. That is why that first talk that I gave to you was about happiness and not about

God. As I had said that day, God and religion are just theoretical concepts to most people. What are real are your desires, beliefs, fears and their ultimate resolution in the results you get. These are the only tangible things that you can work with.'

'That makes sense,' I said, struggling with what I was hearing. Guruji instantly seemed to gauge my confusion.

'Let me give you an example so that you are clear on this important point,' he offered. 'For instance, for a man who lives in a rented house, the desire to have his own home may be of paramount importance. He will believe that he can be happy only when he has his own home. Another person, who has his own home, and who is still unhappy, knows that the belief of the first man is not valid, but even if the second person advises the first person of this truth, the first person will not listen. He will do everything possible, with all his passion and resources, to build his home. Only when he has completed his house will he find satisfaction and only then will he move on with a clear heart to his next project.

'The house is incidental. For someone else it would be a different goal that fires up their passion. All that is important is that only the achievement of emotional milestones has any spiritual value. *You can live happily under a tree only when your desire for a palace is satiated!*'

'Guruji paused to let that sink in. 'And this is how a *Jeevatma* proceeds on the spiritual path—from one satisfaction to another.

'But all this takes time, many lifetimes of banging one's head against walls and doors! Today, though, since we are doing a one-to-one, let us not talk in generalities. Let's talk about you, Saagar ji. What are *you* looking for? What are your satisfactions or pain points, as the case may be?'

'I don't really know,' I said reflectively, 'Earlier my objectives were crystal clear and I always knew what I wanted. I also usually achieved what I targeted, but after my father's death, I have come to feel that I have only been running after mirages, chasing false gods, as they say…'

I could see that Guruji was giving me his full attention as I thought my way through the minefield of emotions that swirled in my heart. 'It seems to me that I have been taking wrong directions all my life. And I feel that I have ended up wasting my life…'

Guruji interrupted, 'Knowing what you don't want is also a step towards knowing what you want! I think you are lucky since you have got over many of the usual things that tie up people all their lives. And you are still young! Now you are ready to begin the real journey. So don't lose heart. Everything you have done and everything that you have experienced till date—the good and the bad; the happy and the sad—have had a role to play in getting you to this particular point in your life—sitting in front of me, ready to take the plunge into the inward journey.

'Remember, your individual soul has been around for millions of years and now, today is the day when, for the first time, it officially seeks to leave the indulgences of the outer world and seek the sanctity of the inner journey. It is indeed a momentous day! Don't you think so?' Guruji's voice boomed and I nodded my head, still thinking about it.

Guruji continued, ignoring my pensiveness, 'As you start on your journey, let me introduce you to a couple of loyal companions who will take you far. Till now in your normal life, reason, logic and doubt have been your tools for discernment. To those you must add two more companions for the inner journey. These true friends are called faith and surrender. Faith and surrender are the two walking sticks that will make your journey easy. Faith in God and a belief that you can reach him is necessary. A book can be written on the nature of faith but for the time being let it suffice to say that, as your faith and belief in God develops, your mind will wrap itself around your belief and bring your belief to reality. The more you believe in God, the more you will act as if He is around and the more you act that way, the more He will be around. You will get physical proof of it in your own unique way. Proof of belief creates a virtuous cycle of faith and leads to surrender at God's feet. As faith strengthens, so does your strong, unequivocal and uncompromised action—and that is the key to progress.'

Guruji continued, 'Let me summarize the essential pillars of a successful spiritual life. First, there must be a deep desire to realize the ultimate truth and that urge must be independent of any escapism from life's harsh realities. Second, there must be proper study of the methods that take you towards your goal; this is where knowledge and books come in handy. Finally, this knowledge must be implemented in one's life by regular practice. To do all this, you need the energy that only faith and surrender can provide.'

'Guruji,' I interjected, 'you have permitted me to ask any question that has relevance for me but I don't quite understand how this works. Since different people may have different questions, how can the answers, which would be different in each case, lead to the same satisfaction?'

'The questions don't matter,' Guruji declared. 'What matters is their satisfaction for the one who asks the question. When a question is genuinely felt from the heart, its satisfactory answer creates a feeling of stillness, a ceasing of that vague sense of unease and restlessness. It creates faith which, as I just pointed out, is essential to walk the path.'

He continued, 'Enlightenment is experiential and it happens when a certain satisfaction takes hold in the soul of the being. Even the smallest of triggers can set off that sense of wellness when the necessary preparation has been done. The trigger is incidental, the preparation important. It is said that Gautama Buddha got enlightened on eating *kheer* (rice pudding). Does it mean that *kheer* is a recipe for enlightenment?'

Again, I couldn't help but laugh.

Guruji smiled and continued, 'I wish that the prescription were so easy! We could get it delivered off the home shopping network in various brands and flavours of our choice! Jokes apart, though, the serious question remains—why did eating the *kheer* work in the case of Lord Buddha?'

I listened intently.

'The answer is that after years of torturing his body and mind and getting no results except that of losing lots of weight, the Buddha simply surrendered—just gave up. The question is: What did he give up? Certainly not his objective of finding the answers he sought! No, sir! What he gave up was his belief that a drop could expand to become the ocean by its own efforts. He gave up his belief that he himself could work out how to escape the pain of *Sansaar*.

'When you are in over your head and finally realize it, two things happen. One, you stop struggling and, two, you stop being so enamoured of yourself. Failure teaches humility and a more open outlook. Both are extremely useful in the pursuit of spirituality.'

'Why is that?' I asked.

'*A drop can never know the ocean,*' explained Guruji, '*but the drop can become the ocean, not by expanding but by dissolving into it!* That's the secret in a nutshell! The drop surrenders its own individuality and in that surrender finds its real nature, which is as vast as the ocean.'

'And this happens only when the *Jeevatma* or the Ego or the deluded soul—you can call it by any name—genuinely surrenders. Unless that surrender takes place, even the attempts of the ego to find God are a fraud that it perpetrates on itself.'

I interjected, 'How is that, Guruji? How can the search for spiritual knowledge and God ever be a fraud?'

'That's a good question,' Guruji replied, 'But the hypocrisies of the ego and its cleverness know no bounds. The ego, believing that it is the highest entity possible, will do anything to defend its existence. To fool the mind, it will even say that it embraces God and surrenders to Him! Yet the ego, being engulfed in darkness, fears annihilation.

'Remember that, however powerful the being, the ego, may become and howsoever proud it may be of its prowess, it knows that there was a time it did not exist and there will be a time when again it will not exist. That's obvious even to the worst megalomaniac. For the being who is so self-focused and proud of what it has achieved, the thought of annihilation is unbearable. It wants to prolong its existence by any means. Most people want eternal life. They go to the gym; they do yoga and Pranayama; many want to search for the elixir of youth. They try exotic techniques—the rich ones even set up stem cell research labs! But all know that the body will fail one day. People, who are obsessed by thoughts of perpetuating themselves, want to know what lies beyond the crematorium and want to believe that even if the body dies, their soul will live on and that they will be able to control even that! For such a self-obsessed being who has confronted the inevitability of death, the afterlife becomes an obsessive search. That person read books, attends talks and meets gurus in the search for finding out what lies beyond death.

'Observe, Saagarji, that this obsession with the afterlife and the journey of the soul is not a search for enlightenment, *moksha or surrender to the divine.* No sir! It is another way for the ego to somehow continue its existence even after death. It is still a selfish and self-preservative act of a limited being. I am sorry to say this, and I don't mean anything personal by it, but the truth is that most people who come here, do so for precisely this reason. They come here not to find God or realization, but to learn how to perpetuate themselves!'

Guruji looked at me and laughed and I smiled back sheepishly. What he had said was spot-on. It was indeed a perfect description of my life and my motives in coming here.

Guruji could probably make out my embarrassment and he said consolingly, 'But never mind your individual reasons for coming. What matters is that you are coming here asking for help. False original reasons change to pious and genuine ones when the light of truth begins to shine! This is why failure is good. Failure makes one examine one's motives honestly.'

Guruji took a pause before continuing, 'So, to come back to the Lord Buddha story, when he realized that he—his mind, body and self—were incapable of achieving his goal, he surrendered. And in that moment of giving up, he got it all.

'You may legitimately ask—if all it takes is to surrender, then aren't all the efforts made in the quest for a higher life useless? But that's not the correct conclusion. Lord Buddha succeeded not only because he surrendered; he succeeded because he became obsessed with the question of ending sorrow and made sincere efforts to find the answer. This question was important to him. The struggle and failure to find the answer tested his resolve. In the first moment that he permitted himself, that first moment of giving up, when for a brief instance there were no thoughts and when satisfaction from eating the rice pudding released a trigger, it created that momentum that broke through the despotic rule of the ego and the stifling nature of his mind.

'This is what he said afterwards, and I am paraphrasing: *Give the body what the body needs, the mind what the mind desires and only then can the soul get what the soul yearns for.* At that moment of surrender, he stepped out of the narrow confines of his ego and found that he still existed! His body still functioned. His mind still worked. So what had changed? Only his sense of self. From the narrow confines of his ego, it became the vastness of the unfettered spirit. His body and mind still obeyed that same ego but the ego itself had become enlarged to embrace the entirety of Creation, or any part thereof that he chose to embrace. The drop had merged with the ocean…'

Guruji's voice softened, as if talking about something precious, 'Once you experience that state, there is no turning back since the joy that you feel is so vastly different from our normal emotional landscape that you are hooked for life. The charms of a normal life pale in comparison.'

'It is a misnomer to say that Saadhus and seekers are renunciates. They are the seekers of that pleasure that is impossible to describe and impossible for the ego driven entity to reach…'

I listened with rapt attention. Guruji was saying so many things at so many levels that I wanted to memorize it all. I also wondered that was it by this technique that he had appeared before me after the first Satsang?

I think he understood my anxiety. 'Let me repeat the three conditions necessary to meditate successfully. One, absence of negative emotions such as fear, grief and worry. Second, *Santosh*; since there is no single word in English to describe the concept, I will use a phrase instead. *Peace with honour*, which is a good way to describe it, although *satisfaction* is also not a bad word. Thirdly, a sense of *Ananda*—which can be described in English as a state of bliss, of non-specific joy, that can only come when one surrenders to the divine will.'

Guruji continued, 'It is no coincidence that all Swamis have *Ananda* suffixed to their names. Vimalananda, Yogananda, Shradhananda, Vivekananda and so on.'

'What is also of note is that different people reach this state of *Ananda* through different means. It has to be completely tailor-made for each person, even though there are some broad highways. Getting there is a bit like threading a vibrating needle. You might be sitting on a rocking chair, I might be clinging onto an angry bull and Gopalji might be riding on a bucking bronco! But once you have managed to thread the needle? It usually stays threaded, however hard life may buck you after that. That's called being centred. Meditation is required to quieten the mind so that you may thread the needle.'

I started feeling overwhelmed. Here I was being given the secret in black and white and I couldn't remember it all. This was too much information. I just couldn't handle it. My brain wasn't big enough and clever enough to take it all in. Fear surged through me. What if I forgot what I was being told? Would I miss the bus in that case? I wildly looked around for the small diary and pen that I usually always carried. This was deep. This was the answer I was looking for and for sure this was in no book that I had ever read. I had to write this down! But my diary was missing. Oh! I had left it outside on the table. Should I go and get it? Thoughts and anxieties raced through me and I started to get up.

Guruji stopped me with a gesture. 'There is no need to write anything down. The Ego wants to make lists so that it can plan its projects! That only strengthens the Ego. Before you start making lists, remember that there is no value to remembering these things! These feelings and states have to come from within and that happens only when the being itself changes. I have told you but a few symptoms amongst many. So don't try to outwardly ape these symptoms to delude yourself that you are in meditation. There are no words to describe the actual state. Ultimately God, meditation and enlightenment are experiential and not theoretical. They cannot be approached like a mission to the moon or as an academic exercise. We are here to experience God and not do a doctorate on him!'

Guruji continued, his voice soft and serene. 'A *To-do* spiritual list; *the eight-fold path of Buddhism; The Yam-Niyamas of Raja Yoga; the Ten commandmentstof Christianity; the Shariat of Islam;* all are but symptoms that appear in a realized soul, they are not the cause or even a course of study. Trying to grab enlightenment by memorizing rules and regulations is like grabbing a fistful of water.'

I was silent and Guruji leaned back in his chair. 'But we are running ahead of the question. As I said, the journey starts when we find satisfaction just as the Buddha did.'

'So, here we are Saagarji. How can I help you find satisfaction on your journey?'

THE STORY OF SCIENCE

'Guruji, you may find it strange but I—I want to ask you some questions related to how the universe was created. I am not sure, though, whether such questions are relevant to the spiritual quest.'

'As I had said the last time, there is no divide between the spiritual and the worldly spheres. The subject of the question really doesn't matter,' Guruji said kindly, 'only the significance that the question holds for you personally. The fact is that everything is part of God's creation and we can use any genuine curiosity about any part to start pulling the thread that unravels the whole thing.'

I gave him a quizzical look and he explained, 'Let me put it this way. If you want to study the human heart, you could do that as a biologist, a cardiologist, a pathologist, a poet or as a lover. As a lover is how God prefers it, in case you were wondering! If we can access the source—the superset—through any genuine means, then all aspects—the subsets—can also be accessed.'

I steadied my nerves, firmed up my voice and plunged in. 'Guruji, I have been trying to understand how the universe was created. Not theoretically or philosophically but practically—in terms of cause and effect.'

'Go on,' nodded Guruji.

Encouraged, I continued, 'You say that every aspect of God must be understood, not only the metaphysical one…' He inclined his head. 'But beyond a point I can make no headway either through the study of science - something I have devoted a long time to, or through the reading of the spiritual texts, which give concepts that sound intuitively correct but give no formulae or calculations to support their explanations as to how the universe is actually created and maintained.'

I threaded my words carefully as I spoke. It was important to convey exactly what I meant. 'Both science and religion may be seeking the same thing—the source of creation, yet there is a large gap between what the scientists say and what the philosophers say.'

I explained the nuances of the conflict further, 'Scientists give concrete formulae but they start at an intermediate stage—the Big Bang—while philosophers and gurus seem to start from first principles, but rarely give a completely worked-out solution. They usually say that God willed it and so the universe happened!

I continued, 'Guruji, that simplistic explanation is not acceptable to anyone with a rational mind. Even my 12-year-old niece rolls her eyes at that! This incompleteness in spiritual thinking gives an opportunity to scientists to be dismissive of the spiritual-metaphysical thought process as wishful thinking.'

I rushed on, 'I can't say I agree with them, but if spiritual explanations could provide a logical answer down to the last practical details about how the universe was created, then this chain would be complete…' I tailed off, unsure if I was making any sense.

'Hmm...,' hummed Guruji. 'Why can't science answer these questions?'

'Guruji, scientists have been unable to create a theory that explains everything from the beginning or from a unified source.'

I further explained, 'Since the start of the universe—the point of the Big Bang is itself intermediate, it leads to several unanswerable questions. What happened before the Big Bang? What created the Big Bang? And at the other end—why do we have hundreds of fleeting particles in the soup of creation? Or why do we have so many different types of forces that are required to work together in coordination to form the universe?'

I warmed to the theme, recalling the days when I had delved deep into these mysteries. 'Or how and who created the materials and the laws and who coordinates between them? All this leads to the ultimate question: What is the original material, if any, from which all matter is created and is there an original force from which all the forces of the universe emerge? Scientists admit that they haven't reached the source but they claim that since it is unknowable either by science or by the philosophers, it is not important.'

'Interesting,' murmured Guruji, 'I was not aware of this conflict between philosophers and scientists.'

I continued, 'But even in what the scientist's claim as their domain—basically everything after the Big Bang onwards—their explanations have started to ring hollow after a hundred years of failure to find a unified theory. Modern physics remains split into the Classical–Quantum divide, each with its own fundamentally differing sets of laws. And the situation has actually worsened instead of getting better as the years pass. Even as classical and quantum theories continue to remain incompatible, more and more phenomena are being discovered that are poking bigger and bigger holes in the existing theories.'

Even as I spoke, I wondered if I was throwing out an impossible challenge. How could anyone, however enlightened, not only understand the complexities of the problem but also be able to offer an alternate explanation? Still I ploughed on. 'For example, we know that all types of matter is made of various combinations of only three particles—electrons, protons and neutrons, but this explains only about 30 per cent of the actual mass of the universe. So what's the balance 70 per cent made of? It is no surprise that this unknown rest is labelled as Dark Matter, since scientists essentially don't have a clue about what it is!'

I continued after a pause to marshal my thoughts, 'There is also the question of this mysterious energy that is flinging the universe apart even as the laws we know suggest that the universe should be collapsing back upon itself! This energy, of which we know nothing, is again—not surprisingly—named Dark Energy.'

'Also, Guruji,' I soldiered on, 'these things are not small entities that we could dismiss as errors or approximations. They are the largest entities in the universe by far. Come to think of it, we don't even know why light has a certain fixed speed…'

I continued my ruminations, 'Since there are so many ever-widening gaps in the scientific world view, there has to be a fundamental flaw in the scientific approach. That's what I think. It strikes me that maybe we should approach the problem from the other end—the spiritual end, and see where that takes us…And in that the scriptures seem a great starting point since they offer holistic explanations. We could try to work out the math from there…'

'What I understand from you,' Guruji remarked after I had finished, 'is that scientists are unable to explain the universe from a common source and you want us—the gurus and philosophers—to do the job that scientists are unable to do.'

'Yes, sort of,' I admitted sheepishly. Guruji sounded sarcastic—or was I imagining it?

'Why is this question important to you?' Guru asked.

'Hmm, that was a tough one but I gave it a go. 'Guruji, ever since I can remember, I have wondered about the purpose of my life. Where do I fit in? That is, if I fit in at all. And what of this world, does it have any purpose at all, or is it just a *random reversal of random chaos*, as the atheists claim?'

'And this is not just a theoretical question for me. I am desperate to believe that the universe does have a purpose, since then it stands to reason that if it does then I, myself, would have a purpose as well! And that confirmation would be such a relief for me...'

I spoke as though a tap had been opened inside of me. 'I have realized only recently, since the death of my father, that all my life has been a struggle to find this meaning and purpose. This has been the unconscious desire behind every quest of mine. I may have achieved a lot of material things but today they are like ashes in my mouth. What is the worth of these accomplishments unless I know the ultimate purpose of it all?'

I continued, passion driving my words, 'My father's death—and he was quite a well-regarded man—tells me that all things are transitory. Success, money, fame, everything that I have chased till now offers only temporary relief. None of these things can mask the inevitability of our annihilation. So today I ask myself—what is meaningful in this blind desire to achieve?'

I paused, gathering my words, so that I could say this as effectively as possible. 'For me to be happy, my life and my effort should have some purpose and some absolute value. And how could my life have any purpose if the universe itself is without meaning? So if I could get a sense of the workings and intent behind this vast creation and my place in it, then I could lead a purposeful and a happy life.'

I stopped, overwhelmed with the depths of my feelings. I was choking with emotion and my throat felt completely dry, like sandpaper.

I cleared my throat and plunged on, driven by my own demons, not caring how I sounded. 'I feel like a misfit, blind to the real meaning of life. I find it difficult to believe anything or to contribute meaningfully since I don't know what is worthwhile. Chasing my petty ambitions in light of the inevitability of death seems a waste of time. A sense of fear and grief buffet me and I feel lost. I feel no joy and I live my life with a vague sense of unease percolating whatever I do. I feel as if I have taken the wrong train or a wrong turn somewhere. I do things not from my heart but because they are expected of me. I live a second-hand existence, always taken aback by life's circumstances.'

I paused and took a breath. I had spoken so fast that I found myself breathless, 'If only I could understand the whole structure of creation and my personal role in it, I could find meaning in my life.'

It all came out in a rush, as though I had wanted to say this all my life, but hadn't known how.

Guruji closed his eyes and went silent. I had seen him do that often in the few months of interaction that I had had with him. He had said once, '*Meditate more than you read and read more than you speak.'* Most of his talks were interspersed with periods of silence, the pauses intermittent yet peaceful. I didn't know what to think or do, so I waited; my innards shuddering with the relief of having articulated what I scarcely knew existed in my heart.

Finally Guruji opened his eyes and smiled. 'Your question is acceptable to me. What comes from you is a desire of your heart and not just something you wish to sharpen your debating skills on. I haven't thought about God's creation quite this way till now—in terms of the nuts and bolts of construction. But that should be no barrier to exploring the question. We can carry out this inquiry together.

He continued, 'As I have said many times, there are a million ways of worshipping God, and trying to understand his creation is one of them. Therefore yours is a valid question.'

Guruji smiled again. 'And as you were speaking, I went into the inner world, to the level where Creation is being done and I saw with my own eyes how it is being carried out. So come, let us explore this together!'

'Where do we start, Guruji?' I leaned forward in my chair eagerly, feeling as though we were about to go down the proverbial rabbit hole.

He replied, 'Explain to me what the scientists know for certain. That could be our starting point. From there we could go backward or forward as our inquiry takes us.'

I pondered over where to start. The trouble was that physics was a vast subject with hundreds of years of study and zillions of theories and experimentations to sift through. Thousands of physicists were engaged round the clock in searching for answers to fundamental questions. Yet, could I cull it down to the basics?

I mentally summarized the broad conclusions that modern physics had come to after 600 years of study and research.

One—that the totality of the physical world could be reduced down to just four basic building blocks: Protons, Neutrons and Electrons being the three material particles and the Photon, being the fourth non-material entity that provides the energy for the first three to move.

Two—that four basic forces explain all the interactions of the material particles in the universe. The hundreds of complex interactions that scientists saw through their microscopes and telescopes were spawned by the permutations and combinations of what were only four fundamental interactions.

Three—that physics is divided into two broad zones. Though mutually incompatible, they are both separately required to explain the universe. At one end is the domain of classical physics which explains interactions between large objects through vast stellar distances, and at the other end of the spectrum is quantum mechanics whose domain is the sub-atomic level—a dimension so small that it makes even the tiny proton appears a giant in comparison.

Four—that there was no grand unified theory that could explain everything from a common source. That, of course, was the quest—the Holy Grail of physics that was often referred to as the Theory of Everything.

And finally—that new discoveries were pointing to a situation where the universe was again becoming largely inexplicable. Dark matter, dark energy, black holes, quantum entanglements, action at a distance and the origin of mass, amongst other unknowns, all pointed to things that we had no idea about.

Yes, this would be the summary sheet of modern physics.

I took a deep breath and started. 'Guruji, we know that the universe is made up of combinations of protons, neutrons, photons and electrons. Protons, neutrons and electrons are further composed of sub-atomic particles. And the photon is not a particle at all; it is but a pulsating packet of energy.'

I glanced at Guruji as I spoke. He was giving me his full attention. That gave me the confidence to continue. 'We also know for sure that there are four major forces that maintain this universe. These are the forces of electro-magnetism, gravitation, the strong nuclear force and the weak nuclear force. Together, these forces create the bulk of all the interactions in the universe and help maintain the structure of the universe itself.'

Warming up to the subject, I continued, 'Various theories have been propounded by scientists to explain all this. The main ones are Galileo's Theory of Relativity, Newton's Three Laws of Motion, Einstein's Theory of Relativity—both special and general, Quantum Mechanics, the Standard Model and the exotic String Theory. Put together, these theories explain most of what we know, although recent developments are showing that we know far less than we thought.'

Guruji stopped me. 'Saagarji, since we are trying to go into understanding the fundamentals of science, the names of the theories are not important to me. I would rather be explained what these theories actually say. When you do that I will compare your description with what I have seen with my inner vision.'

Hmm, I thought, this should be interesting! Would Guruji be able to understand what I would be saying? And more importantly, would I be able to explain these complicated theories adequately to him?

How to do this? I wondered to myself…The trick would be to make the story of science meaningful rather than technical. Parroting it out like our teachers used to in school would not do the job. I would have to narrate the story of science as if I was describing a detective chasing a murder suspect in a novel!

I gulped some water and started. 'Guruji, we humans have always had the urge to understand the world around us, we have always wanted to know how our world was created and what would happen next.'

'Go on.' Guruji nodded encouragingly and I continued, my voice getting less stuttery. 'This has been a timeless quest for man and it carries on today as well. It is as if we humans have been genetically hard-wired to seek our origins.'

I continued, trying to make what I said as interesting as possible. 'As we examine our world, we see ample evidence of a system in place and therefore it would seem logical to assume that there would be a controlling agency. What else could explain this delicately balanced functioning of our universe? Everything around us—the circle of night and day; the cyclic nature of the seasons; the patterns in the growth of crops, even animal migrations—it all points to a system that runs in perfect order.'

My voice grew stronger as the memories of my years of study flooded back. I had forgotten nothing!

'Guruji, Scientists and philosophers since time immemorial have been chasing our world down to its essential parts. The basic aim of both scientists and philosophers is to go down to the fundamentals of creation, till what we arrive at is the base of this universe.'

I looked at Guruji. He nodded, a smile warming his eyes, and I wondered, for a moment, if he already knew everything

I was telling him! Never mind, I thought—a revision never hurt anyone!

I continued, 'Let me recount a brief history of modern science to you since that will summarize all aspects of the scientific journey...and it will also lay the base for what we want to discuss.' I added as an afterthought.

As I spoke, I realized that I was rather enjoying myself! This was familiar territory. I continued, 'Copernicus, Kepler and Galileo were amongst the first to shake off the dogma of the Dark Ages and follow this method of unbiased scientific inquiry. They correctly postulated that the earth revolved around the sun, as did the other planets. They also postulated laws that described this motion so accurately that they are still in use today to predict the movement of the heavenly bodies.'

'Newton, who many people call the greatest scientific mind ever, carried on this work, compiled all this knowledge and further refined and improved it to give us the base—what is considered as modern physics today. The three laws of motion, the law of Gravitation and Calculus are his main contributions to science.'

I again sneaked a look at Guruji. He was giving me his full attention. Reassured, I continued, 'In physics, two broad directions were explored. The first direction headed towards the study of the cosmos. Stars, planets, galaxies, our own sun and the vast distances between each of these—in short, everything that was large in scale and size. The other direction headed towards the study of the microcosm—the world, as the name suggests, that can only be seen through a microscope. So at one end of the spectrum, scientists were building better telescopes to peer further into the universe and at the other end, they were also building better microscopes to look deeper into the substances that surrounded us.'

'The power of the machines grew but scientists soon came to the fundamental conclusion—that however powerful the machines became, they would never reach beyond certain limits. The secret world of innermost and outermost matter would always hide one step further than the instruments could reach. Why did they conclude that? The answer lies in the fact that a machine that was made up of matter can never see something that was smaller than the scale of matter. But our scientists were nothing if not clever! They speculated and created ingenuous and indirect experiments that would confirm their speculations. They called them Thought Experiments. The endeavour was to somehow reach the bottom of the soup of creation—to reach the smallest, indivisible and therefore most fundamental of particles. In those days the atom was considered that particle and was the designated Holy Grail of physics.'

'Interesting!' commented Guruji as I took a breather. 'This shows that man has always been a seeker. What may vary is what he seeks. But the urge to seek seems eternal. If only we could orient our seeking to the highest possible purpose, we would be realized in no time. Never mind; it doesn't matter as long as man keeps trying. One day he will reach his final goal after knocking his head on all intermediate ones! And it's not man's fault entirely. *Kaal*, the manager of the universe, makes sure that we are kept suitably distracted from the real goal. But let me not make you digress from your fascinating story! Please, do continue, Saagarji.'

'Relentless experimentation over the centuries,' I went on, 'led to steady advancements in the knowledge and the theories of science. By the 18th century, it had become fairly clear that the material world consisted of two main parts. The first part being matter and the second part being the forces that acted on that matter. It also became clear that most of the common substances we saw and used were combinations of more basic substances and scientists invented ways to separate complex materials into their simpler components. A table, called the periodic table, was created and scientists diligently filled it with those basic elements that could not be reduced any further by any means known at that time.'

Guruji interrupted me, 'By basic, you mean a substance that cannot be broken down further?'

'Yes, Guruji. These irreducible substances were given different names and their smallest particles were called atoms, which means indivisible—in Greek or Latin, I forget which!' I answered with a laugh as I continued, 'This simplified the mindboggling variety of substances found in the cosmos down to a combination of just over a hundred unique basic elements. But Guruji, the story doesn't end there. Experiments indicated that the substances discovered, when examined individually, weren't monoblocs either. They appeared more like a lattice with empty spaces inside. As scientists peered inside this lattice of the atom through a series of indirect experiments, they discovered an even more striking fact: these hundred or so differing building blocks were themselves further constructed from a combination of three basic sub-atomic particles. Scientists called these the proton, the neutron and the electron.'

I paused to emphasis the point I was making before continuing. 'Scientists ultimately were able to prove that all the substances of the periodic table were simply permutations and combinations of only three fundamental particles. For example, the element Hydrogen—the first and the lightest element in the periodic table—is built out of just one proton and one electron circling the nucleus, while Uranium 235—one of the heavier atoms and the one that is used to make the atom bomb—is built as a combination of 92 protons, 143 neutrons and 92 electrons circling in many orbits. The significant thing is that these three basic particles—the electron, the proton and the neutron, are identical across all the elements. Theoretically, you could take one proton from the Uranium atom and replace it with one proton from the hydrogen atom and it would make no difference.'

'Yes Saagarji!' Guruji's eyes twinkled 'What you are summarizing, rather well I might add, is part of a standard physics high school syllabus. Even if my school going years were a long time ago but I still remember this part!'

I smiled back sheepishly, 'I thought that I would cover all this just so that all these facts are on the table…'

'Do carry on.' said Guruji and I continued. 'Yes Guruji. The point to take away is that atoms of different substances may have strikingly different characteristics but the bottom line is that different atoms are composed of the same three particles. The difference is only in the permutations and combinations.'

I went on with my story, 'Scientists initially concluded that even though the atom was composed of three distinct components, the combination was stable and thought to be indivisible. If that had indeed been so, then scientists would have arrived at the fundamental particles of creation and the scientific quest would have been over. Not so! The fun was just beginning. This belief, like many others of those turbulent times, soon suffered an irreversible setback.'

'How so?' asked Guruji, sounding intrigued.

'Almost by accident,' I replied. 'A certain substance was discovered that glowed an unearthly greenish light. The amazing thing was that this glow wasn't the reflection of light from any outside source, but it seemed to be coming from within the substance itself. And the light emitted was strange. It could be stopped by nothing—not even by the opaque wrapping of a thick sack that would otherwise keep even the harshest sunlight out. Detailed examination by Madam Curie and her husband, Pierre Curie confirmed the initial observation that the light was being emitted from within the substance itself. Now the million dollar question was—where was this energy coming from?

'This was finally worked out by Marie Curie and she was able to prove that the emission of this light energy was the result of a spontaneous decay in the atomic structure of the substance itself. She named the material Radium, in recognition of the fact that the substance was spontaneously radiating energy.'

I finished my rather long explication by concluding, 'This substance is what causes the greenish glow that we see in wristwatches and alarm clocks, which helps us see the time in the dark.'

'Such watches were very popular when I was a student,' observed Guruji with a chuckle. 'But the smartphone killed them!' I laughed with him before continuing my narrative, pleased that it was going smoothly.

'This was a dramatic discovery,' I elaborated. 'It showed us that substances could spontaneously break down into lighter elements while emitting energy. The possibilities were endless. If one element of the periodic table could spontaneously decay then it was possible that other elements could decay or be broken down as well. Not to mention that this was the first live example of the conversion of matter into energy. Guruji, as we all know, this led to the invention of the atom bomb and the advent of nuclear energy. Both these applications are nothing but a man-induced breakdown of the Uranium or the Plutonium atom.'

'The discovery of Radioactivity, as it was called,' I went on, 'led to the scientific quest opening up again. The indivisibility of the atom, which had been an accepted fact at that point in history, was proven to be false and the search for a common minimum base started all over again.'

I took a pause before trying to inject some humor, 'Scientists again asked themselves—"Mirror, Mirror, on the wall, which is the most fundamental particle of them all!"'

'Yes,' laughed Guruji. 'It must have been frustrating for the scientists to have to start their quest afresh after thinking that it was nearly over.'

I replied, 'Yes Guruji, and this is a common pattern in science. Just when scientists think they have arrived at the highest peak of knowledge, or the lowest common element, as the case may be, they find that there is another higher mountain still left to climb…'

'Or a further depth to be plumbed,' Guruji interjected, 'and this is true not only for science but every other aspect of life as well. Even in spirituality this is the common refrain. The spiritual seeker has always wanted to believe that he has reached the final frontier, the final God! But only on reaching it does he find out that there are still many gods left to conquer! But do carry on.'

I continued, 'Today the search is at a point where it is known that the three subatomic particles—protons, electrons and neutrons—are composed of further smaller particles.'

I paused to collect my thoughts, since I was now getting into the real unknown part of science—the part that modern scientists were grappling with today.

Here goes, I said to myself and dived right in, 'What lies underneath the proton is a strange new world, Guruji, far removed from the earlier one. This innermost world resembles a world of magic, where protons disappear when broken down!'

'What do you mean?' asked Guruji.

'Officially,' I explained, '…The remnants of a proton are called quarks but since these quarks have a very short life, it is akin to the proton disappearing when broken into pieces. This is the equivalent of breaking a single piece of wood into two pieces—but finding that the act of breaking makes those two pieces disappear. That's why I called it magic!'

As I said that, I recalled my conversation with Dr K all those years ago…

'The original question raises its head once again—where does all this come from and what, if any, is the common source?' I wondered aloud. 'And, Guruji, that's not all. Once the proton breaks down further, it does not lead to a further simplification but rather to a further complication of the state of affairs. As scientists are discovering to their chagrin, the world below the scale of the proton consists of literally hundreds of extremely fleeting particles that scarcely have an existence. Scientists give them strange names: Quarks, Leptons, Gluons, Bosons etc. The situation today is such that scientists have been forced to admit that their assertion that space is empty is probably not true. Instead, the nothingness of space is speculated to be pregnant with possibilities and if you boil empty space with energy, you could theoretically produce matter from nothingness.'

I continued, 'And the scientific explanation is equally incomplete when it comes to the four forces of nature. As I mentioned in the beginning, the four forces are the electromagnetic force, the two nuclear forces—strong and weak, and the force of gravitation.'

'How are the scientific explanations for these four forces incomplete?' asked Guruji.

I replied, 'The model of the atom that scientists have constructed is able to satisfactorily explain the force of electromagnetism as a part of its design. Electricity is explained as the flow of unattached electrons, while magnetism is a twisting force that develops when electrons spinning around the nucleus create a perpendicular thrust, rather like a vertical axis that is created by a spinning top.'

I paused to organize my thoughts before continuing. 'The explanation for the nuclear forces is more indirect. They are explained not empirically—that is, not by direct observation—but purely by deductive logic. Nuclear forces have never been measured and they are thought to exist only because there is no other way to explain the structure of the nucleus of the atom—the way it appears in experiments. The logic is that if positively charged protons attract the negatively charged electrons to create the stable atomic outer structure, then by the same logic, all the positively charged protons sitting squashed together in the tiny nucleus should be repelling each other with great force. That should make the nucleus unstable and liable to fly apart. But we know for a fact, through experiments, that the nucleus of most atoms is a highly stable entity. Scientists have tried hard but they have been able to break the nucleuses of only the Uranium, Thorium and Plutonium atoms—only three elements amongst more than a hundred that are known, and that too has not been an easy task. Enormous energy is required to do so.'

'If my memory from my school days serves me right, what you are describing about the attraction between the electron and the proton—isn't that Coulomb's Law?' asked Guruji.

'Yes, Guruji,' I replied, even as he continued as if clarifying things in his own mind.

'And if I remember correctly,' he mused further, 'Coulomb's Law states that opposite charges should attract each other and like charges should repel each other. Isn't that so?'

'Yes, Guruji,' I said again.

'And that is why,' he continued, 'negatively charged electrons circle the positively charged protons in the nucleus. And this is also why the protons within the nucleus should fly apart, as you said, since they are all positively charged! Is my understanding of what you are saying correct?' asked Guruji.

'Precisely,' I said, relieved that Guruji had understood what I was explaining.

'Please continue…' said Guruji and I did.

'To explain this anomaly,' I offered, 'scientists were compelled to invent a new type of force. They called it the strong nuclear force. The term *nuclear* relates to the fact that this force acts within the confines of the nucleus and the term *strong* indicates that this force is stronger than the electro-magnetic force. Scientists speculated that an extremely powerful attractive force must exist, and that this force must be stronger than the electrostatic force of repulsion between the positively charged protons. Thus the nuclear force was thought to prevail within the nucleus while the electrostatic forces prevail over the longer distances within an atom.'

'Mind you, all this is pure deduction. The actual nuclear force has never been measured,' I concluded my mini speech. 'Guruji, so this is how the three forces have been explained by scientists as of today. Gravity, of course, has not been explained as yet.'

'I thought that the force of gravitation is also well known since the time of Newton?' asked Guruji.

'No, Guruji, it is not,' I replied. 'We know how to calculate the force of gravity very precisely, and that's why people think that we know it. But we don't know anything about its nature or where it originates from,' I replied.

I stopped. It had been quite a long talk and I wasn't sure if Guruji had grasped all the concepts.

I waited for Guruji to say something and after a while he spoke. 'So, Saagarji, we have these three building blocks and we have a set of four forces that together make up matter and the functional universe. Is that right?'

'Yes, Guruji. And we have energy in the form of photons.'

'Hmm…' said Guruji and went into a long silence. I waited.

It was quite a while before Guruji opened his eyes and looked at me as if from another world.

'I think it is time for me to put the whole thing together in the right perspective…'

THE THEORY OF EVERYTHING

I leaned forward with anticipation as Guruji started. 'It is obvious to me that protons, neutrons and electrons come from an underlying source. The forces you mention could not be the cause of creation but are simply the manifestations of an underlying cause.'

I replied, 'Guruji, we do know that protons, electrons and neutrons are constructs of subatomic particles which come from the strange underlying world I just mentioned, but how can we conclude that the laws are the consequence and not the cause of creation? Scientists think of it as the other way around. Einstein and Planck, two famous scientists, in fact joked that God created matter and Newton's three laws of motion, and the universe started functioning!'

Guruji spoke, 'I will get into that later, but the first thing I can say is that we cannot start from here as these facts are intermediary facts.'

'Yes, that's a fair statement, but in such a situation, from where do we start, Guruji?'

'Let's start from what we know. Something that is incontrovertible and unconditionally true through induction or direct deduction, and that which does not require complex mathematical derivation.'

No math! Wow! 'Why no math, Guruji?" I demanded. 'Isn't math the language of science? Without formulae and quantification how can we quantify this creation? And isn't that our aim?'

Guruji smiled, 'Math may be the language of science but it's not the language of creation. I say again—complex mathematics has no place in creation. Whatever needs to be calculated is at an elementary level, a yes-no type of calculation.'

'Why is that, Guruji?'

'Whatever happens in the universe can be explained by a set of relationships that the scientists call laws. But are the laws actually used to run the universe? The simple answer is: No.'

Seeing my puzzled look, he explained. 'The laws of physics simply express an underlying reality. Just as your image in the mirror is a reflection of you but is not you, and the temperature of your body is an indication of the heat contained in your body but is not the heat in the body, similarly the laws of physics are a reflection of, rather than a cause of how the universe behaves. If the underlying reality changed, then so would the laws of physics. The only reason the laws appear constant is because the underlying cause remains consistent in the long run.'

I must still have looked uncertain, because Guruji continued patiently, 'Saagarji, we humans have been observing the universe intelligently for a few hundred or at most a few thousand years, while the universe has existed for billions of years. Why do we assume that the laws have been the same quantitatively for all that time? Why couldn't the speed of light have been different in another time?'

'But scientists say that it is a constant!' I protested.

'Scientists say that it is constant but do they say why it is constant at 300,000 kilometers per second or thereabouts? Maybe they are right about the constancy of the speed today but that constant could also be changing or evolving over the billions of years that have passed since the universe came into existence. Is that not possible?'

'How, Guruji? Isn't that just wild speculation on our part?'

'No, Saagarji,' Guruji said firmly, 'I am speaking scientifically. Until such time as scientists can explain exactly why the speed of light is 300,000 kilometers per second, this constancy will always be under question.'

I asked, 'Guruji, so what you are essentially saying is that unless we are able to understand the underlying causes, we cannot truly understand the laws, and if we do understand the underlying cause, then we would be able to derive all the laws of the universe?'

'Yes, precisely! And I am also saying that the laws are the reflection of some underlying fundamentals that scientists are as yet not aware of,' Guruji replied.

So if we understood those underlying reasons we would arrive at the Theory of Everything, I thought to myself.

'And I am also stating,' Guruji told me, 'that the four forces that you just described are not external to the matter they act upon, but emerge from the construction of the matter itself.'

'How can we say that for sure?' I asked, since I didn't understand how he could have come to that conclusion.

Said Guruji, 'Let me give you a practical reason as to why the laws of physics cannot be external to the matter they act upon,' Guruji said. 'If that were the case, we would need to have a central controller. That controller would first be communicated the mass of atoms, based on which it would calculate the applicability of the appropriate laws. Then the conclusion would have to relayed back to those particles. This scenario would require a pre-existing system and a medium for communicating these laws through time and space. And that's not all. The speed of communication required to implement this system, the way we observe, would violate the laws themselves.'

I didn't understand a word but I did understand that that controller would be the God that all religions worshipped. Why would Guruji be arguing against the concept of God?

'What do you mean?' I asked. 'I presume that the controller would be God himself?' And why would you be against the concept, being a guru and all? I added silently to myself.

Guruji answered my questions both spoken and unspoken with a laugh. 'I do believe in God, but not a central command-post type of God, that's all. The reality, by logical inference, can only be that every part of the universe is intelligent and, by implication, conscious, the laws of physics reflecting the sum total of the inevitable and very basic actions that are happening in its every pore.'

'But Guruji, aren't all these just assumptions that we are making? What basis do they have?' I was forced to ask. After all, if I had set out to challenge the assumptions that the scientists and the theologians made, we couldn't be guilty of the same crime—in effect replacing their arbitrary set of assumptions with our own arbitrary set.

Guruji replied, 'I am not making any assumptions about the nature of the universe as yet. We are just talking about the practicalities of creating and controlling a large system in an orderly manner and in a way that the laws, which are only the symptoms, aren't violated—that's all I am trying to do right now. Let me ask again: can we have a universe where results are dependent on calculations or formulae made by a central command? Is that possible?'

'Why not?' I asked mulishly. Science was very clear that the laws of physics governed the running of the universe.

'If we have a central command mode, then requests and orders would have to be transmitted across vast distances. In effect, the central command would be doing calculations for planet earth, for the hundred billion stars in our Milky Way and for the 100 billion estimated such galaxies in the universe that each contain a hundred billion stars!'

'I blinked, quite overwhelmed at the picture Guruji was painting as he went on, 'It boils down to this. If one object strikes another, like two balls on a billiards table, then who decides to implement Newton's laws of motion? Would it be a supreme central commander or the balls themselves?'

I had to smile at the imagery as Guruji continued. 'So the question is: Is there a man on the moon, a super computer or God sitting somewhere who figures out things, passes messages not only to our planet but to each and every phenomena that happens in the entire universe?'

'I assume that God, being omnipotent, can do that!' I said, a bit peevishly.

'Let's study the whole thing through logic,' said Guruji soothingly. He could make out that I was having difficulty with this. 'If God was running the whole show from a central command mode, then messages would flash from the billiard balls to that commanding authority and that commanding authority would be sending back the instructions, right?' Guruji asked as if he was explaining things to a child.

I didn't really understand the arguments that Guruji was throwing like thunderbolts and I guess it showed on my face.

'Ok,' he conceded, 'let me take a specific case to make it simpler. Let's take gravity. Science says that nothing moves faster than the speed of light, yes?'

'Yes,' I replied. 'Even gravity obeys the speed limit of light.'

'Therefore,' said Guruji, 'if there was a centralized command post that receives requests, calculates and then issues instructions, then it would first receive the request from the two balls in question at the speed of light, apply the formula and then send back the instructions, again at the speed of light, right?'

'Yes…' I admitted as I thought through the maze of words Guruji was throwing at me.

Guruji smiled triumphanly, 'That leads to an anomaly. The two balls interact gravitationally with each other at the speed of light, but if the instructions were sent to and received from a central command then that process would be at least thrice as long, wouldn't it? The instructions would first go to the central command at the speed of light and then come back at the speed of light and then the action would take place at the speed of light. That is three times longer, –at least, than how it happens in reality! What do you think, eh?' smiled Guruji impishly.

I suddenly understood what Guruji was alluding to. It was a brilliant yet simple point. Sending and receiving instructions wasn't possible, as that at least tripled the time that the original action took. That meant that the original action itself precluded the central command model.

'This one fact proves that there is no central command anywhere,' Guruji continued. 'The God-on-a-throne concept is practically and logically not possible. Yet the fact is that the universe remains in order. The question is—how does it do so?'

Clearly Guruji was being rhetorical, so I kept silent.

'It can only be,' Guruji continued his analysis, '…that each pore of the universe is able to take these decisions on its own—decisions that honour a basic design principle. The laws that we see are the cumulative sum total of these minute actions that are taking place consistently all the time, all over the universe. At the particle level, a member of the universe interacts only with its neighbour. If the neighbour pushes, the particle gets pushed and it pushes someone else! That's why we need no maths…'

I was still mystified and he figured that from my face.

'Tell me Saagarji, what do you do when you are hungry and you find yourself alone at home with no-one to cook up a meal for you?' asked Guruji.

'Huh…' I said under my breath. This was obviously going to be a metaphorical question so I better be careful, I thought to myself, 'Ummm Guruji, I would go into the kitchen, open the cupboards, find whatever snacks I can…and eat them… or I would take a couple of eggs from the fridge, boil them and make a meal out of it with some bread and butter...and I would make myself a cup of tea. That would do the trick quite nicely.'

'And what do you call this activity?' asked guruji.

'What do you mean?' I enquired, confused.

'I mean, do you have a name for this activity and is there a logic to how you would behave?' Guruji's voice was impish but for the life of me, I couldn't figure out the trap.

'What logic could there be Guruji? Except that I am hungry and that dictates what I do.' I replied.

'Do you not follow any mathematical principles as you go about searching for your food? Are there no mathematical formulae involved in your behavior?'

'No, Guruji, and now you are pulling my leg and I can't understand your point,' I protested, a bit flustered. I couldn't for the life of me figure out where he was going with this. An image of John Nash the schizophrenic genius chasing pigeons and writing down algorithms of their behavior flashed through my head.

'Saagarji, the point I am leading up to is that you may not be consciously using mathematics but mathematics is emerging from your behaviour. The scientists call this the Fibonacci series…kind of!' laughed Guruji. 'What is the Fibonacci? Take whatever is available and create something out of it.'

I sat there stunned as Guruji continued, 'Further, remember that where there is choice, there is intelligence at work.'

'How?' I asked, totally intrigued with what Guruji had just said.

'The choice at the particle level may be extremely rudimentary but it still exists,' he clarified. 'The choice of what to do when something happens to that particle has to be inborn and cannot come from an outside source. The actions and their responses have to be completely local. And that, my friend, means that there is intelligence residing in every pore of the universe even if that intelligence is of a very basic level. There is no other way for this to work.'

'But Guruji, if the intelligent consciousness, of which you speak, is very basic then how can such elementary actions and responses create such a complex universe?'

'What of it?' he shrugged. 'Isn't the complex computer world created by combinations of only two numbers—zero and one?'

I thought about that. In the computer world, 0's and 1's were the only two elements. Yet, using the logic written down by the programmer they were enough to create every combination that was the basis of all the characters, all the alphabets of all the languages, all the numbers from zero to infinity, all the 36 million shades of colours and all the logic required to create the World Wide Web. The movies we saw, the conversations we held, the businesses we ran, the coding and hardware and everything else we did on the computer was a product of only two basic numbers—zero and one.

Seeing my bemused look, Guruji smiled. 'Let me put it simply. Do you see the sunset?'

'Yes, Guruji, I do.'

'Do you think that God calculates it or does it happen because of the interactions of light, air, water vapour, clouds and many other things?'

'Obviously it's an interaction...' I said rather reluctantly.

'Mind you, it is an interaction that follows certain rules and regulations that are inbuilt into the basic particles that interact. That's an important thing to remember,' said Guruji, not at all put off by my reluctance. 'What if you had to create the exact same sunset on a computer? How difficult would that be?'

I considered Guruji's question. The answer was straightforward. It would require highly complex calculations and the hardware needed would have to have extreme capabilities. I wasn't even sure if there was a computer, as of today, that could do the job.

I answered, 'Guruji, it would probably be impossible. We would probably need an ultra-high-speed, supercomputer and a highly complex program that factored in every possible variable. The number of variables would also be very large. What you ask is actually being attempted. Scientists have been trying to create realistic models of global weather so that we could predict the exact weather but a totally realistic model exists only in the movies. Simply put—the computing power and the programming complexities required are beyond our capabilities as at this time.' I shrugged my shoulders, 'It may happen in the future. Who knows?'

'Yes, Saagarji,' said Guruji with a satisfied look on his face. 'And do remember that we are not talking about just one earth but the entirety of the universe—sunsets, sunrises, middays, creation, destruction and trillions of other activities and actions.'

I let this vast thought settle in.

Guruji continued, 'So Saagarji, what can we conclude from this inevitable logical analysis?'

I kept silent, my brain trying to find some logical inconsistency in what he was saying.

'Since every pore of the universe knows how to behave, it can only mean one thing—that every pore of the universe is inherently intelligent and therefore by implication conscious.'

I pondered over the ramifications of what I had just heard. According to Guruji, the laws of physics did not run the universe, it was run by a conscious and intelligent entity—the universe itself!

'How does *that* follow?' I wondered.

'Intelligence cannot exist without consciousness.'

'Why not and what is consciousness?' I asked.

'Consciousness has many meanings but at the most basic level it simply means to have awareness.'

I was perplexed, since inanimate objects such as robots also had a certain kind of awareness. They had artificially designed sense organs and they had a programmed intelligence—artificial intelligence as it was called.

'But Guruji, what about artificial intelligence, in that case?' I pointed out. 'Even computers show high levels of intelligence. They are intelligent enough to defeat human chess grandmasters, in fact.'

'Don't confuse calculative powers with intelligence,' Guruji advised calmly. 'Consciousness means that you have the power to make a choice or to discern between different things based on your desire for a certain experience. You might think that a complex computer program has that power but no computer program can ever be designed to take care of a basic possibility which every conscious being has.'

'What is that, Guruji?'

There was a theatrical pause.

'What?' I prompted, impatient for answer.

'Someone switching the electricity off! Can even the most sophisticated program control that?'

I laughed involuntarily at the image Guruji had created.

'Also please remember,' he added, 'that a computer is loaded with all kinds of programs and software but a human has to decide what program to switch on. For instance, even the smartest computer in the world cannot say to itself, 'I don't feel like doing weather forecasting today so I will play a chess game with Kasparov and for that I will have to call him on his phone and challenge him to a match. And since I don't have his phone number, I can hack into the Moscow phone directory to retrieve it. Or I could send him a friend request on Facebook and wait for him to accept it before I can challenge him to a match! And what if he doesn't want to play with me, a non-entity with no experience? What do I do then? Maybe I can hack into and take over Vishvanathan Anand's ID?'

I found myself chuckling and shaking my head with amused chagrin. 'Please note, Saagarji, that each individual task that I mentioned can be easily done by the computer if it is ordered to do so,' he observed, 'but the ordering and sequencing of these activities is desire driven—the desire to play chess with a grandmaster in this case. This kind of desire-driven thinking runs through the mind of every conscious being and even the lowliest form of life. Machines, on the other hand, are alien to the concept of desire. They don't even have an instinct for survival.'

He continued, 'Deep Blue, the computer that can defeat chess champions cannot do what even a 12-year-old human can do—plan to bunk a class to see a film! And it is not that our brains have more calculative power—they clearly don't. It is simply because we are conscious and have a stake in being alive, unlike the computer.'

'But Guruji even a human can be switched off,' I demurred. 'Isn't death that switching off? A soul needs a body to live and if we kill the body the soul is ejected automatically. Isn't that akin to switching the computer off?'

'Hmm...' said Guruji and retreated into one of those long silences.

I sat and thought quietly about what I had been hearing. This was very different from what I had expected.

Guruji's words interrupted my thoughts. 'Tell me, Saagarji, what came first—music or the musical instrument?'

A chicken-and-egg question! I thought to myself.

'Uh…music, maybe?' I ventured.

'No!'

'Then it must be the musical instrument,' I riposted.

'No!' Guruji shot back. 'Neither! What comes first, every time, when anything is formed from the formless soup of protons, electrons and neutrons, is the desire to create that object. It is desire that sculpts any object like a potter does with his wet clay. In the case of music, first comes the desire to create music, which is followed by the creation of the musical instrument and that's when music flows.'

I listened quietly. I was listening to a discourse that flew way above all the philosophy I had ever read.

Guruji continued, 'Just as the urge to express music must precede the creation of any musical instrument or even the rules of music itself, similarly the urge to live, to experience and to express through any and all means can come only through consciousness. The instinct to live, to survive under any circumstances also comes through that consciousness. Consciousness is that potent seed that creates everything that it needs. Like the bow of a mighty ship it cleaves creation before it, with its immense desire. Consciousness is unstoppable—something that lives and expresses itself under all circumstances, in any form, as a tree, a bird, an animal or a human or even as a rock! Consciousness has no shame. It will do anything to exist and expand—cannibalize anything to gather itself further! Therefore the Fibonacci series is so simple and so compelling. Take what exists already, use it to become something more, something else. Can anything turn this switch off?'

Guruji continued like a river in flow. 'Imagine, Saagarji, a seed that has lain fallow for thousands of years, in an Egyptian tomb, because it has not found the right type of nourishment. And then one day the tomb is opened, the seed taken out and planted—and lo and behold, it grows! How did the seed know that now the conditions are right? Think carefully, Saagarji. The only answer can be that there is a consciousness and intelligence within that seed that waits for things to be all right. It waits and watches for the time to be ripe. This is the difference between a machine and a conscious being. Only when a computer program starts expressing that instinct to live and experience, will it be able to challenge the dominance of humans and only then can it be called intelligent, not before!'

I thought about what we had discussed. The example of the seed lying fallow for thousands of years and then springing to life was a powerful example, as was the Fibonacci series analogy... And it meant that there was a logical basis for the existence of consciousness. This was a big step since this was something that the scientists denied as existing.

But that created a question for theologicians as well.

'Guruji,' I wanted to know, 'if that is true—the bit about God residing in every pore, why do we worship God as a form or a figure? And why does that form closely resemble the human figure? Why do we give names to that entity? Names such as Lord Narayan, Lord Krishna, Jesus Christ, Allah, Jehovah or some version of a fatherly figure who sits on a throne and hands out rewards and punishments...' I trailed off.

'That, Saagarji, is slightly beyond the scope of the question we are discussing right now,' he told me. 'We can talk about the nature of God once we finish talking about the nature of

God's creation. God is my pet subject, but what we are talking about right now is *your* pet subject! Let's stick to science and retrace our steps back to first principles. What can we say categorically about the universe that is true, whatever may be the circumstances and however limited our understanding?'

I was now totally confused. All that I had heard was creating a complete spin in my head. What I had assumed as fundamentals had been chucked into the dustbin. Since all my information was second-hand in any case, how could I vouch for anything as the untrammeled truth? And how could I separate pure facts from conclusions?

Guruji waited for me to speak, but when it was clear that I wouldn't, he said, 'Let me rephrase the question. What I am asking is that when we observe the universe through our senses, can we come to some basic conclusions that don't depend on any theory or any experiments?'

'But Guruji, as you have pointed out many times, our senses are limited. Even with the best telescopes and microscopes, we can see only so far, so deep or so magnified. How can we ever be sure that our knowledge is complete enough to make categorical statements?'

Guruji replied, 'I mean can you say something categorical about the universe even with your eyes closed? Something that is obvious?'

'We do know that the universe is an orderly kind of place and follows cyclic patterns…' I started tentatively.

'Yes, yes, that's a good start,' said Gurui encouragingly,

I continued, 'It exhibits certain and predictable behaviour and patterns and also seems to be evolving in a certain direction.'

Guruji spoke, 'Just the fact that the sun rises every day and the seasons chase each other with clockwork precision is enough to prove this point, isn't it? These observations are obvious and we don't need any scientific experiments to prove them, do we?'

'No,' I acquiesced.

'Then prima facie we can derive a few qualities about the universe,' he reasoned. 'One: that it seems to exist by design—that there is intent behind it, a purpose that exists even if we are not aware of it. Two: that it is structured with a few basic laws explaining its behaviour. And finally, that it seems to be evolving from point A to point B. The journey could be either cyclic or one-way. We don't know but change is obvious. Can we assume that the above observations are correct under all circumstances?'

'Yes, I think so.'

'All this points to the fact that there must be a Creator. Doesn't it?'

'How does that follow?' I demanded.

'How do you have intent, order and an orderly transition in a random system?'

'Can't that just be a coincidence? Sheer chance? Or simply that our universe is that specific one in a trillion where everything seems to be by design, while it is actuality not?' I asked. This was the standard argument that atheists used in every TV debate.

'Say that again. I didn't get that,' replied Guruji.

'Scientists say that our universe is perfectly balanced, not because there is some intent behind it, but because it is just one in an infinite series of universes and by sheer coincidence conditions are perfect in this particular one.'

'Oh that's nonsense. That's no different from the monkeys on a typewriter argument. You know, the one that goes something like if an infinite number of monkeys type on an infinite number of typewriters then one of them will type a play of Shakespeare and that would be just a coincidence. The question that atheists never ask is: Who created the monkeys, who created the typewriters and the English language in which the play is written and, of course, who created Shakespeare?'

That's what Science Baba had also said, I recalled.

'You know what's wrong with the atheists?' Guruji asked me.

'What?' I asked.

'That they are simply ungrateful. Every single thing in the universe, including their own very existence, is proof of the existence of that cosmic consciousness, but they deny it.'

I nodded. 'Yes, they call it coincidence or chemical reactions in the brain! I don't agree with them, but isn't that a logical argument that anyone can make?'

'Think about it, Saagarji. A certain situation could be chance but what happens if it is evolving in a predictable manner? Could that also be chance?'

'Why not?' I challenged him. It was important to clear up this point.

'Okay, let's analyze it from the point of view of the law of probability since that is how the extent of chance is measured. If I throw a dice and a six comes up, then that's chance, right?'

'Yes,' I agreed.

'A one in six chance, to be more precise,' said Guruji and I nodded. 'But what if I throw the dice six times and every time a six comes up?'

'It could be that the dice only has sixes printed on it!' I tried to joke my way out of it.

Guruji took me seriously. 'Okay,' he conceded, 'let me refine my argument. What if we throw the dice six times and it comes up as a perfect sequence? One, two, three, four, five and six—and this repeats every time we throw the dice? Could you classify *that* as a coincidence?'

I thought about it. Every time the dice landed in sequence, the probability of it happening would recede further by a factor of 1/6 and soon would be approaching infinitesimal figures. If I threw a dice 100 times—something that could be done in a few minutes—the odds of getting the right sequence would be 1/6 raised to the power 100, a number that is extremely small—one in a trillion, trillion, trillion, trillion, trillion, trillion, trillion, trillion! In fact this number would tend towards the infinitesimal within a few seconds of beginning the game. Nature had been playing this game for billions of years and that too on a trillion-faced dice!

If it was chance, it was one hell of a chance.

Guruji completed my thoughts. 'This is what most atheists forget. Chance may be superficially used to explain a static picture—one throw of the dice and the perfectly balanced universe came into existence. However, can that one throw explain a logically evolving picture that follows laws and rules? Come to think of it, can chance be used to explain why the offspring of a human is always a human? Or that of a horse always a horse?'

I played devil's advocate. 'The atheists say that the setting up of the system and its logic is sheer chance, but once the system does get set up, after that it has to follow the logic and orders that were set up in the beginning—by chance of course!'

Guruji snorted, 'A system that changes over time would always require an overseeing intelligent controlling agency that keeps the system on track by observing the behaviour of the system. And that is the Conscious Intelligence that I just described. I advise you not to get into debates with cynics. It is futile to argue with people who do so only with the purpose of proving they are right. Instead try to figure things out for yourself since only that is important. As Bernard Shaw famously said, it is futile to wrestle with a pig; you will only get dirty and the pig quite enjoys it!'

I chuckled as Guruji continued, 'What I am saying is that this universe is a live, functional, self-corrective and self-aware system and the overwhelming conclusion can only be that the orderly running of the universe is by design and not by chance.'

I mulled over what I had just heard. It was a strong argument, no doubt, and even if I didn't accept it completely at this moment, I could certainly go with the flow and hear what Guruji was saying.

And then I heard something that changed my life.

THE THEORY OF EVERYTHING
PART II

'So then how did creation take place, Guruji?' I asked, eager to hear the answer.

'If I recall correctly from my readings of physics when I was a student, a long time ago, we know from science that before the Big Bang took place, there existed nothing, not even space,' said Guruji. 'The Big Bang was the point at which creation burst forth from the size of a billionth of a pinhead to a functional, fully stocked universe in the fraction of a second.'

'Yes,' I agreed. This was a well-established fact.

'Now, if there is a Creator we would have to assume that he would have created this world from within himself, as before creation nothing would exist that resembled creation. Would that be a good assumption to make?' he asked.

'Yes, Guruji.'

'Can we assume this without reservation or exception?'

'Yes, Guruji, I would say that we could.'

'So we can summarize as follows. There is a Creator who is conscious, who is intelligent, who has a desire to create this universe and then goes about creating it methodically from his own essence and without having a central command module.'

'Yup,' I said. 'That sums it up well.'

Guruji continued, 'Mind you, Saagarji, we are not taking the religious, blind faith kind of route here. We are simply following a logical thought process to its conclusion just like scientists claim they do.'

I nodded my head in agreement. Nothing that Guruji had said till now had anything to do with religion.

'Let's take it further. The *created* rests in the *Creator* but it would be different from the *Creator*—the seed being different from the tree, even though it may have the potential to reproduce the tree exactly.'

'Again, yes!' I replied.

Guruji continued, 'As I was saying, a moment comes when this endless potentiality cleaves something different out of itself—a seed or a space, we may call it. This seed comes from this potentiality, but stands apart from it. Like a cube of ice flowing in water! Or like a giant Peepal tree that sprouts a seed. This thing that we may call the supreme consciousness sprouts the universe in a small part of itself. Imagine such a thing, Saagarji.'

I closed my eyes and tried.

Guruji asked, 'What should happen first?'

'What?' You tell me, you are the Guru—I invited silently. This is way beyond my pea-brain!

'Since nothing existed before in that ever-lasting seed of nothingness, the first thing that the Creator would need to create is Space itself. The dimensions—length, breadth and height—would come into existence and like scaffoldings that hold up a tented hall, volume would be the first to be created. Suddenly you have a separate entity in what was earlier an undivided, intelligent consciousness. A kind of bubble that is different from the rest. And what would that difference be?'

After a pause, he answered his own question, 'To be different from its origin, it would have to have the opposite qualities—it would be unconscious instead of conscious, divided instead of unified and ignorant instead of intelligent. Rather like a messed up Rubik's cube! Doesn't that sound familiar to our state of existence?' Guruji chuckled.

I laughed back and said, 'Yes! That sounds exactly like the world we live in!' And also like the state of my mind right now—I admitted silently to myself.

Guruji joined in the laughter and continued on happily, 'Essentially what has been created is an object on which work is required to be done to get back to its final state, rather like a CKD (completely knocked down) aero-model kit that you can order on the internet to build for yourself.'

Guruji continued, 'It's not a coincidence that the seers, the saints call this world *karmasthana*—a work place. Now that you have a place—a workshop, you can start working. The only condition is that the net work done must be zero. Whatever you do, the opposite is also done automatically, otherwise creation cannot be sustained. We can call it the ultimate "buy one, get one free" offer, and as Don Corleone so famously said, an offer you just can't refuse! You can call this the law of conservation of spiritual mass. The net impact of all the work done is zero and the Creator has to do nothing except to hold this division in place. Won't that be the simplest way to do it?' asked Guruji.

'I didn't quite get that.' I replied.

He explained, 'If you want to build a mountain, you have to dig a hole don't you? Where would the earth to build the mountain come from? From that hole! The result is that the net work done is zero. It's all just a rearrangement of matter.'

Wow, I thought. That's the law of conservation of energy simply explained!

'Get me a piece of paper,' Guruji ordered.

I took out my trusty square notebook, the one I used to jot down my designs.

'Draw a circle.'

I did.

Guruji carried on, 'Let's assume that space has already been created and we are in the first slice of time after the Big Bang. We have no materials yet, nor any laws of physics. Let us also assume that this newly created space is nothing but an elastic medium. And why is it elastic? Because it wants to contract back to its original form but something energetic is holding it apart.

'Somewhere in this space a pulse starts beating. From a circle of radius 'D', a force pulses both outward and inward. Since both these pulses are equal and opposite, the net force is zero. Yet the geometry is such that the pulse that heads outwards dissipates into the distance, pushing out all before it, while the pulse that heads inwards from the perimeter of the circle, comes together into a crescendo, pulling in everything from the surroundings. Let us assume that this pulse beats in a regular rhythm of a certain frequency, creating two regular impulses of push and pull in the surrounding elastic space. We could call these pulses repulsive and attractive forces also, since one of them pulls everything towards itself and the other one pushes out everything before it. Since the force that pulses inwards comes together at a point and the force that pulses outwards dissipates into the distance, the inward force would be slightly more potent than the outward force, although the difference in the two magnitudes would be very small.'

As I finished drawing the diagram, Guruji asked. 'What do you say, Saagarji?'

I pondered over the diagram. It was relatively straight forward geometry.

'Seems fine, Guruji,' I replied.

Guruji continued, 'What would happen to an object in space as it is impinged by these pulses periodically?'

'I expect that any object in the vicinity would experience a rocking-the-boat kind of movement with a gradual tendency to be pulled in towards the pulsating circle, since the attractive pull would be slightly stronger than the repulsive push?' I ventured.

'Yes...precisely.'

I wondered where all this was leading.

Then came the shocker.

'Can we call this pulsating point a proton?'

'Hold it! What?' I literally jumped out of my chair.

This was wild. My mind raced over all the stuff that we knew about the proton. Luckily I had boned up on it only this morning from Wikipedia, in preparation for this meeting. This is what Wikipedia had to say: *'The proton is a subatomic particle with the symbol p or p+ and a positive electric charge of 1 elementary charge. One or more protons are present in the nucleus of each atom. The number of protons in each atom is its atomic number. The free proton (a proton not bound to nucleons*

---

[4] https://en.wikipedia.org/wiki/Proton

or electrons) is a stable particle that has not been observed to break down spontaneously to other particles. At sufficiently low temperatures, free protons will bind to electrons. However, the character of such bound protons does not change, and they remain protons.'[4]

Scientists further stated after experiments that the proton was a highly stable particle that had an extremely long life. And when protons were smashed in a particle collider they broke down into smaller particles called quarks. Two up quarks and one down quark to be precise—whatever that meant. And of course, the strange part was that the quarks had an exceedingly short life span and disappeared almost instantaneously when the proton broke up. The unanswered question was: how did three completely unstable and short-lived particles combine together to form the most stable particle in the universe? This was one of the great unsolved mysteries of science. Another of the 'we don't know yets,' by the scientists.

Did Guruji's way explain the characteristics of the proton better? I thought through what he had just said. Essentially Guruji had defined the proton in a completely different way—as a pulsation and not as a material entity. As if someone was methodically and periodically pinching and releasing an elastic sponge. If the proton was a vibration as he said, what would happen when you smashed a vibration? I tried to visualize it. I imagined a stable steady pulsation in space and I imagined an object—another vibration being the only possibility—coming in at high speed and hitting this stationary vibration. With my mind's eye I could see the answer. That first stable vibration would break into some forms of unstable vibrations that would go twanging off into space. Like a jack-in-the box flying off as soon as the can was opened. No one could predict where the pieces would fly off to. And here was the significant point. If the proton was a material object that exploded, pieces of the breakup should be found somewhere around. But since actual experiments in particle accelerators could not find the leftovers, the results were impossible to reconcile with the proton as a material particle. But what about the proton as a vibration model that Guruji was offering? That offered a more convincing explanation. Like a whirlpool dissolving in water, a proton would simply melt away, like the quarks did in particle accelerators.

Guruji continued even as I fought battles with what I was hearing. 'What we have is a pulsating entity that consists of two forces running in opposite directions, their net effect pulling on the surrounding medium. Although this entity is balanced, yet the original act of creation of the proton should throw off a countervailing pulsation as well. Something that is an inverse pulsation to the first one.'

'Why, Guruji?' I interrupted.

'Simply to create an opposite action to the original action. And what would that be, Saagarji?'

I sat and thought. A proton was two up quarks and one down quark and its opposite, the mirror image, should be two down quarks and one up quark. That sounded vaguely familiar. Where had I heard of one up quark and two down quarks before? I racked my brains…Hold it! Wasn't that the composition of a neutron? I asked Guruji for a minute and googled it on my phone. Yes! There it was! Two down quarks and one up quark constituted a neutron.

Hmmm…interesting, I thought to myself. So if the neutron was the mirror image of the proton, then shouldn't it have the opposite characteristics? That is, shouldn't the neutron have a negative charge, since the proton had a positive charge? And why did the neutron have such a short lifespan as compared to the proton that had a very long life? That didn't gel with the known facts about a neutron…

Guruji, on seeing my furrowed brows, commented, 'Stick only to basic thoughts right now. Don't add your existing pool of knowledge to what I am saying. Remember we are starting from scratch. All we have right now is a pulsating circle in a dense elastic medium. There are no pre-existing forces or materials here as yet. Right now we are talking about only simple mechanical movements.'

'Okay,' I said.

'First, mirror the behaviour of the proton pulse…' Guruji said, 'From the circle we drew.'

I started thinking. If the proton was a combination of a pair of movements that started from the perimeter of a circle with diameter 'D' then what would be the opposite movements? Well, instead of two forces pulsing out from the perimeter of a circle of Diameter 'D', it would be the other way around. Two pulsations would start but this time one would start from the centre of the circle and the other should start from 2D—twice the diameter away from the centre of the circle. The first movement would pulse outwards towards the perimeter of the circle while the second movement would pulse inwards towards the perimeter and—hey, hold it! They would hit and neutralize each other at exactly the perimeter of the circle! Again I ran over the visualization in my mind's eye. Yes, this should be correct. This movement that I had just imagined in my mind's eye would be the mirror opposite of the one that had created the proton.

And importantly enough, this model explained why the neutron would have no net charge. But one major question remained: Why did the neutron have such a short lifespan?

I tried to calm myself down. Thoughts were running like startled rabbits through my head. The implications were huge. Prima facie, Guruji's model was explaining things that science had been unable to explain—ever! This was new! This was path-breaking! I again closed my eyes and imagined a proton pulsing rhythmically. As it pulsed, it threw off an opposite swirl. What would happen to that swirl? It should go off veering into space and die away, somewhat like the whirlpools that the oar of a boat creates as it chops through the water. This would mean that the proton was the original creation and the neutron was simply a byproduct. But that raised the subsequent question: how did the neutron have a long life within the nucleus of the atom but a short life outside?

And then it came to me like a revelation! As the protons in a nucleus pulsed, they threw out neutrons as opposite reactions. Every group of protonic pulses created an equal number of neutronic pulses! Two things could happen to the neutron. One—the emitted neutron would hit the neighbouring protons and bounce back and forth between the group of protons that were close together in the nucleus. And the other possibility was that the neutron would not hit a neighbouring proton and would escape into space and die away…And this explained what had never been explained before—why there was no neutron present in the nucleus of the hydrogen atom! Since there would be no neighbouring proton to bounce back the emitted neutron, it would be lost to space…

Wow! I said to myself. Guruji's model explained a fact that scientists had no answer for: Why is the Hydrogen atom the only atom not to have a neutron? The answer as per science was unknown but as per Guruji's model was that the Hydrogen atom was the only atom that had only one proton and therefore the neutron that was produced with every pulse of the Hydrogen atom proton was simply radiated off into the surrounding medium.

But Guruji's dependence on the elastic medium was troubling. The Michelson–Morley experiment and many other similar experiments had conclusively proved the non-existence of ether. Patience! I told myself. All in good time. I would cross that bridge when I came to it.

'Yes, Saagarji,' Guruji was mind-reading as usual. 'The neutron's behaviour and nature, as shown in experiments, support the postulate I am making. That's the only way a neutron can be an antonym of the proton in its structure and yet have a short lifespan. Oh, and have no charge either.'

'Yes, Guruji,' I grinned back.

Guruji smiled back. 'The logic is simple, sunlight bathes the sky even at night but we see the night sky as black. The reason is that there is nothing to reflect the light that is passing through the night sky into the retina of our eyes. But what we do see is the moonlight which is nothing but sunlight reflected from the surface of the moon into our eyes.'

I smiled weakly at Guruji. He had explained, without even working up a light sweat and without even touching a pen and paper, a fact that had foxed scientists. The trouble was that the implications of this model were completely destructive to the existing well-accepted tenets of modern science. I decided to carry on with my questioning and leave the mastication of what I had heard for later.

'How are electrons created?' I asked Guruji.

'Electrons and protons are the only two original creations. That is why they have such long lives. The other particles, neutrons and positrons, are the counterbalancing movements—reflections that fade with time.'

'And what about quarks?' I asked, 'How do they combine to form protons?'

'Quarks and all such fleeting particles are not real. They do not combine to form protons.'

'What!' I said, 'How is that possible? What you say is completely against what the scientists say.'

'Huh,' said Guruji. 'If I am wrong, then please show me one experiment where scientists have combined quarks to create protons. What they have been able to do is only smash protons to get quarks. Isn't that so?'

'Yes, but—so what?' I replied and Guruji reacted patiently.

'Listen carefully to what I am saying, Saagarji. I am stating that the basic units of creation are the protons and the electrons. They are created as a whole and not as a combination of smaller entities. When they are smashed, by nature in the cosmos or in the lab by scientists, we get those hundreds of quirky and unstable entities that are given these strange names by scientists. The basic point is protons and electrons are the stable, fundamental units of creation. They are the wholesome entities that combine to form molecules and all the complex materials we see in the universe. Let me repeat—*My contention is that the proton and the electron are the fundamental building blocks*. You may smash them but you get nothing useful in return. And this is the inflexion point in science. The search for the smaller particles below the proton and the electron is doomed and it only takes scientists further and further away from the search for the fundamental particle…'

I sat quietly. Listening to what Guruji was saying...thinking of what I was hearing and the person who I was hearing it from. I could only fall silent in the face of the inescapable logic of what I was hearing. How was this man sitting before me, casually explaining things that had perplexed humans for centuries? *Was this how ancient Rishis operated when they wrote all the stuff they did?*

But this man in front of me hadn't finished shocking me with what he could see in his mind's eye! And it must be quite an eye!

'This pulsating point would attract everything in its vicinity, won't it?' Guruji continued while I was still mentally gasping for breath.

'But protons are supposed to be positively charged and they should repel other positively charged particles.' I said plaintively. 'Coulomb's law says so!' My years of scientific study and beliefs were beginning to smoulder at the edges.

'Can we replace the word *positive* with the word *attractive* for a minute and take this argument wherever it leads us?' Guruji said soothingly. He could probably make out that I was having a tough time letting go of my burden of already learnt knowledge.

'Yes,' I replied, 'Why the heck not? Since we were out to overturn conventional wisdom, why not go the whole hog?'

'Let me summarize what we have discussed about the proton and you will see why I am saying what I am saying,' said Guruji. 'We have a pulsating point in space that pulls and pushes all surrounding objects rhythmically. There are only two other types of objects in space—electrons and other protons and both are pulled in, since the attractive force is slightly stronger, as our diagram indicates.

'Notice that protons may come close,' he continued, 'but they will not fuse since they are independently pulsating entities. And remember, there is nothing else in our dense elastic medium. The only forces we have are the ones that are pulsating from inside the proton and the electron.'

I opened my mouth to speak and then shut it. Guruji had just shot down the concept of the most powerful force in the universe—that of the nuclear force. He deemed it unnecessary! In his model, the complication of the nuclear forces was not required to hold protons together in the nucleus.

Guruji continued, 'The trouble with the way science has postulated the structure of matter is that they think of matter as something inert and the forces that act on the matter as something alien to this matter. That's not true at all. The fact is that each unit of matter—and there are only two types, the proton and the electron—are nothing but pulsations of specific strength and design that are creating ripples in the elastic medium in which they exist. Since the points of vibration are distinct they can never merge with each other. The protons get pulled together because of the net attractive force, but they can never fuse together. There is no need to invent the strange and contrived entities called the nuclear forces, since even without that force the nucleus is stable as per the explanation that I am giving,' Guruji said softly, with his eyes sparkling.

Yet I had to protest. 'Guruji, you are explaining something that has already been explained. Your explanation sounds robust and, let me admit, intuitively correct, however, unless this theory explains something new, I mean some fact that the conventional theories cannot explain, I see no reason to switch over to this new theory…' I trailed off, since what I was saying sounded slightly rude but I had to say it, nevertheless. I had to stick to my guns, since that was the scientific way, after all.

'Saagarji, hold on! There is an advantage to this model.'

'What?' I asked.

'We can explain the force of gravity and we can explain the speed limit of light through this model. It's all clear to me.' Guruji was suddenly all smiles.

I looked at Guruji with amazement.

'If we replace the word *positive* by the word *attractive*, we would solve two major problems,' He told me. 'It removes the problem of having to explain how positively charged protons don't fly apart when stuck together in the nucleus and secondly, it leads to an explanation of the great unexplainable in the standard model—the force of gravity!'

I looked at Guruji goggle-eyed. He was speaking the language of a seasoned scientist.

'But how can we call something *attractive*? That's not a scientific word!' I complained. 'Positive attracts negative and negative attracts positive. How can something be generally attractive? And gravity has been defined as not a force but a tilt in the space-time continuum by none other than Einstein himself!' I added as an afterthought.

'Saagarji, you haven't thought through your science properly.' There was gentle reproach in Guruji's voice. 'There are many things in the world that are purely attractive. A whirlpool in water is always only attractive. It pulls in everything, doesn't it? So does a Black Hole! And have you forgotten the force of gravity which only attracts?'

I shut my mouth that had started to hang open.

'Let us proceed further,' he continued calmly. 'A proton is sitting in space, pulsating. It attracts anything and everything. Free electrons running around are the first to get attracted and an electron soon starts rotating around the proton. The moment that one electron marries the proton, the attractive power of the proton is consumed and it no longer has the power to attract any other electron. A stable union is formed. We call this union a hydrogen atom. And what is the nature of electrons? They are energy junkies! They suck in energy and eject it out like jet engines and use the thrust to move around. The greater the energy available, the greater is the speed of their movement. Now imagine the situation from the perspective of an unattached electron. It is riding the empty elastic medium, which we call space, using the energy it gains from radiation—photons, that is. Suddenly it gets the attractive pulse of a nearby proton. It starts rotating around the proton. In a sense it feeds off the energy that the proton generates as it pulses—something like a daredevil rider in the well of death in a circus. The original speed or energy of the electron and the attractive pull of the proton combine to put the electron in a stable orbit around the nucleus.'

'But, Guruji,' I interrupted, 'Why doesn't the electron spiral into the nucleus?'

Guruji answered, 'This is because the proton is essentially shoving out two opposite waves—one attractive and the other one repulsive. The two waves that are emanating from the proton, one pulling and the other pushing, have a phase difference and that creates ripples in the surrounding medium. Electrons can generally be found in the troughs of those ripples.'

I didn't understand and I said so. Guruji replied, 'Please draw the sectional diagram of two waves that have the same wavelength but have a phase difference. You will find troughs and peaks. Electrons will typically be found in the valleys where they will continue to reside till a large energy differential forces them to eject either to a higher or fall to a lower orbit. In that sense their orbits are quantized. All-in-all the electron will be found in a convenient trough wherever the centrifugal force is counterbalanced by the attractive force.'

'Okay,' I said, trying to take in all this.

'But do you notice something interesting, Saagarji?'

'What?' was all I could manage to croak, since everything he was saying was interesting—not to mention confusing!

'The electron may be using the attractive pulse of the proton to circle around the nucleus, but it can't be everywhere at once. As the proton shudders out one attractive pulse, it sends out the two waves in all three directions. The electron rushes around its orbit sucking up the energy generated, but it can't be in all the spots at once. And the electron can only go in a two-dimensional circle while the pulse is radiating in three dimensions. Therefore a certain amount of the attractive force will leak out, however efficient the electron may be in sucking in all the energy.'

'Yes, that sounds reasonable...' I said, trying my level best to sound intelligent.

Guruji interrupted me with, 'This leftover attractive power that leaks out is nothing but the force of gravitation.'

'How does that sound?' Guruji asked, his eyes twinkling.

I was stunned...

'Now you know why I was insisting on calling it an attractive force as opposed to a positively-charged force!' he pointed out cheerfully. 'And this is why gravity is so intimately linked to mass, since the mass of the universe is essentially the sum total of the mass of all the protons inside it.'

This was crazy! This was awesome! Guruji was actually offering an explanation for the force of gravity. And interestingly he was explaining it as a force—as Newton had done—and not as a tilt in the space-time continuum as Einstein had postulated.

'But hold it,' I thought to myself. That would mean that if protons lost their electrons for any reason—science called them ionized—then their gravitational pull would be stronger and a lot stronger at that!

I croaked, 'Does that mean that if we had the same number of protons but this time without the electrons around them, then they would exert a greater gravitational force than those with electrons?'

'Hmm...' Guruji thought for a minute before replying. 'Yes, I would expect so. That could be a good experiment for scientists to conduct and a good way to test this theory. Can you devise an experiment to test this?'

I thought about it. We could take two equal portions of Hydrogen gas, weigh them to make sure that their weight was equal, and then ionize one of them so that its electrons escaped the container. The gas without its electrons should have a heavier weight if this hypothesis was correct. Even an ordinary weighing machine of a decent sensitivity should be able to measure the difference. Suddenly another thought struck me, which would be an even more elegant way to test this theory. The logic would be as follows.

When any substance is heated, it expands. This is a well-known fact. The logic is that when an electron orbiting an atom gains energy, it jumps to higher orbits. Since the perimeters of the orbits have now expanded, more gravity should leak out as the electrons would have to cover much wider areas to consume the energy of the proton's pulsation. That should make a heated material heavier on a weighing scale. I racked my brains for any known scientific research on this. I could half-remember something that I had read a long time ago. Yes sir! There was! The planet Mercury showed an anomaly in its orbit around the sun that was hard to explain. Mercury, being close to the sun, experiences extremely high temperatures. Essentially Newton's formula for the calculation of the force of gravity between the Sun and Mercury was being distorted for some reason. Scientists didn't exactly know why. Could that be a proof of what Guruji was saying?

'Worth exploring…' I said to myself. To Guruji I said, 'Yes Guruji, I think an experiment can be devised to check this out.'

'Let us meditate on this, Saagarji, before going further.'

I sat and thought about what I had heard. My mind was whirling, not meditating! Testing what I had heard against what I knew as scientific evidence, trying to find some loophole.

I couldn't locate any obvious flaw.

The most amazing part was that Guruji was reducing all this down to a simple pulsating movement of only two entities—the proton and electron and, of course, the elastic space…

I awoke from my reverie. It was time to bring out my reservations about ether—the medium that Guruji was so heavily dependent on for his explanation.

I voiced my misgivings. 'Guruji, there are two problems with what you are saying. All that you say depends on the existence of an elastic medium through which all this happens, but no such medium is known to exist. In fact ether, as this medium is called, has been proved convincingly to not exist by the Michelson–Morley experiment. And your hypothesis is also in direct contradiction with Einstein who explained gravity as a sag in the space-time continuum rather than as a force.'

'Let's take the second objection first,' said Guruji cheerfully, not at all perturbed. 'You said that thinking of gravity as a force is outdated since Einstein explained it as a bend in the space-time continuum. Isn't that the basis of your objection?'

'Yes, Guruji,' I replied.

'There are problems with Einstein's explanation, Saagarji. Thinking of space as a tarpaulin seems convenient on a YouTube video but in reality can anyone explain why this trampoline bends only downwards? Why this partiality for the downward direction? Is there a force that pulls everything downwards? That would be like explaining the force of gravity by assuming another mysterious downward force! And how many tarpaulins will you stack up one over the other to explain the thickness of the universe and what happens in between the layers of tarpaulins? That is, if you have to do inter-tarpaulin travel as comets do or as even our satellites and aircraft do when they travel across the North and the South Pole, which are perpendicular to this space-time fabric! Not to mention the fact that there is not a shred of physical evidence for such a structure. Mind you, a structure that is strong enough to hold a star or a planet in its embrace at a certain plane but gossamer enough not to be discovered by the most delicate of instruments!'

Yes, I said to myself. This was essentially what I had argued with Professor Sood, so many years ago. It was gratifying to have my adolescent question ratified.

'Scientists say that gravity also travels at the speed of light and not instantaneously.' I half muttered to myself since that wasn't connected to the immediate discussion.

Guruji latched on to it. 'That is redundant in any case!'

'Why?' I enquired meekly. 'How can gravity instantly establish itself between objects that are freshly formed and are far flung from each other?'

'Please think it through,' he admonished. 'There are a lot of superficialities to what you are saying. First of all, the universe is converting a lot of mass into energy as stars burn in their thermo-nuclear fires, but is energy congealing to form mass anywhere in the universe? Einstein does give the relationship between energy and mass but in the excitement no-one notices that it seems to be mostly a one-way relationship. Nothing in that famous equation $E=mc^2$, indicates that you can only do this one way. But that is the observable reality in our universe…'

I asked, confused, 'What is that? I didn't understand.'

'The fact that mass is being converted to energy but energy is not being converted to mass,' he answered. 'This raises the interesting possibility that all the mass was created in the beginning and it is slowly being converted into energy. Like a large bank balance from which only withdrawals are taking place, it will ultimately run out and so will our universe! And if mass was created in the beginning then all that is happening is a subsequent rearrangement of gravitational relationships rather than creation of new ones. That's why I said that the word *instantaneous* is not relevant in the case of the force of gravitation, since all the mass created has been around for a very long time. No new mass equals to no new gravitational relationships…so whether gravity is instantaneous or it travels only at the speed of light is basically a moot point.'

'What about stellar nurseries where new stars are being formed?' I ventured, still perplexed.

'That's not new mass, just a reorganization of stellar dust into a more compact area. Were I a scientist, I would probably call this the law of conservation of gravity!'

My head was spinning. I went through my checklist. In a short afternoon I had been offered an alternate explanation of the nature of protons, electrons and neutrons, I had been explained why the nuclear force was unnecessary to explain the stability of the nucleus of the atom and I had been given an alternative explanation for the force of gravity. And since electromagnetism was already explained…could it be the theory of everything? And there was another startling conclusion. Pulsations couldn't just happen on their own. There had to be something or someone who caused these pulses to beat regularly and eternally. Guruji called it an all pervasive, conscious intelligence.

'This is revolutionary, Guruji,' I couldn't contain my enthusiasm. 'Maybe we need to write a paper on this and submit it for scientific scrutiny.'

Guruji shrugged. 'What for? I have no interest in it. For me it is not worth the paper it is written on!'

'Why not?' I asked, stunned. Guruji was shrugging off what seemed to me a revolutionary new theory of everything. Scientists would kill to present this paper to the world…This was the Holy Grail of physics!

'Just imagine! If the theory of the universe is so entrancing to you, how enchanting would the Creator be?' My thoughts were interrupted by Guruji's words.

I gave him a quizzical look and he explained, 'Suppose a famous painter lives permanently in your house and he makes painting after painting on a daily basis. What would you do if some guests came to visit? Show them the paintings or introduce them to the painter?'

I said sheepishly, 'I would, of course, make sure that every guest of mine meets my famous guest.'

'Precisely! That's what I am doing as well!' said Guruji with twinkling eyes. 'Introducing you to Him! And believe me, when we have the Creator in our hearts, everything else pales in comparison. I for one can think of nothing else.'

Guruji continued, 'For me, the importance of this conversation and of answering your heartfelt questions is only this—that you come face to face with the reality and inevitability of the Creator. That you accept from your heart that the universe simply cannot exist unless there is a Creator. My only purpose in this debate is to help you believe in Him, so that after today, you are unable to deny Him.'

Guruji's eyes penetrated mine as he spoke. Although impersonal, they pierced through me, propelling me into a distance that seemed to vault infinity.

'Saagarji, have no confusion. I answered your question not to help you publish a scientific paper. I did so only because you genuinely wanted to know how God created the universe so that you may understand the purpose of existence and how you fit into it. Wasn't that your original query?'

'Yes,' I replied.

'Now I have done my job. I have explained through logic that which you call the theory of everything. I have shown you how the only way the universe can be created and can be run is by and through God himself. Everything—the physical, the mental, the emotional and the spiritual—has emerged from the Creator. Your body is a subset of God's body; your mind is a subset of the universal mind and your soul is a splinter of the soul of God. And that is true not only of you but of everything in creation. Even a proton is nothing but a soul that has been given the task of pulsing in and out of existence by the Creator a trillion or more times a second. A splinter of God is made to believe that it is a proton and it finds meaning in pulsating for billions of years. Another splinter believes that it is Saagar, that it has this body and mind to command and do the things it wants to do. And this splinter does that diligently. Can you not see this, Saagarji?'

'Yes, Guruji,' I said simply. It was true…

I sank back into my comfortable seat. It was as if soothing rain was washing over me. Just knowing and believing that this world could not exist even for an instant without the Creator changed things for me. There had to be a God, and a grand design, for the universe to exist, and that meant that I had a purpose as well. All I had to do was to find it. And that was not all. Whatever had happened to me or would happen to me, good or bad, would also have a Godly purpose.

In that instant I was healed, my mind and heart finally coming to rest from my restless unending search. The vague sense of unease was finally gone as if it had never existed. I held a delicious secret in my heart, a knowledge that scientists would kill for—and yet I also knew that in itself the knowledge was worth nothing. This knowledge was as valueless or as valuable as a symphony written on sheets of paper. With no one around to play the notes, those sheets would be worth nothing, but if someone picked them up and played the music that was written on them, an entire universe could be created. Living in this universe was worth nothing unless we didn't connect to the source.

I had been given a golden opportunity to realize this fact.

I opened my eyes and looked at the man who had made it possible. I found him looking back with unshuttered eyes, as he usually did.

He said softly, with a stare that seared my soul, 'Why does the Creator do all this, Saagarji? Why go to all this trouble?'

I waited for the answer.

'The answer can only be that He desires to create this universe and that desire is what fathers everything that exists. And what happens when he has created this universe? He populates it with himself. Creation is the vessel that he creates out of Himself, so that his soul—He himself, can enter and reside in it. The universe is like a house that is built so that someone may live in it. From the body of God comes the body of the universe and from the mind of God comes the consciousness that runs the universe. Who are you? Who am I? Nothing but a part of the universal soul. We are He himself—unlimited, endless, eternal—living in this limited body and universe only to provide a portion of the experience to our Father who views what we experience through the window of our individual soul.'

'Never forget this basic fact and never overemphasize the house. Remember that you live in this body only because you are deluded that this body is you. Delusion is the only way that you can be kept here.'

Guruji continued speaking slowly, emphasizing every word, 'No jail can thwart the yearning of an enlightened soul that longs for its true home, so God created, through *Kaal*, the ultimate illusion. Maya, as we call it. Maya keeps the soul entranced. The idea or the design is such that the soul remains identified with this creation of God rather than with God Himself. The trickery is no doubt clever, but it can succeed only as long as the soul is deluded and is tempted by this world of sensation. Once a soul realizes this chicanery, it finds the easiest way to leave. That's the state of enlightenment.

'And what's the job of a guru? To help you become aware of your delusion. To help you get rid of the personalized form of what is essentially universal delusion. The Guru does this so that you become the opposite of what you are today. *Unified instead of divided. Conscious instead of unconscious. Endless instead of limited. Instantaneous instead of painfully slow and clumsy.* How does that sound, Saagarji?' Guruji raised enquiring eyebrows.

'Like being in heaven!' I smiled back, unshed tears brimming in my eyes.

Guruji smiled kindly, his voice a gentle murmur, 'When you realize this truth, not theoretically but from your being, you will be able to move galaxies with a wish, since you are an irresistible force moving a puny object! Realization is as simple as that. Like getting up from this chair and sitting in the next chair!'

DEVOTION

I sat there as if pole-axed, my whole body shuddering with these immense thoughts, my being vibrating like a flimsy net tied across the maw of an erupting volcano.

This is what it feels like, my conscious mind wondered, to chase a dream and find it coming true. I felt a deep sense of achievement and satisfaction flowing through me. The satisfaction of having found out the theory of everything—my childhood goal, of having reached a cherished milestone; I felt at peace in my heart. An 'all is right with the world' *kind of feeling came over me. This was a delicious secret that I hugged close to my heart. I felt a new sense of purpose, an elegant reorientation and certain knowledge that I wasn't just a random reversal of random chaos.*

A thought arose—that there was no fear, no loss, no tragedies in life, just the cycles of creation going on. I hadn't lost anyone. My father's soul was just on its own journey. We had been fellow travelers on a journey called life and we essentially derived ourselves from the same source.

Thrills chased through my body like bolts of electricity. I couldn't explain even to myself what I felt as I sat there before Guruji. It was as if I was resonating immensely and in that resonance, I lost my petty self.

I felt as if I was flying through the sky, yet there was no fear of falling. This was my own space, my territory and I was the lord of all I surveyed. I could see, in front of me and around me and through me, creation pulsating in-and-out of existence, a trillion beats a second—and yet I could count every single beat. Creation and annihilation dancing in harmony and the whole fabric of creation pulsing in and out of existence, creating the hum of the cosmic motor.

Guruji's voice rang out from another dimension.

'Saagar, do you find your life hard? Do you find it a struggle? Do you find that whatever you pay attention to improves but the other aspects suffer?'

'Yes, Guruji.'

'That's because you are living your life clinging onto that net of wires called creation, much like a trapeze artiste! How can life be easy if you have to spend most of your energies hanging on for dear life?'

'True, Guruji.'

'Let it go!'

'No, Guruji, I will fall. I will die!'

'What if I tell you that you will not die? Not because you are special or anything, but because you simply cannot die. No one can kill you! Now can you let go of the fear born of ignorance—the conditioned response that keeps you hanging there?'

I gritted my teeth, tried to let go but couldn't. My fingers were claws, refusing to obey my command, holding the ropes in their death grip.

'You may be hanging on for dear life but the ground is just six inches away from your feet! Let go, I command you.' Guruji's voice boomed again—and yet I couldn't let go. Instead, I sobbed and said to him, 'I am scared, I don't know what will happen, I want to trust you but I don't know how to...'

Guruji's voice softened. 'Let go! Feel one with the eternal spirit that sustains and nourishes each one of us.'

Still I clung on, stubbornly, and his voice became soft like the murmur of water flowing gently down a mountain stream, 'Alright, then. Let go and I will catch you...I promise...'

And with that I did as he asked.

I fell. I was in free-fall and there was no-one to catch me and the ground wasn't just six inches away. Guruji had lied. I panicked as I picked up speed, plunging towards an endless but inevitable bottom. I felt as if I was fainting and I felt my innards convulsed sickeningly. The taste of bile filled my nostrils as I picked up speed towards the bottom—that must exist, surely? I gasped at the air whooshing by, like a man drowning. I couldn't breathe. Was I having a heart attack? I couldn't die. Not like this—ignorant, unfulfilled and betrayed! I wouldn't let go of this life, I decided frantically, but how could I hold on when there was absolutely nothing to hold on to? My fingers turned into claws and my nails ripped off my fingers as they clawed for my survival as I slid down that immense cavernous tube of nothingness.

My life flashed before me. It had been of no use. So much promise unfulfilled...What was the use of this wasted life? What was I holding on to? I was tired, tired of somehow staying on top of things, trying to make sense of senseless things. Better to die and let it all go. I felt myself give up, then. Let me die, I prayed. Let me sink into a comfortable numbness.

I felt myself slide into a mire of sleep. I felt myself losing consciousness. And yet I was wide awake as I watched myself sink. I saw my fears, my worries and sorrows blow away like dry and dead leaves in an autumn wind. What were they, in any case? Just a tattered bundle of petty concerns that no one else gave a damn about! Let them go, I told myself. They were irredeemable in any case. I sank down further. Hopeless. Sedated. Squelching into a comfortable morass. Further and further into the earth as my feet scrabbled for a bottom that didn't exist.

And then at some point in that fall, I stopped falling. I looked down but I still couldn't see the bottom. I could see my body falling further. I watched it fall away into the endless pit and slowly disappear from sight. Was I dying? Leaving my body? It was strange to watch something go that you believed was you. And it felt alright. If I could be without my body then why was I so worried about it in any case? And it wasn't just my body that seemed to be missing. I couldn't feel that worried, anguished, sorrowful nature that had been so much a part of me all my life. Where were they—my body and my mind? If I could exist without them, then it obviously meant that I had no need for them; I was eternal. Was I special, then? Was I God?

As that question arose in me, I saw the answer arise as well. No, you are not particularly special, I was told—just as special as everyone else. The only difference is that you can see yourself for who you are. The others can't as yet.

We are all one, I recognized in that moment. Just deluded. And if we are all the same, then how could I lie, cheat, kill, betray another? That would be like betraying myself! And what need did I have to do any of that— just to preserve this unnecessary body and mind? I had no needs. I was complete…all I could do was help someone more deluded than I was…only that was a job worth doing…

I opened my eyes with a start. Maybe it was a dream—a wonderful one, no doubt, but a dream nevertheless.

Guruji was smiling at me. The words he spoke next proved that it hadn't been a dream…

'Yes, Saagarji, if you realize that all beings are one, you will automatically follow all the rules.'

I felt tears rolling down my cheek. My father had died and I still felt his loss, but we weren't separate in any case. We were only going through our own cycles of birth and death conditioned by our pet peeves. It was no big deal! As I let that particular sorrow go, all other sorrows I had been clinging to also followed suit…

My eyes closed again and I found myself sitting in the lotus position, still and immense as a rock. Even as I sat, I was outside my body, looking down on it. It seemed immense, glowing an intense golden brown, a perfectly proportioned torso, flowing out into arms and legs that showcased their strength and sturdiness simply by the way they looked. It looked like the form of a young bodybuilder in his prime, rather than the skinny and ungainly body that I remembered as mine! And it wasn't just my body that I could see and feel. I could feel the reverberations of my heart that was beating in this steady rhythm that resonated with the pulsations of the universe. And as I glanced around, I could see Guruji sitting right next to me. The universe felt like nothing but an extension of my body. I felt that all I had to do was to shift a bit and the world would shift too. I tried it. I tilted my weight and I saw the universe slide. 'Careful' said Guruji, tilting in the other direction to counter balance, 'You just caused an earthquake! Read about it in the newspapers tomorrow!'

This is what the earth element is, I recognized. Stable, inert, immovable and completely dependable. Its job? Providing a platform for God to rest the universe upon.

As I revelled in my strength, my stability, my invincibility and ability to move mountains on a wish, I felt myself flow like lava. Everything about me was quicksilver—like a pool of mercury heated beyond its limits. Everything merging and flowing together, wiping away differences and barriers. Long-held opinions, beliefs, angers, fears, and anguishes disappearing. Yet it felt cool and refreshing, life-giving and healing the sorrows of the world. Oh, this is what the water element is like, I thought with surprise. Ever-flowing, life-giving, forgiving, merging all differences…

And then I felt a heat emanating from within. A deep fire, like a furnace, As if I was entering into the heart of the Sun itself. My inner core was invincible and cool but my outer being was intense—like a thousand blazing suns. I felt the energy percolating through me and out of me and throughout the universe. This, I understood, was the fire element—Shakti. This is what provides the energy to do things. As I went within the fire, I could feel the cells of my physical body dancing like sparks in a blaze. I could feel my body being deconstructed and then being reconstructed in a different way, I could feel the balances of the tattvas *(elements) being restored and rejuvenated. My body felt light and strong. An ache that had been my constant companion ever since I had dislocated one of my shoulders, 15 years ago, miraculously disappeared—healed in an instant.*

And as that passed, I felt a wind beginning to blow through me. A great gushing, shrieking melody that breathed in and out rhythmically. Prana Vaayu, *I recognized. The universe is alive, it breathes just as I do. The moment I recognized that, everything went still. There was just immense space. Silent, quiet, peaceful, forgiving, nurturing. The womb of creation from where everything emerged and where nothing ever changed. The cradle where everything is born…*

I looked around that vast emptiness. Wait! What was that? The emptiness seemed to be full of translucent bubbles of bright sparks, glimmering like fireflies, pulsating in and out of existence. My vision zoomed in closer, as if my eyes were a telephoto lens. And suddenly I was within one of those bubbles, diving in. I was zooming into an entire universe. Galaxies zipped by and I went past stars and solar systems, zooming in further and further till I knew I was within the heart of the proton itself. There it was—pulsating, thumping out its heartbeat steadily as the fabric around it crinkled in waves, just as Guruji had described...the entire cosmos was pulsating in a steady beat…

I gently zoomed out again and the cosmos receded and became a faint bubble silhouetted against countless other bubbles…

I was finally at peace, I wasn't that small puny being called Saagar who struggled with his life. This was who I really was. This immensity. This sublime entity who could travel at the speed of a wish. This was my heritage, my ancestral property. I was lord and master of all I surveyed. I could move things with a wish. As I looked around and up, I spotted a gateway on top at a far off distance. What is that? I wondered and in an instant I was there. Oh! This is how Guruji does it! Travel at the speed of thought! How simple it really was. Just let go of your petty self which is scrabbling in the dirt and you can be this immensity that can go anywhere and everywhere you please…

I looked around and I could see an opening in the distance. An ethereal light was emerging from it. I headed closer. What lay beyond? I could hear a melody coming through it. A vibration that sang through my body. This new immense body that I had—could I go through that door with these new powers of mine? Just as I thought that thought, I saw the familiar form of Guruji standing there. He was smiling. 'Don't you think you have had enough fun for one day, Saagarji? Come, let's head back. We can do the rest another time.'

'Yes, Guruji,' I responded, elated to see him. He was my guide and guru. Without him I was nothing.

He nodded at me and I found myself descending through a narrow and increasingly constricted space—and suddenly I was awake, in my own body, sitting on the soft carpet.

Guruji was not in his seat. I stretched. I felt wrung out but elated. What an experience! Out of habit, I looked at my watch. Wow! It was 5 in the evening. I had come here at 11 in the morning. Could I have been sitting here for 6 long hours?

Guruji walked in and handed me my mobile phone. 'I had it removed so that you may not be disturbed.' He smiled at me. 'How was the experience, Saagarji?'

'Amazing!' I said and fell at the feet of the man who had shown me a new world. There were no words to express my gratitude, so priceless was this gift. Guruji helped me up and made me sit down on the sofa. I was trembling all over with energy flows popping all over me.

'Saagarji, you have had this experience because for a few moments you were able to leave your petty ego. This is a gift from God to the one who can do that. It is a welcome home gift. This is an indicator of what your life can be, if only you align yourself to God's path and sublimate the physicality that weighs you down.'

'Yes, Guruji. What can I do to always be in this state? I don't ever want to be lost to this experience again and I don't ever want to make even an inadvertent mistake.'

'Don't worry,' he assured me kindly, 'once the current starts flowing, it claims you as its own and guides you till it forever transforms you. But don't think that the work is complete; actually, it has just started. The sincerity of your seeking and the quality of your being—the way it is at this point in your life—has opened the door that otherwise remains firmly shut to unworthiness. This vision and this experience have been shown to you because you are now worthy of walking the path back to your essential self. There will be many realizations and transformations along the way. There will be experiences that you cannot even imagine right now. There will be many further rejections of falsehoods and notions that are only the ego's false dreams and there will be things, events and people coming to your life to help you on your journey.'

I listened to Guruji's words. He was trying to tell me something, even warning me. I asked humbly, 'Guruji, I am a nobody who has been blessed by the infinite kindness of the Creator. It has not been my capability that has brought me here. In the future, as I walk this path, I fear that I may commit a transgression in my foolishness. How do I ensure that I never ever do that?'

Guruji smiled, 'You have just been shown the entirety of creation. You have seen how it is a single living being. How everything is connected to and depends on everything else. You have also realized that creation starts as just an idea. The Lord, the Creator lovingly creates this universe and many others out of the desire to create and experience Himself. He sends his own self to create and be created. It is He who is the material, the workshop, the designer, the designed and everything else in between.'

Guruji continued in a resounding voice, 'As the Lord says in the Gita, He is the father and mother and grandsire of the universe. He is the object of knowledge and the purifier. He is the syllable Om and He is the Vedas. He is the goal, the sustainer, the master, the refuge, the witness, the abode and the most dear friend. He is the Creator and the annihilator, the very basis of everything. He is the ritual, the sacrifice, the offering, the sacrificial fire, the clarified butter that is offered and the ladle that makes the offering…

I, you and all this'—Guruji gestured around the room—'are He Himself. If you keep that sense of oneness in your heart and remember that everything you see around you is nothing but yourself in another form, you will never go wrong. You may not fully understand and realize the vastness of what I am saying; that is the work that is yet to be done. That Oneness, that Love, when realized, completes you. But even if you understand this theoretically, it will keep your journey honest and true. I can tell you that as long as you sincerely seek, you will be guided. So my advice is to live normally just the way you always have, but now dedicate all that you do to Him—the supreme guide and provider. Do that and gradually this state will become second nature to you.'

I leaned back in my chair. My heart overrun with thrills and my eyes brimming with unshed tears of joy. Boy, what an explanation! What an experience! I wished at that moment that my grandmother was alive. I now knew what it meant to have a real guru. The same life seems so different and alive when you understand the real reasons and only a true guide could help you see that.

I looked at my guru. What a man, what a life—a selfless dedication to helping others. After all, what did he have to gain out of this? But then I had learnt the answer to that question. He couldn't help himself. It was simply one brother helping another. Or a man whose wealth was endless helping another to discover the same vein of gold.

Guruji smiled, reading my thoughts once again. 'I do get something out of this. I will tell you that I am also being judged by God by the number of souls I am able to bring to the glow of enlightenment. The more souls I bring, the more pleased will my Heavenly Father be with me. I am doing this to please Him who, I might add, is your Progenitor as well.'

Guruji fell silent. So did I. There was no need to say anything. Only to be thought and experienced and welded down into my soul.

I finally got up silently, touched the feet of the man who had given me everything that I could imagine—and everything that I could never have imagined.

AFTERMATH

I came back from my reverie and found myself at my desk. The sun was on my face—a sign that it was noon—and I found the young man sitting across the table.

I said to Ashish, 'What a life it's been since that day with Guruji…'

'Was this the time you started on the path of being an inventor?' asked Ashish.

'Yes. Pretty soon after that. That was the start. That day unlocked me. Not just spiritually but in every other way as well. Ideas, feelings, and a million other things started flowing through me effortlessly as if I was a perennial river. Every moment, every thought, every feeling gradually became one of gratitude and happiness. A feeling of blessedness percolated through me, just for being alive. Even the bad stuff that had happened in my life was good, strange though it may sound!'

I recalled those momentous days, as I spoke to Ashish. It was like a film reel running, so strong were the memories. 'It was a process that unfolded over the next several months. I sat with Guruji every week, meditating, and learning to fly through the inner worlds and understanding them. Guruji even took me through that doorway from which I had heard the celestial music coming that first time and I discovered the worlds beyond. We also discussed the Theory of Everything in more detail and we completed every aspect of it.'

'Yes,' interrupted Ashish. 'I was meaning to ask you about that. There are many things in the Theory of Everything that you haven't explained and there is also a basic confusion that I have…'

'What things?' I asked.

'Things such as the explanation for the speed of light, the Michelson–Morley experiment, black holes, action at a distance…' Ashish said, referring to his notes. 'Could you please talk about those?'

I cocked my eyebrows at Ashish, teased, 'You want to know all my secrets!'

'Not if it is a secret you don't want to reveal!' came the pert reply.

'Hmm…' I said and thought about what Ashish was asking. I came to a decision.

'I have only described those parts of the Theory of Everything that reveal the nature of God and the fact that this universe cannot be created or sustained without there being a Creator. My explanations of the Theory of Everything are at odds with many scientific theories, which are still considered valid. So for my explanation to be true, many existing theories of science have to be disproved. And to do that, I will have to engage in a far more rigorous exercise than your readers may be able to handle in this interview...We could, however, take it up for later, as a separate article, if your magazine so desires.'

'But...' interrupted Ashish, 'Sir, I am very curious about the explanation for the constancy of the speed of light. Why 300,000 kilometers per second? If you could explain only that? Just for my personal understanding?'

'Alright, Ashishji. Let us understand the concept of the speed of light. Tell me, how is speed defined in science?'

'Distance covered by an object divided by the time it takes to cover that distance,' answered Ashish promptly.

'Yes. That is what it is. Now, as you may recall, I have already explained that the universe consists of an elastic fabric through which light travels.'

'Yes, sir,' said Ashish deferentially. 'However, you haven't explained how the Michelson–Morley experiment is flawed... and that is a necessary condition...'

'Yes, yes,' I interrupted, 'But I won't do that now since that will make this discussion too technical. For the moment, let's just accept my assumption and continue with my postulate. We can proceed on the understanding that my postulate would be deemed correct only if I can prove that the Michelson–Morley experiment is flawed.'

'Okay, sir,' said Ashish, 'Fair enough...'

'So as I was saying,' I continued, 'there is an elastic medium and all that lies in that medium—protons, electrons, neutrons, etc—pulsate in and out of existence at a certain beat, or "frequency" as it is called in the nomenclature of physics.'

'Okay,' said Ashish, listening hard.

'You would recall,' I continued, 'that I had the vision of the universe as a pulsation?'

'Yes,' replied Ashish.

'The universes pulses—and what are the two ends of that pulse? At one end is nothingness and at the other end is creation. That means that the universe is flashing in and out of existence a trillion or more times a second and all objects in the universe appear and disappear at a certain frequency. It's Lord Shiva's drum or *dumroo*, as our scriptures call it.' I paused to let the point sink in before continuing. 'The universe shimmers like a hologram and in each shimmer or pulse, a photon can travel the distance of one unit…'

'What does that mean?' asked Ashish, his brow furrowed, 'I didn't quite understand.'

I thought for a while. I would have to find another way to explain this complex concept.

'Okay, let me explain this through a thought experiment. Let us imagine a group of marching soldiers. Let us assume that they can take a stride of any length since they are all supermen! But let us impose two conditions on them. First, that we have laid out a series of equidistantly placed stones in their path. They can step on only those stones. Second, that they have to march to a drumbeat, just as an army contingent marches in the Republic Day parade. Is that clear?' I asked.

'Yes, so far,' said Ashish and I continued.

'So what would be their speed as they march? Simply the distance between one stone and the next divided by the time between two drumbeats—right?'

'Uh-huh. Yes,' said Ashish, clearly concentrating on every word I was saying.

'That is how it is with a light photon as well. It steps from one node of the universal fabric to the next at every drumbeat or pulsation of the universe.'

I paused for a bit again so that this could sink in.

'Can you visualize it, Ashishji?' I asked to make sure that he had understood what I was describing.

Ashish answered, his brow furrowed, 'Yes, kind of…'

'Okay…' I continued, '…So the speed of light is simply the distance between two nodes of the elastic medium divided by the time period of the pulsation of the universe.'

Ashish gave this some thought before exclaiming excitedly, 'Yes sir! I see what you mean! If we assume that the distance between two lattice nodes is D and the time of the pulse is N…Though we may not know these values individually, we do know that if we divide D by N, we will get the figure of 300,000 kilometers per second.'

'Yes, precisely!' I smiled. 'And what if I increased the distance between the stones on which the soldiers march and keep the drum beat at the same frequency? Won't the speed of the march increase since the distance covered in each drum beat is more? And what if I slowed down or speeded up the drumbeats frequency? Won't it impact the speed of the march as well?'

'Yes sir!' Ashish said excitedly.

I continued, 'Note the implications, please. If my hypothesis is correct, then in the beginning, when the universe had just been born and when its size was much smaller, the distance between the nodes would also have been much smaller. Hence the speed of light should also, by logic, have been much slower. The million dollar question is—could the speed of light have been 300,000 kilometers a second when the size of the universe was just a pinhead? I would say NO! And I would further say that as the universe expands, the distance between the lattice nodes increases. As a consequence, the speed of light becomes faster and faster…'

Ashish interrupted, his eyes shining brightly, 'I understand! The same logic must work in reverse as we go into the past towards the Big Bang…The distance between the lattice nodules would shrink and the speed of light would become slower and slower.'

'Correct!' I told him. 'Again, this gives a robust explanation of how light must have behaved in the early universe. If we were to believe the scientists and accept the fact that light has always travelled at a speed of 300,000 km/sec whatever the size of the universe, then the pea-sized universe must have been a blinding kind of place with a single photon passing you billions of time a second, bouncing off the walls of the tiny universe!'

I paused for effect. 'See the inconsistencies and logical fallacies in what the existing theories say when examined closely?'

'Yes, sir,' Ashish agreed, suddenly pensive. 'What you are saying destroys the very basis of the age of the universe calculations, since the constancy of the speed of light is a key component of that calculation.'

'Very astute of you,' I remarked. 'There are so many staggering implications of what I have just said that I feel sorry for the scientists! And if I ever do decide to make all this public, then we will be releasing the fox in the chicken farm! Maybe that is one of the reasons for my laziness—I don't want to destroy someone's illusions!'

Ashish grinned back. 'I don't agree with your noble sentiment, sir! I for one can't wait for that day, if and when you decide to do this, but I must bring your attention back to the Michelson–Morley experiment, since your theory completely rests on disproving that.'

'You are persistent but I will resist the temptation to brag. I won't get into a detailed explanation of why the Michelson–Morley experiment is flawed but I will leave you with two compelling thoughts.'

'Which are?' prompted Ashish eagerly.

'One—why do proton beams, when shot out at high speed in particle accelerators, oscillate like waves instead of travelling like projectiles? After all, if space is empty then the trajectory of a material particle should be that of a projectile and not a wave oscillation. The only answer could be that just as a speedboat bounces up and down while travelling through the sea, the photons of light, the beams of electrons or protons will oscillate only if they encounter the elastic fabric that my theory depends on. There can be no other explanation for the oscillation.'

'And the second?' Ashish asked after mulling over what I had said.

'Einstein's own statement when he presented his theory of relativity. He clearly states that he postulated that theory only because the absolute point of rest—the basis of the universal coordinate system—could not be located. Einstein clearly says that because of the failure of the Michelson–Morley experiment in detecting ether, the concept of relativity is the only way to calculate the movement and location of all objects in the universe. The negative result of the Michelson– Morley experiment is thus central to the need for the theory of relativity.

I continued, 'Imagine the scenario if the Michelson–Morley experiment is wrong. The implications are staggering. Einstein's theory of relativity will become redundant, in that case, by his own words! And our dear scientists will be running around like chickens with their heads cut off! What I am saying, my friend, is a very big deal in the annals of physics. Everything that has been worked out in the last 100 years is up for grabs!'

'And you are saying, sir, that you can prove that the Michelson–Morley experiment is itself flawed?' asked Ashish, looking awestruck.

'Yes,' I said simply, 'But no more on this, or we will get sucked into a scientific debate that you will find hard to understand.' I closed the topic firmly.

Ashish looked as though he wanted to argue, but thought better of it. Instead, he ventured after a pause, 'I wanted to also ask you about the term Creator or God that you frequently use. Who is God? Is he Lord Vishnu, or Lord Shiva or the God who visited Abraham? We have so many gods and I am confused about which God you are referring to.'

'The God I refer to is the Creator of all,' I responded. 'Even the Holy Trinity of Brahma, Vishnu and Mahesh have been created by Him through the agency of Maya—the female creative principle. The Lord I refer to is the Creator even of *Kaal*, who is the first step in the creation of the universe. The mindboggling fact is that our souls, yours and mine, are nothing but slivers of that Creator. They have been in existence since before the universe was created! We—our souls, that is—are older than even the deities we worship, The gods are themselves just souls like you or me, the only difference being that they have been assigned specific duties. The gods have been brought into existence by the Creator to carry out the various tasks of creation, maintenance and recycling of the universe. The saints and seers call creation "Brahm". The Creator and we—the individual souls, have an existence which is beyond Brahm itself. The area that lies beyond *Brahm* is called *Par-Brahm*. That is an eternal place not subject to the cycles of creation and destruction. That is from where we come. The irony is that the Creator—the Lord of all, lives in us, unrecognized and unacknowledged! Isn't that strange, Ashishji? That we are so unaware…that we look for relief and blessings in all places except where they are to be found?'

I continued, 'The good news is that no one who genuinely seeks can be ultimately denied, but the bad news is that God hides in plain sight simply because we don't seek him. We seek everything but God!

'To get back to the end of my story, to sum it up, what essentially happened that day was that for the first time, I got clear proof that I, that is me, was a separate entity from my body and mind. And I learnt that I could, with my own will, jump across the chasm and take the inner road whenever I wanted. The inner world was so seductive that I was hooked. I got into the habit of meditating at every opportunity. Twenty minutes was all that was required, sans the preparation, and whenever I had a bit of time in the midst of my work, I would sit and meditate. Flights, taxis, trains, hotel lobbies—all were great spots. In the office, I would disappear into the toilet and meditate. People thought I had constipation!'

Ashish laughed involuntarily and I joined in.

I continued, 'Guruji gave me many tips and practical guidelines to help me master the techniques. Over the subsequent weeks and months of meditation, I travelled across the inner worlds and saw with my own eyes the wondrous visions of God's creations. There were momentous changes to my personal life as well. It was as if the Creator had taken me in hand and was introducing me to all the things and all the people that were required to help me on my path.

That was also the time I met the person who later became my wife and spiritual companion. She had a major role to play in my explorations of the inner worlds—what I was hinting at to you just now. If Guruji gave me the theory, then I did the practicals with her! And Ashishji, as I mentioned, the transformation is something that is not just mental but something that changes you physically. Your body changes, your senses change and you find all kinds of amazing things happening to you.'

'What kind of things?' asked Ashish, curiously.

I hesitated. These things were intensely personal and not meant to be shared. I *could* mention a couple of things, though.

'The smell of flowers, for instance.' Ashish gave me a quizzical look, so I explained, 'One day I woke up with my senses intoxicated with the smell of flowers. I looked around but there were no flowers to be seen anywhere! Over the next few months I was inundated with the most entrancing fragrance, I was perpetually drunk on it! I finally realized that the smell was not coming from outside but from inside my own body!'

'Wow!' said Ashish.

'Yes,' I said, 'The people around me thought that I was going crazy sniffing around! I even went hunting for that particular fragrance to various perfumeries. I finally found a matching perfume—the fragrance derived from a flower named Parijaat, as I recall.'

'This smell of flowers…isn't it a sign of the stigmata?' asked Ashish with wonder in his voice. 'I saw it in a film.'

'Yes!' I replied. 'But Christianity has no copyright over it. The smell of flowers is a common experience that all mystics from all traditions experience. The basic reason for the fragrance is that, when you increasingly become free of negative emotions, the presence of God inside, starts to take on a more unhindered role. The atmosphere within becomes amazing…Another interesting thing that happened was that I would be woken up very early in the morning by the sound of temple bells. I went to all the local temples around asking about when they began the ringing of their bells.'

'And?' said Ashish.

'The temples did ring their bells but not at 3 am, which was the time I would hear them! I finally concluded that my body was resetting itself at a different kind of frequency and these were the symptoms…

'And here I must re-emphasize the role of the guru. The guru is critical because he first opens the doorway to the inner road, then teaches us the right meditation techniques and then gives us the right guide-map to walk the path back home. DIY is almost impossible in the spiritual realm!' I smiled. 'Many of our karmas are such that they simply cannot be removed without us suffering their consequences and the guru has to intercede with *Kaal* on our behalf. The guru takes upon himself those karmic seeds as an act of infinite kindness. Only a true guru has that capacity. The guru takes our negative karmas upon himself because someone has to pay for them. And he suffers when he does that. This is like the government cancelling the debts of farmers, but for which the tax payers ultimately have to pay!'

'The fact is,' I elaborated, 'that the guru does something for us that no one else would ever do, not even our parents. Our parents are worthy of veneration because they have birthed us and provided us with an opportunity for liberation, but the guru is the one who births us in our final avatar and helps us start on the journey home. His debt simply cannot be repaid. *Tasmai*

Shri Guruve namah, as our scriptures say—that is why the guru is revered...'

'I can see why this is a difficult path,' sighed Ashish.

I replied, 'It is not as difficult as it is intricate. This is why so few are able to succeed. But the determined seeker should not lose heart. Once you have successfully done the three things I have mentioned before, then nothing can prevent your Ego—your *Jeevatma*—from flying. And once you do start to fly, there comes a point when all delusion is lost and the soul realizes that it and the Creator are one. *So Hum—I am Thee*—that is the hymn that comes into the soul unbidden. The caterpillar becomes the butterfly and it is finally free of the cycle of birth and death. The soul merges back into the same cosmic soup from which it had emerged. The cycle that started millions of years ago for the individual soul is complete.'

Ashish listened quietly as I spoke. I could make out that he was deeply affected by what I was saying. I wasn't surprised. Every soul, however enmeshed in the world, just cannot resist what I was saying. Not because I was saying it, but because every *Jeevatma* has a homing device and, like an expatriate who has left his home long ago, even the mention of returning induces emotions.

I continued, 'Just as nothing is more joyous to parents than their new-born starting to recognize them, nothing is more joyous to the Creator than seeing one of his soul children waking up from the drugged sleep of *Sansaar* and starting to recognize Him. The scriptures say that so great is God's joy that he can't help but run out bare-footed to welcome the returning soul.'

I continued my story. 'As one travels on this path many amazing things happen. One loses all fear and one's perceptions become more and more sensitive, not only of the external world but of one's own body as well.'

'How so?' asked Ashish.

I replied, 'I started to experience the consciousness of my own cells. I could hear the murmur of my body as it worked—heart, kidneys, skin, I could feel them all. I could hear the whispered conversations that were happening between the cells of my body! And who was bitching about whom to whom! I could make out that each cell had its own intelligence which worked to keep the cell alive. Each cell was an individual just like you and me, which worried about where its next meal was coming from, just like we do! I could make out that the intelligence of the individual cell worked in tandem with the intelligence of the organ in which the cell was located and they communicated just as I and you are communicating. Ashish, our cells even have a language! This whole thing works, like wheels within wheels, so that the body can function as a highly complex, conscious organism. And this is the model for the entirety of Brahm (creation). This is how creation works—from top to bottom, layer upon layers, from the proton to us...The benefit of this eavesdropping is that you get to know if some cell is unhappy or unwell, and you can take action to heal that cell. Disease comes only when there is neglect in a part of the body or if the cells are too depressed or unhealthy to defend themselves from alien attack.'

Ashish gave me a disbelieving look and I laughed. 'Well, cells can get depressed too, you know! They can also have disagreements with their neighbours—and you can play peacemaker! If you can reach this sensitivity of perception, the rebellion in the body reduces and problems get solved before they become disease. When the body parts work in a good spirit with each other, disease cannot come in and ageing is arrested.'

I thought for a moment before concluding, 'And there is one final benediction. You become aware of not only yourself but of what other individual souls are going through as well. That is, if you put your mind to it.'

'Sounds quite a wonderful state, sir,' said Ashish quietly. 'My life is exactly the opposite of what you describe! All I find myself doing is running like crazy just to remain in the same place, fearing the loss of what I have created after so much of struggle.'

'That's the usual human state, Ashish,' I told him compassionately. 'We all suffered from it—till such time as we understand who we are in the final sense. Only then does the fear drop away. You also realize that you are here for a limited time. You have to go when you have to go. And when you realize that you are here at the pleasure of your Creator, you lose performance anxiety and begin to do everything—whether you know it or not—from an innate intelligence that is there in every living being. That intelligence finds the right, most perfect way to express itself. That's the fourth way of working that Guruji had hinted at in the Satsang on happiness...*Turiya*, as it is called in the *Mandukya Upanishad*...'

I took a pause because I was getting sucked into a topic that had always held the ultimate power of seduction for me, and I wanted to bring this interview to a close. 'Ashishji, let us get back to your interview topic since I can talk all night on this—my favourite subject!' Ashish nodded his assent and I continued.

'As I was saying, everything changed dramatically for me, but what the world noticed was my work. You want to know how I am so prolific with my inventions, don't you?'

'Yes, sir,' replied Ashish, sitting up alertly and reaching for his notepad.

'It is easy,' I declared. 'When your awareness is in tune with God's creation and then when you see what man has made in comparison, you see the glaring loopholes! And the ideas start flowing automatically. I expanded my project management company into an ideas development company. Where would the ideas come from? From everywhere and nowhere! I would read the newspaper and get an idea. I would be stuck in a traffic jam and I would get an idea. I would take a flight and get an idea. I would open a tap in a hotel room and get an idea.'

Ashish interrupted me, 'Sir, can you explain this in a way that'll help me write it lucidly in my article?'

'Okay,' I said, 'The first fact behind my inventions is that there is a common logic to every one of them. And the logic is this: The man-made world sits on top of the natural one. The man-made world should ideally make the natural world more abundant and useful for us. But very often, as the complexity and vested interests of man-made systems increase, the basic purpose of the man-made system is forgotten, lost or corrupted. The system may have been originally designed for certain economies-of-scale, but due to reasons of complexity and neglect, it has lost its effectiveness.'

'How do you mean?' asked Ashish.

'Okay, let me explain through an example. Take the water supply system of a typical city. Any such system in any city is designed to provide safe potable water at home. It is supposed to be more efficient than all the people of the city going to the river to fetch water for themselves, right?'

'Right!' Ashish grinned back and I continued, 'Initially the system does do what it was designed for and achieves what the urban planners call economies of scale, but as the years pass and as the city grows denser and as maintenance issues get more and more difficult to handle, what happens is that the system ends up rusty and leaking and working far below the efficiency level it was designed for. Ultimately, it ends up becoming more of a problem than a solution. I have given a very basic example but this is true for all man-made systems, since most of these systems, unlike natural systems, are not self-correcting or self-healing. The trick and the talent is to see the anomalies and offer solutions for it. Those who can do that, make a lot of money. Flipkart, OYO, Uber, Facebook—all are examples of someone taking a fresh look at an existing system, identifying its underutilized resources, developing a way to use them better and then finding customers for it.'

I shrugged my shoulders, 'I am no different, Ashish. The only advantage I probably have over these entrepreneurs is that I can do what they do but across a wider spectrum of subjects, fields and disciplines.'

'Point taken sir,' the young man nodded. 'Now let's take your inventions one by one and you can talk me through the process by which you invented them.'

'Okay,' I agreed. 'Following the logic I just outlined, it is easy to see that many of the systems around us are in need of improvement.'

'True,' acknowledged Ashish.

'Lets take my first big idea,' I continued. 'This first idea was also the most complex. It struck me that the mega-city was a vast and underutilized resource. Waste and shortage went hand in hand. I examined the subject and went back to libraries to study it. This whole thought process started when I observed the massive flooding in my home city, of Gurgaon in the monsoon. The tragedy was that there was a water shortage for the rest of the year! Everyone knew that there are gross inefficiencies in the way storm water drainage was handled, yet everyone felt helpless. The reality in India is that even if you are the CEO of a multimillion-dollar company, you cannot get even a pothole in front of your house repaired!'

'Totally agree, sir!' he smiled back.

I continued, 'I put down my thoughts and it resulted in a book by the name *Urban Shock*.'

'I've gone through it, sir,' said Ashish, 'While researching you'.

'Then you would know that the book consists of macro paradigms for sustainable development.'

'Yes, sir.'

I laughed, 'In the beginning the book did not do well. It remained but one step ahead of being pulped. People had a hard time believing that we could make the world sustainable without the use of new and exotic technologies. It is only now when I have a crackpot reputation that it has a steadily increasing demand!'

'Sir, that book was a general read but you made your reputation with specific inventions. The Building Environment Management System was the start, I believe,' Ashish jogged me back to the topic.

'Yes,' I replied, 'that was my first patent. The idea behind the green business and *Urban Shock* went hand in hand. The phrase *"Islands of wastage in a sea of plenty"* came to my mind one day while I was meditating. It seemed to me that we humans were first creating a problem and then solving it, but only partially. How not to create the problem in the case of buildings suddenly came to me as a vision as I meditated and I did some calculations.

The results were exciting. My back-of-the-envelope calculations showed that I could save more than 40 per cent of the energy bills of a typical building by putting freely available resources at work. I started with a couple of my brave clients who believed in the idea and were ready to spend that little bit extra. After some trial and error we found that the idea actually worked! Initial disbelief turned to passionate endorsement and my clients became my brand ambassadors. Money started to flow in and that's when I bought this land.'

'As I went about building up my green business, one of the sections of *Urban Shock*, 'Ideas That Don't Cost A Penny', was noticed and picked up by the government. They liked it, especially the not spending too much of money bit! The massive traffic jam—called Gurujam in 2016—induced the government to call in suggestions from private citizens, and I sent a note on how to prevent flooding the following year. I was asked to do a pilot project on a troublesome stretch and my solution actually worked. A stretch of road that used to be under three feet of water remained dry even after heavy rains, and the traffic kept moving. The greatly relieved government appointed me in an honorary capacity to advise them on various urban issues. That's how I became something of an expert and an advisor to the government.'

I sipped at the glass of spicy buttermilk Rupen had brought in while we spoke. 'The idea,' I said, 'behind the green business also led to the invention of the car-shade since the principles were similar. Every summer you can see people scrambling for whatever trees they can find for their cars in parking lots. Why could I not provide a personalized car shade, I asked myself, for each car? Something that could be fixed to the car even when it was being driven and something that could be used conveniently even by women drivers. The trick here was to design something sleek that did not destroy the looks of the car, was easy to deploy, yet not easy to steal...Voila, the car shade was born!'

'Let's talk about the other inventions,' Ashish said. 'How did you think of the airport security system?'

'It was again a simple concept. The idea was to catch the terrorist through his fear of getting caught! A man on a risky mission suffers from a high pulse rate; high blood pressure and high levels of skin perspiration. He may be able to control his facial expressions and his demeanour but not his pulse rate and blood pressure since that is controlled by the subconscious part of the brain. The question was how to detect these readings with a hand-held sensor. It was a piece of cake, actually. Not a difficult job at all, with the technologies already available in bits and pieces. I merely clubbed them together and the security system was born. The Indian Government didn't pay much attention but the Israelis loved it and put it in operation.'

'And how did the idea strike you, sir?'

'I was watching a program on the landing on the moon,' I confided, 'and heard it mentioned that Neil Armstrong's blood pressure had shot up to 240/160 and his pulse rate went to 180 beats per minute as his lunar module approached the surface of the moon. I said to myself—if the fear of death is so potent that it can raise the readings of a trained astronaut who is otherwise sedentary, then why can't we use this auto-response of the body to catch people who are about to do something wrong?'

'Brilliant!' said Ashish, 'But what if the terrorist has taken an injection to stabilize these readings?'

'We have a solution for that too, but that, my friend, is top secret!'

'In that case, sir, let's move on,' he said, sounding a bit disappointed. 'Let's talk about the condom design, sir.'

I was rather amused to see him blush as he said that. 'In the case of the condom, it struck me that the condom, however thin or lubricated it may be, destroys the feel of natural sex as it prevents the friction of the skins of the male and female organs. My idea was to recreate the sense of friction. I found the answer through a double-layered condom. My condom is thicker; designed for the woman and its feel is far more pleasurable. I patented it and here we are! I hope you have tried it?'

'Yes, I have sir,' Ashish grinned and blushed again. 'And I can vouch for what you are saying!' We both laughed. 'And the water heater?'

'The idea came when I was staying in a 5-star hotel in Shimla,' I reminisced. 'It was off-season—wintertime. Very few rooms of the hotel were occupied. The hotel being large and a five-star establishment, was required to have a large and expensive infrastructure for hot water. As I went for my bath, I turned on the hot water tap. I must tell you that hot water has a major role to play in all my inventions since many of my most creative thoughts have come while I am having a hot-water bath or I am sitting in a hot sulphur spring in Manali or some such place! That day I had to wait forever and all this time the cold water kept going down the drain. That, I thought, was rather wasteful. Hotels in Shimla have to cart water over long distances through tankers, and here I was, wasting so much of it just to get to the hot part. Wastage does not make luxury more luxurious and I found myself wondering if this was luxury or the height of hubris?

'As I thought through the problem, I realized that most hotels had centralized boilers that heated all the water at one location. This hot water is then transported across long distances through insulated pipes to each individual room. There are three problems. First, a large amount of water has to be heated at one go and if the hotel is sparsely occupied, a lot of energy is wasted in doing that. Second, the temperature of the hot water inevitably drops as it negotiates the long lengths of pipes. Third, the occupant of the room must run-off the cold water before the hot portion of the water can reach him. So I worked on two concepts. To begin with, I designed a tap that would let the water out only when it was hot, and till then it would redirect the cold water to a storage tank to be recycled later. The advantage of this solution was that this could be retro-fitted into any existing hotel system and that has made this tap design very popular.

'The second design was far more revolutionary. I said to myself; why not progressively heat the water in the pipes themselves rather than in a central boiler? I designed a wrap-around heating system that covered the pipes and heated the water as it travelled through the pipe. This design completely deleted the need for the central boiler. My system worked amazingly well, gave instant hot water and yet consumed very little energy as compared to the older boiler system. It also worked at very low energy levels when the hotel was sparsely occupied. And on top of it all, it was easy to repair with zero down-time.'

'And the earthquake proof design?' Ashish asked, ticking off his list.

'The earthquake-proof design has an interesting origin,' I explained. 'I was in a high-rise building in Gurgaon when the Bhuj earthquake struck on 26 January 2001. The building swayed alarmingly and at the same time I could feel it being vertically lifted like a car going over a speed breaker. Being from the construction line, I knew that the building was in trouble and if the sway reached a certain tipping point, it would topple. I could hear furniture sliding and the building structure creaking, groaning and ripping. Building joints aren't designed to flex beyond a certain point and I could make out that that point had been crossed. From the window I could observe that the trees outside were also swaying wildly.'

'I survived that day but the building was far too damaged to be kept and had to be demolished. It had developed too many cracks in its joints to be safe anymore and was a sitting duck for the next earthquake that came along. Unlike a human body where a cracked bone can be reset, concrete cracks cannot be restored. The trees I had seen swaying outside seemed none the worse for wear, though—and that set me thinking.

'I studied the principles of structure design more closely. I found that the basic assumption always is to make the building heavy enough to resist the maximum movement that the earthquake could throw at it. But what if the earthquake threw in a stronger force than what it is designed for? The engineers had no answers, except to say that they weren't to be blamed since they had designed as per the prevailing structural laws! This, by the way, is the typical response of experts, and that is no consolation to those who are killed. We must remember that earthquakes don't kill people—buildings do, and the heavier they are the harder they fall.'

'The same happened in Fukushima,' observed Ashish. 'The engineers built a 30-foot high sea-wall because the statistical data that was available for a thousand years showed that no tsunami higher than 20 feet had ever hit that particular sea coast.'

'Yes,' I agreed, 'The engineers take decisions based on such kind of theoretical premises on a daily basis. As they say, Ashishji—lies, damn lies and statistics! To me this entire approach seemed dangerously foolish. So I asked myself why couldn't we design buildings with more flexible foundations instead of aiming for heavier and heavier ones? It wasn't that revolutionary an idea! Oil rigs, for one, were examples of heavy buildings sitting on restless foundations. Even a car going over a potholed road was a good example of how earthquakes could and should be handled. That's when I came upon my revolutionary idea—again while I was meditating! I thought of a rigid yet flexible system of transferring vertical loads of buildings during earthquakes. The end result is that when an earthquake strikes, buildings with my foundation design undulate with the flow of the earthquake. The foundation does not transmit the earthquake shakes and shocks to the superstructure. This is like a car going over a rumble strip at speed. You hear it but you can't really feel any major movement. I did some calculations with my structural Engineer and then took it up with the University of Roorkee, now I.I.T. Roorkee. We were able to create models that handled high intensity earthquakes very effectively and we are hopeful that this will soon become an industry standard for a certain class of buildings.'

'Whew!' said Ashish. 'And could you talk about what you are working on at present?'

'Oh! Lots of things! An interesting one is the design of aircraft that can take off from a very short runway. My calculations tell me that this aircraft design would require just one-third of the length that an equivalent conventional aircraft would need to take off or land. Another thing I am working on is Tesla's ideas on free energy. That, I must tell you, is a big one!'

'Wow!' exclaimed Ashish. 'How do these ideas work? If you can share that, of course.'

'It is still in early stages, but I can tell you that the aircraft—it's called the V.S.T.O.L., Very Short Take-off & Landing—works on enhancing the lift of the wing at very slow speeds using existing capacities. The other one—the free energy is at too early a stage to talk about.'

'That leaves us with, let me see,' Ashish consulted his notes, 'the beating-heart bypass, the pollution filter, the virtual tank armour, the Extreme Data Compression, and, uh, the ultimate defender for fighter aircraft.'

I replied, 'The beating-heart bypass is based on the principle that a heart bypass is basically a plumbing job. The difficulties lie in getting to the location of the bypass and cutting open what is essentially a high pressure pumping system. The rib cage has to be opened, the heart has to be stopped, the blood diverted into a heart-lung machine and then the whole process reversed after the relatively simple plumbing job is done. I asked myself: could I puncture an artery without letting the blood leak while the heart was still beating? The answer came in a flash one day and I built my tiny bypass device. I then tried it on an actual rubber hose that had the water supply running at high pressure. It worked! I was able to puncture the pipe, without leading to any loss of water. That gave me the confidence to approach a medical research institution to first do some controlled tests on animals and, when these were successful, we proceeded with human trials, according to the guidelines of the Medical Council of India. The procedure was a success across the test group, it was approved by the government, and now of course is a very standard and safe procedure. There is another heart device that

I am working on currently—the non-invasive heart stent. The logic is that if I have to widen a rather narrow space, why do it by shoving something into that already constricted space when we can handle the problem from outside the artery? But I shall say nothing more than that since the whole thing is touch and go right now.'

'What was next? Oh, the pollution mask. The logic of the pollution control mask is again self-evident. Rather than using a flimsy filter paper or fabric that easily get overwhelmed, I used the cleansing properties of a certain liquid that, shall we say, does the job cheaply and effectively. The system I designed provides you with an unlimited quantity of clean air just on battery power. And women like the fact that the device does not make them look like Darth Vader! Win the women over and you have a large market, as my marketing manager used to say! Sure, there is the inconvenience of carrying that strap-on device but people, especially the asthmatics, don't mind the small inconvenience caused.'

'And the ultimate defender and the virtual tank armour?' asked Ashish, ticking things off from his list.

'Sorry! I can't talk about those. They are top secret! All I can tell you is that the ultimate defender is so potent that enemy aircraft don't even want to approach our fighters from their six-o-clock's. Long-range missiles are also rendered ineffective. As for the virtual armour—well, let's say it is virtual but highly effective in preventing direct hits on tanks, and that too without adding any extra weight to the tank. I am now involved in making a version for the navy. They will be largely protected from torpedo strikes with this device…I am thinking of calling the naval version Dolphin! What do you say, Ashish?'

'Sounds good, sir! Dolphins have been known to butt sharks to death, saving the lives of many drowning sailors.'

'Exactly!' I concurred with a laugh. 'But I'm sorry I can't say anything more than that…'

Ashish again checked his notes. 'And now the last item on my list—the Extreme Data Compression software.'

'Ah, that's my favourite!' I smiled. 'My bread and butter and jam and caviar all rolled into one! I am afraid I can't even hint at the logic though! It is so secret that it exists only in my head. Only the heavily encrypted machine code exists; the source code resides only in my memory! The only place you will be able to read about it is in my will, which I haven't written as yet!' I joked and Ashish grinned back.

'That shouldn't be for many years yet, hopefully!' he remarked, beginning to wind up the interaction. 'Okay, that should be good. I have more than enough for the article. Let me just check my notes one final time…'

ANUSUYA

I leaned back in my chair as Ashish went through his notes and fiddled with the voice recorder.

I had been speaking for three days now and my jaw ached. There was much still left unsaid, but beyond a point you just can't talk about it. The path of self-realization is not something that one could just describe in words but the usefulness of words is that they can plant seeds in fertile minds. The rest requires grace from God and one's guru…

Evening was nearly upon us and another day in my life was done. The breeze was blowing steadily, whistling through the trees; the stars were beginning to show their faces as the light faded. The twin Swargrohini peaks, my co-meditators, looked down at me from their lofty heights.

I yawned and stretched. It had been an intense three days with Ashish and I felt good about sharing my thoughts. Saying stuff helps to work it out through one more level of clarity. The three days had passed easily, reducing the longing for Anusuya that would otherwise have gnawed at me constantly. I looked at my watch. Anusuya should be about to reach…

Anusuya? My wife! As I had mentioned to Ashish, I had met her not long after that fateful day with Guruji. I had gone to a college get-together and she had happened to be there as a guest. I looked at her, she'd looked back and I knew that she was the one for me…How does one know that? Hard to say but when you meet someone special and when you look into their eyes, you see a familiarity and intimacy that is hard to describe in words…

They say that man or woman, both are insufficient on their own to take the inner flight. Like a bird with one wing, it is impossible to fly even with the best of efforts. But what happens when you have prayed hard enough and sincerely enough for deliverance? God grants you that second wing. And when two beings are united in love, so that their souls, minds and bodies converge at one single point in matched pairs, that's when magic happens. Only loving another more than you love yourself breaks the vacuum suction of selfishness that Kaal *traps us with. It is only when you forget yourself completely that the pull of* Kaal *is negated. Just as a body with no mass cannot be trapped by gravity, a person whose sense of self has been submerged in love just cannot be stopped by* Kaal. *We can't see God directly and he is too vast for us to love with a focused passion and devotion, but when we have called him enough and with genuine longing, He shows his face to us through the windows to the soul of someone who looks at us with love. And that is enough. There is no other way. The rest is simply a buildup to that instant…*

At that moment, the door opened. Anusuya walked in and time stood still—just as it had the first time I had seen her. My world lit up. I stood up and welcomed her home…

I turned to Ashish and introduced her. I said, 'There she is—my better half in every sense of the word.'

'Good…good evening, ma'am,' the young man stammered, evidently overwhelmed when she smiled at him. 'Sir was just telling me about how the two of you met…'

'Was he now?' replied Anusuya, looking at me, those deep eyes dancing with laughter. 'I am sure I would have something different to say about that! But never mind, Saagar can say it the way he likes to imagine it!'

I threw back my head and laughed at the hopeful look Ashish cast my way. 'Oh, no! You are not getting me to talk any more, Ashish!' I told him, slipping an arm around Anusuya's waist. 'Not now that my wife is back after one whole week! And, besides, that really is a story for another day…'

ACKNOWLEDGEMENTS

A book is an immense project, a labour of love for the author and an exercise in laborious patience for the people who provide the support structure. If the book be likened to a flower, the efforts of the many silent helpers are like the fertilizer without which the flower could not have bloomed in all its glory. Here is my tribute to all of them…

First and foremost to my father, Narayana Kumar Sinha, who not only instilled in me the spirit of scientific inquiry but whose passing away forced me to look beyond—to those horizons where science can never reach. That is when this book was first born as an idea in my head 20 years ago.

To my mother Sudha Sinha; my sisters Aseema Sinha and Aditi Swaminathan; to my brother-in-law Kumar and my nephew Anish. They may not have realized it but I have sharpened my debating, writing and convincing skills by discussing, arguing and quarrelling with mostly these folks!

To my maternal grandmother, who planted the seeds of spirituality that were destined to lie fallow for decades before sprouting and, ultimately, flowering. She was the one who willy-nilly introduced me to the great Gurus of the Radha Swami sect—Sawan Singh Maharaj and Charan Singh Maharaj, two men mountains whose teachings have been of incalculable value to me and to this book.

To Sangeeta Bahadur—my wife, or Rosie as I call her. Without her encouragement, love and support, I could never have become an author. I was a work-in-progress, as a writer and as a human being, when I met her, and she challenged me at levels that I did not know existed! She helped move me from the world of brick, cement and mortar, to the world of letters and I discovered that ideas could have bigger impacts than buildings! She was the one who gave me faith that there was something worthwhile in what I had to say and helped me through my torturous self-doubts. She is also the first-cut editor of this book and the sounding board for the many spiritual and scientific insights that find a place here.

To my daughter Aanya for being proof of the preciousness of life, that the Mahamritunjaya mantra really works, that I don't know everything and that God works in mysterious ways! She is the one who helps me see things from a completely different and completely valid perspective on a daily basis.

To Shardooli and Niyutsa, my two special girls, who have helped me in their unique ways in the writing of this book.

To Manju Garr, née Gaur, for all the help, support and unstinting approval of whatever I was working out in my head.

To Rupen who, by taking care of my day-to-day requirements, set me free to pursue my musings and my writing, not only in the book but my real life as well!

To my friend Ajay Mehta, whose incisive questioning over the years helped me sharpen many of the concepts in the book.

To Nivedita Sinha for her presence and help through those times when I first saw the flaming maw of *Kaal* swallowing my safe little world.

To Guruji, Dr Arun Kumar—one of the two spiritual engines of the book. His unique combination of science and spirituality and ability to see through to the true nature of my queries acted as a catalyst that fired up my understandings of things physical and metaphysical. This book is in effect a duet between him and me and the ideas he provoked in my head.

To my dearest friend and inspiration Sadhana Surey, the other spiritual engine of the book. She is one of the truly realized persons that I have had the honour to meet and whose ideals I am still struggling to reach up to. From her I have learnt that knowing about God and being one with Him are not necessarily the same thing, and that spiritual progress is not about reaching a difficult goal, but more about self-transformation in the here and now...Many of the deepest insights in this book are due to her unfettered help and unconditional affection. To her and Guruji, I owe a debt that simply cannot be repaid.

To Devapriya Roy, who gently, persistently and diplomatically—much like a mother hen—helped me overcome the blues that all struggling authors go through as they hunt for publishers. Devapriya, I owe you many litres of cow ghee!

To Niyogi Books, my publishers, for showing faith in me and for being so professional and for making my publishing experience an absolute delight.

To my editor K.E. Priyamvada for doing such a wonderful editorial job and being so supportive, prompt and precise about every issue that came up as we went through the editing process.

Books are not people and their place is usually in the bibliography but in my case, some of the great texts that I have had the fortune to read must be mentioned since they have been my guides since much before I met my flesh and blood guru. The *Bhagavadgita*, the *Mandukya Upanishad*, *Srimad Bhagwatam Mahapuraan*, the *Bible*, *Guru Granth Sahib*, *The Book of Mirdad* by Mikhail Naimy, Fritjof Capra's *The Tao of Physics* and Sogyal Rinpoche's *The Tibetan Book of Living and Dying*, are some of the great texts that I scoured for answers to all my Whys and Hows.

To the peerless Dr Richard Feynman, who made the frontiers of science look so easy to reach, explore and understand, and whose famous lectures on YouTube really helped.

And finally, my heartfelt acknowledgements to the Lord Himself—the Creator who is a living presence in all our lives. I will end by saying that He is not just a concept but an all pervasive, conscious entity whose doors are always open to the true seeker—one who searches for Him with sincerity and without guile.

patraṃ puṣhpaṃ phalaṃ toyaṃ yo me bhaktyā prayachchhati
tadahaṃ bhaktyupahṛitam aśhnāmi prayatātmanaḥ

Whoever offers me with love, a flower, a fruit,
I appear in person before that selfless devotee with sinless mind,
and delightfully partake of his offering.

—

Bhagavadgita, 9:26